Diana's Epoch

Terry James

Published by Growingknowing, 2023.

Diana's Epoch

Cover art by Claudia McKinney at Phatpuppy Art Studios

Published by growingknowing

ISBN 978-0-9918686-2-9 (print edition)

Dedication

I dedicate this novel to my late mother, Denise Charlesworth. She loved words. I will always love her.

Prologue

The kitchen was small and crowded. When Petrov sat down, he knocked his head against the single, dull yellow light over the table. The light swung in a slight arc casting shadows about the room. A massive, square man stood next to the back door. He was almost as wide as he was tall. Two aging, well-dressed lawyers hovered between the table and closets while clutching documents in their arms. Ares took the remaining seat.

Petrov was in a good mood. He reached around a lawyer to grab a bottle of vodka. Petrov put out four somewhat clean glasses on the table. He splashed some vodka roughly into each glass then took a swig from the bottle.

"To our success," said Petrov with a radiant smile.

"Success," said Ares as he clinked his glass to the bottle in Petrov's hand and chugged the vodka.

The lawyers hovered uncomfortably but did not take a glass because their hands were full holding folders and documents. They shuffled their arms about to indicate participation in the happy mood. The massive man tried silently and unsuccessfully to blend into the background.

"Is the battery ready? Did it pass the tests?" said Ares.

"Better than we expected. The risk of fire was reduced by 85 percent. The charge time is eight times faster than a lithium battery. With this little gem, we can charge an electric vehicle in the same time as it takes to fill a sedan's fuel tank."

"How did you do it?" said Ares.

Petrov took another gulp from the bottle. "The product worked as I promised. My competitors are left in my dirt. Is that how you say it?" laughed Petrov. "I replaced the graphite with niobium to avoid battery expansion and potential fires. I included tungsten and oxygen in a secret amount. It works. I am not some loud speaking drunk. I am vindicated. No one will dare laugh at my crazy ideas now. I am a true engineer."

"A triumph, to be sure. My lawyers have documents for the transfer of patent rights and control. As promised, I will pay 10,000 dollars in cash and 30 percent of future profits," said Ares. He twisted around with difficulty to take the envelope of money from the large man at the door. The older lawyer put three color-coded folders in a specific order on the table.

"I have been thinking we need a change," said Petrov.

"You want more? I will give you 40 percent. This is an amazing offer. Most inventors get 5 percent. A genius with a proven history could negotiate 15 percent at most. I like you, Petrov. I believe you are a genius, so I will give you 40 percent. You will not find a better offer. If you do, I will match it. You have my word." The lawyers were nodding in agreement.

"I was thinking of something better. We could publish a paper in the public domain. I would make the product free. This would save the world from choking on oil pollution. Everyone would have a Petrov battery instead of a lithium battery. I would be famous."

"Famous, but not rich. My final offer is 75% of profits, and I will give you $50,000 in cash as a signing bonus right now. You will be a billionaire with a 75% royalty. Think of all the good you could do with that money."

Petrov stopped smiling. He ran his hand through his thick hair and stroked the gray stubble on his chin. Petrov looked down, then up, then down again. Ares gestured for the lawyers to leave with a wave of his hand. For a few minutes, the men shuffled about while trying to get to the door without dropping their papers.

Petrov sighed and looked at Ares directly. The eye contact was deep, but Ares did not flinch. Ares showed steely determination.

Petrov grimaced. "My English is not so good, but I have been cheated before. I know about people who offer dreams that are too big. I smell rats. I am thinking this is perhaps crap. You can keep your money. I will find another sponsor to manufacture my Petrov battery."

Ares froze. The two men squinted at each other for a long time. The seconds became minutes, but no one moved. You could hear both men breathing.

"I can see Petrov that I will not persuade you with better offers. You don't trust me. I should have started with vodka, beautiful women, good music, and warm islands. I have lost you, but I do not capitulate."

"I do not know this word, capitulate?"

"I will not quit. You will not get more money. Ares flipped the money across the table. Sign the document. Right here, right now. No more talk."

Petrov smiled. He took another swig, and he spat the drink at Ares.

Ares took a handkerchief and wiped his face. Ares nodded at the massive man behind him. The large man moved with surprising speed toward Petrov but was hampered by Ares blocking the path. Petrov jumped back, shoving the table forward with his legs. Petrov swung the bottle at the bodyguard and hit the overhead light, which broke. The room was utterly black. The kitchen had no windows meaning no moonlight or street lights. Petrov swung the bottle again widely back and forth in the dark, breaking the bottle on the cupboard behind him, and then he smashed the jagged end into the face of the large man.

Men chaotically rushed about as glass, blood, and unknown objects flew around in the darkness. The fight did not last long, but each second stretched in the minds of the three men to an almost infinite length.

"Got him," said the big man finally. Ares found his phone and put on the flashlight. Petrov was in a chokehold. The big man had his arms around the Russian's neck. Both chairs were shattered. The table stood precariously on three legs. The cheek of the large man had a huge gash.

"Sign it," said Ares as he held out a pen. Petrov took the pen hesitantly then tried to stab the pen into Ares in the throat with a quick jab. Ares moved back, and the big man choked harder. Petrov started to spasm as he fell unconscious.

"Of course, the damn Russian wasn't wrong about cheating him. I'll find something with his signature so we can pay a forger. Brodie, make it look like a burglary gone wrong. Let's do it quickly so we can get your face stitched up because you are bleeding on everything."

Chapter 1 - Diana

Diana looked out the front window. The grass was almost six inches. The day was windy, and the grass was blowing. Usually, Diana was fastidious about her chores. I should cut it tomorrow, she thought. Diana had never seen the grass this long, and it was fascinating. The wind played across the grass, and it looked like green, choppy waves. Segments of grass would blow up, crest, and drop back like a conductor of a symphony orchestra. The grass flowed playfully in the sunlight. Diana usually kept everything short and trim to the edges, but the natural flow was more beautiful than she imagined. Diana grinned. My life is so pathetic I am literally watching grass grow!

Diana let everything slide, except school work, since her mother died two years ago. The parting was still painful in ways Diana could never have imagined. The cancer was slow but relentless. Each day, another small part of her mother was gone. Diana's mother weighed less than 70 pounds when she died. She could barely speak. In a raspy whisper, the mother demanded Diana complete university. At first, Diana felt she could not breathe with the emotional pain of losing her mother. Each minute felt like hours of emptiness. Diana was true to her promise and graduated as planned.

Today, Diana was forced into action. She had to find a job and quickly. The focus on her education had drained the family savings completely. Diana grabbed her purse and walked the familiar path through the park to the bus stop on Huntington. She had graduated with a Master's degree in microbiology the previous year. Her latest, desperate idea was to use her school network to find work.

The bus was slow and behind schedule as usual. Diana lost her dad when she was six. The family lived in New Orleans. She was told her dad drowned trying to swim across the Mississippi when he was drunk. They are not sure if the pollution, the river currents, the alcohol, or a passing boat killed him. He swam after midnight; within a few minutes, his drunken friends could not see him from the riverbank. The river was about a mile to the far bank. He swam to win a small bet.

Diana's father was charming, handsome, brilliant, and a marathon runner. On the dark side, he was also a hard drinker, outrageous liar, and bar-room brawler. Burning through life too brightly, he did not live long. The body was found a few days later in poor condition. After he was gone, Diana and her mother moved to Toronto, Canada. They had enough for food, clothing, and a tiny home. They could not afford a car or luxuries. Surviving on the single salary of a junior nurse, they had the necessities, and they had each other.

The bus finally came. Diana got on, and as usual, the bus was full. She squeezed between the students to find a handrail. The earliest challenge Diana could remember was during her first winter in Canada. She came home from school, and she was pelted with snowballs by five kids across the street. Some of the snowballs were had bits of ice in them. She was hit by many missiles despite walking fast and avoiding eye contact. Diana rushed into her home and asked her mother for help. She was being assaulted by a mob of kids.

Her mother smiled warmly. "What will you learn if I fix it? You will learn to seek help from powerful people whenever you face a problem. You will not learn to solve your own problems. You will not be independent. Ask yourself, what would a leader do? One small girl cannot beat five kids. How can you win? Go outside, and I want you to find a solution. What can you *learn* from this adversity? What would a leader do differently?" These are two questions Diana would hear whenever she had a problem.

The bus was moving up Victoria Park Avenue. The driver kept asking the people to move to the back of the bus to make room for new people. The driver was an optimist. The bus was completely packed. People moved a bit, but no magical new space emerged.

Diana returned to her thoughts. She had gone outside and looked for tools. She found the cover to a garbage can could shield her head and upper body. The lid was not big enough to protect her legs. She found a few things she could throw. If she held the shield, she could not hold many objects to throw. The five kids could hold 10 objects if they had one in each hand. She could only keep one or two. The solution was not good enough. Behind the garbage can, she saw a hockey stick about twice her height. She grabbed the shield and hockey lance and moved to the front of the house.

The enemy outnumbered her, but she had fortitude. She blocked the snow missiles effortlessly with the shield. She raised her stick and started a slow run across the street as the snowballs came fast and furious. Her enemies began to panic. They hit her legs many times, but she was picking up speed. She lowered the stick and charged at the biggest boy. He turned and ran. The rest of his army scattered in all directions. For the first time, Diana felt the triumph of victory against overwhelming odds. She knew, intuitively, that the big boy could have won if he was willing to risk being stabbed by the stick. Diana might have got one good hit before he would hurt her. It did not matter now as she had faced them down. The kids never confronted her again. She knew she could be a leader. She rejoiced without making a sound. She felt the song of satisfaction and independence sing strong and true.

The bus climbed slowly up the hill to the university. Along with almost all the occupants, Diana alighted from the vehicle and proceeded to one of the many entrances. Diana had no classes or appointments. She was hoping to speak to whomever she could find. She needed work to pay the mortgage and student loans. Diana could easily find a minimum wage job, but a temporary position would never pay enough to survive. She would fall further behind and continue to get foreclosure notices and late fees. Diana would lose their small home in a few weeks now her mother's savings was gone.

Diana took the familiar stairs to the Microbiology Department. The rooms were covered in dust and tarpaulins. Workers were renovating the building. Diana got a lump in her throat. The school trip was her last resort. She had exhausted other options. She must have sent 200 resumes out in the previous week. She turned and wandered a bit lost about the building. She poked her head in and scanned the cafeteria. She saw Professor Maynard hobbling toward the faculty lounge. Maynard was at least 70. He was a brilliant biology professor and sweet, but he was disconnected from life outside academia. She could talk to Maynard anytime because he was a neighbor.

"Diana?"

Diana turned and saw a mid-thirties woman with trendy pink glasses and a smile as wide as a rainbow. Diana was visibly relieved. Perhaps, her friend could help. "I am so happy to see you, Professor Osborne."

"Please, call me Angela. Diana, I did not expect to see you. Why are you here?"

"I need help finding a job. I am a bit desperate if I am honest with you," said Diana.

"That is hard to believe. You were my best student. You were valedictorian. You ignored the boys and focused with pure intensity until you solved every assignment. How could you have an issue finding a job?"

"I can find crappy jobs as a waitress or retail clerk. I need a real job as a scientist. I am offered short contracts for a few weeks or months, and then I am back to begging and searching. For every job posted, they get 200 applicants from across the globe. I am exhausted looking for a full-time job. I don't have the resources to wait a few months between contracts while working temporary jobs. I cannot work for a few dollars an hour like the people in the Asian or South American countries. We have a higher cost of living here."

"We need to get out of the corridor. I will buy us some coffee and donuts, and you look for a table." Diana had some hope that her networking idea might work. Diana loved her classes. Angela was hilarious and the best teacher ever.

Angela came back with Diana's favorite coffee, French Vanilla from Tim Hortons. The two women reminisced. They bonded despite the difference in age and power. While the conversation with Angela was scintillating, the topic of a job was not broached.

"Diana, I admired the way you not only conquered every assignment but provided leadership and help to your small team of women. We have brilliant students who earn top grades on every assignment. We do not measure the influence and maturity that one student provides to everyone around them. You are a leader. You brought people together and energized them to deliver more. The sum of the parts is greater than the whole within your sphere of influence."

"Talking about leading, do you have any leads for me? Can you call a few contacts? Can you help me find work?" asked Diana directly.

Angela looked defeated. "Diana, I was dreading this moment. I am a Ph.D. candidate who works at three colleges on part-time contracts. I teach the same courses as tenured professors but make a third of the money, with no benefits, vacation, or overtime pay. I must reapply for my own position every four months. I am barely getting by myself."

Diana looked blankly. "Are you telling me that the faculty who tell us to get a good education so we can get good jobs don't actually have good jobs themselves?"

Angela bit her lower lip. "Not all the faculty," she said softly, "just the younger faculty. The older professors have tenure. The remaining 70 percent of us are temporary help and poor."

"What is wrong with this world? You are talented, smart, highly educated, and poor," Diana said with both hands raised to the sky in a gesture of anger at the false gods of academia. "We are both doomed. I must find a way to solve this problem."

"I thought you were set. You won that job at Boopoint as our top graduate," said Angela.

"I thought so too. The job was an unpaid intern; unpaid slave, if you call it what it was. I worked for six months for no salary. They had 10 unpaid interns. I heard two executives talking on the elevator. They did not see me. They laughed that they got the equivalent of five years of work for free. The one person they hired full-time was the nephew of a senior executive, Marcus Hydrome. The rest of us had no chance to win the single full-time job no matter how hard we worked. It was never a competition. It was a setup to exploit nine people for six months on the promise of a job that would never happen."

"That is disgusting," said Angela.

Diana pursed her lips together in a tight line and gathered her purse. "If you hear of any science job, literally anything full-time, please call me. I will carry books, get the coffee, and wash test tubes if it leads to full-time science work." Diana took a resume from her purse and gave it to Angela.

Diana was losing hope. She understood if Angela found a science job, why wouldn't she take it for herself? Diana had assumed that a history of excellence would provide a path to a good job. She was wrong. The ordinarily confident Diana was afraid. She could lose the house and be evicted by winter. Diana had a sudden vision of all her worldly belongings sitting in the snow. Where could she go? She had no family to call. Diana had no mother or father and no uncles or aunts. Even if she had family, she would not want to be a burden. Diana's heart was breaking. She had no choice but to go home and take inventory what she could sell. Failure was more than a vague threat. Diana wanted to be strong, but she knew she would cry if she had to sell her mother's jewelry. She had so few precious objects from her mother. Diana needed to be tougher and turn her swelling fear into opportunity. But how?

Chapter 2 — Go see mom

Could she risk talking to him? Diana heard him tinkering in his dark garage. She knew the risk. Last time, after their little talk, she obsessed for more than a year. He always smiled warmly with his sea-blue eyes. The conversation would be innocent, a little joke, the weather, and you gradually realized he had dropped an explosive idea that would consume your life for years. At first, you think the idea is intriguing. You smile because new ideas are fun. You dream about the idea. You check to see if he was right. Pow. You are obsessed. Your life has changed forever. Last time, he talked about jellyfish. Could she dare speak to him again?

She finished mowing the lawn. The day was sunny. For once, she was not thinking about the boulder of debt on her back. Today, she was 25, healthy, young, five feet, and brunette. She dressed casually in running shoes and T-shirts because she was a proud science nerd. She wore her hair in a ponytail. She enjoyed the sparkles on her bright pink shoes. She wore glasses because her academic performance was more important than being chic.

Today she felt like she could mow a hundred lawns. She could smell the freshly cut grass. She wiped the sweat from her forehead with her forearm as she walked across to the dark garage. She had energy, an excellent brain, and could conquer any mountain.

"Good morning, Professor," she said. He was tinkering as he had for years.

"Good morning to you, Diana. Please, call me Lazarus." He smiled warmly, of course.

"How long have you worked on this project? Four years?" she asked. The professor's machine looked like a flying saucer supported by wheels stolen from a baby carriage. He had put fancy seats, knobs, and dials in the machine, but those wheels were better suited for a toy car.

"Oh, about 16 years."

"What's this thing sticking out the front?"

"That's the torus."

"What is a torus? It looks like a big truck horn."

He grinned, "Something like that. I was about to take my vehicle for a test run. Would you like to join me?"

She looked more closely at the vehicle. A test run was worthy of a laugh. He would be lucky if the machine rolled down the driveway. Could the vehicle roll to the end of the street without falling over? How scary could it be?

"How far?"

"I built it to see my mom. If we could make it to mom, I would be happy."

"Sure," she said. She was a bit scared, but she was a fierce woman and ready to climb any mountain today. "Sure," she said again.

"Jump in," he said. He helped Diana into the seat. He walked around and jumped in too.

He pushed a button. The button turned green but without any engine sound. "Failed already," she thought. She smiled as she wondered if the only thing working was the green light.

Surprised, she felt the vehicle edge forward at the speed of an ant. They rolled down the driveway. He turned onto their small residential street.

"Can you put your seatbelt on? You loop the belt over each shoulder and buckle into the strap pulled through the middle of the chair." She had seen this kind of belt in a movie about fighter jets. Why use a superior belt if you are traveling slower than an old woman walking with a cane? As she looked down to manage the seatbelt, she felt something brush against her hair. She jumped a bit and turned to see tree leaves touch her cheek. She looked at the tree before looking over the edge of the vehicle. They were 15 feet in the air.

"What?" she said too loudly.

"Sorry, I was focusing on the controls." He tipped the steering control, and the vehicle gradually descended to about six inches above the ground.

"We are flying!"

"I know. Isn't it exciting?"

She calmed down now they were at street level and moving at a walking pace. Slow and low was not scary. "Stop sign coming up." She watched him fiddling with the many controls. According to the dashboard, the vehicle slowed to a crawl of about 5 Km/hour. "Stop sign," she repeated.

"I know, but how do you brake a helicopter?"

He was right. You cannot throw an anchor out of the window. There is no brake on a helicopter. He kept angling the T-bar controller with the left hand as he tipped the steering control up slightly. The machine slowed, edged through the stop sign, and rolled onto Sheppard Avenue. She desperately leaned forward to check for oncoming traffic. Sheppard Avenue was a four-lane road that was usually busy. They were lucky because of a break in traffic.

He picked up speed to 30 Km/hour and moved into the left lane. The first traffic light was green, so they pushed through without risking death. The next intersection had cars stopped to turn left. She felt her foot pressing with increasing pressure on an imaginary brake pedal. He looked worried as he moved the T-bar with one hand and the steering column with the other hand, but this time they stopped successfully.

While they waited for the cars to move, Diana looked more closely. She noticed things that were not there. No side mirrors. No mirrors at all! No radio. No headlight switches. No windshield wipers. No parking brakes. No windshield!

"This is a good time to turn our convertible into a sedan." Lazarus twisted around to pull on a brown belt behind them. A plastic cone powered over them, covering the top and sealing hermetically.

She noticed some parts of the vehicle looked like a homemade amateur project, and some features suggested sophisticated engineering. The cars started turning left, and they followed onto Victoria Park Avenue. After about half a mile, he pulled onto the ramp for the highway.

"Are you going on the highway? Isn't that a bit risky?" Her voice, she knew, was an octave higher than usual. She felt a mounting crisis but was unwilling to admit it to herself.

"We have to see if we can travel at high speed. I don't want to bicycle the whole way."

She did not feel confident. What they were doing might be dangerous. The vehicle moved onto the highway and sped easily to 100 Km/hour. The engine made no hum, clunk, or shudder as they went faster. Since they floated above the ground by about 20 inches, there were no bumps, dips, or wheel noises. The ride, she realized, was smoother and quieter than a prestige automobile. The vehicle floated along at the speed limit with no effort. The Professor moved the machine into the middle lane and then floated into the fast lane. The cars in the fast lane were speeding around 120 Km/hour. She heard no engine noise at the quicker speed.

"What powers this machine?"

"The engine is a bit complex."

"I am a scientist. I just graduated with a Master's degree in microbiology. I was top of my class. Try me." Diana was annoyed - men and their engines.

"The engine uses a quantum field controlling gravitons as the base engine. We travel at high speeds in any direction by leaking some dark energy repulsive gravitons from the rear of the machine. The torus at the front provides an anti-energy field to remove motion friction by creating a vacuum immediately in front of the vehicle."

Diana had studied physics enough to recognize some of the terms, but she was vastly out of her depth. Less annoyed now, she was more embarrassed, "Anti-energy?"

"Yes, you know, negative energy. You could call it a little antimatter field just sufficient to cancel air friction. Nature abhors a vacuum. The vacuum directly in front of us pulls us forward while removing drag. At these speeds, it does not matter; but at record-breaking speeds, the friction from the air can generate heat of up to 3,000 degrees centigrade."

"How fast can we go?" Diana felt tense again despite the smooth ride.

"That is the point of the test run. I am hoping we just zip past everyone."

The traffic ahead was slowing, which was normal on the 12 lanes of the 401 highway. Traffic snarls on this stretch of road were constant and usually for no apparent reason. You might stop dead and then travel at high speed. They pulled up next to a sports car. The driver was revving the engine and playing music loudly. He gave their vehicle a long look. He winked at Diana and revved his engine louder. Diana rolled her eyes - men and their machines.

"Should we take him? We don't have to wait. Shall we fly over these people in front of us?" Lazarus asked.

Diana laughed. She could fly over a traffic jam. "Yes, yes, yes. I always wanted to fly over traffic. Do it. But wait." She leaned forward, pointed at the sports car driver, and gestured with a flick of her head that he should follow them. "Okay. Let's zip over everyone."

The Professor pulled the vehicle above the car in front of them by three feet and then pushed the T-bar forward. They jumped to 150 Km/hour. They were flying ahead of thousands of vehicles. The acceleration from zero to 150 in less than a second should have powered them both back into their seats. She felt like they sat still while the other cars drove backward. The movement tricked her brain into seeing the Earth move while they stood still.

They were flying very fast. Diana thrilled as they zoomed ahead of the long lines of cars. A tractor-trailer was ahead. Before she could say anything, the Professor pulled higher, and they went smoothly up and over. A large sign before them broached the entire highway. They were heading straight for it with no time to react. Diana raised her arms in front of her face to brace for the crash. The vehicle, almost by itself, moved higher, and they floated over the sign as well. Diana's face was pale, but slowly the color returned. The Professor reacted with fantastic speed. She did not even see him adjust the height higher. They stayed at the higher level to avoid other trucks or overhead signs.

They zoomed ahead for 10 minutes until they passed the traffic jam and then settled back to the street level. The Professor slowed to the speed limit and traveled west. She realized her plan was working. For the first time in months, she forgot about the giant boulder of debt dragging her into an emotional and economic swamp of no return. She was on a wonderful, gut-wrenching exciting ride. Diana relaxed and smiled as she looked at the landscape. The cover was a window on the top and sides so she could stare at the sky as easily as the road. The Sun warmed her face.

Diana looked at the man next to her. They had never been close. He was about 40, so 15 years older than her. He looked fit with his hard biceps and a tight stomach. Although his curly blond hair and pale blue eyes were almost sexy, he was too old for her. He was probably handsome when he was younger.

"Do you have a license plate? Could the police stop us? Is this vehicle road-worthy? Do you have tail lights?" She could guess the answers.

"No license. Yes, the police could stop us. We are not road-worthy, and I have no lights. I don't think of this machine as a car but an ultralight airplane. Ultralights are little airplanes made in garages by hobbyists. The engines are homemade versions of a lawnmower engine. The regulators have only a few flight rules for ultralights."

"Perhaps, we should not be traveling on the road?"

"Good point, Diana." He turned off the road, across a grassy ditch, over a guard rail and flew directly to Lake Ontario while increasing the speed to 300 Km/hour. The machine worked perfectly at the new pace. The sunlight glinted on the lake as a few boats sailed below them. He moved the vehicle lower so she could have a better look. Over the first moments of panic and near-death, she was now enjoying the trip. She felt the brilliant Sun, watched the sailboats, and enjoyed the exciting free ride across the country.

"We can go up to 1,600 Km/hour as the maximum speed for the first level engine. The next stage engine can move us much faster, but I must warn you it will be an adrenaline rush. Are you up for it, or should I turn back?"

"I thought we were going to see your mom? I was looking forward to meeting her."

"You will like her. She is a gentle soul who loves tea and reading. My friends like her more than they like me. My friends exchange email conversations with her and don't copy me."

"Fine. Let's go see mom." Diana laughed.

"As I said, the engine has two stages. I flip the plastic cover to expose this red button for stage two. Don't ever push the button by mistake. Once I push it, a delayed reaction of about ten long seconds will pass before we feel a difference. Our machine will disengage from gravity. We will drift away from the planet. Once our gravity engine re-engages with the planet, our movement away from the planet will slow. When fully caught in the planet's gravitational field, we will be pulled in and catapulted forward at high speed. If you think of a skydiver, once you jump from the plane, as you fall, you continue to gain speed until you reach terminal velocity. If, of course, everything works as expected. Are you ready?"

"This is probably the craziest thing I have ever done. Just hit it, and turn me into an amateur test pilot?"

The Professor pushed the red button then sat firmly in his chair. He tensed his jaw as the seconds seemed to extend and extend. Diana braced herself. She waited, and when nothing happened, she turned to speak. The vehicle started to move at a heart-squeezing speed. The acceleration continued as they moved up and backward through clouds. They kept accelerating. It was as if the Earth just tossed them away and kept going. Up, up, up- more and more.

The planet was getting smaller. She started to panic despite trying to stay calm. The acceleration continued; this was a space launch. The vehicle hovered as the Earth moved further and further away. They were in space. Space! She felt nauseous. She had thoughts of floating away forever into deep space. The idea of being lost in space squeezed her mentally. She felt like the planet's gravity let go. She felt cold although her palms were sweating. The Professor pressed a blue oxygen button on the console.

The vehicle hovered, and just as he had said, the rubber band of gravity embraced them, and a pull took hold as predicted. They were in the grip of gravity. The ship began to re-enter the stratosphere. She recalled his comment about 3000-degree centigrade temperatures at high speeds.

"Normally, you must enter the atmosphere at just the right angle, while spraying freezing liquids on the hull to keep the friction temperature from melting the metal. If you calculate wrong, you can bounce off the atmosphere and back into space or burn up. You may have to re-enter a few times if you don't get the angles perfectly correct. I am counting on the torus vacuum to remove those issues."

"Do you know it will work, or are you putting faith in hope?" she shrieked.

"No hope involved. I tested everything in the laboratory with simulations and prototype models. We are on the first real test flight. The proof of concept worked well, but this is the real test."

The vehicle moved forward. The speedometer moved: 50, 100, 200, 400, 800, 1600, 3200, and kept going. Diana was concentrating on the speedometer. They were rushing into blue sky at 10,000 Km/hour and speeding up. She scanned the front looking for melting metal. The machine was moving smoothly. No violent vibrating, no rivets rattling, and no panels ripping off. The speedometer numbers kept climbing. They were flying at over 20,000 Km/hour and still speeding up. Her heart was beating so fast and loud, she felt she would pop. The speedometer was still going up but at a slower pace: 30,000. 33,000, 33,100, 33,200 .... peaking at 33,500 Km/hour.

"That was a bit disappointing. I thought we might hit 40,000 or 50,000. The total theoretical speed is 65,000. Since this is a test flight, I wanted to be a bit cautious."

Diana was stunned that he was talking so calmly. They were in the fastest flying machine ever built. Diana was in an adrenaline rush. What an extraordinary understatement. She tried to speak, but no words came. She was gripping the armrests so hard her hand started to spasm. She was almost panting. Diana closed her eyes, and she concentrated on slowing her breathing.

"Are you okay? You look a bit freaked out?"

"Wrk. Wort." Words were not forming correctly. Was she having a stroke? She took a long slow, deep breath. "What is the fastest anyone has gone?"

"Good question. The fastest military airplane flies at 3,540 Km/hour. The fastest rocket was the X-15A at 7,242 Km/hour, and the ...."

"We just broke the airspeed record by going 30,000 Km/hour faster than any record?" she interrupted him.

"No, not that much. The space shuttle re-entered at 17,000 mph, so about 27,358 Km/hour in scientific measures. We are only around 6,000 Km/hour faster than the record."

"Only 6,000. Sheesh, I feel cheated."

"Well, like I say, I was cautious."

She marveled at how he did not hear the sarcasm in her tone. He might be a great physics professor and builder of engines, but he was unaware of people's feelings.

She watched them move through clouds. She saw three cargo ships near the horizon. "How long to mom's house?"

"At this speed, we should be there in 15 to 20 minutes."

"Where is she?"

"Pretoria."

"Do you mean Pretoria, South Africa?" Diana asked with wide eyes.

"Yes. I thought you knew my mom was in South Africa."

"You took me on a test ride from Canada in the Northern Hemisphere to South Africa in the Southern Hemisphere?"

"True. It sounds like a stretch when you say it that way, but the trip will be less than 30 minutes. We are moving quickly.

Which way do you want to go? We can fly down the middle of Africa or hug the coastline. Have you been to Africa before?"

"No. I always wanted to go one day, perhaps join a safari to see animals in the wild. Could we go down the middle of Africa?" Her voice was shaky. She was still unsettled. This was why she hesitated to speak to him in the garage. You drop by to chat with a neighbor, but in his case, your whole life starts moving in a completely different direction. This wild trip was more unsettling than the jellyfish incident. If she was honest, the trip was also the most exciting adventure of her life. She was moving through a vast range of emotions but decided to make the best of the experience, given she had no choice at this point.

"Your wish is my command. The middle of Africa it is." He turned the vehicle, and they were flying over the ocean to the coast of Africa. He was flying about 200 feet above the sea. Dolphins swam and dove alongside a cargo ship. One dolphin moved out of the water, dancing backward on his tail. Its body was above the water except for the tail. She had no idea they played like that in the wild. Dolphins must love to perform. Sadly, she got only a brief glimpse of the dolphins given the vehicle's speed.

They left the Atlantic Ocean and powered across a lush green Africa. "Ivory Coast," he said with a nod of his head. Diana looked to her right side and saw a vast circle with a beautiful domed building. Mansions and estate buildings were positioned in a circle. "I think that building is Yamoussoukro. I am sure I mispronounced it." They were traveling almost 10 Km every second. Within three minutes, they were over Abuja in Nigeria.

Diana admired a colossal mosque in Abuja. She saw a massive gold dome with geometric patterns built around the trees, and four huge minarets surrounded the cupola. Each minaret reached high into the sky. The vehicle kept up the incredible speed. He flew two thousand feet in altitude so Diana could see more. There were animals everywhere. Hundreds of baboons were strolling across a road, and she saw thousands of wildebeests running across a plain. "We are crossing the Nki National Park and the Odzala-Kokoua park. We will also cross the Kruger National Park soon. Kruger is my favorite," he said.

As they left the Congo and neared the border with Zambia, a rocket soared up, looped in increasingly wider loops, and finally puttered and fell. At their speed, she had to look behind her to see the rocket drop. Diana admired the beauty of the fireworks before having a horrible thought.

"Is someone shooting rockets at us?" Diana asked. She bit her lower lip unconsciously.

Chapter 3 — Afternoon tea

"We did not file a flight plan. We are an unidentified object. We were trespassing in Congo airspace. Congo has rebel problems. I am not sure if rebels were firing at a suspected government plane, or the government was firing at a suspected rebel aircraft," said the Professor.

"They are trying to kill us," shouted Diana.

"It was a heat-seeking missile. Our engine does not burn fuel but uses gravity waves for power. The missile could find no heat to target except its own emissions. I suppose that is why it looped. It was trying to hit itself. There is the other thing."

"Other thing?"

"We are traveling faster than any rocket. We are moving faster than the outer range of the targeting system. A jet fighter firing a rocket will still not have enough combined velocity to catch us. We will arrive and leave before the targeting mechanism can lock onto our vehicle. They cannot intercept us or catch us at this speed. You are safe because I am not slowing down for you to get a better look at the majestic sights of Africa. They simply cannot catch us."

"I see." She needed to take the words in and process them. We filed no flight plans. We could be considered hostile by any national defense service. We should be safe if we go fast.

Diana could see a vast mist and several rainbows above a forest about 20 miles ahead. As they got closer, she could see the mist coming from a spectacular waterfall.

"Victoria Falls and the rain forest. In this forest, we see rain all day, every day. It is not actual rain but splashing and condensation from the waterfall," he said. "We will be in South Africa soon."

The vehicle sped over fewer trees, the foliage turned sparser to brush and bushes. The soil was red and dusty, with hills and mountains on both sides. Lazarus slowed down as they flew above another game reserve. Rivers were smaller. She saw about 20 elephants slowly moving toward the water. The smaller elephants used their trunks to hang on to another elephant tail ahead of them. Colorful birds were flying out of the trees. A few substantial grey birds the size of large turkeys flew above their vehicle.

"Ladida birds. The real name is the Hadeda Ibis, but everyone calls them Ladida because of the sounds they make," said the Professor.

She could see highways below and a suburban area. The vehicle slowed to about 150 Km/hour. They had been slowing for 20 minutes. The Professor pulled out his phone and brought up the Maps app. "Mom is nearby. There we go – Newlands Park." He smiled as the vehicle descended on a small road next to a shopping mall. They drove at about 50 Km/hour around a corner, flew over a 10-foot security gate, and across a driveway to the front lawn of a small cottage.

There was an escape of air when the hood was released. The Professor jumped over the edge and came around to help Diana from the car. Diana wondered if she was traveling in a car, an airplane, or a spaceship.

An older woman was working in the garden. She looked about 60 and was tall for a woman. She held a hand over her eyes as the Sun blinded her from seeing them. "Lazarus? Is that you? Why didn't you tell me you were coming? I am not dressed for guests". She looked down at her muddy hands. "I am a mess."

"Mom, we just dropped by for tea. Please let me introduce Diana. She is my neighbor in Canada and came along for the ride."

"Well, this is all a big surprise. I am pleased to meet you, Diana. What a lovely surprise. When did you fly into South Africa?" Mom was grinning widely and hugged Lazarus warmly.

"Oh, about 10 minutes ago. We got here and came straight to see you."

"Lovely. Lazarus, could you put the kettle on while I get cleaned up?"

They entered her small, warm, cozy cottage. Lazarus brewed tea in the kitchen. With a slight limp, Mom walked to the bathroom. On the wall, Diana saw pictures of Lazarus as a schoolboy. He wore an English school uniform, a school tie, a school cap, and polished black shoes. The cap was a bit skewed, and one shoelace was untied. Diana saw many ornaments of Africa, statues of elephants in a circle, a warthog carved in an unusual type of verdite stone, and a few needlepoint seascapes. A considerable book collection was on the wall with an eclectic collection from Agatha Christie's detective novels to scientific rants about the next pandemic.

Mom returned with combed hair, a clean dress, a pearl necklace, and wool slippers. She plopped into a cozy leather seat with blankets on the armrests. The Professor came in with the tea. He followed a ritual in pouring the tea, milk, and sugar with precision and detail.

"Mom has strict rules about the order of milk, tea, and sugar. The time needed for steeping and every other aspect of the tea performance must be perfect," he explained while looking at Diana. "I made you a spicy ginger tea. I hope that was a good choice? It is my favorite, and you can only get it here." Diana smiled and sipped the tea. The tea had a kick. The ginger was strong but sweet; however, not for the timid. The tea was delicious.

"Tell me all about yourself, Diana?' said Lazarus's Mom.

"Not much to tell. I just graduated with a Master's degree in microbiology six months ago."

"There must be more. You are on the cusp of an adventure. I can tell. What else?"

"Are you sure you want to hear more?"

"Please."

"I studied hard. I skipped time with friends. I missed parties, movies, and boyfriends, so I could have a successful life. In high school, I was top of my class. I went to a prestigious college and won many accolades. I graduated cum laude as the valedictorian and won a scholarship. The plan was to pursue a scientific career. I hope to make a few small discoveries to add to scientific literature. Most of all, I need money, or I will lose the family home and cannot pay off my enormous student loans. I call that debt *my boulder*. Every day, more interest is due, and my boulder grows in weight. I am tethered to poverty and possible eviction until I can find a full-time job."

"How much do you owe?"

"Just over one hundred thousand dollars. I feel buried and helpless."

"With all your academic success, you must have some offers."

"I was given a work term as part of my scholarship. I worked for a large chemical company. When I got there, I found 10 top students working for them from top schools worldwide, but only one job was available for the top performer. The rest of us were working for free for six months, for the *experience* they called it. The competition was fierce. The person who won the full-time spot, I found out much later, was related to an executive. I am not sure it mattered how much work I did."

"That does sound like a boulder. Are there no jobs at all?"

"There are some jobs. Just enough that we blame ourselves if we don't find work. For every full-time job, there are hundreds, even thousands of applicants. Of course, you can always work on the gig economy."

"What is the gig economy?"

"Temp jobs. Delivering pizza. Waitress at a restaurant. Retail clerk. They call it gig because they never give you full-time work with benefits. They carefully offer you one or two days, never full-time work. The jobs are just that, jobs. Not a career. No possibility of moving up the career ladder to more responsibility. All my friends are in the gig economy, and they are all brilliant, ambitious, and eager to work. We are skilled, but some scientists in Brazil, Vietnam, or China will work for less. We don't get hired. My boulder grows larger."

"I have been ignoring you, Lazarus. How long are you staying? I can make up the guest room. Why did you not tell me you were coming for a visit?"

"The trip was spontaneous. Normally, as you know, I'd need a two-day flight from Canada to South Africa with two days to return home, which is four days without any time together. It was just too long. I have been working for years on a faster way to see you. If I could make the trip faster, then I could drop by for tea, pick up some groceries for you, replace a light bulb, and fly back in time for work tomorrow."

"That would be lovely, but it is impossible. A bridge too far."

"He did it. We left this morning and got here in a couple of hours. It was the most amazing, exciting, nail-biting, gut flattening, mind-blowing, scary, fantastic journey ever. It was totally amazing. I was shocked, angry, thrilled, and afraid- all at the same time. It was awesome in every cell of my body, from my hair to my little toe," said Diana.

"Is this true?" Mom looked at the Professor.

"Indeed. It is, but sadly an hour from now, I need to take Diana home as promised. She just came along for a quick test drive. We will be gone, but I plan to see you a few times a month."

"That is wonderful," said Mom.

The room went silent. Each person was thinking of how this would change what was possible. All three of them reached for their tea at the exact moment, sipped a little, then put the teacups down at precisely the same time. They laughed at the synchronicity. They were happy. A was mother reunited with her son, and life was grand.

Everyone in the room realized the world was smaller, boundaries to travel were changed forever. Mom spoke first, "I have a thought. I saw something in the newspaper today. There is a competition for the fastest land speed record, and the prize is $100,000. The race is somewhere in the USA. Lazarus, do you think you could help Diana? The prize money would pay the full loan."

"I could never take the whole prize. At most, I could take half, but I don't deserve even that much," said Diana.

"You can fly us home. I will show you the controls," said Lazarus to Diana.

Diana was anxious again. She was scared as a passenger. Could she drive that machine at 30,000 Km/hour and not get lost in space?

"I must warn you. We did not file flight plans. The Americans are tough about border controls and airspace. You can keep the entire prize, but you must agree to take full responsibility for any risks going to the contest."

"When is the contest?" asked Diana. Mom flipped through the newspaper on the coffee table and pulled the page with the contest story.

"It says the contest is tomorrow afternoon."

"I must teach at the college tomorrow, but if you want to take the machine, you can. Diana, there could be obstacles we have not considered."

"Like what?"

"I don't know, but please check it out thoroughly before you go. You may need to make some preparations. I will leave that part to you." There was another pause in the conversation.

"Lazarus. You kept this project very secret."

"Mom, I did not want to get our hopes up until the machine worked."

"Yes, but how does it work?"

"It is a bit complicated. One large part is motion without moving. One part is suction into an induced vacuum, and the last part is graviton repulsion."

Mom looked at Diana. "That is typical of my boy. He talks in riddles and then waits for us to beg him to clarify his cryptic little hints. Does he do that with you, too?"

Diana laughed. "He does and worse. He makes spectacular, unique observations about nature and then leaves. I found myself obsessing for years about his jellyfish observations."

"Really?" said the Professor.

"We are waiting, my boy."

Diana looked at the Professor differently. He was about 40, but his mom still saw him as her little boy. She pictured him at 40 with his school cap and half-tied shoelaces. The image made her giggle.

"How can I explain motion without moving? Hmm. Think of it this way. The Earth is spinning at about 700 to 1600 Km/hour, depending on how far you are from the equator. What if I could cancel gravity so the Earth moves, but we do not. If you see a train next to you leave the station, you feel you are traveling when you are not. The movement is relative to the train beside you."

"There are three obvious issues with that idea. First, when you stop gravity, why don't you just fly off the planet into the abyss? Second, 700 Km/hour is about a commercial jet's speed, so you would take just as long to get to South Africa. Finally, how could you fly in the opposite direction of the Earth's orbit if you wanted to go in that direction?" said Mom.

Diana watched the conversation. Mom was not old and confused. The Professor's Mom was sharp, and her brain was laser-focused on the issues. Her body was slow and stiff, but her mind was flying fast. The older woman may also have lifted her boulder with the land-speed idea. Could any of this be real? Could Diana really drop the debt boulder?

"The idea first came to me when I realized gravity was the weakest of the natural forces of nature. Gravity is weak compared to magnetic or nuclear forces. With some research, I theorized that gravitational forces are spread across the ten dimensions of space. Gravity is not binary. Gravity is not like a light switch that goes on and off. Gravity is more like a dimmer switch that can be dialed up or down to alter the forces. The percentage of gravity controls the answer to your first question. We don't switch gravity off and fly away. We turn down the knob a few degrees and let the planet shift under us."

"That still leaves us with the second issue."

"Yes. The Earth is spinning but is also moving around the Sun at about 65,000 Km/hour. As you said, if we disengage gravity completely, we stop moving, and Earth flies away. When we re-engage, as long as we don't take too long, we are dragged back into Earth's orbit at tens of thousands of kilometers an hour. We would burn up at that speed when we hit the atmosphere or travel at high speed within the atmosphere, and that problem took many years to solve. I found a way to create a small vacuum directly in front of the ship using negative energy. This idea solved the second problem."

"My son, I know you can do anything you set your mind to."

"For your third issue, two of the ten dimensions shown to us by string theory have a repulsive gravitational force. Our experience of gravity between objects allows for only attractive forces. If I leak some repulsive gravitons from these two dimensions to the far side of the machine, we can move against the spin of the orbit."

"I am so pleased you spent your time focused on overcoming the natural laws so you could see me." Mom was so full of pride you could almost touch the pride emanating from her.

"There is a third complexity that could cause annihilation by something as small as a raindrop or a flying bug. I suggest we leave the remainder of the scientific discussion for the next visit? I need Diana to fly me home. I have work tomorrow."

The Professor stood up. Mom and Diana followed. They ambled to the machine while Mom kept talking about her garden. The proteas were blooming, and she did not want them to go without seeing the flowers.

"Please call me Denise," she said to Diana. "Thank you for the visit. I hope your boulder rolls away in a few days." She gave Diana a handshake and a little hug.

"Lazarus." She gave him a big, lingering hug. She had a little tear in her right eye, but she said nothing.

Diana started to climb into the passenger seat, but he stood and gestured to the driver's side. She went around and took the pilot seat. Lazarus jumped into the passenger seat. Everyone waited for Diana to turn the machine on. Diana had meant to ask more about possible annihilation.

Chapter 4 — Look for a pelican

She pushed the start button, which turned green. She put a seat belt across each shoulder, but the next step brought trepidation.

"Turning left or right is the same as driving. If you move the steering column up or down, you move up or down. The tricky part is braking. You need to slow your speed with the T-bar while gently moving the vehicle up. Why don't you practice by driving in circles around the parking lot?" said Lazarus.

She drove around a tree in the middle of the parking area. She moved the T-bar one notch forward, and the vehicle drifted slowly along. Every 10 yards, she tried to bring the machine to a stop. She could see why he struggled with his first stop. It looked easy, but she found having the right touch difficult. She expected a few fumbles, but after nine or ten failed attempts to stop, she felt she might never get it. The craft was still drifting forward while she glanced back at his mother. She felt embarrassed. Was she going to fail? Diana huffed in frustration.

"You are doing fine. It took me twice as long to get it right."

He was helping her, not laughing at her mistakes. She felt more confident. She gritted her teeth and doubled her effort, but she failed again and again. She was about to give up when it worked. She stopped. She tried again and stopped again. She picked up speed to a running pace and successfully stopped again. Diana beamed. She did it. She could fly this insane contraption and possibly pay off a lifetime debt in one afternoon.

"Okay, let's roll over to the security gate," he said. The vehicle moved at 2 Km/hour forward and came to a stop at the security gate. A large fellow in a uniform came out of the hut and walked to the main entrance. "Try going up and fly over the gate." She did. The vehicle moved smoothly up at the same speed as it moved forward. The guard jumped back, his eyes wide, as the machine slowly rose above him and moved over the gate. He smiled widely and waved at Diana. A gardener and a maid were chatting nearby. The guard shouted for them to look. Diana glanced back as she headed down the road toward the strip mall. She moved the vehicle to street level.

"Take the next two left turns, then follow the traffic signs to Windhoek, Nambia."

"Are we going to Windhoek?"

"No, we are going to cross the Atlantic Ocean, but the highway to Nambia is moving us in the right direction. Windhoek is the biggest city in Nambia, so that is the name we will see on the signs."

Diana followed the signs. The traffic was not heavy, but the suburbs had many roundabouts and bumps in the road to slow traffic. At first, she approached the speed bumps slowly out of habit, but she started to speed up since they just floated over them. Once on the main highway, she moved the T-bar to speed up to 200 Km/hour, and she took flight above the traffic by about 30 feet to avoid traffic signs. When she felt comfortable at this speed, she moved up to 300 Km/hour, and they flew directly toward the coast. The area around Pretoria was similar to any big American city. They flew past many highways, roads, rows of houses, gas stops, and business malls. The flight was boring. She would have loved to see lions and other majestic animals.

They continued for an hour, watching the suburban green grass and trees turn to semi-arid brush and sand. Diana felt comfortable. She relaxed more, and she got comfortable. They moved higher to about 50 feet to avoid hitting low flying birds. Diana moved the vehicle slightly to the left and then to the right just for fun. He smiled but said nothing as she became more confident.

All was going well when a large white bird with a massive wingspan of about 10 feet dropped directly in front of them. Diana had no time to react. She watched in shock as the collision became inevitable. Diana raised her arms to protect her face. It happened in only seconds, but mentally the time extended. She felt as if the accident was taking place in slow motion, as if her mind was taking a series of photographs, with each picture bringing disaster closer. She waited for the crash, the shattering of the windshield, and the explosion of blood, bone, and metal.

There was no splat. Diana experienced no bursts of metal and debris. The bird was gone, and the vehicle continued. She looked around wildly. Were they dead? Did she have a mental episode? Did she fall asleep, and this was a dream? It seemed so tangible. Lazarus was smiling an inane smile.

"You are alive and well. If you recall, I said negative energy creates a vacuum directly in front of the machine. The bird was directly in front of us so was hit with negative energy to create a vacuum."

"What? Yes. What?"

"The vacuum is not just there to deal with orbital re-entry air friction. You cannot travel 10,000 Km/hour into a bug or raindrop. The small object would hit with such velocity the energy might penetrate the machine, pass through our bodies, and explode in such a mess we would never survive. I had to create a vacuum for such an incident. A raindrop could annihilate us. You see now why it took me 16 years of tinkering in the garage. The problem of flying 12,000 kilometers across half the planet in two hours is not trivial."

"Bird," she said. She was in shock.

"I know. I did not anticipate a 20-pound pelican. I have no idea what that bird was doing flying 1,000 kilometers inland. I tested for small collisions, not 20-pound flying objects. That bird was a surprise."

"Big bird." She knew she was not making sense, but the words just dribbled out.

"Diana. Take us up higher. Do it. Do it now before we hit another bird."

She jolted back and somewhat mechanically followed instructions. She moved the vehicle higher, and they flew in silence for about 15 minutes. The flight was dangerous. She should never have let herself feel comfortable. The African Sun, the gentle movement, had lulled her into comfort. She was the pilot. She had to stay alert, or they would both die in seconds. She was the captain of this plane.

They flew across increasingly dry land. Namibia is mainly desert - golden beach sand for miles in every direction. A thousand miles of beach with no water or food. You see the odd hill, the occasional metal shack, but the place is a desert. It is strange to have a sea of water alongside a land so utterly arid.

"Sperrgebiet," he said. "The only national park in the world that prohibits people. You have 20,000 square kilometers of desert. No vehicle is allowed to leave once it enters because of the diamonds. They are afraid you will smuggle out diamonds somewhere on the truck so no truck can leave. There are so many diamonds; people say you can walk around and pick them off the ground."

"That looks like deer?"

"Yes, there are some springbok, gemsbok, and even a few hyenas. I suppose they survive in this desert because there are so few people. If they catch you taking a diamond, you get a 15-year prison term for one small gem."

"Nambia has an area called the Skeleton Coast because so many people sail in and die of thirst. The only water is from sea fog. People try to sail in and steal diamonds. The police find lots of shipwrecks and skeletons along this coastline. Did you want to stop and look around?"

"We better not."

"Good decision. My mom toured here when she was younger. She said the trip was rough, hot, and difficult. A few people are allowed in with a special permit and only with a tour guide. Anyone you see is probably a security person driving about looking for lost or dying adventurers. "Why don't we take the jump to space and pick up speed for the journey home?"

Diana was dreading this moment, but she knew it must come. She closed her eyes. She sang a little mantra from a popular song her mother loved to play. "I am a woman. Hear me roar. I am strong. I can do anything. I am invincible." With firm resolve, she flipped the plastic cover to the red button. She closed her eyes again, sang her song, and pushed the red button.

As before, nothing happened. They sat braced for what was coming. The slow seconds ticked for ten long ticks. There was a little drop in speed as the planet beneath them started to pull away. Diana understood what was happening. The first engine emitted gravitons on the underside of the vehicle. Without gravity, the vehicle ascended out of the Earth's atmosphere. Now the vehicle maintained a relatively slow speed. The planet spins on its axis but also orbits the Sun. The Earth's spin is hundreds of kilometers per hour, but the planet's speed around the Sun is 65,000 Km per hour. They felt like they were flying backward at thousands of kilometers an hour; however, it was actually the planet flying ahead. The land looked smaller. The clouds looked smaller. She had done this before but could not help but feel panic growing as she saw Earth, her home, her only home, fly away. The planet looked like it was almost gone when the pull began. Gravity was re-engaging. A slow but ever-growing pull that sucked them back. The elastic band of gravity extended, and now they were snapping back with speed as the intense fury of gravity caught them in a web of force. The speedometer started to spin 1,000, 5,000, 10,000, 20,000, 25,000. The super-acceleration started to slow the increase in thousands until it topped close to 34,000 Km/hour. The experience reminded her of a video she saw about using gravity with a slingshot approach for faster space travel.

"We are moving a bit faster this time if I recall our last epic trip. I will need to examine the machine to understand the variation," said Lazarus.

Diana stayed firmly against the seat. She could not casually talk when she was the pilot. She wished he would just shut up and let her focus on driving at the insane speed.

"Why don't you fly toward Brazil. We can cross the Atlantic and then fly along the seaboard north to the coast of Canada."

She didn't answer him, and she didn't look at him. She kept her eye on the sea ahead. Time passed, and the sea was all you could see in any direction. She found nothing to do and nothing to see except the sea.

"I went to sea to see the world, and what did I see? I saw the sea." He laughed. "Mom taught me that little ditty."

They crossed the Atlantic in 15 minutes. Turning north, Diana moved along the coastline. The Sun was shining. As the water moved, the sea glinted with the Sun. She felt her initial anxiety replaced with a sense of accomplishment. She was flying a plane for the first time. She had control. She was the master of her destiny and the destiny of her odd neighbor. She was breaking speed records. She moved the machine to about 30,000 feet above sea level.

"You know, this technology is a breakthrough innovation. You should file a patent and sell it to the highest bidder. You could be richer than kings and queens."

"Yes. I could, but I have concerns. First, a worldwide patent would cost about $100,000. Second, you must file your designs and specifications to prove you made a truly unique invention. As soon as you file, patent lawyers find and copy any designs that look valuable. These corporate lawyers want to steal your ideas. They replicate your design, change one or two minor things, and claim a new invention. Worse, they sift backward through past designs, looking for any similar components so they can threaten to sue you for patent infringement. They say you violated their past patent. The government finances and runs the patent system so poorly that the patent system creates more harms than benefits."

"What do you mean, harms? That sounds like an exaggeration."

"As an example, say you are the CEO of an oil company. Someone makes a huge innovation in battery designs. You buy the patent without any intention of using new batteries to prevent a global warming crisis. You buy the patent to prevent people from using new batteries instead of oil. The patent system is being used to prevent energy improvements and maintain oil profits."

"That is awful."

"The solution is so easy. You have a law for patents; use it or lose it. If you don't bring new technology to market within five years, you lose the patent, and the technology is free to the world. The law would help bring innovations to the world that could improve our lives."

"Wow. I am sorry I asked. I was hoping to invent ways to use microbes to solve food, energy, or even lifespan problems. I have dreams of science prizes and wealth. I want to make a difference. I want to leave an improved world for my children."

"I saw a report showing 40% of cancer cures are not studied because researchers are unsure if there is a patent violation. They do not want to face a lot of litigation. How is the patent system dangerous? When the system hurts human survival and prevents cures to horrible diseases. You should plan how you release your ideas to the world."

"No one in my science classes taught us about the underbelly of finance, power, and control. I feel innocent when talking about this stuff."

"Look, the Caribbean islands. We are getting closer."

Diana could see the long island of Cuba ahead. As they approached Miami, they could see more boats and ships. The many boats bobbed up and down. From above, it looked like almost everyone must own a boat. She smiled. They were flying above it all. Below, tiny people enjoyed a little sailing.

In the East, she saw a massive aircraft carrier. Two jets from the carrier flew toward them and gained altitude quickly. He was right. With each passing second, the jets fell further behind. She turned her head, but within minutes, she could not see them.

"You saw it too? We are on the radar of the American navy."

"Should I be worried? Are they going to launch missiles at us from some military satellite in space?"

"There are no space missiles. That was a waste of money. It is too difficult to target one fast-moving object with another fast-moving object and accurately hit it."

"I saw something on TV showing they could do it."

"That demo was a PR stunt. They gave the seeking missile the trajectory of the target missile." The professor laughed. "Given the shape of our machine, they are probably having trouble deciding what to report. I can hear them now. "Yes, we saw a flying saucer. It was moving too fast for our fastest jets. Our pictures are blurry because of the speed. The aliens are coming!" I wonder if they will report the alien sighting in some bland way; perhaps saying a *visual anomaly was detected,* but a close inspection revealed nothing."

Diana laughed with restraint. She was concerned American jets had tried to pursue them. She felt the navy was unlikely to give up easily. She laughed despite her worries because they probably did look like a flying saucer.

"With Canada only 3,000 kilometers ahead, we should start slowing down."

Diana nodded and pulled the T-bar back to increase the gravitational pull on the vehicle. They were almost home, and she could be eating dinner in an hour. Diana was nervous about the American air force. Should she go north until they reached Nova Scotia or take the shortest route through New York State to Toronto? New York would be too congested. Since they had no radar, she could not see approaching planes except visually. It was too dangerous to fly close to New York. They slowed from 34,000 to 10,000 Km/hour when they got near New York. It only took a few minutes to reach Maine. She decided to fly across Maine and Vermont to Lake Ontario.

She saw two more fighter jets on her left. This was the second attempt. Even at 10,000 Km/hour, the jets kept falling farther back. The Americans were not giving up. They were sending jets that were likely armed with machine guns and missiles.

"We have a tricky problem. If we keep slowing down, the jets will catch us. If we do not slow down, we will fly past our destination in a few minutes. What do you want to do?"

"What do I want to do?" said Diana.

Chapter 5 — Land speed record

Diana realized the obvious. She was in charge. Diana was the pilot, and it was her call. She was the captain when it was fun flying across an open sea. She was also the captain when things went wrong. She thought quickly, and she concluded that the boss does not have to make every decision."

"I am open to suggestions."

"It will take only six minutes to reach Toronto at 10,000 Km/hour, so I suggest we hold this speed for two minutes and then slow as fast as possible to 100 Km/hour and drop down to the highway. If they are looking in the sky, they won't find us. If they look to the road, we will be invisible in plain sight. They will see tens of thousands of vehicles, and each vehicle will provide us with camouflage. We will be one leaf among ten thousand."

"Right." She decided against Lake Ontario. She let the machine fly at 10,000 for two minutes until she saw the highway ahead. She pulled the T-bar back and dropped altitude. The change in speed pushed them deep into their seats. The flight was more exciting than a roller coaster. She felt like screaming with fear and excitement. She did scream, just for fun, "Whoooo. Rock and roll, here we go."

They dipped fast as the speed fell furiously. The ground seemed to rush toward them, and adrenaline rushed inside them. She had to fight with the steering to align the vehicle with the road. They dipped a bit and overswung, then swung back as she tried to get the alignment right. Dropping to the highway, she became increasingly aware, required skilled flying. She had to get her momentum to match the ground traffic momentum to avoid running straight into the rear of a truck. She was hovering about 20 feet above traffic, watching for overhead signs, making turns to follow the road, and aligning with the traffic speed. She was too focused to think about the danger. She dropped to road level but quickly moved up to go over a slower-moving truck. She settled back down a few hundred yards beyond the truck.

"Whew. Made it," Diana said. She felt her palms were wet with sweat. Sweat soaked her armpits. A ridiculous thought, she wondered if she had an unpleasant body odor? "I would not want to do that again. Do you think we lost them? We don't look exactly like other cars?"

"I expect some traffic cameras will get pictures of us, and if they notice, we might find ourselves on the news. I do not know if American fighter jets will enter Canadian airspace. I am fairly certain they won't fly low over congested areas. They will definitely not open fire on suburbanites driving cars down the highway. We are safe for now. There will be some postings on social media of the flying saucer. Do you think most people will see us as just a prank posting?"

"Not if we keep flying around."

"I planned to use the machine every two weeks to see my mom. I plan to drive my car to work and hide the machine in the garage. For tomorrow, I will leave the garage door closed but unlocked. You should know that I have many defensive measures to protect the machine from falling into the wrong hands. Please take this little brooch that looks like a two-inch black beetle.

Without this beetle, you cannot fly. It works like a remote, keyless entry system for a car. If there is no key on your body, the machine won't start. The key is a bit sophisticated. Just keep the beetle in your pocket, and all will go well. Without it, the machine will not cooperate."

"Okay. Are you sure you don't mind me flying off on my own?"

"You can take the machine. I trust you. Please be sure your planning is thorough."

She looked at the beetle. "This brooch looks exactly like the real machine but smaller."

"It is exactly like the real machine. I built a small prototype for cost reasons and did all the testing and improvements on the beetle. A few hundred prototypes did not work."

Diana now looked at his coat more closely. The buttons on the coat were all beetle prototypes of different sizes. He had beetle ornaments on the sleeves, beetles on the coat lapels, and coat button beetles. The beetles looked like miniature adornments or odd buttons, but they were all prototypes of different sizes. Diana made a mental note to ask him about the beetles another time.

She turned her attention to the traffic. The remainder of the journey was calm. They traveled slowly despite light traffic. No one needed more excitement. The test flight was successful and that was enough. They spoke little. When they got home, the Sun was setting. A beautiful pink sky with whisks of light cloud provided a celebration in shades of intense pink. They were tired from too much excitement. Diana felt like she had run 20 marathons. The verbose professor was smiling but subdued.

"I still cannot believe you would trust me with this awesome machine," said Diana.

"I made your mother a promise that if you asked for help, I would help you. She was very persuasive. I never break a promise. I keep my word as a matter of honor and reputation. You need help. As promised, I am giving you some help."

Diana did not know. She was never told about the promise. Was her mother thinking about the need for a bowl of sugar or some garden shears?"

They parked the vehicle in the garage and went their separate ways.

The land speed trials are on the Bonneville Salt Flats, 40 square miles in Utah. He told her twice to prepare, so she spent a few hours mapping the approximately 3,500-kilometer journey along a route to reduce unwanted attention. She did not want fighter jets joining in on the journey. The plan was simple. Keep the trip as short as possible, fly high, and fly fast.

She rolled the machine out of the garage. She closed the garage door, jumped into the machine, and drove on small backroads to the lake. It was after rush hour, so traffic was light. The trip to the lake took about 15 minutes. As soon as she got to the lake, she hit the red button, built speed up to over 30,000 Km/hour, and flew across Canada to Winnipeg at high altitude. She got to Winnipeg in about four minutes. She banked south to Utah for about two minutes to reach the Utah border, slowed down fast, and drifted to street level. She drove slowly to the Bonneville raceway.

Diana was unsure what to expect but was surprised to drive by a casino. She expected to find a farming community of primarily religious folk. She found the salt flats easily. The area was 30 or 40 miles with low hills in the distance and a few small water areas. She parked and walked up to a gathering of people. Daina was looking for a check-in desk.

"Are you here to race?" said a middle-aged man with a large brown beard.

"Yes."

"What event?"

"I was hoping for the land speed record."

"Go to staging area four. We will have some questions, and we need to inspect your vehicle. Wear this on your jacket." He gave her a red ribbon. "If you need to change into racing gear, there is a tent over there," he gestured with his thumb.

"Racing gear. Is that really needed?" Diana thought. I just raced across most of the country in six minutes. Do I need a racing suit to do it? She sat on a foldout lawn chair for about 20 minutes with her vehicle alongside. She watched three men in white coats, no doubt officials, moving from station to station talking and laughing. These people were a community. She was the outsider, the unknown, in this society.

She looked at the team next to her. The driver wore a racing suit, and he had a balaclava pulled up around his head. He gave her a wink when he caught her looking. Diana quickly looked away. He tossed a full-face helmet in a circle to loosen his arm joints. She wore a T-shirt, sweater, tight jeans, and pink running shoes. Diana thought of herself as a nerdy science geek, not a fashion icon. She was beginning to think she did not prepare as successfully as the professor had asked.

The three officials came to her station. "Hi, I'm Jim, this is Bobby, and the big guy at the end is Frederick."

"Just call me Freddy," said the big guy. He was about 6 feet 2 inches and looked about 6 foot 2 inches in circumference at his equator. He stretched out his hand to Diana with a big grin.

"So, show us what we have here. Is this the vehicle?"

"Yes," said Diana.

"Is this wheel driven?" Diana was not exactly sure what he meant. Was he talking about a ground-based wheeled vehicle or an engine driving a shaft to deliver torque to wheels? She assumed the latter.

"It is on wheels, but there is no driveshaft. The engine is a bit complex. Actually, two engines can each provide power to the machine separately."

"Okay, a hybrid engine. We need to know, so we enter your vehicle in the proper category," said Jim.

"Are you fuel-based? Is this engine using rocket fuel, standard gasoline, or are you electric?" said Bobby.

"No fuel is used. Electric is the best answer," said Diana. She was feeling very unprepared. She had inadvertently ignored the professor's advice.

"Good. That explains why I do not see any fire extinguishers. Oh, that looks like one," Jim said while pointing to the oxygen tank used when the machine went to high altitude.

"We need to see the engine, then we do a safety inspection, and finally, we will ask to see your driver's license."

"I cannot see the hood release?" said Jim.

Diana had no idea how to look at the engine. She was winging it. "You just slide underneath."

Jim slipped out of his white coat and slid underneath. "My, my, my, my," Jim came back up. He whistled for a full minute and shook his head. "I am not sure if this is a joke, but your engine is more complex than my decades in car shops can handle. Take a look, Fred."

Fred walked off and came back with the car jack. He pumped the machine up one foot, then slid under with a flashlight. Diana heard some grunts. Fred was humming and mumbling and making 'ah' and 'oh' sounds galore. After ten endlessly long minutes, Fred emerged. "Lady, I am a physics professor at MIT. Your engine is the most sophisticated engine I have ever seen. It looks like a miniaturized cyclotron particle accelerator. If you told me you could fold space, generate mini-black holes, and create antimatter particles, I would be skeptical but would not laugh. What is your source of power? All I could see was a few tiny lithium batteries. There is not enough battery power here for a vehicle. You might have enough power to start an engine, but not much more. I would not call this an electric engine." He paused for a few seconds, then asked in a whisper, "Is this machine radioactive?"

Diana gasped a little. Had she been flying around in a radioactive capsule? Was her chance of having a deformed baby quadrupled? She stuttered a little while the three men waited for an answer. "I said it was complex."

"...and you were right," interrupted Fred.

"What is this big circle thing in the front? Is this a huge horn in case someone gets in your way? It looks like a truck horn, and you supersized it?" said Bobby.

Diana was happy Bobby was changing the topic from a radioactive engine. "It is a torus."

Fred looked askance. "It is a torus, but a torus is just a term for a geometrical configuration. What does it do?" Diana looked a bit perplexed. "Don't tell me. Let me guess. It is complicated."

"Yes. It is a bit complex."

"You know," said Bobby. "I think we are looking at a flying saucer. Did you get help from aliens?" Bobby giggled at his own joke. It was surprising to hear an official giggle.

Fred was not laughing. He looked worried.

"I see you have an excellent safety harness for the pilot. I do not see any brakes? Do you have a brake chute?" said Jim. Diana again looked puzzled. "You know, a big parachute that gets launched if you need to slow down quickly," added Jim.

"No chute," said Diana.

"Do you have fire-resistant underwear, bodysuit, gloves, and full-faced helmet?" said Jim.

"No. Perhaps, I could borrow some fire-retardant clothes? The machine is not fuel-based, so I thought it was unlikely to burst into flames."

"Have you done a blindfold test?" said Jim. We must be sure you can stop the engine, unbuckle the seatbelts, and release the cockpit latch when smoke or shattered glass is obstructing your vision."

"I have not passed the blindfold test. I am attempting my first land speed run."

"My last question," said Bobby. "Can I see your driver's license?" Diana gave him her license. "This looks like a standard license to drive a car on a city street. The license I want to see is the graduated speed license. You need a class A license if you want to go over 400 mph. If you want to go over 300 mph, you need a B license, and for 200 mph, you need a C license. You need two successful tests at each stage before you can travel faster than 400 mph."

"From my reading, the current land speed record is 763 mph, about 1,100 Km/hour," said Diana. "I would need an A license to break the record."

The three men were grinning. "Did you expect to break the record on your first attempt? Just checking?" said Bobby.

"I hoped I could."

They all laughed. The three men laughed long and hard while slapping each other on the knee and back. They started to speak, saying one word such as 'today' or 'first attempt,' and howled again for a minute. Diana was a bit uncomfortable as she looked at station five. The machine there was a rocket on wheels. There were four or five mechanics, some engineers doing calculations, and a pile of about 30 tires. The people all wore matching uniforms. Diana felt like a little girl and the butt of a joke. She was so unprepared she should give herself the most outstanding chump of the year award.

Finally, Fred calmed down enough to speak. "You obviously cannot compete in any land speed trial. We can let you race in the acceleration trials. We are looking for the fastest time for the quarter mile. For a production car, a Tesla would do it in 10.4 seconds. A Suzuki Hayabusa can do it in 9.3 seconds. The Busa, Hayabusa for the correct name, is not a production car and can run at maximum output for only four to six seconds. Does that interest you? Do you think you could beat those times?"

"Yes, I want to do the acceleration test." Diana was hopeful of a chance to show she was not a young fool. She would not win significant prize money, but she could leave without shame.

"One important question before I approve. Please tell me I was not poking and touching a radioactive core when I put my face inches from your engine?" said Fred.

"I would not want to sit on a radioactive core. You can see there are no cooling rods," Diana said while trying to remember what the professor told her. "The first engine uses quantum fields, and the torus uses anti-energy."

Fred nervously moved his hand across his red beard, and he pulled a bit at the end. He took a deep breath, then said nothing. He took another breath, then said, "I might be a fool, or you might be a genius, but I have to see if this flying saucer can move faster than a Tesla. I especially want to know if you can go fast on wheels that look like you plucked them from a baby carriage."

The three men walked to the next station. Bobby kept looking over his shoulder and giggling. Diana wanted to slap him, but she felt she did not deserve to be in the competition and a war with an official was not wise.

Diana spent a few hours watching massive engines blast rocket fuel while making ear-ripping noises. The smell was awful. The noise was painful. She now understood why station five had 30 or 40 tires. The car pulled away so fast it could strip the rubber off the tire in seconds. Smoke and burning rubber smells were drifting in the wind after every trial. The race consisted of two steps. You cover a 10-mile track in one direction, and then after 30 minutes or less, you make the return trip. They average your times, which addresses any speed due to wind blowing behind you.

Finally, Diana got her chance. She had chosen a standing start. She pulled up to the line. Apparently, there had been a lot of chatter about her entry, so everyone was watching. Diana pushed the green button. There was no noise. She put her hand on the T-bar, waiting for the green traffic light to give her the start sign. Since there was no engine noise, the crowd thought she was not ready. One of the officials started to walk over to her when the signal turned green. Diana rammed the T-bar up and took off at 700 Km/hour. Since the first part was moving west, she could use motion without moving. The silent engine held the vehicle still while the Earth was spinning. She had a standing start of 700 Km/hour without a sound. She counted one hundred, two hundred, three hundred, four hundred. She must have done the quarter mile in under five seconds, or about half the Busa's time. She slowly turned around and drove back to the crowd. The official time showed 4.8 seconds.

Diana had broken a world record for acceleration. The crowd was throwing hats and jumping. A small group of mechanics ran to her. As Diana got out of the car, they lifted her onto their shoulders. She got grease on her clothes, but she did not care. They threw her into the air. Someone sprayed her face with champagne. Everyone around her was screaming. Diana enjoyed the thrill of a win after the poor first impression. They thought she was a joke. Now, she was a triumph. The crowd gathered around her shouting questions. People took photos.

She saw Bobby walking away, talking on a cell phone. She was pleased to see he was not giggling. He looked grim.

"You asked me to call you if I saw anything special," said Bobby.

"Yes. What is so special?"

"There is this girl."

"A special girl. I am so glad you called. Is she the one? I am damn busy. Get to the point or get off the phone."

"Yes, Sir. This girl just broke the acceleration record, the world acceleration record. I do not mean by a tenth of a second. She cut the acceleration record in half from 9.3 seconds to 4.8 seconds."

"That is impressive, but why should I care? I am paying you for more than information about speed records."

"She did not use fuel. No rocket engine, no gasoline, and no batteries. Something new."

"Now that is interesting. I want the details. You just earned your fee. What is the name of this girl? What is the power source for the machine? Send me everything you can about her and her engine, and I will double your fee."

"Yes, Mr. Ares." John Ares turned around and waved for his associate at the far side of the room to continue. The large man with a scar on one cheek used one hand to hold someone in a business suit against the wall. When the large man saw the wave, he bent at the waist, pulled back both hands into fists, and in seconds hammered the person 20 to 30 times in the stomach. The man in the fine suit coughed blood and slid to the floor.

Chapter 6 — CEO

Leo entered the CEO's office. John Ares, looking dapper, walked around his enormous desk with a big smile. Ares was trim, clean-cut, and seemed genuinely happy to see Leo.

"Leo, I am so glad to meet you."

"My pleasure, Mr. Ares."

"Please, call me John."

Leo was taken aback. Mr. Ares was treating him, a rookie, the youngest member of the marketing team, as a friend. Ares had a reputation as a ruthless executive. The rumor was Ares left a long trail of bodies behind him as he climbed to the top. The man was nothing like his reputation. Ares was friendly and charming.

"Leo, I am sorry it took me so long to meet you in person. Are they treating you well?"

"Yes, Sir. I am sorry it took this long to meet you too."

Ares paused, then laughed. Ares liked courage and felt good about his choice of Leo.

"Leo, I have an opportunity for you. Do you want to hear more?"

"Absolutely. "

"Good man." Ares pushed a button on his desk and a large monitor displayed on the wall. Ares clicked a few items on a tablet, and a picture of a pretty young girl was shown. "This girl has access to an engine that does not use gasoline or batteries.

We need to buy that engine. We need to find the plans for that engine. We need to find out everything we can about her and that engine. Can you do that?"

"She is pretty enough. I might enjoy this assignment."

"We are an oil company. Technologies that do not use oil are not welcome. We have to shut it down quickly. Buy the engine, buy the plans, hire the designer, and buy the patents, if any. My lawyers are trolling for patents now. At this time, all we have is this photograph."

"No name?"

"She won an acceleration speed test. Unfortunately, when she found out there was no prize money, she gave a false name. Diana Rocket. She also slipped away from the crowd before the award ceremony. No one saw her leave. No one saw her drive away despite the area being a salt flat with a clear view for 20 miles. She was there, and then she was gone. I have my security team working on a name and location."

"What about resources, John."

"You will like this. I am giving you a blank cheque. This is too important to be cheap. Hire investigators or lawyers if you need them. You can rent a fancy hotel room. Take this woman to the opera or lay on the beach with her. Romance her, wine and dine her. Just make sure you get that engine back here."

"Did you say lay around on the bitch or the beach?"

Ares paused. He waved his finger at Leo. "I like a brazen operator, but I am not messing around with the success of this project. You win, and I will reward you. I will give you a promotion from marketing intern to project leader. I will give you stock options. I will pay for all your student loans. How does that sound?"

"You won my commitment when you said the magic words about paying my student loans. I will win if I have to crawl naked over broken glass."

"Now we are talking. How long have you been here, Leo? Two weeks?"

"Yes, John."

"I have a reputation that is fully deserved. I am loved by my friends and feared by my enemies. You do not want to become an enemy. I am giving you unlimited money to get this done. Do it or else."

"May I ask why you picked me? You do not know me."

"You had a hard start in life. It was just you and your mother living in Palestine. Life was hard with no father. You got a degree in chemical engineering from Oxford despite limited schooling. You struggled. The CIA tried to recruit you, and you turned them down. You are as smart as they come. You know about poverty, oppression, and struggle, but you are a winner. You are so good-looking that almost every woman in this building swoons when you walk by them. Smart, handsome, resourceful, tough. You remind me of me. I am betting on you. This Diana Rocket, or whatever her name is, will be tempted. You have all the cards. Win her trust and buy her machine. Succeed and jump ahead of every intern. Fail, and find yourself on my enemies list."

"I can't imagine how you could know some things that I never discuss with close friends. You did your homework. I will not fail."

"You will call me every day with a 60-second update. I don't want a long list of things you tried. I don't care how hard you tried. I want to hear about what worked. In 60 seconds, tell me about the progress. You call every day with no misses. If you need help, tell me that too. I don't want to hear long stories, especially excuses. You get to the point quickly."

"Yes, Sir." Leo felt the friendly part of the relationship was over unless he won.

"The man behind you is Brodie. He is my security solver. You report to Brodie, and don't worry about your existing manager. Ignore him. Brodie will get you what you need. Airplane tickets, cars, phones, listening devices, muscle, ... anything you need, you should discuss with him. He is my eyes and ears in the field."

Leo turned quickly. He had not heard or seen the other man. The guy's neck was as thick as Leo's thigh. Big and hard. He had a scar that crossed from his right cheek to his ear. Brodie's eyes were blue and cold. Brodie gave Leo a nod but said nothing.

"I will start right away," said Leo.

Brodie pulled a business card from his pocket and tossed it into the air. It flew directly at Leo. Leo caught the card between two fingers and flipped it into his pocket with a swirl.

"That's the way. Win, and win with style," said John. Brodie said nothing but gave Leo another nod.

Chapter 7 — Coffee time

Diana sat in a neighborhood coffee shop. She was sitting next to a fireplace in a very comfortable, deeply cushioned chair. She did not have the money for fine meals or bars, but her one extravagance was the weekly fancy coffee meeting with college friends. Yasmin was the first to arrive. She bounced in and put her hand on the top of the chair and vaulted into her seat. Yasmin had a hearty laugh and large breasts. Yasmin was black and perhaps gay. Yasmin never talked about religion or sexuality in the five years they were friends. Diana felt they could share any confession or thought if salient. Diana did not push friends.

"How are things?" asked Diana.

"Good. I convinced the yoga studio to give me free access if I cleaned the studio on weekends. I also persuaded the martial arts studio to give me free lessons if I taught the kids on Saturday mornings. No one likes to teach the little kids."

"I forget the name of your martial arts. Screamer? You learn to scare the bad guys with a lot of screaming?"

"Very funny. Escrima. It is fighting with sticks and knives. How is your job search going?"

"Ugh. Moan. I sent out over 200 unsolicited resumes to major science organizations in town," said Diana.

"I had a friend check my resume. I tried using social media to reach past my friends to every acquaintance since grade one. I am hoping one of these acquaintances can help me find a full-time job."

Faith and Pi came in together. Faith was born in Canada; she was pretty and a little chubby. Faith was full of life, enthusiasm, and a bubbling personality. Pi was five foot nothing. Pi had long, shiny hair that flowed to her lower back. Both women were Asian. Pi was born in Bermuda. Pi had wealthy grandparents who fled when the communists took control of China. The family lost everything when Pi's mother became ill. When Pi was young, the family moved to Buffalo in New York to start again. They waved at Diana and Yasmin before going to the front to order. Pi would always order jasmine tea. Faith often got a chocolate donut and French vanilla coffee.

"They want to make me the store manager at my antique clothing job. Still part-time, but I will be a manager with no benefits, which is somehow better," said Yasmin. "They let me pick my schedule and pay me $15 an hour. My math tells me I will have my student loans paid off and enough for a down payment on a one-bedroom condo before my 81st birthday. Yippie."

Faith and Pi sat at the table. Pi gave Diana a nudge and whispered, "Look at the hottie by the window." Diana looked. He was striking. He had green-blue eyes, black hair, and a flawless complexion. Faith winked at Diana and Pi, then pursed her lips and feigned blowing a kiss at the stranger. The girls laughed.

The door burst open, and Milton came in loaded with a heavy backpack and a bicycle helmet. After a brief fight between the backpack and the double doors, he emerged unscathed. Milton tipped his head side-to-side as a greeting to the women and went to the counter. He paid for his coffee with loose change. When Diana met Milton, he was a pimply-faced boy with a pale complexion and allergies. Working as a bicycle delivery person, he was now lithe and muscular. He had a tanned face, and the allergies had disappeared. Milton had straight, thin, brown hair. Most of the pimples were gone, replaced with a few freckles. Milton had a sparkling smile and perfect teeth.

"Always last to arrive and first to leave," said Yasmin.

"He wasn't like that before the baby and the wife. Now he is always flustered and struggling to keep up," said Diana.

"My friends, please tell me how the miserable job hunt is unfolding for each of you?" said Yasmin.

"No job for me. My parents are freaking out. I took a job as a waitress at a Chinese buffet until I find something better. Part-time, of course. My parents think I am not trying hard enough to find a real job. In my culture, children give some of their salaries to their parents as a reward for the sacrifices parents make," said Faith.

"Nothing. Still looking," said Pi softly.

"Hey, folks. Sorry I am late," said Milton. "I got a last-minute delivery and had to take it. "It doesn't pay much, but the bicycle delivery gig keeps me fit."

"How is the job search, Milton?" said Diana.

"Horrible. I am so busy on the delivery gig Mondays and Tuesdays, the retail sales job on Wednesdays and Fridays, and the burger joint on Thursdays. I babysit on the weekends so Jody can work. I am exhausted all the time, so I can't find time to look for a real job. I am swirling with three jobs, the baby, almost no money, and I am accelerating to a spectacular career failure. Same as last week."

"I am tired of hearing about misery from everyone.," said Yasmin. "They keep publishing surveys about how many STEM jobs are needed, but never ask the companies where they want to hire. They just assume American companies want to hire American workers. It is not true. They want to hire workers where the pay is lowest. We should fight back."

"Yes, fight," said Pi.

"Yeah, Milton. Why is capitalism failing us? You are an economics major. What is wrong? Why can't we have a good life like our parents? Why are we drowning in these low-paid, temporary jobs?" said Faith.

"It is not capitalism. Capitalism builds wealth. I think it is our leaders," said Milton. "You have all these dictators and corrupt leaders. They steal. They give special deals to their friends. They fix prices. Suppose we remove the bad leaders in the world. In that case, all workers could ask for money without fear of being executed or imprisoned. If workers overseas got more money, our workers here could get more money. Free trade would work both ways."

"How do we get rid of dictators?" said Yasmin.

"Well, we can't kill them," said Leo smiling confidently. Everyone looked up. "I was sitting over there by the window all alone. It was obvious this is the cool table. I would be honored if I could join you? I see you have coffee but no snacks. Why don't I order a round of chicken wings and pizza for everyone?"

"Don't forget the chocolate cake," said Yasmin. She gave Diana a nudge with her elbow.

"I'll be right back with gifts," said Leo.

"I think he was looking at you, Diana," said Pi.

"Every woman for herself. Scoot over, Diana. He can sit in this chair next to me," said Faith. "Did you see that tight man-butt?"

"And, he does not favor murdering dictators. He can't be all bad," said Yasmin.

When Leo returned, he carried a three-layered chocolate cake cut into 12 slices. "Here is the chocolate cake for my lady," Leo said and plunked the cake in front of Yasmin. A waitress came right behind him with two bottles of wine, one red and one white, and glasses for everyone. Faith opened her hand and gestured to the empty seat between Diana and herself. Leo smiled and sat next to them.

The waitress rested her hand on Leo's shoulder. "I will be right back with the food. If you want anything else, my name is Suzy. Just give me a wave, and I'll come running." Yasmin and Faith exchanged glances and rolled their eyes.

The group ate vigorously and drank with equal gusto. Their glasses tinkled, and they wished for better prospects. Leo was the outlier. Leo was obviously employed and working full-time. Diana looked at his expensive blue suit, silk tie, and shoes shined to a mirror finish. He was about the same age as them, a man in his mid-twenties, yet he was successful. Leo had what they aspired to achieve. Like Leo, Diana wanted to have a career and an opportunity for advancement.

"You know, there are things about having a real job and not this temp gig stuff that I don't think about but should. It would be nice to feel valuable instead of replaceable," said Diana.

"I would love to have some respect. One day of respect would go a long way. I am constantly worried about being evicted from my crappy apartment," said Milton. "I have a

Masters in Economics. I should know enough about money to keep my wife and child protected and warm."

"At the grocery store where I work, they did something new called contract flipping. The temp agency the corporation uses was changed. Since we have a new temp agency, all the temp people have to reapply for our existing jobs with this new temp agency. Since we have not worked for the new temp agency, they consider us new, so reset our salaries to entry-level. I have worked at the same store for two years, but I am paid as having zero seniority or experience. They have so many ways to cheat us."

"Why don't we make a list of demands? If the world's dictators don't have free elections in 30 days, we kill them. By 'we', I mean the disenfranchised youth," said Yasmin.

"Revolutions are always bloody. It would be better if powerful people treated us with justice and kindness so we could skip the protesting, killing, and rioting," said Leo.

"What I don't get is why the conservative party is called the right-wing. The conservatives don't care about us. Conservatives only care about rich people. There is nothing right about that ideology. We should be called the right-wing, and the conservatives should be called the wrong-wing or left-wing," said Yasmin.

Leo stood up. "Suzy, could you bring us two bottles of champagne? There are six of us, so should I change that to six bottles of champagne?" Leo scanned the group for any nods. What he got was a lot of giggles and laughter. The group was getting louder. The corks for bubbly wine popped. Little conversations broke out among them.

"I should probably mention to everyone that I had a bit of an adventure with my neighbor," said Diana.

"Oh, a romantic adventure?" asked Faith. Everyone suddenly stopped talking.

"Oh no. He is much too old. Nothing like that," said Diana. She blushed. "He took me for a ride in his new car, airplane, not sure what to call it," said Diana.

"You don't know if it was a car or an airplane?" asked Milton.

"A bit of both. I call it an adventure because of the speed. This machine was fast. It was so fast you had to grab the nearest handhold in terror. I had a fantastic time," said Diana.

"Fooling around in cars is how it starts," said Faith. Everyone laughed. Diana blushed. Faith stood up, holding a champagne bottle, and did a little dance. Faith leaned in and kissed Leo on the cheek. "Sorry, I shouldn't have done that," she said to Leo. Moods were spinning out of control.

"We should play spin the bottle," said Pi. The group went silent while considering the idea.

A woman came up and stood next to Leo for a few minutes. He looked up. "I like you," she said to Leo. "You are the best thing here."

Everyone laughed and could not stop. They knew it was rude. They didn't want to be uncouth, but it was a long time since they had such a good time. They couldn't prevent themselves from laughing. The woman walked off with a snort of derision.

"Who was she?" someone asked Leo.

"I don't know. I have never seen her before."

"Oops. I am in trouble. I have got to go. I'm a married man," said Milton waving as he bundled his things under his arm and headed to the door.

Pi stood up. "I am having the best time. We should plot the death of heads of state more often. I really have to go too." Faith looked at her watch and grimaced. Faith did not want to go. Faith wanted to hump Leo, but she was sharing a ride with Pi. Faith stood slowly, gave Leo a slip of paper, and whispered, "Call me."

Yasmin took a last swig to empty the bottle of red wine, and then without saying anything, gave Leo and Diana a wave.

"Wow! That was quick. I thought we'd party until 2 or 3?" said Leo.

"We work many hours to earn very little. We can't party much anymore," said Diana.

"I will take the hint, but why don't I give you a ride home?"

"You don't know where I live. I may live in Alaska."

"What a coincidence. Alaska is on my way." Leo said it with a serious face, but his eyes twinkled.

"Well, I don't live in Alaska. I am just a few blocks from here."

"Would you prefer to walk?"

"Sure."

As soon as they walked into the night air, Leo took Diana's hand. It felt so natural. She felt they had been friends for a decade. The air was warm. A musty smell of moisture was blowing in from nearby trees. "The moon is enormous tonight. I think I can touch it." Diana reached out with a grabbing action.

They walked a few blocks without talking. Diana was enjoying the moment. She was too nerdy to get much attention from the boys at college. Perhaps it was her fault because Diana did not have much tact and may have inadvertently crushed some delicate male egos. This time she was the one to walk away with the handsome devil. Was he a devil?

Leo walked her up to her door. He moved closer, and she could feel his breath. She wasn't breathing at all. He leaned in and gave her the softest, most gentle kiss on the lips. She felt weak in her knees. He squeezed her hand warmly, kissed her again very quickly, and slipped his tongue into her mouth for a half-second. When she opened her eyes, he had turned and was walking away. He was across the street and under the trees before she fully grasped the intensity of the moment.

Chapter 8 — Steal the machine

As Leo walked around the first turn, a black car pulled alongside him. Leo got in the car and reached for his cell phone. "CEO 60-second update. Brodie ran image recognition software from the photograph you provided, which provided us with a match to a high school graduation photograph. I made positive contact with the subject tonight. I confirmed she is the girl we want. She got the machine from a neighbor. He is a Professor, and I have her address. We plan to have Brodie steal the machine tonight. With luck, you will have the machine tomorrow."

Leo gave Brodie the address for Dia na. "Do you need me?"

Brodie shook his head. They drove in silence for 20 minutes until Leo was dropped off at the hotel. Brodie said, "I will assemble a small team and some equipment. I will call you tomorrow with the results." Leo saw Brodie slowly pull away into the night. Leo was glad Brodie was not chasing him.

Leo walked to his hotel. The lights were bright, and an enormous chandelier was at the center of the room. A spiral staircase offered a walk to three floors of meeting rooms, restaurants, and shops. Leo found himself thinking about Diana. He would love to show up at her door in an hour and kiss her again. The idea was exciting, but he had to stay focused. Leo could not mess up his life with love and kisses on the first day. Leo took the elevator to his floor.

By the time Leo got to his floor, he had changed his mind. He gave Diana a call. "I just called to tell you how much I enjoyed tonight."

"Me too."

"I especially liked our goodbye."

"Yes. It was nice." Diana grimaced. Nice. Just nice. It was way better than nice. Why could she not think of a better word?

"Well. I wish you sweet dreams. I will be thinking of you."

"Thank you for calling. I was not expecting to hear from you so soon."

"Okay then. Goodbye."

"Goodbye again." Diana hung up the phone. She felt fantastic inside. No debt boulder tonight. She felt, once again, she could climb a mountain of metaphors. She could conquer her world.

Three men climbed out of a black van across from Diana's home. The men were all wearing black shirts and slacks. The men sprinted up the driveway to the garage.

"The machine we are looking for looks like a small car. It is a two-seater. It is not in the driveway. It would be too big to go through the front door, so it has to be in the garage," said Brodie. Brodie pulled on the garage door, and it was unlocked. He pulled it up about three feet, and the men slipped under and into the garage. Each man pulled a small flashlight. The place was a mess of boxes, bottles of insect spray, old paint cans, garden implements, and fertilizer bags. The garage was dirty, smelly, and filled with junk. There were no cars or engines.

"Not here. The Professor must have rented space somewhere in the city. We have no choice. We will take the Professor, and we drill him until he tells us where to find the machine," said Brodie. The men slipped out of the garage and went back to the van. Brodie grabbed a clipboard. The two men behind Brodie took a big box on a dolly out of the back. They walked up the driveway again, and Bodie rang the doorbell. They could hear noises after a few more rings.

"Who is it?"

"Delivery," said Brodie as he stood back into the shadow.

"It is late," said the voice. The door opened six inches, and an older man looked out.

"I need you to sign this," said Brodie waving the clipboard blocking the view of his face.

The door opened wider, and Brodie punched the man in the stomach. He groaned, winded. The two men stepped forward, and they put a hood over the man's head. Brodie dropped, picking the man up by the ankles. The two men in front each grabbed an arm, and they carried the man down a few steps and dumped him into the now open box. He did not cry out. He was still gasping for breath. In less than 10 seconds, he was put into the van. Brodie went back and closed the front door. He picked up the clipboard. The van reversed to pick Brodie up, and they were gone. The whole episode took less than 60 seconds.

The van drove into an industrial area and backed into an abandoned shipping dock. They wheeled the box into the building. Banging and shouting was coming from the box, but the place was isolated. The sounds from the box were muffled by the hood and cardboard. The man was wheeled into the building, pulled from the box, and bound to a metal chair with handcuffs. A bright light was directed into the man's face. Brodie removed the hood.

"What the hell?" said the man.

"Are you the Professor?" asked Brodie.

"Yes. I am a Professor." The Professor could not see the man in front of him because he was blinded by the light. He could hear someone was behind him.

"We want the machine. Give us the machine, and we will take you home."

"My mother is 93 years old. She has dementia. I cannot leave her alone. She could turn on the oven. She could burn herself with hot tap water. She could burn down the house. She could take too many pills. She could die. You have to take me back. Right away," he was talking faster as he went, with more and more frenzy.

"We will take you back as soon as you tell us where to find the machine."

"What machine?"

"Just tell us."

"I have lots of machines. Mass spectrometers, liquid chromatographs, CISPR, centrifuges. You have to be more specific."

"The machine you gave to your neighbor. The machine that moves without gasoline."

The Professor looked puzzled. "I don't know."

"You do know. You have a bundle of nerves just under your earlobe. I will punch it with my knuckle, and you will feel a lot of pain. I don't want to hurt you. Start talking."

"I don't recall giving any machine to any neighbor. Can you be specific?"

"Stop playing stupid," Brodie pushed forward the knuckle on his middle finger, used his thumb to brace it in position, and punched the Professor just under the earlobe. The Professor went rigid. He seemed to spasm.

"Ah. Damn. Stop."

"Hurts, does it not? That was a light tap. If I take my thumbs, I can push on that nerve under both ears until you tell us what we want."

"I am a Professor of biology. I know exactly where the nerves are. I know exactly the damage you can do pressing on that nerve. You can kill someone."

"Then tell us where the machine is. Wait. You are a Professor of biology? You are not an engineer of some kind?"

"No. I am not an engineer. I do not know how to build machines that travel with or without gasoline. I know about microbes: bacteria, viruses, and fungi."

"You did not give Diana, the girl next door to you, a machine."

"No. There are lots of students and Professors in the neighborhood. We are just a few blocks from the university. You could walk there in twenty minutes or ride a bike in five minutes."

Brodie turned and walk back a few steps. He thought for a few minutes, then returned.

"When we looked in the phone book, you were the only Professor living next to her."

"There are at least three Professors I can think of on the block. Some just give the phone company their names and not their title. Some do not use the title professor. They can call themselves a doctor if they have a Ph.D."

"I have to think. Are any of these Professors engineers, or people who could build a new engine to drive faster?"

"I don't know. We often just wave or talk about the nice weather. I would have to remember."

"I could kill you but that would attract an investigation. The smart move would be to recruit you. If you help us find the machine, I will pay you a lot, Professor. Get Diana to reveal who gave her the machine? Do it so she does not suspect you are working for us. If you help, we will pay you. If you betray us, we will kill you. You know how easy it was for us to get to you. Do we have a deal?"

"Let me see. If I help you, I get to live. If I don't, you kill me. I will take the first option."

"Good thing we did not let you see our faces. Damn. What a shitstorm. I can't believe professionals like us could make such a mess of it. I'm am sorry, Professor."

"It is okay. Just get me back so I can check my mom is safe."

"I have done hundreds of kidnappings, beatings, and torture and never got the wrong guy. Not once."

"Look, it is okay. Really. Just get me home. I need to see that my mom is safe."

"Guys, get the hood." Brodie unlocked the cuffs.

"Do I have to wear a hood?"

"Yeah. We don't want you to know where we took you. It is only a short drive."

"How do I contact you if I find out anything?"

"Don't worry about that, Professor. We will contact you."

Chapter 9 — Plans within plans

Leo and Brodie discussed the failure and formulated a new plan. They were reluctant to provide an update to the CEO. They kept thinking of reasons to delay the update in the hopes of more positive developments. Feeling grim, Leo called. "CEO 60-second update. The plan to snatch the machine was a failure. I will contact the subject again tonight. I have a backup plan. Diana's main need is a full-time job. She is smart and broke. I recommend HR contact her, fly her to New York for an interview, and hire her full-time at Enworld as a project leader. We can give her access to lab equipment and let her pursue some pet science projects. This will give us significant leverage. Once she has tasted the apple, she will find it difficult to go back to the unemployment line. As a bonus, maybe her project makes money. As a ..."

"Leo, I was listening to your message. I like the backup. Steal the machine if you can. We will hire her. We will win her loyalty. If she can convince the Professor to help explain the technology, we can move much faster. The machine alone will justify any hiring costs. Besides, a full-time job is only temporary if you don't make it through the probation period. Do it. Oh, and Leo. 60 seconds, not 6 minutes." He hung up, here and then gone.

"Thanks for not mentioning it was my disaster. I remember my friends," said Brodie.

"No biggie, Brodie. As soon as I get better intelligence on the correct Professor, I will call you with the details. I have to call Diana, see her, and hopefully pry the information from her without making her suspicious I am a corporate spy." Brodie gave Leo a nod, and he left.

The room felt isolated, a bit lonely. After the excitement of the initial contact, Leo suddenly felt like a stranger in a strange city doing a strange job. This was not the marketing work he wanted. He phoned.

"Hi, Diana?"

"Hi, Leo?"

"I have been thinking of you. Can I see you?"

"How about we meet at the coffee shop at 5?"

"Absolutely. I will look forward to it."

"Okay. See you soon." Diana did a little spin and put the phone down. She was walking to the kitchen when the doorbell rang. She switched direction and did another little spin just because it was fun. Diana opened the door and saw Maynard, the Professor from the house on her left.

"Good morning. Sorry to bother you, but I have to tell you something. "

"Professor Maynard. What is it?"

He was looking at the ground. He looked up at her and then looked away again. "I am trying to find a way to tell you something important. I am not sure you will believe me, but this is important for your safety."

The smile on Diana's face evaporated. He looked worried. "Start anywhere."

"I was kidnapped yesterday. These goons were looking for a machine. They thought I had some machine that travels fast.

They thought, for some reason, that I had given a machine to you. They threatened to kill me if I did not find out where you got the machine?"

Diana held on to the door frame and did not feel strong. She felt scared.

"I pretended to cooperate. I wanted to warn you. Please be careful. Don't open the door to just anyone like you did now. Have a place to hide and an escape route."

"Are you safe? Is your mother safe?"

"Yes, we are fine for now. If these guys approach you, please do *not* tell them that I warned you. Tell them that we spoke, but you did not know what I was saying. Whoever gave you this machine, you have to warn them right away that these guys are dangerous, ruthless, even deadly, and they want that machine at all costs."

"I will. Definitely," Diana said. She was talking mechanically while feeling empty. She had not processed the impact of this development on her life. She knew everything was going to change. "What will you do?"

"I am a Professor of biology. I am almost 70. I cannot physically fight a team of corporate thugs. I have skills and knowledge. I am going to my lab now, and I will look at my books and resources. I will not let them harm me with no consequences. I have dangerous bacteria and access to flesh-eating fungus. There is no cure for the fungus, and I have access to bacteria that kills or maims. I will isolate some dangerous products. I will find a smart delivery system so I can destroy them without creating unintended victims."

"Oh." Diana was shocked. They had taken a quiet, studious man and turned him into a potential killer. He moved slowly but was not slow thinking. He could also turn his skills to pain and destruction rather than health and instruction.

Diana felt responsible. She was the reason the machine was discovered. She rushed to win prize to pay off her loan. Fools rush in. She had no prize money; however, now both Professors Maynard and Lazarus were at risk. How did it come to this?

"Don't worry about me. I am sorry to have to tell you. If I can help, let me know. I am just next door."

"Thank you, Professor. I am grateful." Diana watched Maynard walk away. He walked, tentatively with a small bend from the waist. How could anyone threaten that kind soul? He was a man that spent spare time tending his garden.

Diana went next door to the other Professor. She still had the brooch to start the machine. Diana knocked on the door. She tried the doorbell. No answer. She used her cell phone to find his college phone number.

"... and that was the main theory. Hello? Yes?"

"It's Diana, your neighbor. Are you busy?"

"We just finished. What is it? Are you ready for another trip? We could fly down the Mexican peninsula on the way to see my mom next week. Would you like to stop at a Mayan or Aztec temple?"

"Professor, can I see you today? I think someone is trying to steal your machine."

"Not to worry. I have defensive measures, sophisticated defensive measures. If you don't have the beetle brooch device, you cannot access the machine."

"I don't want to talk on the phone. Can we meet?"

"I teach until 3 P.M."

"Meet me at the Mirage coffee shop at 4 P.M. That would give us an hour before my friend comes."

"No problem. I love their coconut parfait."

"Please be careful. I think these guys are dangerous."

"Will do."

Diana sat in the coffee shop. She wanted to try the coconut parfait, but it was $5.20, so sadly, she didn't have enough money. Diana got the ginger tea. She liked strong tea. Ginger had some kick, and it was good for your health. Fewer calories she thought, although she knew she was trying to assuage her feelings about poverty. The Professor arrived at precisely 4 P.M. Was he obsessively punctual?

He walked by her on the way to the counter. "I'm getting the coconut parfait. Can I get one for you too?" Ginger and ice cream. Yuck. She could drink one at a time. She nodded aggressively and smiled. She was happier already. He showed the same fearless, calm demeanor on the trip to Africa. Was he just clueless, emotionally shut down, or did he properly understand the danger? Was she overreacting?

He came back with two beer mugs filled with coconut shavings, ice cream, whipped cream, nuts, and possibly some yogurt. The food looked fantastic. Diana loved this place.

"So..." he asked with a shoulder shrug and a gesture with an open palm of his hand.

"There are some big men, corporate thugs. They want the machine. They are dangerous. They are coming."

"How do you know?"

"I cannot tell you. I want to, but I promised I wouldn't. I trust my source. I am sure the threat is real. They want the machine and will kill to get it."

"Do you still have the beetle-brooch device?"

"Yes. Glad you reminded me. It is in my purse somewhere. Here it is."

"I am going to give you three more. These are not just remote starter fobs. These are complete miniature replicas of the machine. Usually, scientists develop a functional machine, then work on miniaturization. Since I lacked the funds, I began with a small and much cheaper prototype. Do you remember the pelican?"

"Yes. Of course. I thought I was going to die by being pulverized by a 20-pound bird."

"These little beetles can do the same thing. The torus at the front of the beetle will create enough negative energy to build a vacuum directly in front of it. Any threat will turn into a vacuum. I am giving you four devices for protection. Keep one hidden in your home as insurance. Keep one on you and handy. As you can see, I wear them all the time on my clothes. I can grab one and use it if any one attacks me."

"Where did the pelican go? Turned into dust?"

"I don't know. I could never find dust when I tested the beetles. Natural law states energy cannot be created or destroyed; energy can only change form. Fire becomes ash, but you always have remnants of some kind when energy converts form. The pelican went somewhere that is *not here*. The form of the pelican perhaps changed, but there is no evidence remaining to examine. I don't know where the pelican went. It went to *not here*. We need more study to understand as there are many strange behaviors with anti-matter. Positive becomes negative, forward becomes backward, and the most interesting, time runs in reverse. Up to now, it has been too difficult to create more than tiny amounts of anti-matter, so we have limited understanding."

"You are saying we don't know what happened to the pelican. Vaporized, but no dust remains. Could the bird be ported into reverse time somehow? Whatever reverse time actually means?"

"Yes, the forward-backward, positive-negative, and the flip of time has been established in testing. This is not simply a theory. I want you to take this little program." He handed her a small USB storage stick. You insert the stick into a computer, and you can download instructions to the beetle. The program is not fancy. Basic instructions can be entered like fly up or down, look for heat or light, state the size of the torus field as two inches or two feet."

"I don't know how to program computers."

"You don't need to. The program asks what you want, and you pick from the choices. Play with it a bit. You do not want these devices to fall into the wrong hands."

"Why would you trust me?"

"Timing. You came into the garage just as I was about to fly away. I thought the company would be nice, and having a witness to a successful flight would be helpful. We turned down the same path. Our journey is now shared. I am committed and must provide you with protection since I put you in jeopardy. I knew there were risks by exposing the machine to the greedy. I did not realize the magnitude of the risk and now have to respond accordingly. This is on me."

Diana turned the beetles in her hand. "You did not suggest I fly across the country and enter some speed contest. I exposed myself." She noticed the beetle legs allowed you to stick them to any surface like a real insect. She sipped her parfait. The beetles could cancel an attacker without the need to hide a body. The attacker would respond if you reached for a gun, but the beetle could take someone out before they knew they were in danger. The beetle was not just a fantastic flying machine but also a formidable weapon. Diana could see the reasons for his reluctance to tell the world about his scientific advances. The technology could destroy birds, people, tanks, planes, walls, and buildings. The technology could take you to your mother in minutes instead of days, and it could just as quickly destroy a city in minutes, not days.

"I am going to put you in my Will. If something happens to me, I want you to be the steward of this technology. We cannot let any warmongering nation get near it." He reached into his bag. "This is my Will, signed and witnessed. I created this document yesterday just in case. I have included a plan that is detailed and on the memory stick. If these guys kidnap me, I want you to control the machine. I will give you access to my savings account if I am incapacitated. You will use the money to look after my mom, my only living relative. Can you do that?"

"Yes. Am I the right person? There must be someone better?"

"The plan spells out everything for the machine. If they get me, they won't get the machine because of defensive measures. The memory stick has many pictures of flowers. Each picture is hiding the design specs, blueprints, and technical papers. I have included a social plan. I want this machine to change more than travel. I expect the technology of this machine to change the power dynamics of the world. We see the rich using their wealth to gain more power and more wealth. Their greed is destroying not just lives but also communities and our planet. This machine will allow the stewards to become wealthy and powerful. This new technology should be used to build a better world, not destroy the existing world."

"I see that more and more. All my friends agree. It is time for regular people to do something drastic. We have all these dictators stealing our wealth, polluting our planet, and taking too much. It is greed without any limits or proportion. Take, take, and take. It is sickening."

"Yes, democracy is the key. The issue is more than dictatorship. Think bigger. We need democracy everywhere. Just read the plan."

"I will. I will read it with great interest."

"As I said, there are pictures of flowers on the memory stick. If you display any photograph, you will see each flower includes a bird somewhat camouflaged by flower colors. If you click on the phoenix bird, the flower will bloom, and the picture will change into the plan documents. You should copy the pictures and keep the memory stick hidden."

"What do we have here. Are you two plotting to take over the world?" said Yasmin.

Diana sat up straight. She was startled. Diana was so focused on the discussion she did not see Faith and Yasmin approaching. She glanced nervously around.

"I was just kidding. Seriously, are you plotting some nefarious intrigue?"

Diana and the Professor laughed a little too loud. The Professor had a silly grin like he got caught doing something naughty.

"I was surprised. I didn't expect you. I didn't see you coming."

"I am Yasmin. This is Faith," she said and held her hand out to the Professor. He stood up and shook her hand firmly.

"Please join us," he asked.

"We are tired. We stood in line for almost an hour, waiting to get our renewed driver licenses. My feet hurt," said Faith. "If they are going to have long lines, they should have some seats."

"Something I teach my students. When you read a book or listen to a politician speak, pay attention to what is *not* said. The part that is left out is the important part. When a new politician promises tax cuts, he does not say what will be cut to make up for the lost tax revenue. If he promises tax cuts and then explains that line-ups for government services will be twice as long, we will know what we get if we vote for him. Would we still want the tax cut?"

"Good point. And that tax cut, it is not like every worker gets $12,000, a flat amount by dividing the revenue from the tax cut across all workers. No, he gives some billionaire stock investor six million and gives the rest of us 300 dollars. We lose six million in services and gain 300 dollars in the tax cut. It is not much of a bargain," said Faith.

"Who are you?" said Yasmin to the Professor.

"My fault. I forgot to introduce him. This is Professor Lazarus, my neighbor," said Diana.

"Please, just call me Lazarus."

"I remember. Is this the guy that took you for a ride, and you weren't sure if it was a car or a plane?" said Faith. Diana and Lazarus exchanged glances.

"Hi everyone. I didn't know this was a group party?" said Leo looking at Diana. She glanced at her watch. It was almost 5 P.M.

"Serendipity. Destiny alone brought us together," said Yasmin to Leo.

"I am Leo," he said to the Professor.

"Sorry. I am not myself. Leo, this is Lazarus. Lazarus, this is Leo," said Diana.

"Pleased to meet you, Lazarus."

"We were just talking about paying more attention to what is not said in books and not said by politicians. What is not said is the most important aspect of the whole text."

"That is true in my business," said Leo. "I'm in marketing."

"Oh. You are a professional liar?" laughed Faith, and she touched his arm.

"I am not; that is the politician's job. I am a teller of tales, myths, and dreams of a better tomorrow," said Leo with a chuckle. Everyone smiled.

"What do you do, Lazarus?" said Leo.

"I am also a dreamer. I love to dream of a better life, better government, and better technology. I spend my whole life dreaming. Some people call it a vision, while others call it research. My boss sometimes calls it a waste of money."

"Oh, are you a movie producer, author, or perhaps a professor?" asked Leo with intensity.

"That thing you said about paying attention to what is not said seems important, but I don't understand the logic. How can you hear what is not said? How can you see what is not displayed?" said Faith. Leo squirmed in his seat.

"You are right," said Lazarus. "In the book *Alice's Adventures in Wonderland*, the king asks Alice if she saw anyone on the road. Alice tells him she saw nobody. The king replies that her eyesight must be perfect. He can barely see somebody, yet she can see so well she can see nobody. The author, Lewis Carroll, was a mathematician. The little vignette shows the illogic of language versus the pure logic of mathematics."

"You sound like a Professor, full of wisdom?" said Leo.

"Take democracy. We say we all believe in it. Research shows that decisions made using democratic methods are better than dictatorships. If democracy is so good, why don't we practice it more than once every few years in some election? Did the employees in your team vote and elect the project leader of marketing, Leo?"

"I had no say in picking my boss."

"Did anyone vote for your religious leader? Did you pick your priest, rabbi, or imam? How about the CEO? Employees and customers don't have a say about who is picked for CEO? The community where the company is located does not pick the CEO. The shareholders have a vote, yet most do not vote. It is not one vote per shareholder but one vote per share. One person with a million shares can vote a million times more than 1,000 other shareholders. The vote is not a democracy where every person is important and counts equally."

"Yet the system works," said Leo.

"A system where we all praise democracy, but we don't practice democracy at work or when we worship. We do not practice democracy daily. We say we will die to protect democracy but do not vote for our multinational conglomerate leaders. Some of these companies have more money and power than half the nations in the world."

"This is the system that made us a rich country," said Leo.

"Is the system making all of you rich? The average CEO salary in the 1960s was 20 times that of the average worker. Today, the average CEO salary is 354 times the average worker salary. Is the CEO of today working 200 hours a day more than the CEO of 1960? Are they taking more than a fair share? You are being left behind. All of you are being left behind. The lobby groups ensure it is government for the corporations by corporations. You just think your vote makes a difference. Your tax dollars are used to fund rich companies with subsidies, which explains why university costs so much. This is not the system that made this county rich. This is a corruption of our system. We have some national leaders who are dictators, but you can see dictators everywhere. The ratio of psychopaths in corporations is four times that of society. Many of these leaders are greedy psychopaths and should not have power."

Leo thought about his CEO, and the description was a fit. He had a CEO who sanctioned death squads and theft. He was, at this minute, helping the CEO steal the Professor's machine. Actual theft. Not creative corporate innovations, just plain break and enter, break the door with a hammer, steal what you want, and kill whatever is in the way. Leo felt ashamed. He looked at the women, and they were struggling. He was part of the problem, not part of the solution.

Diana's phone rang. She spoke for a few minutes, then got up and walked to a quiet corner to talk privately. Leo suspected he knew who was calling. He had to try again to confirm this guy was indeed the Professor they wanted.

"What subjects do you teach, Professor? Are you a business teacher?" said Leo.

"I teach physics."

"Yes, and he took Diana on some trip in a vehicle that might be a car or might be plane? Apparently, it was a lot of fun," said Faith.

"You are Professor Lazarus Arnold? You wrote a paper on thermodynamics?"

"No. I am Lazarus Solomon. I have not written papers on heat. My papers are on multi-dimensional string theory."

"Oops. I think I left my phone in my car. I will be right back," said Leo.

As Leo left, Faith said, "My heart is breaking. I would love to know Leo better. I dreamed about him last night. We were boating on a lake and got lost together."

"Be careful. I don't think Leo is all that he pretends to be," said Lazarus.

"Why?" said Faith.

"Because he was so determined to learn Lazarus's name and profession. He is not just chatting. He has an agenda," said Yasmin.

"I like him," said Faith.

"You are smitten, is what you mean," said Yasmin.

"Maybe, but just a little bit."

"You cannot be a bit smitten. You are smitten, or you are not. It is binary."

"I cannot believe it. Finally, after almost 400 resumes, I got a call. They must have liked the resume because they are flying me to New York tomorrow. All expenses paid. I can pick up the ticket at the airport. They want a project leader for some new team," said Diana.

"I am soooo envious. First, you get the most handsome guy in the world hanging on your every word. Second, you get a job interview," said Faith.

"They are building a new division. It will be made up of new graduates to pursue and innovate in any direction they want. They want to see if young people can improve their product innovations. And best of all, it is full-time. I think I have gone to heaven. This must be a dream."

"Life is not fair. The rule is lucky in love or lucky in money. Not both," said Yasmin.

It was a short walk to the car. Leo pulled his cell phone from his pocket. "Brodie, is that you? We got him. The name is Lazarus Solomon. He is a physics Professor. Okay. Okay. You will steal it tonight? Good. Sounds good. We can sync up tomorrow. Send me a text where and when. Okay. Sure. We will talk soon." Leo put the phone away. He suspected Diana just got a job interview at Enworld. With luck, I will be back in New York, and my student loans paid off in a couple of days. I am doing creepy horrible things, but the payoff is life-changing. I hope I can live with myself after this is over. Guilt is nasty.

Leo sighed and walked back to the Mirage. Mirage was a suitable name for him too. When he got to the restaurant, Diana was too excited about the job offer. She wanted to go straight home and pack for her trip. She gave him a quick peck on the cheek and left. Leo was not accustomed to being dumped mid-date, but it was for the best given his mood.

Chapter 10 — This time is different

Brodie and the team pulled up again in a black van. They wore black clothes. It was 3 A.M. All the lights in the house were out. The nearby homes were dark. They moved up the driveway and almost stepped on a raccoon. He was a big animal sitting comfortably. The team paused as the raccoon looked them over and showed no fear. Sitting still, the raccoon licked his foot. Brodie shone a flashlight into the raccoon's eyes. The raccoon just sat there.

"I could kick him," said one of the team.

"I don't want him to make a noise. Squealing and crying will draw attention," said Brodie. "Try the garage door. See if it is unlocked." The guy ducked down, moved along the wall, and tried the door. He shook his head.

"Screw it. I am going to ignore this guy the way he is ignoring me." Brodie walked within inches of the raccoon and tried the side door. It was also locked. Fortunately, the porch lights were not on. Brodie pulled a cattle prod from his belt. He held it to the door, and there was a short, loud popping sound. The lock for the door had been punched into the garage. Brodie turned the door handle and went in. He looked back to see the raccoon saunter away in the moonlight. Brodie shook his head in amazement as real life is never like the movies. You run into obstacles you could never imagine.

There was no way to get the machine out without opening the garage door. He had no choice. He pushed the button and waited. Finally, they had a stroke of luck. The door was one of those whisper models. The door slowly opened with almost no sound. The team came in and looked over the machine, but they could find no hand-brake or gear shift. There was a starter button, but it was nothing like a car. They could not jump-start it. They tried to wheel it out, and it moved easily. Brodie laughed. This was too easy.

The team moved the machine down the driveway. They had just cleared the garage when the machine rose about 10 feet. If Brodie jumped, he could touch the machine's bottom with his fingertips but not get a grip. The team looked at Brodie. How could they stop it from hovering above them? This was new.

"We need rope," said Brodie. One of the team scampered back to the van. He returned with a coil of nylon rope. They threw the rope over the top and caught it on the other side. "Now, we can pull it down," said Brodie. The machine came down about two feet, then popped back up another 10 feet. Two of the team lost their grip on the rope, but one member was still hanging on. The machine kept moving up. "Let go," said Brodie as loud as he dared. The man looked down, saw it was more than 15 feet, so he kept hanging on. He tried to climb up the rope. The closer he got to the machine, the faster it rose until it was over 200 feet in the air. The man lost his grip and fell to the driveway. Given the horrible position, one leg was broken. Brodie cradled the wounded man's head. Brodie's hand came away wet with blood. He looked up at the machine about 50 feet above him.

"Damn, this is a bust," said Brodie. "Grab him by the waist. They carried the injured man to the van. The wounded man made no noise when they lifted him. Brodie knew he was dead. This was another complication. Brodie took the man's pulse. Nothing. The injured man's heart had stopped. Brodie sat with his team in the van. He watched the machine as best he could in the dark. The machine descended slowly until it was just above the ground, and then it returned to the garage. The garage door closed. The machine was programmed to return to the base in the garage.

"The first mess was my fault. I would like to say this was out of my control, but it was not. I underestimated our opponent. This was my second mistake. If he is smart enough to develop the fastest machine in the world, he is certainly smart enough to create an anti-theft device. This machine jumps at least 10 feet away from any unknown person and keeps jumping as long as you are too close. It killed one of my men, so I must think of a different plan. Brodie started the van and drove slowly down the road. Another failure.

Chapter 11 — My deepest longing

Leo and Brodie sat together in a diner planning what to do. Brodie had lost his stoic demeanor. The two men were annoyed, frustrated, and concerned about the required one-minute update to the boss. They had a rough plan, but the CEO might hate it.

"I am not sure how he will react," said Brodie. "This could be bad."

"I told him I would win with style," said Leo. "I am doomed, but we have no choice. I cannot sit here and let this feeling drag on indefinitely. I am calling him." Leo dialed, giving Brodie a sign of prayer with his hands.

"This is a 60-second update. Diana was excited about the job interview. She will be in New York today. We failed to take the machine. The machine has defensive measures."

"Leo. John Ares. Are you telling me you failed twice?"

"Yes. We have a third plan."

"You said you were a winner. You said you would crawl over broken glass to win."

"Yes, sir. I am going to put you on speaker. Brodie wants to talk."

"Please do not blame Leo," said Brodie. "It was my failure, not his."

"That is not like you, Brodie. You never fail. How hard can it be to subdue a middle-aged Professor and take one of his toys?"

"I thought the same. I underestimated the Professor. We lost one of our men."

"They are ex-SAS. These are the most highly trained killers on the planet. How could a Professor take on three special forces men, injuring one, and win the battle?"

"Killed. The man is dead."

"Dead! Christ. What happened?"

"Every time we approached the machine, it jumped 10 feet into the air. We tried to use ropes to pull it down, but it kept going up with our man, Snake. The machine dragged him half a mile up. He fell and smashed his head open like a watermelon falling off a truck," said Brodie.

"I need that machine."

"I will not underestimate him again. I expect that the machine has many traps. We cannot know how many ways he could hurt or kill us. If he is smart enough to develop the fastest machine, he is smart enough to lay many dangerous and unexpected traps. There is only one way to do it," said Brodie.

"Speak," said Ares.

"We need to get the Professor to cooperate. If you could wine and dine him, you could persuade him to help us. You have formidable skills with people," said Leo.

"Hmm."

"We could follow the plan that worked in Cairo. You offer him the world. If he is difficult, I grab him when he leaves. I will offer him a fist to emphasize the value of your offer. We will hold him until he changes his mind," said Brodie.

"That could work and might cost less in the long run," said Ares.

"Also, if we set it up a week or two from now, Diana could help persuade him. She would be on our side if she takes the bait today," said Leo.

"We are not calling it *bait*. We are calling it a job offer. Here is what I want. Brodie should have a team watch for any movement of the machine. We need eyes on it day and night. Leo, you keep close to Diana and keep us informed. No more failures," said John. He ended the call.

"Whew. We managed to delegate upward. The boss is now the one to deliver. That went better than I expected," said Leo. "Without you, Brodie, I would be fired."

"My past service cut us a break. We cannot fail again."

Diana was happy. She felt important. She was traveling to New York with a ticket paid for by Enworld. She rolled her two bags to the curb and looked for a taxi. She saw a limousine driver holding a sign with her name on it. This was getting better and better. She had a paid limo to Manhattan. They were putting her up for one night at the Hilton Millennium at the UN Plaza. The hotel was not the closest hotel to the job interview building. When she asked for that particular hotel, they agreed immediately. Diana was not sure why she needed to stay in a hotel. They could have saved money. She could fly in and out on the same day. At least, if she did not get the job, she could explore New York for a day. It took both her and the driver some effort to put the one bag in the car's trunk. He must have thought she packed rocks in the bag. She expected him to complain, yet he showed no emotion.

Diana had no trouble finding the interview building. As she sat waiting for her interview, she checked and rechecked her outfit. She had struggled to know whether to wear pants or a skirt. Should she wear heels or flats? She was never comfortable talking about herself. Job interviews do not allow for modesty. Our culture does not smile on people who are too confident. You must sound confident yet not arrogant when you talk about your achievements. The balance between confidence and arrogance is a fine point of judgment.

"Diana?"

"Yes."

"I am Mrs. Valkery. I am doing your interview. Follow me to my office."

Diana followed. She wondered if there would be three people at once shooting questions at her, or would there be multiple interviews back-to-back. Usually, the HR questions were easy. The technical probes were more challenging. Finally, the manager would ask questions that were often unpredictable. Sometimes she found personal chemistry with the interviewer, sometimes not.

"Did you have a good flight, Diana?"

"Yes, it was lovely."

"First time in New York?"

"Yes. I find the idea of New York exciting."

"You got lucky. We have nice weather today."

Diana knew this was the Human Resource expert asking mild questions to relax the candidate. The more challenging questions would start in a few minutes. Why have you not been working in your field for the last two months? Why did the intern job not result in a long-term hire? When the technical person shows up, you never know what area they will drill you on. Sometimes they just jump around to different topics until they find a weak area, then drill and drill the weak spot. Diana was nervous.

The interview seemed perfunctory. The casual questions continued much longer than Diana expected. Finally, the woman talked about the job.

"The job is a new division. We want to see if our innovation level improves if we build a team of young people who are not trapped by years of set procedures and methods. For this reason, you can take two weeks to write a one-page business plan for the research you want to do. You can spend as much money as you want."

"As much money as I want!" said Diana. Her mouth gaped initially on hearing she had a blank cheque. She had to close her mouth.

"There is a catch, of course."

"Of course."

"You can spend whatever you want, but you must show a profit in 12 months or be fired. You can hire a team of two or three if we approve your project proposal. We are not a university. As a business, we must make money. Our corporate mandate is about profit and only profit. While improving knowledge or helping a community is a noble cause, we follow the corporate mandate. We can be sued by shareholders if we do not focus on profits."

"I understand."

"You must deliver a project proposal which must be signed off by management within 30 days or, as you can guess, you will be fired. We like projects to be 90 days or less. In a research position, we understand some research takes longer. Please be sure you have something tangible to show every 90 days."

"That sounds good."

"We have a corporate condo. You can live there for 30 days for free while you find a place of your own. We have people to help with any moving logistics. Can you start on Monday?"

"I have the job. Just like that."

"Yes. Do you have any questions?"

"I was expecting I'd be waiting for a decision."

"I was expecting you'd ask about salary. The salary is $150,000 a year, plus three weeks of vacation, and the usual medical benefits. We have a training fund of $10,000 a year, which you can use for new training or pay off student loans. Is this acceptable?"

"Yes. Absolutely yes. I am thrilled to be working at Enworld."

"I can see that. My secretary has more forms. Fill them in and enjoy a day in Manhattan. Welcome to the team." She smiled. This young woman accepted the initial offer without bargaining simply because it was stated as a fact, not an opening offer.

"May I ask how you picked me?"

"You were suggested with the highest recommendation from one of our most important people. I am the senior manager of HR, and I have never had such a high recommendation. I never do interviews except for executive positions and you."

"Wow. I am so happy. I can't wait to tell my family and friends."

"I hope to see great things from you. Can you tell my secretary to send in the people for my next meeting, and don't forget to do all the forms before you leave." They shook hands. Diana walked back and missed a turn. Diana was so excited her hands were shaking. She spoke with the secretary and collected more forms. She finished the new forms eventually.

It was a sunny day as she walked onto the street. She was in New York. This place was the center of the world in some ways. If you found fame in New York, you were famous everywhere. Ten million people on one little island. Everywhere she looked, there were famous streets, parks, galleries, and buildings. She was surprised there was not more pedestrian traffic on the pavement. The U.N. was across the street from the hotel. She had a room at One UN Plaza on the 30th floor. This was going to be her second adventure.

She took the elevator to her room. From the window, she could see all the flags of the world's nations outside the UN building. Her window was shut, and there was no lever to open it. She already knew that by enlarging a web advertising photograph of the rooms so she could see the type of window. Diana went to one of her bags and pulled a small metal tool shaped a bit like an Allen wrench. Feeling with a finger near the bottom of the window, she found a small hole. Diana put the wrench in the hole, cranked a bit, and the window released. With a few turns, she opened the window about ten inches. A gust of fresh wind came into the room. The air was so refreshing. You don't notice how stale the air is with air-conditioning. This high up, the wind was strong and somewhat clean. She went to the zipped bag, the heavy one, and opened it. Inside were thousands of pages. She took an armful of papers and tossed them into the wind. It took a few trips to throw the thousands of flyers out the window. She closed the window and put her empty bag in the closet.

She could see the papers blowing everywhere. Some flyers went up, some danced in circles, yet ultimately, they all drifted down to the street. Papers went everywhere. The message was delivered, and there was no possibility of taking it back. Message sent. She was scared, but she was committed. She felt guilty about polluting the street with paper, but mostly she was afraid.

Chapter 12 —Planetary constitution

Guy Lacan was head of the United Nations (UN) Security team. Although the UN is headquartered in New York, the land was granted to the UN as an international territory and is not part of the USA. Many security groups collaborate with Guy's UN security team. The New York Police, FBI, CIA, and all the national security teams for different international leaders work with the UN. Each security manager wants their security needs to be the most important.

The new threat was a bit different since it was a death threat, not for any particular leader, but for any leader who was a dictator. How many national leaders were dictators? Guy felt at least half the leaders were targets, which would make heightened protection almost impossible.

The threat also specified how to determine who was a dictator. The criteria w ere interesting because the fake elections held in many countries did not exempt anyone from being added to the dictator list. The author of the threat had carefully considered who was a democratic leader and who was a dictator. If Guy was honest, he liked the explicit rules to determine actual dictators from leaders who drape themselves around a pretense of being elected.

Guy had to file the threat, but he had no intention of taking any specific actions. There were threats every day, and on some days, the threats surfaced by the hour. Guy opened a new file for the document. He expected most security teams were aware of the flyers since thousands had been scattered about the UN Headquarters building in Manhattan. Guy scanned the threat and then forwarded the document to the usual group. With that task done, Guy turned his attention to more specific and current threats of the day. The dictator threat gave leaders 30 days to hold an election, so no immediate action was needed beyond sharing the information.

//

Every leader not democratically elected has 30 days to hold a free and fair election per the articles below or be terminated with extreme prejudice.

Articles of Planetary Constitution

Political Leadership

a. Anyone imprisoned for political ideology must be released immediately so that they can run in the election. If people do not like their ideas, they can vote against the idea.
b. The media, press, radio, and TV stations will provide all political candidates with equal access and time. The press will give balanced coverage of all parties without judgment.
c. Big money will be removed from the election so undue influence is not sold and corruption introduced. A flat amount of government funding will be given to each candidate to spend so no influence can be bought. All political expenditures for any campaign will be posted per sub-article h.

d. Term limits will be less than 5 years and at most two terms after which the candidate may not serve in any capacity in the government.
e. No lobby groups are allowed to influence the government. If a corporate industry wishes to promote an idea, they can tell their employees who can individually vote for the idea.
f. All vote counts can be witnessed by equal numbers of people appointed by each party. Third-party observers from outside the nation, such as the UN, can observe to ensure the election is fair.
g. The courts may not be used to intimidate opponents during, before, or after an election.
h. All campaign expenditures will be audited and posted online for full transparency.
i. Polling stations must be accessible and every employee must be given sufficient time off to vote. Voting is compulsory for all citizens with stiff penalties for failure to vote.
j. The same form of eligibility and identity for a voter applies in all areas of the nation and must be reasonable and fair.
k. If a monarch is the current national leader, they can remain in power provided they win the election. If people want a monarch, they can vote for the monarch.
l. War is mass murder and a failure of leadership, so war will not be tolerated. Any dispute can be resolved through the United Nations, World Court, International Court, or negotiation. A leader who disputes the election using armed rebellion will not be

tolerated.

Chapter 13 — Coffee time again

Diana and her friends had a little goodbye party to celebrate her success. Yasmin bought a vanilla cake. Pi ordered a bottle of red wine, and Faith bought chocolate strawberries. They hugged. They linked hands and sang "We Are the Champions."

"Finally, our tales of woe arrive at a happy ending for one of us," said Yasmin.

"Don't say 'ending'. I have more news," said Diana.

"I have to start Monday. Good thing I don't own much, so packing my belongings should take about 20 minutes. After 30 days, if I have a successful business research proposal, they may approve hiring two to three people for my team. I'm going to need some hard workers; people I can trust. If you don't have a job in four weeks, can move to New York, and don't mind working with me, we could be a team."

"Hurrah. Hurrah," shouted the women. They got a few hostile looks from other patrons, but they were too happy to contain their joy.

"We are on our way to the promised land," sang Yasmin. Her friends looked at her. She had a beautiful tremolo in her voice. She had hidden how beautifully she could sing. The young women were enjoying drinking wine and eating cake. Yasmin bumped Faith as she was about to bite into her cake, and Faith ended up with cream and icing on her nose. Faith took a handful of cake and mushed it into Yasmin's hair. It might have ended badly, but they both laughed at each other, and then everyone laughed.

"What happens with Leo?" said Faith.

Diana looked serious for a minute. "What is the point? I am leaving for New York. He will be here. I will be there. It would be too hard. It was not meant to be."

"Would you mind if I call him? Only if it is fine with you?" said Faith.

"I suppose," said Diana reluctantly.

Milton came banging and clambering through the double-doors. He had his heavy bag over one shoulder, his phone in one hand and bike helmet in the other hand. He was struggling with the door.

"You know, I hate that door. It is like it has some personal vendetta against me. I can never enter in triumph."

The girls exchanged glances. "The door is an inanimate object. The door has no feelings. It is just a door," said Pi.

"Tell that to the damn door. It always attacks me," said Milton.

"Why don't you have some cake," said Faith to Milton.

"Ah, cake. This will be the best part of my day. Congrats, Diana." He grabbed a plate, took one bite, then closed his eyes to savor the bliss.

"I have some other news. Do you remember our conversation about dictators?" said Diana. "I did a scary thing. I need to know if we can be close friends, sworn to secrecy, all for one and one for all, just like the *Three Musketeers*?"

"Of course," said Yasmin. Everyone nodded.

"Long ago, we agreed dictators were the problem. While in New York, I secretly distributed flyers around the UN that threatened to kill any dictator who did not hold fair elections in the next 30 days."

"Good," said Pi.

"I agree," said Yasmin.

"Oh. That seems risky. Is it a crime to threaten a world leader with death?" said Faith.

"How secretly?" said Milton with a mouth half full of cake.

"I was cautious. I was nervous there might be street cameras on some business entrances, so I made sure I was away from any street-level view."

Milton nodded.

"I am glad. Now the dictators have something to worry about if they are stealing power and money. Let them lose some sleep," said Pi.

"It is not really a threat. Dictators can have a fair election, and then they are in no danger. Besides, anyone who won an election fairly is not threatened. The crooks and cheats are threatened. They should be arrested by the World Court. I think it is fine," said Faith.

"I am so glad I have your support. I had only a short time to prepare. There were only 24 hours before my flight. I expected I would not get the job and probably never go to New York again. It might have been my only chance."

"It is just a threat. There does not have to be any follow-through. We don't have to kill anyone," said Milton.

"Exactly," said Diana. "I have something to show you. I got it from Professor Lazarus." Diana removed a beetle from her sleeve. She put it on the table. She hit a button on her phone, and the beetle moved into the air. Diana took a sugar cube and tossed it at the beetle. The cube disappeared. Diana tapped her phone, and the beetle floated back to the table. "This is not a magic trick. The beetle can fly. The beetle can vaporize objects in front of it. I know we have been friends forever. I know I can trust you. I think there is a way we can stop talking about improving the world and actually do it."

"Wow. That is another whole level. That is serious stuff," said Milton.

"I like it," said Pi. "Enough talk. Enough corruption. Why does the world tolerate such monsters when we know they are corrupt? Leaders who live in 500-room palaces while their people do not have running water or electricity. If the World Court does not fix it, we should. How does the Russian President have a $300 million vacation home when his salary is just a few hundred thousand? According to the Panama papers, he has half a billion dollars offshore. How is that possible unless he is stealing hundreds of millions? The stolen money could help pensioners, orphans, or students. The stolen money belongs to the people."

Pi was the smartest of them. They all knew it. She coasted through the most challenging mathematics courses. She was usually so quiet you might forget she was there. They did not realize how angry Pi was at the obvious injustices of the world. The liars and cheats enriching themselves while so many empathetic opponents to corruption sit endlessly in jails.

"I am going to keep one of these beetles. I will share the other beetles with you, my friends. I am doing this to make us stronger. If something happens to me, you will be able to carry on."

"What is going to happen to you?" said Faith.

"We never know when it is our time. I may be hit by a car. I may succumb to an illness. I am hoping nothing bad happens. I am taking insurance by sharing this technology and the plans."

"Plans. What plans?" said Milton.

"I have posted some pictures of flowers on my social media. Download the pictures, and then click on the bird. You will find the flower blooms and changes into a document showing a plan for a better world. Read it. I would like us all to meet and discuss the plans once you have all read the documents. If you don't like the plan, I understand, and we will proceed without you. If you like the plan and want to do something, I am glad because I need your help. You can make suggestions. There is more than one way to improve. I offer this plan because it is the best I have seen. I was overwhelmed when I read it. Please, help me." Diana had not posted any of the flowers that contained the blueprints of the machine. She had published the flowers showing ideas of how to alter society and world governance.

The friends ordered more drinks. Since Diana now had a job, she ordered a bottle for each person. They laughed. They cried. Milton had to leave early because of his family and work commitments, but you could tell he wanted to stay. The women partied more. They started drinking shots. Usually, this group would study until the early hours. Today, the study was over, a new phase of life was beginning. At 3 A.M. Diana's phone beeped, so she glanced down at the screen. There were nine or ten text messages from Leo. She would call him in the morning.

Chapter 14 — Dinner and a kidnapping

Three weeks later.

John Ares, CEO of Enworld, asked Diana to dinner. He sent her an email with the invitation. Ares said he had a personal interest in the success of her new department. This was a new initiative, and he was full of hope about the potential. He wanted to hear about her plans and progress. Diana had her proposal ready and kept reviewing and improving the proposal. She dreamt about what could be done. Diana thought about it on the subway, elevator, and at home. Every waking moment she had ideas and would capture them in a voice memo. She knew her future, and the future of her friends depended on an outstanding proposal.

Mr. Ares had selected a nearby restaurant with an outstanding reputation for seafood. It was one of the many endless treasures in Manhattan that you keep discovering as you spend more time in the city. Just two blocks from work, you venture into a small alley. You go down a narrow staircase to a basement that opens into a warm, rich restaurant of surprising size. It had a red carpet, well-cushioned leather seats, and suave help in tuxedos to meet every whim of your palate.

Diana was not much for fashion, but she spent too much on a black velvet evening dress. She wanted one dress to help provide an image of class. The dress was cut to the knee, fit snugly around her body and legs, and could be adjusted at the shoulders to reveal more decolletage or provide a conservative view. Diana dressed conservatively with a simple strand of fake white pearls. Diana had never talked to a powerful, affluent leader. She was nervous as Ares could make or break her career.

She was 15 minutes early, but she could see him in a cubicle when she emerged from the staircase. He waved her over. He was a good match for his posted online photographs. He was a bit gray at the temples, slim, and trim. He wore an expensive Italian wool suit and huge warm smile. Diana was surprised he knew her on sight. He got up from the table and shook her hand firmly with both his hands. She felt instantly relaxed. He just had a manner about him that made you feel like you had been friends for a long time. She went from nervous and intimidated to a bit more comfortable.

"I am so glad you agreed to dinner instead of an office meeting. In the office, I am always getting interruptions or being pulled into meetings. They already have my schedule booked solid, with tons of meetings on top of more meetings. I am hoping we can have an hour or more of good conversation without watching the clock. I can hear about your project, and I can get to know the leader of my new division."

"I am flattered you have time to spend with me. I cannot imagine the demands of running an organization with over 50,000 employees operating in over 42 countries."

Ares smiled again. The table was circular and meant for three people. They were far apart, but it was easy to hear him as the layout was intimate with all the little nooks and turns and wood panels. "Do you drink wine? I could order a bottle, or we could have mixed drinks?"

"Wine would be nice," said Diana.

Ares waived, and a server was there in seconds. "The usual," he said. The server nodded wordlessly and left.

"I am eager to hear everything. We have about 30 minutes with just the two of us, and later we will be joined by a third person. I am glad you came early."

"Oh," Diana wanted to ask him who was coming, but she was desperate to see if he liked her ideas. She only had a few minutes before someone might hijack the conversation, so she parked her curiosity and started her speech. "I have two ideas. The first is a big moneymaker. The second is more difficult, bolder, but comes with bigger rewards."

"Excellent. I like where this is going already."

"My research shows we can create food 800 times more efficiently using algae instead of beef. The nutrition is better, the growth is easier, and the costs are lower. This is established in small-scale experiments. The challenge is the taste because people love the taste of beef. Many researchers in this area are purists. They would never consider a mix of algae and beef. They are politically averse to beef for many reasons, such as animal cruelty, objections to artificial hormone treatments, almost hatred of factory farming methods, etc. We will use enough beef, about 20%, to capture a meaty taste. The other 80% of the food will be algae protein. Our costs are 600 times lower than factory beef but healthier."

"I absolutely love it. This is exactly the kind of innovation we wanted, and we can save the planet by reducing the number of cow farts."

Diana was filled with joy. She was almost shining at the positive reception. She was animated and bouncing in her seat. He totally got it. He was aware of the global warming study showing methane released by cow farts was large enough to be a factor in climate change. The cow has multiple stomachs processing food repeatedly and releasing methane gas at each stage. Methane is the second most important greenhouse gas is in global warming and more potent than carbon dioxide. He got it in the first two-minute pitch.

The waitress came with the wine. It was a sparkling ice-wine usually provided as a dessert wine. The waitress popped the cork, poured two glasses, and put the bottle in an ice bucket. Diana had seen this wine before but could not afford it. The sparkling red wine was $180 for a tiny bottle of Cabernet Franc. The bottle was a quarter of the size of a standard bottle. She took a sip and was transported by the taste. The wine was sweet, sparkling, and exploded in her taste buds.

"Amazing, isn't it. I know it is meant for dessert, but I just love this stuff and couldn't wait. Now tell me about the bold idea."

Diana realized Ares did not have the temperament to be patient. He wanted what he wanted, and he wanted it now. Ares understood *now*. He looked a bit mischievous. She thought he looked like a 60-year-old kid with his hand in the cookie jar.

"There is the challenge of eternal youth that has persisted for thousands of years. Many companies offer poor substitutes that improve our looks by small amounts for a few years, but the old age epidemic always wins. We die old and ugly."

"You plan to find the secret to eternal youth. I can see the value. I could sell people the solution to old age. What I need to hear is the *how*."

"Exactly. The current fixes are just sad. They put retinol, an acid, on your face. The acid gives your skin minor burns requiring the skin to use the healing process. The new skin is fresher, less wrinkled, and genuinely looks a bit younger. The issue is that this is borrowing from the future to look better now. The Hayflick limit gives our skin cells about 50 replications to renew from damage. With each replication, the renewal of new skin replacing old skin takes longer. An acid might give you a small quick fix, but repeated usage takes longer to show the same results. It is not a real fix. The acid does not give you younger skin."

"I am listening." He took another small sip of the wine, closed his eyes for a few seconds to savor the taste.

"I was challenged by a neighbor years ago to look at jellyfish. This almost brainless species has a unique ability to reverse aging. The Medusa jellyfish can grow younger. They can become younger, regressing to even earlier life stages such as a polyp. This is like us deciding if we want to grow younger to be a teenager again or perhaps go all the way back to an embryo. What my neighbor asked me was how do we measure the age of jellyfish? The jellyfish could look ten years old, but it may be hundreds or even millions of years old because of thousands of regenerations."

"I see you have an innovative way to study the problem. You are not working from a dream and wishful thinking. Why do you think you can solve what no other cosmetic or pharmaceutical company has solved? This would be a holy grail moment."

"I did not come up with this idea when you hired me three weeks ago. I thought and studied the problem obsessively for years since that first conversation with my neighbor. Life is the challenge of biology. Life is about the self-preservation instinct of our species. The meaning of life is the philosophical purpose of humanity. I know the issues, and I know the team I need. Faith is a genetics major. Yasmin is a bioengineer. Pi is a genius, and I am a biotech graduate. We have the skills to do the job. I have the plan. With 97% hard work and 3% luck, we can do it."

"I love confidence. You will have your team. As of now, consider your project approved. I will send HR a text telling them to give you whatever people you want."

Diana raised both arms in triumph. "Yes," she said. She took her glass of wine and chugged it.

"I am loved by my friends and feared by my enemies. You are a friend. If your experiments are a success, we will take your group and spin-off a new company with you as CEO. If you want the job, you will take it from a small idea to a functional international conglomerate. You will have 20% of the stock and a stock option plan. If and-only-if you succeed with your research, we would do an IPO, meaning a new company listed on the stock market with you as CEO. Does that interest you?"

"Oh my God. Yes. Yes, please."

"Then it is settled. We are partners in crime."

Diana laughed, smiled, poured herself another ice wine. "I admit I was nervous and scared when you asked me to dinner. I had no idea what to expect."

"Now, I have one small favor to ask. As you see, I have invited a third person, someone you know. I asked Professor Lazarus to join us. I was hoping you could tell him a bit about our company, how you like working here, and anything else you want. I want to hire him if I can. He is brilliant. I do not believe people have any idea of how smart he is. We could reward him in ways no university could afford to do. Do you think he'd like to work with you and me at Enworld?"

Diana was not prepared for this question. Her first thought was the machine, then Maynard's beating, then Lazarus's opinions about corporations, leadership, and greed. She was flooded with ideas and not sure what to do. She had an overwhelming need to protect the progress she had made, protect her friends' jobs, and the jellyfish obsession project. She was experiencing cognitive dissonance. How could she meet all objectives at once? She was running out of time. She had to answer soon as Ares was a *do-it-no*w type of leader.

"Yes. I would love to tell Lazarus what support you have given my friends and me. I think we could improve the world together. We could make obscene amount of money at the same time."

"Ah, music to my ears. I was hoping you would say that. You see, Lazarus has been on my radar for some time. I would love to support his ideas and reward him richly."

Your first blatant lie, thought Diana. You don't want to support him, and you want to steal his ideas. You would already have stolen the machine if he had not outsmarted you. In sixty seconds, Ares had gone from her confidante, patron, and friend to a deadly liar. She was working for a devil. Could she tango with this man and not become live bait?

"Ah, there he is," said Ares. "The man of the hour."

Diana looked up. She could see the Professor in his tweed corduroy jacket. No tie. He had nice wool pants but sandals.

He didn't dress up for Ares. He was wearing the same clothes to this expensive restaurant as he wore to the local coffee shop. He ran his hand through his curly hair to make himself more presentable. Whether he was in McDonalds or Tiffanys, the Professor looked the same. What was first class and exclusive about Lazarus was not his clothes but his mind.

"I am so pleased you could join us," said Ares to Lazarus. "Please call me John."

"I was in town already as one of the speakers for a conference. When you said Diana was going to be here, I had to come. I was curious what the two of you are planning?" Lazarus shook Ares' hand and gave Diana a little wink at the same time.

"What was the topic of your speech?" asked Diana.

"A bit boring. Multi-dimensional space-time gravitational waves from a mathematical perspective. Boring nonsense to most people. What is needed is less mathematics and more proof-of-concept testing. I was suggesting some testing ideas."

"Could you give me an example of a practical use?" said Ares.

"Sure. Since we have a biologist and the CEO of an energy conglomerate at this table, I will give you an example we can all enjoy. The Earth is running out of non-renewable resources. There is only so much copper on Earth. The whole capitalist system will slow down because we will just run out of non-renewable resources like copper. You cannot endlessly supply products to eight billion people. One day, you will go to the store to buy a cell phone, and they will tell you that they are all out of cell phones because there is a shortage of rare earth used to make cell phone screens. They will suggest you come back in a month, and maybe they will have more supply."

"Ouch. That will hurt," said Ares. "You can always make a new cell phone by taking an old phone from someone else."

"Sure. Good point, John. You could steal or buy old products. The issue is with recycling; you only get a portion of the resources back; you never get 100% extraction. On each recycling, the portion returned gets smaller, but the costs get bigger. Recycling methods always follow the law of diminishing returns. We are going to run out of all non-renewable resources."

"How can biology fix it?" said Diana.

"The solution is we can take resources from asteroids. Our solar system's asteroid belt is untapped and an enormous source of precious minerals like copper, diamonds, gold, and other non-renewables. We don't do it because space travel is expensive in part because of the fuel needed. It is also expensive and difficult to mine on asteroids due to limited gravity. A jackhammer in almost zero gravity, micro-gravity, would not penetrate the rock but fly backward off the asteroid and into space. The solution is microbes. You have microbes that eat minerals and so inadvertently mine the resources as a byproduct. You fly by and seed asteroids with microbes and then come back a year later to pick up the resources the microbes processed."

"Truly brilliant," said Ares. "The first company to do it would control the supply of the metals and other precious resources. If you control the supply, you control the prices. The company would own the world. The only issue is the cost of travel."

"I may have a solution to the travel problem, but I think you were aware of that, which is why you were so eager to meet me," said Lazarus to Ares.

"What I would love is to hire a top thinker such as yourself. Whatever the university pays you, I will double. No, I will triple your current salary."

"I don't think happiness is determined solely by money. Sure, the first $50,000 makes a big difference in buying shelter, clothes, food, and other necessities. After that, the value of money declines in providing happiness. I am happy now, and I love my job. Money is not everything to me. There are lots of people with lots of money who are not especially happy or healthy."

"Well, I don't give up that easily. Have some wine, and tell me what I can do to persuade you. I have many resources. How can I help? Diana, what do you think? Are you happy at Enworld?"

"Mr. Ares, I mean John, has been supportive. He has hired me, promoted me, he wants to hire my friends as part of my team, and he has offered me great incentives if our project succeeds."

"I am happy to hear that. What are you working on?" said Lazarus.

"The first idea is a way to feed more people at less cost, with better nutrition, and less environmental footprint."

"That is outstanding, Diana. I am so pleased," said Lazarus.

"She is a superstar in the making, Professor. Notice she gave no hint of how we will do it, so our intellectual property is not at risk. Diana is a gem. I am so lucky to have her on the team. I wish the three of us could be a team. We could make a difference."

"I believe in capitalism. I believe in a free market. Mr. Ares, you bought battery technology not to compete in batteries but to shut down battery improvements. You sold no batteries. You prevented anyone else from selling the improved batteries so you could sell more oil. This is not capitalism or a free market. You enriched yourself by preventing the invisible hand of capitalism from helping all of us improve," said the Professor.

"That is a bit harsh. I believe in capitalism. It is more complicated than you are suggesting," said Ares.

"Of course, saying it is complicated is an excellent retort that is impossible to disprove. If we keep polluting with oil, global warming will lead to more floods. The floods will wipe away millions of coastal homes, and stronger hurricanes will blow away homes. The higher storm surges will destroy freshwater with seawater. We will see more pestilence and hardships for millions of starving people. Not using batteries may be complicated, but so is global warming," said Lazarus.

"Fifty percent of people do not believe in global warming," said Ares.

"Yes, and 99% of scientists do believe in global warming. Why is there such a big gap between what the public believes and what the scientific experts believe? Shouldn't both groups believe the same facts? Are newspapers not doing their job?"

"There are more ways to envision the world than yours alone, Professor," said Ares.

"My view is that Enworld is funding lobby groups to spread misinformation about global warming. Now you may deny it, but there is a standing offer, I call it a bribe, that Enworld will pay any scientist $10,000 if they go to a conference and deny global warming. You created the disinformation. You fund the disinformation. While Enworld pays people to deny the science, at the same time, your own scientists are planning for a world where global warming has destroyed the Arctic ice. You want to run oil tankers through the Arctic as soon as the ice melts in the summer because it is faster. Is that correct?" said Lazarus.

"It is a conundrum. Is there no way I can tempt you to work at Enworld? You could work on global warming mitigation?"

"Fortunately, I can mitigate global warming now. My machine can run without any oil or hydrocarbon fuel. I can power an aircraft carrier without oil. I can run jet aircraft without fuel. I can run cars without gasoline. We can, within a year, just keep hydrocarbons for essential needs like making plastics. Oil is too precious to burn," said Lazarus.

"God no. I have to win your support. You are talking about destroying everything. Diana, you have been quiet. Could your projects use the help of such a smart professor? Help me. Professor Lazarus is describing a terrifying world. My company would collapse, and tens of thousands of employees would lose their jobs, including you."

"Professor, I believe more can be done with collaboration than competition. Is there some common interest we could find?" said Diana. "While you both ponder the possibilities, if you gentlemen don't mind, I have been drinking too much wine, and I need to go to the lady's powder room. Please play nice until I get back." Diana slid out of the booth and left the two men.

She did not really have to go to the bathroom. She had a scary thought. Did Leo also work at Enworld? She pulled her phone from her purse and brought up the Enworld employee directory. She searched for Leo and found his name. He was a junior employee in the marketing department. Diana felt sick.

Ares was behind it all from the beginning: Professor Maynard's beating, the job offers at Enworld, and the near love affair with Leo. It was all Ares conducting her life. She had been led like a dog on a leash. How could she recover? How deep did the whole plan go?

"Now that she is gone, we can speak plainly. You will get on board or else. I can call the President of your university and offer him endowments, but only if he finds a reason to terminate your tenured job."

"Do your worst. I will sell my technology to a people-friendly government like Canada or Norway for enough royalties to buy Enworld 50x over. Of course, within a year of my machine being manufactured, your stock will be worth a few pennies. Whatever country I pick to work with will be the richest in the world. I think a country that cares more about people than corporate greed would be a good choice."

"Fine. If you don't care about yourself, I will hurt Diana. I will kill your dog. I will destroy your mother and your friends. You will work with me, or you will be an enemy. I destroy my enemies with the flick of a hand."

"What you should consider is that if I am smart enough to build the fastest machine in the world, am I smart enough to build a powerful weapon?" The Professor did not wait for an answer. He got up and left.

As soon as Lazarus turned his back, Ares sent a text message to Brodie. "Take him. We need him alive but don't be too gentle. He needs a lesson in respecting his superiors." Brodie got the text and signaled his team. One soldier crouched behind the van, which they parked alongside the entrance to the restaurant. They had two men in the alley near the street. The other side of the path was a dead-end. With luck, if they approached, he'd run into the dead-end. They could take him without any view from passing traffic.

Diana came back to find Lazarus gone. "Sadly, your Professor had a snit. He left before we could enjoy our meal. Very rude," said Ares.

"Don't worry, I'll get him back," said Diana, and she ran off before Ares could object. It was hard to run in high heels. She was not used to high heels, but she did her best. Ares tried to follow but was slowed down moving around the circular table.

Lazarus expected trouble as soon as he saw the alley entrance. He pulled one of the beetles free and held it in his palm so that it was not visible. He came through the door and looked up and down. There were two big men at the top of the alley near the road. They came menacingly toward him. They did not have weapons. The giant mercenary had one hand in a fist and punched his open hand while keeping a steady gaze on the Professor. They made no attempt to surprise him. The gesture was a direct threat. The Professor took a few steps toward them and smiled. The big man with a scar across the cheek jogged forward with both hands in fists. The Professor raised his hand, pointed the beetle, and clicked it. There was a popping sound, and the big man was gone. The second man hesitated. The Professor clicked the beetle again, and the second man also popped into the void.

A sound from behind Lazarus of the door opening made him spin. As he turned, he caught sight from his periphery of a third mercenary. Where did he come from? Lazarus did not have time to respond. There was another popping sound, and the third man was gone. Lazarus had braced to be walloped, not saved. He looked at the door and saw Diana holding a beetle. She had saved him from a beating, torture, and likely indefinite confinement except when allowed out to help Ares improve the machine.

Diana's mouth was open, and she held her trembling hand up in a gesture of horror. "What have I done?"

"You saved me. You saved me from a bloody beating and kidnapping. I cannot thank you enough."

Diana was overwhelmed. She did not know what to do next. With emotions overflowing, Diana ran into the Professor's arms. She hugged him and put her head on his chest. She was breathing hard. In a few seconds, she felt the hug was inappropriate. She pulled away, but her beetle was tangled with one of the legs of a beetle on his lapel. She stopped, but he did not notice and moved back. Diana's beetle twisted and clicked, and Lazarus was gone. Diana stood alone in the dim light of the facade. She did not want to believe what had happened. A silly snag of clothing, and she had killed him. He died, not from the mercenaries, but her stupid, insecure hug.

Diana turned to face Ares. He was coming up the stairs. As soon as Ares saw her, he knew something was wrong. He assumed Brodie had snatched the Professor. He was worried she saw the takedown.

"What happened?' Ares asked.

"I don't know. I came up the stairs, and Lazarus was gone. I looked up and down. No sight of him." Diana was afraid of Ares. He was a ruthless liar and would kill or beat anyone in his path to glory. He was a monster. She had to step nimbly around this monster and not prod the dragon.

"He will be back when he calms down. He left his phone on the table," said Ares. "Come on. We don't want to waste the whole evening. Tell me more about jellyfish." Ares turned, and

Diana followed. She felt wobbly. Diana held on to the handrail and tried her best to act as if nothing had happened. Since Ares did not know her, he probably could not tell how upset she was. She had just killed a caring person. Actually, she had killed two men. She should have told Lazarus how much she respected him. He gave her a plan to save the world, and she gave him death.

Chapter 15 — Why did you send us the bird?

Lazarus found himself in a white room. The walls were not painted white but a misty, milky translucent color. The wall was not a solid color but gave the impression you could see through the mist into an endless horizon if only the fog would move. Lazarus walked up to the wall to touch the cool, nylon texture. A twelve-foot door with no handle was in the corner. There was no furniture. The room was bright but with no direct source of light. One felt like the whole room was under light rather than a specific light bulb. He did not realize it at first, but the silence was intense. No sound. No talking, no street noise, no birds - just pure silence. The room was large, perhaps 30 by 20 feet. When Lazarus walked to one wall, the opposite wall seemed to retract as if the dimensions were adjusting as he moved. Am I in purgatory? Am I in heaven, or am I dead? Lazarus pinched the skin on his arm, and he felt pain. He felt alive but disoriented.

"Hello. Anyone? Anyone listening?" Lazarus shouted. There was a responding crackle of static. "I am Lazarus." Again, the static crackling response. Lazarus went to sit down on the floor. As he lowered, he felt the shape of a simple chair. Lazarus looked but saw nothing there. He slowly lowered his weight, supported by a column of air. The chair was comfortable in a way he had never experienced. The soft chair adapted to your posture as you moved. He laid down, and the chair supported him in a horizontal posture. He sat up, and the chair supported his back.

Lazarus walked about the room. He touched the wall, and the mist swirled about his finger. He put both hands together, placed them on the wall, and spread his arms while still touching the wall. The fog cleared, and he could see a pelican in the next room. Lazarus was beginning to suspect he was not dead but ported. Lazarus walked to the opposite wall, made the same gesture, and could see one of his assailants. The big guy with the scar was screaming and punching the wall with a speed and intensity that gave Lazarus some fear. He could never have survived an attack from that man. He would have been beaten unconscious before he had a chance to think of weaving or ducking. Lazarus was concerned. What if they were put together? Would he be killed?

The cackle returned, but it was more defined. The cackle kept changing to form more distinct sounds from different languages. Lazarus listened carefully. Lazarus called out the letters of the alphabet. The cackle changed into pronounced letters that sounded like his own voice. The voice matched Lazarus in intonation and timbre.

A six-inch control panel popped out of the wall with three colored buttons; green, blue, and red. The word *hapiness* was misspelled on the panel front. Lazarus pushed the green button. There was a hum, a short sound that vibrated about him, and he had an intense experience that felt like an orgasm. It was more of a mental than a physical experience. He pushed the green button again; the same hum, the same vibration sound wave washed over him, and the same intense pleasure. Happiness was misspelled, but the pleasure was a touch of joy.

Lazarus pushed the blue button. There was another series of sounds. The sound this time was more mathematical. The closest description would be Bach's Prelude in C for harpsichord. He did not feel different and had no intense experience. Lazarus pushed the button again, and the same tune was played. Lazarus thought the button was defective. He did have a general feeling of elation. He felt happy in a subtle, non-specific manner. Could this feeling be the same as being in love? Lazarus had not been in love for a long time. Being in love, the higher energy, the sublime feeling of goodwill, the overall optimistic outlook. Yes, that was precisely what he felt. He felt the subtle uplifting happiness that comes with the first kiss of love. The feeling was gradual but was sustained. He felt happy and energized.

Lazarus hesitated to push the red button. Red was usually a color of caution. He did not want to lose this feeling of being in love. He walked around the room, did a few push-ups in his high-energy state, and when nothing else happened, he jogged over and pushed the red button. A red ball bounced twice on the wall and sat still. The wall was functioning as a computer monitor. The monitor above the ball showed a picture of a man thinking, and the ball started to roll an inch. Lazarus smiled. The third type of happiness was to *think*. This was ideal for a professor.

He stood near the ball and swiped his hand across the ball, and nothing happened. He focused on the ball and imagined it moving. The ball wobbled a little. He focused with full intensity, and the ball rolled about one inch. He could mentally move the ball. There were no wires. Somehow, the wall could trigger brain waves in his system to create an orgasm or the feeling of love. He developed a brain pattern by thinking of moving the ball. For the next hour, Lazarus kept focusing on the ball. He managed to move it about six inches with lots of tiny wobbles and vibrations. The effort was exhausting, yet he was satisfied with his success. He smiled. The third dimension of happiness was the satisfaction of achieving a goal.

He went to the wall and opened the mist to see the pelican. The pelican was eating something. He went to the other wall to see the killer. He had his back to Lazarus and was gesturing and talking to another of Lazarus's assailants.

The wall now opened another drawer. This time Lazarus saw a large vase of water, a platter of brightly colored grains, and three colored vials of pills. The picture on the wall showed a person drinking and eating the products. Lazarus downed the water because he knew he was dehydrated. He ate the grains, which tasted like oatmeal and berries. He hesitated to swallow the pills. Was this candy or pharmaceuticals? Would he die? Could he digest any of these things, or would some alien bacteria eat his gut and bones? He tried one pill from one of the vials.

"Greetings." A voice emanated from the wall, but there was no apparent source. The sound was from all sides, up and down, left and right. The accent was identical to his own. "You are in quarantine."

"Greetings to you. Where am I?"

"You are in class M401 of the ninth multiverse. We are the galaxy of Hyperion9 in the solar system of Nef22, the fifth planet of the second sun. Do you know how you got here?"

"Not exactly. I have a machine that can isolate gravitational waves by folding space. I created a torus with negative energy to build a vacuum in front of the machine to pull the machine forward. By accident, I was caught in the negative energy and ported here."

"You did not use a black hole for the travel?"

"No."

"Are you the scientist who invented the machine and the port device?"

"Yes."

"We are honored to have you with us. In our multiverse collective, scientists are the most respected of all professions. Since you invented a device that can transport across universe boundaries, your name will be added to the List of Universals. You may travel to any universe at no cost, as required by inter-universe protocol. You will be given the Amulet of the List and all the privileges of that office. We are honored you chose us as a destination. We are the low and most young."

"I don't deserve such honors. I am a scientist. I did invent the machine. However, I had no knowledge or goal of traveling across a universe boundary."

"The science to span a universe is almost always found through serendipity. Only the first one of the List of Universals predicted the outcome correctly. All eight members on the list found insights by providence."

"How is it that you speak my language?"

"We have been to your universe, galaxy, and planet. Many of your languages are in our catalog. We could not communicate until our system heard you speak enough of your language. We knew what language to use from our catalog. When you spoke your alphabet, you were most helpful. I don't really know your language. I speak my own tongue, and our system translates forward and backward into your language. We have a question. Why did you send us the bird?"

"Unintentional. The bird was on a collision course with the machine, and we were traveling too fast to swerve. The torus anti-energy ported the bird to avoid annihilation."

"Why did you send us these soldiers? Some here think they were scouts for an invasion?"

"Absolutely not. They are mercenaries. They were sent to capture and torture me to reveal the secrets of the portal machine. They were ported because I could not avoid capture. They were sent away. I did not know if they would survive the trip. I did not know where they would be sent."

"That was my analysis too, from listening to their conversation. Given your story, we will keep you separated from the others."

"I am grateful. I am Professor Lazarus Solomon. What is your name?"

"I am SF03."

"What happens now?"

"You must remain here for 10 days. You are in quarantine. We found 129 types of hostile bacteria in your body, mostly in your digestive tract but generally in almost every organ and muscle. We have found 749 types of dangerous bacteria outside your body, mostly on your skin. First, we will attempt to remove all known microbial pathogens. If you survive, you may enter our world. Naturally, we could never allow those germs into our community."

"Agreed," said Lazarus. He walked to the vials of pills and took them all. He looked at his skin with horror but assumed they had talked about the billions of random bacteria every human carried with the aplomb of the ignorant. Did the alien say, 'if I survive?'

Chapter 16 — It is just an enzyme, stupid

Ares sent Brodie at least 20 messages in the 24 hours after the attempt to grab the Professor. The messages became more strident and panicky. Ares kept checking his phone for messages constantly, but Brodie did not respond. Brodie's team did not respond. Leo reported no movement of the machine and no visuals of the Professor. Ares was worried. He did not have the device that threatened his industry. Ares did not have the designs of the machine. He had argued and lost contact with the only person who understood the machine. Now he had lost his security team. Brodie had never failed until he was tasked with controlling this Professor. No blood, no signs of a struggle, and no body was found. The team was gone with no clues left behind.

What worried him the most was Brodie knew too much to be lost. Brodie knew where the bodies of his competitors were buried. Brodie knew about the kidnappings of Enworld executives when they dared oppose Ares. Brodie had the blackmail photos of so many politicians and judges. Brodie, under the influence of the wrong people, could put Ares in prison forever. Ares had not felt this level of fear for decades. Without Brodie, Ares knew he was vulnerable to losing his fortune, reputation, and freedom.

Over the next few days, Ares sent more than 100 text messages. On the second day, Ares hired 12 people from four different security teams to find Brodie. For obvious reasons, Ares did not want to involve the police. There was still no news and no leads. Ares was not used to feeling afraid. He would focus on finding Bodie and then worry about the Professor.

The only happy development was the research by Diana was making unexpectedly fast progress. Diana had promised to help Ares find the Professor. With some pressure, Ares had convinced Diana to disclose what she knew about the Professor's friends and relatives. Diana told Ares that Lazarus had a parent, maybe a father, whom Lazarus cared for greatly. Diana said she knew the parent was living out of the country. She thought it might be Europe but was not sure. At least, thought Ares, I have won Diana's full trust. She doesn't think of me as a killer.

Diana hired Pi, Faith, and Yasmin. She assigned Pi to look at jellyfish since that was the most challenging problem, and Pi was the genius. The rest of them focused on the algae. They knew the challenge. They had to go from the laboratory experiments, which were their comfortable realm, to a production facility generating enough money to pay their salaries. The clock was ticking. They had to generate enough profits within 12 months. Issues they could control quickly in the lab were often challenging in the field. Diana had bought a small farm in New Jersey to start growing large amounts of algae. The pond was almost immediately contaminated with pond scum and other unwanted micro-beasties that altered the product's taste.

Pi was the one making the most progress. She had isolated an enzyme called telomerase that the jellyfish used to trigger the body to reverse the aging process. With the millions of chemical reactions in the body, Pi had somehow found the specific chemical trigger to reverse aging. The aging of cells ran backward once exposed to the enzyme. The body made the cells younger and younger by rebuilding a small part of the DNA called the telomere. What made the problem easier was humans and jellyfish both use DNA and telomeres to control aging. Nature was efficient. Why invent a new method to build life? The blob of transparent goo that made up a jellyfish body used DNA to control life, the same essential building blocks humans used. Pi had the enzyme to reverse aging in humans. Everyone was excited. The challenge was finding a delivery method to recharge the billions of cells.

Despite the management challenges, Diana needed to hide the machine as a priority. She struggled. Diana felt guilt, overwhelming guilt that she had killed the Professor. It was an accident, but she had ported the Professor when her only goal was to save him.

As the executor of his will, she would inherit all his money and his home. She would need to care for his mother. Would the police be suspicious that a will signed a few days before he *disappeared* was too much of a coincidence? They would suspect she killed him. In truth, she had killed him. She did belong in jail. She could not sleep, but she had to pretend and go through the regular daily functions to protect her friends and the Professor's secrets.

Diana had checked the web. When a person goes missing, they must be missing for seven years before they are presumed dead. She would not be able to sell the home or allocate his funds for seven years.

She knew the top priority was to hide the machine. On the first weekend, she took the train to Canada and went back to her old apartment. She had moved so quickly; she had not had time to sublet the place. The lease was for two years. When it was dark, she jumped the fence into the Professor's backyard. She knew where he kept his spare keys as it was specified in the will. She slipped in the backdoor. She assumed the house was being watched, but perhaps all this caution was not needed. The problem was if she took the machine out of the garage, it would be seen. She had to hide it without moving it. Diana had not been in his house before so did not know what she would find. She had a small flashlight and taped the device so only one pencil thin beam of light projected.

There were books everywhere. Books on the floor, books holding up plants, books under the couch, and books in the kitchen. She kept kicking and bumping into more books. She crept around until she found a door to the garage from within the house. The garage had no windows, so she turned on the garage lights. She took the wheels off the machine. The windshield was already down. It was difficult, but with the engine on to support its own weight, she could angle the machine through the door. The fit was tight, and she was turning and pushing at one point. For a minute, she thought it was permanently stuck in the door jamb, but she was able to push it through. Diana was sweating profusely with the effort. There were French doors on the side of the house. When she opened both doors, she could ride the machine out and across the fence into her backyard. She struggled again to get the machine into her old home.

Where could she hide a machine the size of a small car? It is not like you can just park it in the living room, and no one will notice. Diana sat on her old couch with the machine sitting on the carpet where the coffee table used to sit. This was not an easy problem. She had to hide this machine, and she had to sublet this house.

Chapter 17 — You missed the war

Lazarus was bored much of the time for the first week. He would play the mental game with the bouncing ball, but the game physically drained him. Lazarus could not understand why a mental game was so physically exhausting. He was taking his pills. On occasion, he would part the mist to watch the mercenaries next door. The three men shared the same room now. Lazarus could hear them if he put his ear to the wall, but he did not want to listen to them most of the time. Most of their conversation was swearing and threats to his life, God, the system, and each other. The youngest of them spent most of his day touching the green button to have a mental simulation of an orgasm. The young guy was giving himself hundreds, possibly thousands, of orgasms a day. "Death by orgasm,'" said Lazarus to himself.

The limited interaction and lack of activity made Lazarus crave conversations with the SF03. The discussion at first focused on security as the aliens had concerns about attempts to colonize their world. What was most important, of dire importance for Lazarus, was learning information to improve life on Earth.

"Good news, Lazarus. Our council has decided that your mercenaries were not sent here to colonize us. Some of us thought they were advanced scouts to assess our ability. After talking to you and listening to them, we are sure that is not correct. The next concern was that they were infected with hundreds of pathological microbes as a way of invading us. Since everyone from your planet has the same microbes, we dismissed that concern too. We believe you do not remove the microbes because your species is too ignorant to know what microbes are dangerous. The council has agreed that your planet is not a threat. You may enter our society once your dangerous microbes are removed. We will not allow the mercenaries to enter our society since they would infect us with damaging emotions, thoughts, and actions. They are an emotional and ideological risk vector as well as a biological threat."

"I understand," said Lazarus. They may kill each other if they don't die from overuse of the green button."

SF03 laughed. "Yes, the younger one used the green button over 21,000 times yesterday. He is addicted to pleasure. Pleasure is the simplest and least fulfilling form of happiness."

"21,000 times. Yikes," said Lazarus.

"We have seen you move the red ball from 6 inches the first day to 24 inches today. Your intelligence is multiplying."

"The red ball exercise is developing my intelligence?" said Lazarus with surprise.

Yes. Every inch adds about 10 points to your mental intelligence. You have added 180 IQ (intelligence quotient) points since you arrived. We use this game to develop the minds of our children."

"How far can the ball roll?"

"There is no limit as far as we know. Some of us roll the ball for miles. You would think our brain could only perform to some finite limit, but we have never hit the end of the journey. The ability of the brain to interconnect permits billions and billions of connections. Intelligence growth can be an exponential explosion rather than a finite journey."

"This explains why I find the game so exhausting. I am lifting weights to develop a huge brain muscle instead of big arm muscles."

"Exactly."

"Can I ask when I will be free from quarantine?"

"We have removed the less persistent bacteria, but you have some entrenched bacteria and viruses that are resisting and adapting. If they adapt too quickly, instead of antibiotics, we will have to give you competing bacteria that are not pathogenic. The competing bacteria will be faster at removing the bad germs but might have painful side effects. The competing bacteria would consume the same food as the bad bacteria and starve the bad bacteria to death. The bad bacteria cannot easily adapt to the competition except by finding a less competitive environment. You will need to be in this room for at least two more weeks."

The two of them talked about music, literature, art, and science. Lazarus felt it was more of an assessment than a discussion. They were sizing him up, and he was the benchmark for his entire species. SF03 was working when he talked to Lazarus.

"We, the low and most young, did not expect your planet to survive past the first planetary stage of extinction called Stage Up. We dismissed your planet as unlikely to survive."

"Why?"

"The first stage, Stage Up, usually results in the extinction of an intelligent species. The smartest species will dominate the world and begin overbreeding. It is what you call Darwin's

Survival of the Fittest concept. The best species compete for resources, and the weaker species become extinct. Even as your society discusses saving species, you have hundreds of species becoming extinct every month. When we last assessed your planet, you had over eight billion people consuming space, water, and food. You were killing every other living thing on the planet to make space for more humans."

"We are turning our whole planet into a garbage heap. We are a plague of locusts turning forests into deserts," said Lazarus.

"Stage Up is a challenge. Each planet has only so many non-renewable resources. The amount of iron, copper, manganese, and other resources is finite. You must learn enough about science and smartly use the resources you have, so you can learn to travel to new planets. If you have not learned how to explore space before you run out of resources, you can never go to space, and your whole species will die when the resources run out."

"We could recycle."

"Recycling only buys you a bit of time. Each round of recycling redeems less than 100%. You will run out unless you can get to other planets for more resources. This is the first stage of planetary extinction. We felt you were going extinct because you did not spend enough on science and knowledge. Your species enjoys religions, mythologies, sports, movies, and stories. You spend your resources on luxuries that you throw away rather than spend your limited time and resources on knowledge, education, and science. Most people give their charitable donations to religion. Religion will never give you more resources from other planets. How much knowledge have religions provided about space travel in the last 1,000 years? The second biggest charity is colleges, but the money is spent on football games instead of science studies. Sports and beer will not help you use those few precious resources to escape the jail of living on a single, dangerous planet. Most rich people spend resources on more big homes they rarely live in than education for your smartest humans. We saw little hope for significant space travel from your planet. Lazarus, you were the outlier. You were the surprise. You could save your entire planet if you could harvest resources from space. You could travel to another livable planet, an exoplanet, to ensure your species survive the Stage Up extinction."

"As a scientist, I would not complain if our leaders spent more on science. If our survival on Earth means we spend less on sports and beer, then I agree Earth is doomed. Your assessment is reasonable."

"You are humble. Good - for we too are the low and most young."

"I am going to have to ask you to explain that epithet."

"Soon, that epithet will belong to you too, if you are lucky."

Lazarus was taken aback by the conversation. Humans were in a race for survival. The human species had to learn enough to harvest the solar system or run out of time and resources. We have the needed intelligence, and we have time left. We behave like that kid next door who keeps punching the pleasure button until dead. Lazarus went to the wall and pulled back the mist curtain by an inch. The kid pushed the button another 20,000 times. The big guy was getting angry about it. The two of them started shouting. The voices got louder. The kid lost his temper and took a swing at the big guy with the scar. It was a mistake because the big guy bounced him about the room with a few punches and some grappling.

Lazarus had seen enough. If humans continued a life of pleasure, spending our time on sports, beer, and stories of everlasting spiritual life, we would simply cease. Our lives, the lives of our children, and a thousand generations of grandchildren, the lives of all humans would be snuffed out. Sadly, the prayer from an Aztec priest to the God of the Corn Bird, or some such deity, would not save humans. Lazarus shook his head. "All religions predict an end of days, and if you believe, the prediction will certainly come true." Lazarus gritted his teeth. He was determined to pass the message to world leaders. Would they listen? Would they believe?

Chapter 18 — See the prince

Diana was going to Saudi Arabia on the corporate jet with Ares. This was her first experience traveling as one of the rich and famous, except she wasn't rich or famous. A limo picked her up from her house. She was driven to a small local airport. There were no long security lines, no long baggage check-in lines, and no harried airline employees trying to fix every missed connection and emergency change. The employees were relaxed, smiling, and welcomed people to the airport. A pilot held the door open for her. With available seats in the airport lobby, she liked it already.

Diana knew she was not needed on the trip. This was John Ares's way of trapping her for hours on an airplane, and she would have nowhere to run. He could interrogate her endlessly about the Professor and the machine. It would not be fun, but the perks were seeing how the other side lived.

The pretense was to propose to the Saudi prince an agriculture venture in a country with almost no significant farming. The government could grow algae in seawater if Diana could use sea algae instead of lake algae. Diana was convinced Ares did not care if the Saudis went for the proposal. Enworld was a major oil company and had hundreds of projects refining and distributing crude oil. The algae project was incidental.

Ares was not the only person with ulterior agendas. Diana had her own plan. She was eager to meet the Prince and implement phase one of the planetary constitution. This week would be a coordinated strike for democracy and improved leadership. Every member of the team was in place and had a target objective. The Russian President was attending a UN Security Council meeting tomorrow. Pi had volunteered to stay in New York. Yasmin was attending an art auction of African antiquities expected to raise large amounts of money for the South Sudanese President. The Syrian President was also in the country. He was attending a peace conference in Washington D.C. where the major players would carve up his nation to suit the powerful. He would be speaking at the UN General Assembly to defend his use of chemical weapons and landmines on his own people.

Diana was pleased to help Milton. He and his family had moved into her old apartment in Canada. She had paid the rent for the rest of the year, and the lease ran for two years. Milton was being evicted from his one-bedroom apartment and was desperate. As a bonus, in keeping with the leadership plan, Diana and the others had combined resources to buy Milton and the family a week in Orlando, Florida to see Disney World. Milton was so happy he cried. Diana could not hire him at Enworld because he had no science skills, and her project had no need for an economist. The paid holiday came with a commitment. The North Korean Supreme Leader Kim Tim Bit would be in Disney World at the same time. The Supreme Leader was in the country as part of the failed nuclear treaty negotiations. With a security contingent of more than 20 secret service people of his own and protection from the US government, this would be the most challenging target.

"I hope you have enough shrimp platters and champagne" said Ares.

"Yes, sir. You will be drowning in shrimp," said the concierge.

"So not like last time?" said Ares.

The concierge gave a silly grin but said nothing. Diana walked up to the plane. Everything was so casual, and you could walk where you wished. You can chat with the pilot as you wait for the plane to be fueled.

"Ah, my protégé," said Ares.

"My Lord," said Diana with a curtsy.

Ares laughed. He was pleased with himself for asking her. She was nice to look at, and she was solving problems. Not like the useless piece of crap, Leo. For two weeks, the daily updates were the same; we have no sighting of the Professor. The Professor was not at his office and not at his home. There was no movement of the machine from the garage. Leo was essentially a waste of money, and Ares did not expect a positive result. Ares had left Leo watching the house for 12 hours a day, mostly as a punishment. He could picture Leo sitting for 12 hours a day staring at an empty home. Worse than prison. Prisoners are free to let their attention drift. Ares finally relented and sent Leo a text. "Enough. I'm pulling the plug on your failure. Meet me at the airport tomorrow at 10 A.M. We are going to Saudi Arabia."

Ares was more concerned about Brodie. It was as if Brodie and Lazarus were no longer on the planet. No trail was found by the 12 security experts. No cell phone activity. No facial recognition looking at the video scans from nearby retail stores. How could someone not be caught on some security camera from some store somewhere in Manhattan? You cannot walk one block in any direction without a camera from some building capturing your image. There was no credit card activity.

The security team told Ares they had never encountered this kind of disappearance. In all their experience, there was always some evidence at every crime scene. The victim and the perpetrator always leave something of themselves behind. There are scratches and drops of blood, torn buttons not noticed in a scuffle, a few hairs are grabbed, or glasses break and are left behind. You might find a discarded and hastily hidden weapon, a cigarette butt, or perhaps a tossed piece of paper. Something is always left behind by all parties. All they could find was half a boot print behind a van from one of the soldiers. There was some spit at the top of the alley from Brodie. Dead end. The Professor and the mercenaries were gone. Two weeks and no findings.

Diana and Ares boarded the plane. They took seats facing each other while Diana was facing toward the pilot. Diana was relieved. She would get sick if she had her back in the direction of motion. Two Enworld executives joined the party. An elderly gentleman, the chief operations officer (COO), came first, and he was followed by the chief financial officer (CFO), who clearly had problems with a sore back. Diana had met him once before, and he stood throughout their 30-minute meeting because of his back pain. The pilots were doing the checks, and everyone was checking the time. Diana looked out the window and saw Leo running to the plane. She was surprised she still found him handsome despite his manipulative games. He was a liar. Leo bounded onto the plane and went to the back of the aircraft for the remaining seat. He nodded quickly to Diana but averted eye-contact.

There were bottles of wine and magazines in the storage areas about the seats. One of the bottles was an expensive wine. Diana could not tell the difference, but the executives knew the premium wines from the outstanding vintages. The CFO smiled broadly, waved the wine above his head, and tucked the wine next to him. As soon as he went to the bathroom, the COO slipped out of his chair and stole the wine. Ares smiled at Diana. For the next few hours, she watched the gamesmanship for the prestige wine. They stole it back and forth. They connived, argued, cheated, manipulated, and took enjoyment from the game. If this is what they will do for a bottle of wine, what would they do for an important business deal? Diana was disgusted. These executives had to win. They had to win even if it meant cheating a friend for a prize that didn't really matter. Monsters.

Finally, the moment came. "Diana, have you heard from Lazarus since the dinner?" asked Ares.

"Nothing, John. I am increasingly concerned." Diana opened the text messages to Professor Lazarus. "Look," she said as she scrolled quickly. "Professor, can you call me?" was sent two weeks ago. "Are you okay?", "Did you get my last message?", "Can you get back to me soon?" "I am worried." She scrolled through 30 or more messages. Of course, Diana knew when she sent the text that there would be no reply. Diane had ported him. She felt miserable with guilt. Diana knew he was *not here*. Had she killed him or sent him into the void? "As you can see, I have sent him so many messages, and he never replies. I tried him at work. I tried him at home. I am so worried. He was a friend. We spent years just greeting each other as we came and went, but recently we had an adventure."

Ares raised one eyebrow at Diana.

"No, not that kind of adventure. It was not like that. Lazarus was much too old for me. He must be thirty or forty."

"When I married my third wife, she was about your age when I was 42."

"Hmm. She must have really loved you."

"No, not really. She loved my money, and I loved her body. It worked out well for about four years. People think of a trophy wife as a pretty but empty-headed bimbo. She was a stunning beauty, and she was no bimbo. She has a Master's degree in English Literature. She speaks five languages. She sings opera, and she is rich given her four-year investment in me. I miss her sometimes when my fifth wife cheats on me. My third wife never cheated. She got tired of me cheating and dumped me. To be honest, I deserved to lose her. I send her messages sometimes, but she never replies. We make mistakes, and we pay the price."

Diana smiled inanely, but she felt nothing but disgust. She was working with the devil. Should she flatter him, tell him how much she liked his red tie, shiny horns, and pointy tail? She saw Leo studying a magazine with zealous intent. He was another fake. He was trying to avoid looking at her. She noticed his magazine was in Spanish, and he was holding it upside down. How could she be taken in by such a fake? He was like a fluorescent paint-by-numbers painting. He glowed in the light but faded compared to real art. She watched the executives entertain themselves by seeing who was the best thief and liar. These are the captains of industry. These are the kind of leaders we didn't vote for who take almost all the money. Diana felt like screaming.

"Did you fly in the Professor's machine," said Ares.

"I am sure you know that I did. I cannot keep any secrets from you," said Diana and gave him a little punch on the shoulder and a giggle. She hated herself for playing the doll, but she had to focus on the end goal. Yes, the ends justify the means, a phrase used to justify all sorts of awful crimes from mass murder to petty theft.

"Tell me about it," said Ares.

"It is incredibly fast. It can fly. It moves in complete silence."

"No sound at all?"

"None. You do not even hear the sound of the wind. Completely silent. He uses gravity particles and anti-matter to create what he calls motion without moving. A silly phrase really because motion is always motion relative to some object."

"That is just stupid. That is exactly the kind of frustrating over-intellectual nonsense that makes me want to crush these intellectuals."

Diana thought it was exactly the kind of genius that allowed him to invent a way to explore the stars at almost no cost. Ares was cunning but no genius. Lazarus was the real leader even though he never aspired to any leadership role. Lazarus would ask that we pick someone better if he was offered a leadership position. Lazarus would feel the weight of leadership to protect and improve the lives of the many. Ares never felt any weight except his boot on the neck of a competitor.

"I wish I could fly in it again. Unfortunately, Lazarus has some complex security grid around it. I think it may use nuclear fusion energy. If the machine is not started correctly, it could blow a hole 500 miles deep and 500 miles wide in the city. I find the machine terrifying but flying in it was the most exciting experience of my life." Diana knew most of what she said was a lie, but she tried to say it with such a deadpan expression he would at least consider there may be some element of truth to her story. She was not sure if he believed her, but he stopped asking questions. If she was lying, he would learn nothing. If she was not lying, he could gain nothing without the security protocol or the Professor's help. She hated herself for not being honest, but she understood this was an intellectual game of chess that put real people at risk.

Diana looked out the window as they crossed the Atlantic. The trip was more fun with Lazarus. They soared and dipped. They watched the dolphins play. They shared scientific truths. The journey across the Atlantic took minutes and not hours. She watched the sun glint on the moving waves. The beauty of nature was so much better than the best painting. The colors were deep blues, shades of blue, all shining in ripples and waves. The extraordinary beauty of nature always impressed her. She sat back and fell asleep listening to the babble of the executives about her.

Diana did not know how to wear a hijab, but room service helped. On her floor in the Four Seasons Hotel in Riyadh, her entire floor was for women only. She was told current rules required only modest dress, not a specific Islamic outfit. She went down to the hotel lobby, and she met with the other Enworld Ares entourage members.

"You are in luck. We are eating at Al-Yamama Palace. It is a working palace, not just a residence for royalty," said Ares. The whole group went to a limousine.

"The palace was in town. Diana could not believe the majesty and beauty of the building. Diana walked into a magnificent lobby of Italian marble floors, mosaics, and crafted wall panels. The marble had an intricate design with many colors in the center. The wood panels were done by Saudi artisans. It looked like even the tissue dispensers and wastebaskets were silver.

"Impressive, isn't it? This is one of several palaces for Saudi royalty," said Ares.

The hosts were gracious. Diana was famished. They sat at a long table with the influential people in the middle. Opposite the Prince sat Ares. The two men knew each other or gave that impression. They talked about the weather, cars, and life. The table had tea and water poured for everyone. A small dessert of candied nuts was alongside each plate. Diana waited as the bosses talked. She could hear the conversation, the polite preamble that filled the air with words but did not offer the deal or reach an agreement. The bosses talked, and everyone listened. Diana was starving. The dessert was looking more and more scrumptious. She hoped, then hoped some more that Ares would stop blabbing on so everyone could eat. Diana realized her hope was just that, hope alone. She decided to be brave, and she took a quick fork of candied nuts when she thought most people were not looking. If someone saw, they were too polite to say anything. The taste was heavenly. She ate as slowly as she could while the bosses went back to something about BMW cars. More chat. More smiles. No eating. She took another quick bite. She tried to savor every little bit. This process continued, and when she looked again, the entire dessert was eaten. She looked down the table to the perhaps 20 people, 10 on each side, and noticed their desserts looked complete and available.

When the food finally arrived, the food was fantastic. Lobster and lamb, even the rice, was excellent. They had Basmati rice mixed with orange segments and cranberries. Some people called this jeweled rice. With everyone busy eating, Diana took the small beetle brooch from her dress, bent down, and put it on the floor. She tapped her phone, and the beetle drifted over to the Prince's long white robe and latched on to the bottom just on the inside of the folds. Perfect.

Leo was sitting next to Ares, and Leo was fluent in Arabic. Another surprise thought Diana. Who was this Leo person? Is Leo his real name? Diana was sitting next to the CFO, who kept squirming around, probably from back pain after the long flight. The meal was so wonderful she felt she would never forget it.

After the main dish, Ares talked about the algae solution as a way for Saudi Arabia to export food and cheaply feed the many migrant construction workers. The Prince smiled at Diana. He agreed the opportunity should be explored. He asked Diana if the algae food would taste good. She was enthusiastic in her answer that it would taste as good as a filet mignon. He again agreed they should pursue the opportunity. She had read thousands of articles, and she had amassed answers to hundreds of challenging questions. Her expertise was not needed for a 60-second question-and-answer session. She had clinched her first international export deal, but the effort was so minuscule. Was it easy come and easy go? Will anyone remember the Prince wanted the algae food?

After many hours, the meal was over. The men and one woman stood, and they retired to the lobby. Ares entourage chatted in the lobby for about 15 minutes as they waited for the limousine. Diana pulled her phone and tapped the button. As she stood there, waiting, the initial change was not dramatic. Two men ran across the lobby, and soon more men started running about the hall. All the doors were being shut with some shouting. The palace was moving into a lockdown turmoil. A guard came toward them and ushered them with arms wide into a nearby room. More and more people were pushed into the same room. The crowd grew to about 500. There were whispers. Leo waved the Ares team into a huddle and whispered, "The Prince is dead. Some kind of epileptic fit or heart attack."

Chapter 19 — War

Lazarus was getting better with the red ball. He could make it wobble, bounce, move up and down, and go around in circles. Lazarus understood the game better. The exercise does not make you more intelligent with every inch of ball travels, just every *new* inch the ball travels. Lazarus could make the ball jump around for 20 to 30 inches before exhaustion made him stop. Many people think intelligence is genetic. You are born with a level of intelligence, and nothing you do can improve what you were given at birth was an old idea. Data has shown a child can add about 30 IQ (intelligence quotient) points across their life. One of the best ways to improve intelligence was doing mathematics. When you work on mathematic problems, you exercise your brain to better your brain muscle. If SF03 was correct, Lazarus was about 300 points smarter. An IQ of 100 is average for a human, and 130 is smart enough to go to university and become an engineer. Lazarus was waiting for SF03. It was time for their daily chat. As soon as he made the wish, he heard the voice.

"Good morning, Lazarus," said SF03.

"How am I doing?"

"Good news. We can skip the painful competing protocol. You are responding well. Most of the bad bacteria are dying. Do you feel any different?"

"No. I feel about the same."

"It does take time. You will have less cravings for sugar and alcohol. You will be more relaxed and less anxious. You will sleep more peacefully. When controlled by bacteria, they like you to do what they want, when they want, so they will wake you up, make you feel hungry when you are not, and run you ragged."

"Now that you say that. I do feel more relaxed, less driven, more at peace."

"It is a subtle feeling at first. Easy to miss."

"I wanted to hear more about why humans were dismissed as having little hope of survival. I understand the Stage Up issue, but I gleaned that there were other stages?"

"Yes. *Stage War*. In Stage Up, you waste resources on silly pleasures until all resources are exhausted. Everyone dies of deprivation. In Stage War, you waste resources on destruction. The resources will last longer if you use fewer resources per person or have fewer people. Wars kill a lot of people. The issue is failing to understand the real enemy. People kill each other all the time for power and money, but the primary war is not people. There is a war among billions of microbes for world dominance in the backyard of every human. These microbes see humans as not consequential or as food. Stage War also has a timeline. You must gain the knowledge and use your intelligence to conquer microbes before they conquer you.

"We have done that. We have antibiotics for the most dangerous bacteria, and we have vaccines for the most dangerous viruses. Microbes were killing us in the millions, but we have beaten them back."

"Take your rubber tree plant. Rubber initially came from a South American tree. You need natural rubber because it has a superior performance to synthetic rubber. Natural rubber is used in over 40,000 products. A Brazilian rubber tree was smuggled to Malaysia. What happened next was a fungus emerged that destroyed the rubber tree. You say you can control microbes, but you could not control this fungus. The fungus destroyed Brazilian production. Today no rubber comes from the continent of America. The only natural rubber comes from Asia. If the fungus finds a way to Asia, the whole natural rubber industry will be destroyed."

"That is a concern. We have never been good at keeping any disease from moving to another continent, especially now with all the air travel."

"The important question to ask is if this can happen to rubber, could it happen to humans? If a fungus attacked humans, would that be the end of humans on the continent of America? Why is no one talking about this possibility? Why is this concern not on every television, every radio, and every newspaper every day? What will happen if a new fungus attacks humanity? How will you respond? When will you respond? Will we have no humans in America, just in Asia? You may be surprised we know this much about your planet, but we leave monitors in every location we visit to send us data annually," said SF03.

"Sadly, I see your point. Indeed, why are we not asking these questions?"

"We dismissed any chance of your species developing into a sustained species for 10,000 generations because you spend your time on sports games, religions, but not science. You do not understand you need to go into space for resources. You do not understand your enemy is not the tribe across the river, but the microbe eating your brain."

"I have a new mission. I must make these stages of extinction known to my species. How is it that you are so advanced?"

"We are the low and most young."

"What does that mean?"

"I am not sure how to translate the names into your alphabet. The closest description is we are class M401 of the ninth multiverse. The letter indicates when we traveled to another universe. The oldest and most advanced classes start with the letter A. As you can tell from the M, we are young multiverse travelers. The oldest are billions of years ahead of us in technology, knowledge, and insight. We are low because we are the youngest and most backward. We are not admired or treated with respect."

"Not anymore. I fear that humans, our Milky Way galaxy, is now the low and most young."

"Correct. Your universe will be class N and intelligent species 001. My people will no longer be the lowest and most young. All we need to do is parade you to at least two other universes, and your status will be proven. Our status will be improved. We can drop that epithet. We will no longer be the most backward. You will have that honor."

"What do you mean by the ninth multiverse?"

"You have a solar system of many planets that orbit a star. You have a galaxy of many stars. You have a galaxy cluster that contains many galaxies. You also have a universe that contains many galaxy clusters. The next level is a multiverse that contains many universes. We have contact with nine multiverses. Next is Synthesis-P, which is a collective of multiverses."

"How far does it go? Is there a collective of the Synthesis-P?"

"Unknown. Our knowledge is incomplete. We lack the instruments to study this question."

"If I understand, the plan is for me to explore at least two multiverses?"

"Yes. I have been chosen as your guide. This is why I have been in rapport with you," said SF03.

"My friend, we will explore," said Lazarus.

"Yes. We are friends."

Lazarus was still having some difficulty since SF03 spoke in the same exact timbre and intonation as Lazarus. SF03 even spoke with the same accent as Lazarus. He felt like he was talking to himself sometimes. While traveling to new universes was exciting, Lazarus felt a bit like a puppy in training. If SF03 was the low and the young, how would the multiverse see Lazarus? Would humanity be seen as the buffoon, the clown, or the class dullard? Would he be asked to perform humiliating tricks for the amusement of the multiverse? It was uncomfortable to be laughed at by a colleague. What would it be like to be laughed at by the nine multiverses? Lazarus was worried. He wanted to go home, and he missed teaching. He needed to warn everyone they are moving at full speed to extinction, not that he expected they would listen. He was concerned about Diana's safety. Would it be pitiful for a grown man to cry because he missed his friends, home, and mom?

Chapter 20 — The king is dead, short live the king

Diana observed carefully. The security people were pulling one person at a time to the front. They would verify your name, address, take a photo, and then ask some questions. Smart. They would know exactly who was here if they needed to follow-up an investigative angle. Would they arrest her? Would she be found out? Could she let a detail slip inadvertently that would implicate her? She was worried. People in Saudi Arabia could be whipped or beheaded by a sword.

She noticed a pattern. The interviews with women were quicker. Women were dismissed as less of a threat. This made her breathe a little easier. She expected the interviews with foreigners to take longer, but they were shorter. A threat from an internal faction seemed the primary concern. People of status were also a focus. If you were part of the royal family, you were treated with deference but serious suspicion.

When Diana was interviewed, the whole process took less than 10 minutes. She was American. This was her first visit, and she was a woman. The assistant interviewer left before they were done. Diana could detect the primary concerns. The focus was the possibility of a rival prince taking the throne. In a monarchy, only a direct relative of the king, such as a brother, uncle, or cousin, would be in line for the throne. Patricide was a popular combination in some monarchies. The dead prince had killed rivals. The security people suspected revenge as the likely motive. It was not impossible that this was a political faction where some tribe was dissatisfied with a ruler. In a dictatorship, the only way for a change of government might be assassination. The next target was a competing religious group. Diana was somewhat aware that the Sunni Islamic prince of Saudi Arabia was funding fighting against Shia Islamic followers in nearby nations. Diana thought the whole state of humanity was sad, and this episode brought many conflicts into focus. Everyone would benefit if people respected and helped each other succeed, rather than helped each other fail.

With her interview over, she was released to leave. Diana's main concern was getting the beetle back as that little bug was evidence that could be traced back to her if found. She had programmed the beetle to seek darkness. The beetle would choose the darkest shadow, for example, under furniture instead of in the open. The beetle would pick an air duct over a shadow since it was darker in the air duct. Moving in shady areas, the beetle was programmed to find its way to the front garden. Diana casually walked to the front of the building. She stood looking at the stars, then casually glanced down to the garden while keeping her head looking up. She pulled her phone and tapped to find the location of the beetle. It was near. She tapped the phone, and the beetle flew to her coat. She kept pretending to tap something on her phone for 20 seconds, then took the leg of the beetle, and hooked it to her jacket. Diana had no way of knowing the exact path the beetle took or the possible exposure. She hoped it went well. She had tested the programming at home and tweaked her programming choices until the beetle found safer options to move.

The men in her party were being released; the CFO, then Operations, and next Ares. Since Leo could speak Arabic, he was the last to be released after a lengthier interview. Leo was perspiring slightly on his upper lip. He looked pale. Diana knew he was innocent, but her view was not shared by the security team. With the entourage complete, the group proceeded to the airport. Leo's charm and confidence had evaporated around Diana. This trip was not helping Leo.

On the news that night, there was a breaking story, the first of many to come. The Saudi Arabian Prince had died in an elevator in the palace. The report said the cause of death was under investigation but appeared to be a fit of some sort. The next morning the news of the Saudi death was interrupted with a report about another dead leader.

The TV networks had secured a video feed of the Syrian President addressing the UN General Assembly at 10 A.M. The video showed the Syrian President walking to the podium. He began speaking for about two minutes when he clutched at his leg. The President did a little dance hopping about as he hugged higher up his leg. He doubled over, he went absolutely rigid, and then his head snapped back, his arms waved as he tried to grab at his neck, and he collapsed while his body jerked about as his head kept banging on the floor. The jerking movement went on for perhaps 10 seconds, and finally, he was still. Security people ran onto the stage. The ambassadors and leaders were panicking, and some leaders ran for the exits. Some were scanning everywhere for other possible attacks.

The news later interrupted with another breaking news segment interrupting the first two breaking news segments. The Russian President died at 2 P.M. while attending the UN Security Council meeting. The Russian President also had a kind of epileptic fit. These reports ran clips over and over. There was an analysis of possible enemies for each leader, medical expert opinions, and potential diseases that can cause epileptic fits.

The following afternoon there was another report. The South Sudanese President had died while attending an art auction of African artifacts in Manhattan, New York. He had also died from an apparent epileptic fit. This was the fourth death in three days, ensuring experts and pundits pontificated.

The next morning there was another death. The North Korean Supreme Leader had died from what looked like an epileptic fit while on holiday in Florida. The Leader was at Disney World and had been killed while swimming in the hotel pool. Five leaders had died in four days. The news was asking who would be next? Five leaders from different countries could not be a coincidence.

Guy Lacan, UN Security Chief, was focused on the two deaths at the UN Building. This was unprecedented to have two deaths on the same day. Guy was under pressure. He gave the signal to continue with the Security Council meeting after the killing in the General Assembly. Guy assumed the Syrian death was a medical issue. The Russian termination was almost identical. Sketchy details from the somewhat uncooperative Saudi delegation had suggested the Saudi prince had died from the same causes. These were most likely two targeted killings on UN territory. Now there was information the North Korean died from a similar attack. Someone was killing world leaders.

Guy sat at his desk thinking. He clicked his pen in a familiar and annoying rhythm. Two quick clicks, then three slow clicks. Two quick clicks, then three slow clicks. He did this repeatedly then spun around to his cabinet. He pulled out a document called *Articles of Planetary Constitution*. There it was: "Every leader who was not democratically elected has 30 days to hold a free and fair election, or they will be terminated...." While Guy was looking over the document, he glanced up at the TV. The TV show was displaying the same text he was holding in his hand. Of course, the paper had been distributed in flyers by the thousands around the UN building a few weeks ago, and it was now more than 30 days.

Chapter 21 — Fifth planet of the second sun

The day had arrived. Lazarus was free to leave his quarantine room. The door slid open, and Lazarus could see SF03. He was big. SF03 was around 11 feet tall. Like almost all animals on Earth, SF03 had two eyes in front, a nose, mouth, and ears. Lazarus did not know what to expect, big or small, human, reptile, bird, or insect. He half expected wings or a hundred legs, but SF03 had two legs and two arms. SF03 looked, for the most part, like a giant human. Although SF03 had green skin, the color of grass. SF03 seemed to be devoid of hair. When Lazarus stood closer, he could see tiny, skinny, transparent hairs spread sparsely about the body but more prevalent on his head. The small hairs moved in groups and individually, not from wind, but as a kind of detection system similar to ears perking up when an animal hears a noise. Next to SF03, Lazarus felt like a small child. He had to look up to see SF03's face. SF03 had deep purple eyes. SF03 looked really fit with solid, tight large muscles similar to a gymnast on Earth.

SF03 smiled warmly, showing perfect white teeth. He handed Lazarus a six-inch necklace on a short steel chain. "This is your amulet to mark you as one of the List," said SF03. "You will be shown respect when people see you are a scientist of merit. In our society, scientists are treated better than leaders, celebrities, or the oligarchs of your world. Only our teachers are shown more respect. Our teachers are taken from the top one percent of our students, the best of the best. Our children are precious. Our children are given the best teachers we can find."

"I understand that. I wish my world showed teachers more respect."

"Teachers are the caretakers of our children. If children are precious, our teachers should be the smartest, kindest, and most decent of all people. We cannot understand why so many nations in your world give teachers less respect than the prime minister?"

"Agreed. I don't know why leaders are respected in my world, given many of our leaders are ignorant, corrupt thieves and bullies thieves."

"I thought I would take you to town. We could visit a doctor to give you a full medical."

"I thought I was released from quarantine because I am in good health?"

"You are not carrying any infectious disease, but we can check you for any flaws. You can decide if you want some fixes."

Lazarus nodded, and they left the building. The skyline was a blue sky with a wide pink glow. One sun was more extensive and rising, and a second sun was 45 degrees higher in the sky. The building behind them was isolated at the top of a hill and surrounded by a low wall. Just beyond the wall, Lazarus could see a few hundred people standing facing the sun, heads back, feet together, in a yoga sun pose.

"Photosynthesis. They are feeding on the sunlight," said SF03. Lazarus was shocked. Of course, they have green skin. They eat or convert sunlight into energy, just like grass or flowers. These aliens may not need to kill animals. They can eat for free by standing in the sun for an hour. The aliens have no need for animal husbandry.

The town had mostly three-story buildings made from the same plastic as in the quarantine room. The plastic was smart because people could sunbathe by removing the mist in the wall or have privacy by allowing the wall mist to swirl. Where the sun hit the roof, there were sparkles like you would see in a crystal. The sparkling seemed to reflect back and forth before moving down a central rod into the home. The glittering of all the houses was a joy to watch. Lazarus could not express the impact of that beauty on him after all the time in quarantine.

There were bright flowers similar to tulips in front of every home and hanging from baskets about the walls. The flower colors matched the color of the plastic walls. The show of color was uplifting. Lazarus enjoyed a mass of bright, warm shades of yellow, pink, red, and blue houses. Somehow, the colors seemed to fit perfectly to create a positive impression.

There were many parks. People in various poses faced the sun. Some people would bend back, twist their arms about themselves, or pose with one foot resting on the standing leg's knee. In one area, the people moved in graceful, gradual, and flowing turns. This team moved similar to the Tai Chi of people on Earth.

They came to a building, and SF03 opened the door. Lazarus could not read the writing. The writing was beautiful, in colorful forms made of swirls and circles. The swirls and circles were made of 20 primary forms on a two-dimensional grid with reels in columns and circles in rows. The intersection on the grid of swirls and circles determined the sound and meaning. SF03 said the color changed the meaning. The color's shade provided a subtle third dimension elucidating degrees of meaning given the degree of tone, hue, and intensity. Lazarus had seen something similar in the Mayan system of writing but without the added complexity of color. SF03 said the color allowed more explicit meaning. The two-dimensional system allowed a nuance that avoided the logical imprecision of the English language. SF03 said the language permitted the removal of most misunderstandings, which prevented hurt feelings, conflicts, and wars. SF03 felt half of the disagreements on Earth were misunderstandings because the English language was ambiguous and imprecise. We have no conflicts from misunderstandings. Our language is logical in syntax and semantics.

Lazarus found himself in a doctor's office. The aliens conversed in their cackling tones for a brief moment. The doctor pointed to Lazarus's amulet of the list and then gestured for Lazarus to lie on the table. There were large machines on all sides of the bed. Lazarus lay down, and the engine hummed as it worked. The table's sides rose about 12 inches, so Lazarus was encased in a type of open-top coffin. The machine hummed and lights flashed.

SF03 read the display on the ceiling. "You have a fungus growing on your right large toenail that our quarantine failed to detect because it is only a micrometer in size. You have a 25 percent partial tear in your right shoulder rotator cuff that may tear completely within five years if you lift something heavy. You have inflammation and a 30% level of damage in the tendon of your left foot, which could at any moment give you plantar fascia pain when you walk. There is a three percent blockage of cholesterol in an artery in your neck. You also have a one-millimeter growth in your lower colon, which could turn cancerous in about 20 years. Your prostate is about 3% enlarged, so in 25 years, you will have trouble urinating. Do you want us to fix anything?"

"Wow. That is impressive. Can you predict 25 years ahead from the damage I have now? I am impressed. Please, fix everything."

"It will hurt for some of these procedures. We will close the top of the bed so you can scream as loud as you want without concern it might bother us."

Lazarus thought they were joking, so he smiled. They closed the lid. Clamps were fastened, so he could not move. A small laser emerged from above him and started to burn the fungus. The pain was not a concern when it burned the nail, but the smell of burning was horrible. When they started burning the fungus under the nail, the pain was intense. Lazarus felt tears coming from his eyes, yet he did not scream. A second laser made the smallest paper cut on his shoulder then pushed under the skin. He felt it was sewing a new tendon to reinforce the tear. The pain of both procedures at the same time was too much. He felt nauseous. Another probe moved into his anus to cauterize the small growth. Now he did scream. The clamps kept him absolutely still. Good thing if you want to avoid a tear in your colon and poop flowing around in your blood. This whole procedure took about 15 minutes, or so it seemed. It may have been one minute, but time moves slowly when someone is cutting and burning you. The lid opened. The pain was not lingering, and he felt more vital than before. He had more bounce, more energy.

"I am sorry for the pain. Your anatomy is different from ours, so our machines are not fully calibrated to your nervous system.

We were afraid to give you a sedative because we don't know enough about your metabolism. We need to be sure you are safe."

"I understand. A bit of pain now to avoid the terror of colon cancer or heart attack in the future is a worthwhile tradeoff," said Lazarus as he wiped away a few tears.

"You are now healthy but not enhanced. Would you like any enhancements?"

"What enhancements would you suggest?" said Lazarus with some suspicion that more pain was going to be visited on his now delicate psyche.

"There are so many. We can give you nanoparticles to roam and repair organs and blood vessels as needed. We can add brain implants to learn languages in minutes or remember massive details with instant recall. We can give you improved robotic joints. We can replace your retina to see infra-red or other areas of the electromagnetic spectrum. Most of us have monitoring bots to track our health. We all have a computer-brain link using nanobots. There are hundreds of improvements. We can modify your DNA to remove flaws. What would you like?"

"What would it cost me? How long would it take? Are there any risks? And this time, I also want to ask how much it will hurt?"

"You are a man with many questions."

SF03 and the doctor talked for five minutes. A woman supervisor came in to discuss the procedures. She made some decisions. She was about 11-foot-tall with the same height and visible strength as the men. Her breasts were the same size as the men, but she did have longer tiny hairs on her head, about two inches instead of just a few millimeters. Lazarus assumed she was a woman given the earrings and a genuinely heavenly smell. A man came in with warm tea for everyone.

"As a member of the list, there is no cost. The brain-computer link will be risky and involves intense pain. The health monitor won't work except when you are on our planet and within communication with our computers. The nanobots to repair your body are painless and instant. The DNA repair is 10% risky and will involve a lot of pain and many years to become fully functional given we designed the DNA without humans as the target."

"What do you mean by 10% risky?"

"That is the chance of death, a 10% chance the procedure will kill you, but a 90% chance it will improve you. The odds are in your favor. The logical action is to do it."

The doctor spoke some more with the supervisor. SF03 added, "The doctor said he can give you a nanobot infusion that is self-replicating and self-learning. This has no risk of death, will improve you, but the improvements are unpredictable. The good news is that the improvement will tailor to your lifestyle. Whatever strains your body, the nanobots will learn and adapt."

"Okay, I will take the nanobots to improve my organs and blood vessels now. Can I take the self-learning and adapting nanobots with me and drink them at a time of my choosing? I will skip the eye operation. I get squeamish when someone wants to cut my eye. For DNA changes, why don't we leave that for another year?"

"Done," said SF03. Lazarus was given an injection of a teaspoon of liquid that looked like a red dye. The doctor left the room and came back with a deep blue vial. He opened a wallet-sized case and put the vial into the case. He snapped finger locks on the case and then took Lazarus by the index finger and pushed his finger on the snapped lock to put a fingerprint lock on the case. Lazarus put the case in his pocket.

"What do you think of the tea?" said SF03. The two aliens watched Lazarus as he took a small sip of the tea.

Lazarus was lost. The tea hit his taste buds with a lingering cascading punch of sugar, a sour lemony taste, then a hard hit of spicy ginger, followed by a honey-flavored sugar. Lazarus was overwhelmed by the sensations and craved another taste of the tea. He wanted it more than anything he had ever put in his mouth. Ice cream, strawberries, chocolate... these were amateur flavors. He craved more of this tea. The two aliens laughed.

"You have just tasted julluwine berry. This berry can own you. You can spend a life growing, caring, and loving this little berry. The berry lifecycle is ensured because all who taste it will want to grow and eat as many berries as they can. We will each have one sip, then the tea must be locked away, and the key given to someone who has never tasted the fruit."

Lazarus nodded. The berry owned him already. He picked up the cup, allowed the smell to enter his system, and he closed his eyes for his last sip. Again, the overpowering cascade of joy. The feeling consumed him utterly and slowly faded to the honey sugar. They each took a small sip. The serving man returned and carried the tea away. Lazarus resisted the urge to grab the tea and gulp it. He exerted all his willpower to be polite and grateful. What he experienced in just a few hours was beyond anything he imagined. What other traps could ensnare his body, heart, and perhaps his soul in this unknown world?

Chapter 22 — Did anything change?

Milton was excited. As agreed, he had stopped over in New York to report to the others. The family had a terrific adventure at Disney World. The mission was successful.

"I thought I was doomed. The Supreme Kim Tim Bit had an entire floor to himself and his security team. They took the elevator in a group so no one could get on at the same time. Tim Bit traveled to the park in his limousine, and whatever area of the park he was in was shut to the public. I could not get near him. I thought I would fail despite all the money the team spent on my travel. I could not sanction failure. Finally, Kim Tim Bit went swimming and that was my last chance. He had the pool surrounded by his security team. From my balcony on the 10th floor, I could send the beetle to the pool and attack the warmest body in the water. The beetle flew to the pool and directly into the Toad's head. A lot of jumping around, and he was dead," said Milton.

"Do you feel any guilt?" said Faith.

"No, he was a dictator. He had people arrested. He had many generals and relatives killed to secure his leadership from the competition. His people starve while Tim Bit is fat. A fat leader in a starving nation says it all. He is so awful he uses the three-generation rule. Do you know what that is?"

"No," said Yasmin.

"When someone is not sufficiently loyal, they can be sent to jail as an entire family and must work for free for three generations. Your wife, children, and grandchildren must suffer in jail for the crimes of the father. I am glad this murderous greedy dictator is dead. I helped free the world and his starving people," said Milton.

"Did you get the beetle back? The beetle could be a clue that would provide investigators with too much information," said Diana.

"The beetle went into his head and out and flew straight back to me. I was on the balcony and spying through the grate of the handrail. I was not visible. I think the whole thing was so fast and unexpected that I had the beetle before anyone realized something was wrong. The security people were diving into the pool and not looking for a flying insect. There was a chance they would see it but did not."

"Yasmin. You were also successful. Anything to add?" said Diana.

"President Mutubby was disgusting. He came in with a young woman and a few bodyguards. He grinned at me like I was a snack. He talked loudly. He was arrogant. I have no guilt. He was a dictator, a rebel, a killer, and a thief. Did you know there is slavery in Sudan? He sat next to me with his grinning teeth. He touched my hand, supposedly to ask the time. I gave him eye contact and told him he was wearing a watch on his wrist while I slipped the beetle into the pocket of his jacket. After the auction, he went into the back to discuss his money from the sale of African culture. I triggered the beetle to swirl up and down his body. They won't find a lot of innards. I made him suffer for all the people he made suffer. I got the beetle back the next day. The beetle was programmed to attach itself under a chair after he fell to the floor. The room had lots of chairs, and he was likely sitting on one when attacked. How about you, Pi?"

"I took a guided tour of the UN Building. I was able to get the beetle into the building. At 3 A.M., the beetle was instructed to burrow three inches into the General Assembly podium. I set the beetle to exit the podium and attack when the Syrian talked. To escape detection, the beetle was programmed to burrow into the floor and travel within the walls of the UN to the Security Council room to kill the Russian dictator. Once the Russian was dead, the beetle was programmed to retrace its path back to the General Assembly podium. We can now attack any speaker at will. And no, I do not have regrets. This Syrian chose a civil war instead of a fair election. He also used chemical weapons on children proving he is a monster. If our leaders had morals and integrity, they would ensure people like him were sent to an International Court and imprisoned for life. The guilt belongs to world leaders whose lack of caring allowed them to watch as he killed hundreds of thousands of his own people rather than have a fair election. That Russian leader was a facilitator for the Syrian debacle. I was glad to remove them both with extreme prejudice."

"The path for the beetle sounds like sophisticated programming?" said Diana.

"It was at first, but once I had the tour, I had the general layout of the building. Remember, the beetle can vaporize what is in its path, so passing into the space between walls is simple. Just make sure the beetle enters or exits from an existing hole to leave no trace of entry," said Pi.

"I feel like I am a killer. Was it worth it? Do you think we were successful in our goal of improving the world," said Diana.

"The news media found our flyer. They are broadcasting it globally and on the web. The message is everywhere. If I counted correctly, 34 nations have stated they are scheduling fair and free elections," said Yasmin. "I believe we are successful."

"I would love for this to be over. If the first message was enough that would be wonderful. We could get back to our lives," said Diana.

"My life is not that great," said Milton. "You know some of those elections may be simple posturing about fair elections. They say they will have a fair election, but will they? They may be talking and no more than talking."

"True," said Faith.

"I think we should give it some time and hope they do the right thing. What is happening in the countries where the leaders are gone?" said Diana.

"The Russians promise a fair election and a return to term limits. There is a power vacuum now the strong man is gone. They always had a pretense of a fair election. We will have to see," said Milton. "The North Koreans had no heir apparent. It is not a monarchy, but leadership always went to a relative of the strongman grandfather. The Toad had no children. Again, we will have to wait and see," said Milton.

"In South Sudan, one of the military generals tried to take over but was killed by the dead President's security team. The security folks are afraid they will go to jail for stealing and murder. It is chaos. I am hoping for an election," said Yasmin.

"No real change in Saudi Arabia. They picked the next in line for the throne as crown prince and the monarchy continues. If we kill more royalty, perhaps no prince will want to be king," said Diana.

"Syria was probably run by the Russians. Since the Russian leader is also dead, it is unclear which political faction will take power or have a fair election. There are at least 13 groups vying for power. We could get lucky," said Faith.

"Milton. Do you think they can trace those flyers back to us?" said Diana.

"I made it difficult. I am not a security expert, but I have been learning many programming skills during this lengthy unemployment period. I am hoping to send a rabbit down a bottomless hole," said Milton.

"Milton. I know I have not been able to secure a job for you here at Enworld, but I have not forgotten you. It is easy for a science project leader to hire science graduates, but I have no role for economists. I am working on it, but it may take some time. Would you be interested in doing a programming job? Are you holding out for an economist job at a major bank?"

"I would rather be programming for you than riding a delivery bicycle on city streets in the Winter. As you know, I am always happy to be near you."

"Hey, you are a married man," said Diana assuming he was teasing her.

"I know. I was the one that got away," said Milton nudging Diana with an elbow.

Diana was unsure what he meant about the rabbit, but she took it as a signal they were safe. I hope something changes given the risks we have all taken. The assassination of leaders probably comes with jail time, executions, and a sprinkle of torture to reveal co-conspirators. It was sufficient to act flippant, but she knew this was the kind of serious stuff that kills you.

Chapter 23 — Small steps

Guy Lacan had worked massive amounts of overtime to investigate the deaths at the UN. While the flyer about dictators was not the most credible threat from a known source of terrorists, it was the only threat that fit with the raft of deaths. The problem was the UN lacked the security infrastructure and funding to do much. He had to reach out to national teams, especially the Russian team under Anna Ivanovitch, and the American group coordinated by Chris Gota at Homeland Security. Anna was the most helpful. Chris seemed to spend most of his time coordinating with the CIA, FBI, NSA, and the many other USA security agencies. Chris had little time left to get much done.

Anna was the most focused. Anna noticed a small smudge in the corner of the flyer. When she enlarged the smear, she made out part of a pattern and was now scanning known groups for an icon or logo match. Anna knew this icon but could not recall the name of the group. She would know soon. Secretly, Anna confessed indirectly to Guy that the Russian President would not be missed. The idea of free, clean, and fair elections was an ideal she embraced but could not express openly. Given the number of similar dictator deaths, Anna felt Russia was not an isolated target by internal or external threats. This was some group fighting for honest elections and an end to fake democracies.

On one occasion, Anna gave a memory stick to a political opposition leader in a cafe. Within minutes after she left, her security team arrested the opposition leader for spying. The memory stick had compromising materials and was used as evidence the leader was spying. Anyone charged with a serious crime was blocked from running in an election. This setup was a favorite way the dead President would remove any politician who dared compete. The election was a pure sham.

The Americans were worried since the Russian leader was killed on American soil. The Americans did not want a war with Russia especially when they were not responsible for the death. The body had been sent to Russia for a state burial and autopsy without any American restrictions. Guy was helpful because he made sure everyone knew the UN was not part of the USA but on international soil. Guy cooperated fully with Anna's Russian investigative team on both the Syrian and Russian death.

"It has been a few weeks since the UN assassinations. We are making progress. The numbers of announced elections keep growing. We now have 56 elections scheduled in the next 30 days. We should send a note to the New York Times thanking them. It is a shame we can't," said Diana.

"We see progress. Some dictators need more proof. Belarus and Venezuela are determined to ignore any warnings. We need a few more examples to 'clinch the deal' as salespeople would say," said Pi.

"Is it too soon to see improvements in the lives of the citizens?" said Diana.

"We do not see more equality, less poverty, or better access to shelter and food, but we hear lots of promises. Now that dictators cannot be assured of victory, t he leader must truly win an election, so they are working harder for votes. There are promises and speeches about a higher minimum wage, lower health costs, and more education access. I think we are winning, but it is too early to say for sure," said Faith.

"Do you think we are safe? The police will probably never stop looking for us. We will have to live with this forever," said Diana.

"Every time we kill a dictator, our chances of being caught will increase," said Yasmin.

"Milton, did your rabbit down a hole work?" said Diana.

"No one has found the rabbit if I am tracking things correctly," said Milton. I cannot use the Enworld computers because they are probably monitored. I must use offsite computers so I cannot watch it all the time. I do want to thank you for the programming job. I am learning a lot about how to write programs to connect all these bizarre science machines into a central databank."

"It is great to have you here, Milton. You are one of the team. I am sure it is hard to be separated from your family. If I can make the assignment more permanent, you could move them here," said Diana.

"The separation is hard, but the relief from the worries about debt, food, and shelter is enormous. For now, the family sees this as moving forward. I had to persuade some people to take partial debt payments until I can catch-up. I am paying the obscene

300% interest rates on the payroll loans first and will pay the 25% interest on credit card debt second. I will focus on the landlord next. I am embarrassed to admit how much of a mess I made of my life."

"Milton, you are a smart person. You are educated. You took multiple jobs. You worked 60 to 80 hours a week. You are not to blame. You are the working poor. You should be paid enough to survive with one job and not think of yourself as a failure. Someone with two or three jobs should not be in a financial mess. You are the victim of a cruel system that is failing too many people. You are not the failure. You were working in a failing system."

"I cannot help feeling bad. The flawed system you describe is capitalism, but I believe capitalism is the best way to help people succeed. I know there are going to be some downturns and some unemployment in capitalism. We are in a booming period of growth but not for me or any of my friends, until the four of you got a lucky break," said Milton.

"Perhaps the problem is not capitalism per se, but the leaders of our capitalist organizations. We should consider that issue more closely," said Pi.

Diana's phone rang, and it was Ares. He had not been the same since the Saudi trip. He had changed after their dinner with the Professor. He was always preoccupied with some mystery project. "Ares calls. He needs another project update. I have to fly," Diana said to her friends.

Diana had good news to share with Ares. The projects were moving fast. Pi was brilliant, and she made every challenge seem easy. They would be stumped and feel defeated. Pi would show up at noon with a solution. As soon as Pi explained the idea, it seemed so obvious. The challenge evaporated.

Diana did not like how Pi came and went as she wanted, but she loved Pi's results. Pi would work until 3 A.M. or straight through the next morning, but she would deliver. Diana was lucky. This team was a blessing. How could so many companies bypass Pi in so many interviews? Pi was quiet, but she was solving the mystery of eternal youth, and she was making it look easy. These companies are so focused on saving money, they miss out on grand opportunities. They just see people as throwaway replaceable commodities. Everything in capitalism, including people, are for sale, replaceable, and without permanent value.

Diana could never get Milton to explain what this rabbit idea was, but she knew if they continued killing world leaders, they would all go to jail. In Saudi Arabia, the police had arrested hundreds of people, tortured many, and some were probably killed. Could that be the reason for the Ares call? Was some Saudi police assassin here to cut out her heart? She shuddered at the thought. She could be going home in handcuffs today. It was just a matter of time. Was it worth it? If it meant improving millions of lives, the answer was easy. The risks and pains were worth it. She might be a heroine to some, but she was afraid every day. She was the big hero who was always scared. Always.

Chapter 24 — Master computer

Lazarus had a sore neck because he was not used to looking up. Everyone was so tall and strong. As a six-foot man, Lazarus was used to looking down. Now Lazarus was looking up at aliens who could crush him. The feeling of being vulnerable was new.

"Tell me about work," said Lazarus.

"Robots do all the boring work. When we sleep, 50 little mice robots come out of the wall and clean the house. They go back and forth eating dust and scrubbing a spill. Little microscopic nanobots remove dirt and bacteria from walls, windows, and floors. Robots drive trucks or fly drones to deliver packages. Robots build, pack, and ship."

"What do people do? How do you earn any money?" said Lazarus.

"We don't use money. We stopped using money long ago. When we could replicate things in 3D printers, we stopped using money. The first family to buy a replicator used it to make more replicators. They gave the new replicators to the neighborhood. Now, if we need something, we print it."

"Money or not, I am concerned robots will create unemployment," said Lazarus.

"If you have one rich person who has 100 workers, each worker pays a tax to the government on earnings. If you replace the workers with robots, you don't have to pay salaries, payroll taxes, sick days, or vacations. Robots work day and night to make more things at less cost. People have no money to buy any of those things because robots have all the jobs. The government has no payroll tax money to support those unemployed people. The rich guy is making things no one can buy. That would be really, stupid. Everyone loses."

"Yes," said Lazarus. "I think our governments do not understand that the system we use now is obsolete as more robots do more work."

"Besides, we don't need factories. We have the replicator. Print what you want at home and skip the delivery cost," said SF03. "The period of transition from human workers to robot workers was difficult. You end up with millions of unemployed people. You can put them in jail, but it is cheaper to pay them to stay home. Jail costs more. You need a universal basic income (UBI) and pay people to do nothing. There were riots, revolutions, starvations, and property crimes until we paid a universal basic income. You should implement the UBI early to save miles of misery and lakes of tears. A Libertarian or Conservative government that likes to keep government small and talks about how people need to be *free* from the government is irrelevant. The Libertarian right-wing philosophy becomes meaningless in a society where most labor is automated by robotics."

"Pay people to do nothing. That would be a difficult political discussion on my world."

"We are still busy. We spend our time learning about science, art, mathematics, music, multiverses, and everything. Life itself is an amazing mystery that still eludes our full understanding," said SF03.

"I am going to enjoy being here. I don't like cleaning my house, and I love learning. Tell me more," said Lazarus.

SF03 smiled. He stood and did some yoga while he talked. He was bending and twisting up and down, left and right. "The real insights come from the software and the robots. No person can compete. A Professor like you might study a difficult problem for years, formulating the right question, collecting the data, running the analysis, and hopefully finding some little truth. Our computers can do thousands of those experiments every second. Our computers use many of the same methods as nature. They alter one small part of an equation, much like a small mutation in your body. They change part of a formula; they switch variables back and forth until they discover a valuable finding. People cannot keep up."

"How can you tell if the software makes mistakes?"

"We don't use the first answer. We have many computers, all using different methods, and each finding their own answers. For example, five computers find their own insights to a problem, and we compare which answer is best."

"How can you tell which is best?"

"How do you think?"

"You use computers and robots to pick the best. You have a master equation that compares the five answers' results and picks the most correct solution. The master equation picks, combines, and weighs factors of the five solutions to find the best combination of answers," said Lazarus.

"Excellent. Exactly right. Of course, we can take years to learn how or what the computers found in minutes. There is satisfaction in people catching up to one element of the calculated progress on issues. We learn to understand what the computers found."

"Is this true in art and music too?"

"Yes. At first, computer music was horrible. You could tell which music came from a computer because it was too perfect. A computer provides a perfectly accurate beat to a song without a single flaw. Humans are emotional; they speed up or slow down a little in places. Now our computers play music with little errors so that we can enjoy the music more."

"I am not sure this is as enjoyable as I thought. If all I am doing is trying to learn some song or formula the computer created 20 years ago, I do not feel I am making a breakthrough."

"We did have some challenges. It is hard to teach a computer the emotional aspect of music. The computer sees emotions as a weakness, an error. The computers struggled to make the correct errors in the right order to create a song that would make humans jump for joy, dance, or become pensive. Computers could not build on the excitement of emotions that is fundamental to a good song."

"The master computer could take the best solution or factors from multiple songs. If the master computer does not get it right, you can always have a committee of multiple master computers work on it," said Lazarus.

"Now you understand."

"And we could get a super-master to decide which of the master computers solutions was best."

"Are you having fun poking at these ideas?" said SF03.

"I was, but I suspect you were teasing me intellectually as well."

"I was, but I was also setting the table. You are in a new world. When I use your words, like a human, I am just transcribing to make it easier for us to communicate. The truth is that all beings are on an elusive journey. We find little truths like we are peeling back the skin of an onion. The universes hide their secrets, and only though 10,000 generations can we begin to approach the Truth spelled with a capital T."

"Now you sound religious. The owner of the truth, the one true truth."

Chapter 25 — Do you like this tea?

Months later.

Anna Ivanovitch was talking to her superior, the Colonel. She had answers, but how much should she reveal?

"This is the actual icon of the group we are investigating. It comes from the Mountain Men Freedom Militia. They are right-wing American gun-loving fascists who don't realize they are fascists," said Anna.

"That is impossible. Do you know why it is impossible?"

"Yes. They are funded by us, Russia. We are their main sponsors."

"Correct. By funding these extreme people, we keep Americans at war with themselves. We conduct a small-arms war of Americans against Americans. It is perfect because no Russians are killed, and America is weaker. The funding comes from Billy Bob Industries in Texas or Hank Rex Guns in Tennessee, but these are fronts for our Russian spies. These American backwoods militias are dumber than wood. They could never kill Russian President Butin in such a complex way in front of 12 world leaders in a highly secure location like the UN. Their best plan would be to walk up to the door with guns blazing."

"It gets more interesting," said Anna. She looked at him then looked down. Anna was manipulating him. She knew he was impatient, but it was a more effective way to make him understand if she made him work for the answer.

"Go on, speak," he said too loudly.

"There are leads that suggest we are not the main source of funding. An Islamic fundamentalist group, ISIS, is also funding Mountain Men. They could be infiltrated by Islamic agents pretending to be militia and instigating the militia in new directions."

"Nyet. That is silly. What leads?"

"There are discussions of funding the militia on the dark web from a group that has ISIS connections," said Anna.

"The ISIS group has strong asymmetrical warfare skills like us. They could be putting out misinformation to fool us. What do you think?"

"I think it is another national security team pretending to be ISIS that is pretending to fund Mountain Men Militia to confuse us," said Anna.

"That sounds more like it. How do we know who they are? This is getting us closer."

"Is it? What if that is what we are meant to think? What if this is some rabbit hole that goes into another rabbit hole that is inside a bigger rabbit hole?" said Anna.

"Damn. When we were the only people turning lying into an art form, we had an advantage. Now that everyone is lying to almost everyone, no one knows anything about what is true or not. Everyone is sending fake information to everyone. We have lost the truth somewhere within truckloads of fabrications."

"And now you know why I was hesitating," said Anna.

"Was the King in Thailand assassinated yesterday killed in the same way, with a missing section of his brain?"

"The police are being secretive, but Guy Lacan at the UN said it was the same method."

"How about Venezuela and the African dictators the week before?"

"Yes, the same. They had winding holes in their brains too, but possibly they had those holes in their heads before the attack?"

"That is not funny."

"May I ask a question, Colonel?"

"Of course."

"If this were President Butin's favorite tea, I would tell him his licorice tea was delightful. Now that he is gone, I might say this tea was foul. Would I be incorrect?"

The colonel looked at her. He moved closer. "One might agree. The old tea was not as tasty as we once thought," he said softly.

"I would enjoy taking a vote on the new tea. For the old tea, we should probably discard what is left in the tin?"

"Good. the tea discussion is concluded. There is no need to talk about old tea mixed with new tea and strange Arab teas. Enough tea talk. We should move along. Stay in touch with Interpol and the UN, and update me if anything new emerges." Anna smiled. She hated Butin. Butin had asked to see her engagement ring and then put it in his pocket and walked away. He was a thief. The new President cared more about working people more than his personal investments.

Diana was increasingly concerned that while the plan was improving things, the improvements were not enough. The risks were high, and the progress was slow. They needed to do more. The plan did not provide a timeline, yet it had many more steps.

Work was the opposite, as the projects were moving faster. The algae sales were increasingly successful. They could grow algae in Saudi Arabia without the contaminants. The dry environment removed the most potent pathogens. They used hydroponics to keep the environment free of unwelcome microbial interference. The flavoring agents corrected the initial unsuccessful product launch. With small DNA changes using a CRISPR machine, the taste was improved and more appealing. The food was ideal in countries with high poverty since the algae grew quickly and at low cost. Ares was pleased. He was giving her increasing autonomy and was faithful to his promises of stock options and shared riches.

She had moved to a new apartment. She had the apartment carefully scanned for listening devices. The security people left a machine she could use to sweep the space on her own. She had catered food and drinks. This would be a crucial meeting to decide if the group should move to stage two of the plan.

Diana tended to jump right into the difficult questions. Today, she would try something different. The team arrived and brought wine. They ate some snacks; platters of crab cakes and coconut shrimp. They laughed, talked as young people often do about movies, songs, and romantic possibilities.

"What about our biggest project? Has leadership improved enough? Are people finding work, doing better than their parents, are things getting better?" said Diana.

"There are fewer dictators. More elections are clean. There is more trust in governments. Things are improving, but I feel we have only addressed the front line. The presidents and prime ministers often seem to be the puppets, not the puppet masters," said Milton.

"Yes. if you want something done, don't talk to the mayor or the governor, you need to talk to the banking lobby or the energy lobby," said Pi. "The elected leaders always say they care about the people, but when they implement a law, the main beneficiaries are the rich and powerful corporations."

"Yes," said Yasmin. "If the main beneficiaries are the regular people, there is always some weasel clause or loophole for the corporations to skirt the intended outcomes. They win directly, or they get a free pass. I feel we are playing a shell game where the prize is never what you want."

"We should go after them," said Pi.

"I agree," said Faith. "They don't pay their taxes. Now they want subsidies from our tax money. They agree to clean up pollution when they leave but don't keep the promise. They blackmail the government asking for millions in subsidies to keep a factory open, and two years later, they close the factory anyway but keep the millions in subsidies."

"They have corporate raiders that steal the pensions of working people. Those workers paid into those pensions for decades," said Yasmin. "They buy the company by using the employees' pensions as collateral, pay themselves huge contracting fees which adds to the debt, and then file for bankruptcy to move on to the next victim. The company pension is taken by the creditors, the executive fat cat million-dollar paychecks are protected as sunk expenditures, and the employee pensions essentially stolen. Many corporate raiders are scum. They don't build companies, they don't create jobs, they raid, and destroy companies and jobs."

"Hey, folks. This is going too far. This is the system that made our nation rich," said Milton.

"The system that made the nation rich was slavery, colonialism, and greed. A nation filled with poor people drowning in student debt and temporary employment does not feel rich for most of us. You know it is true from your own experiences, Milton," said Yasmin.

"There are some abuses, but you cannot turn us into a communist country," said Milton.

"I am not a communist," said Diana. "I don't think we are talking about the form of government. Russian leaders abused their people under the czars as a monarchy. The Russian leaders abused the people when they were communists. Now, Russian leaders abuse the people under a capitalist system. The form of government keeps changing, but what never changed was the top Russian leaders took too much, and the people suffered too much."

"We should send out some flyers, and 30 days later, execute a few greedy pigs," said Pi.

"Whoa. Slow down, folks. I am not okay with this," said Milton.

"We are moving fast. We should look at the plan and decide what to put on the flyer," said Diana.

"I am not comfortable," said Milton.

"We won't move forward until the flyer is ready. We will take a vote and discuss this more before there is any action. Milton, you will have a chance to persuade us. If you have a better approach, we want to hear it. We want a world where most people are happy and not just the top 1% of the super-rich. There is enough money for food, shelter, and education for everyone, but we are not sharing it properly. We want to live in a world where people do not work three jobs to support their children. We want to work, but we want to have time for a family. Give us a better plan, and we will embrace it, Milton. I am sick of the excess. I am tired of a culture of greed and materialism. Buy, buy, until everything and everyone is thought of as another consumer object. I am not a thing that you can buy or toss away anytime you want even if HR thinks like that, " said Diana.

"I agree something is broken. I am glad we are going to talk more," said Milton.

The team went back to talking about sports, drinking, and laughing about the world. Life was good again, and the worries were behind them for now.

Chapter 26 — He is no longer here

Lazarus was staying in the home of SF03. Watching SF03's family, he learned more in a few minutes than he had in the weeks of quarantine. First, the large translucent panels used as walls in his quarantine room were the same material used in the wall, ceiling, and floor of SF03's home. What Lazarus thought of as a wall was a fully functional computer screen. The simple taps he made to move mist to see into other rooms also allowed you to bring up photos, computer applications, or even make phone calls. You could scan your brain or bones on the wall. You could talk to someone and see their face 1,000 miles away. You could have pictures of the sea or waves move across the walls.

SF03 said plastic was coated in nanobots so it would never get dirty. The bots removed dust or grease and kept the surface sanitary. The panels also created energy by acting as solar panels. The wall could automatically dim or open to allow light to flow as you wished or open to provide a window.

The flowers in front of the house were not organic. The flowers were a mix of technology and living material that cleaned the air by capturing toxins and converting the toxins into breathable air. Every house had flowers, not just for the beauty, but to clean the atmosphere.

SF03's children played games that were too complex for Lazarus to follow. He taught them chess, which they learned in about 10 minutes. Lazarus won the first game with the younger boy and never won another game. Lazarus knew he was smarter from the red ball exercise. When he usually played chess, he would think about five or six moves ahead. Now he was thinking about 15 moves forward before the possible combinations became too complex to track. Lazarus realized he was thinking like a small child compared to these aliens.

SF03 sat on an air couch next to Lazarus, and he opened a screen on the plastic top of the coffee table. Lazarus was still adjusting to the idea of sitting comfortably on furniture made of airflow that adapted to your movements. SF03 moved his fingers back and forth to bring up a panel with some 40 different titles. "I know you cannot read the writing, but these are the options for our visit to another universe. I could help by telling you a bit about each universe so you could make a more informed choice?"

"Good. Anything you say would help."

"There are many choices of universes such as singular, fractal, turbulent, chaotic, stationary, expanding, self-creating, colliding, fake, dying, ... the choices are many."

Lazarus was utterly lost. He was a physicist, and he was clueless about space, time, and matter in the multiverse. "Could you give me some suggestions?"

"I said we were in the ninth multiverse class M401. The older the universe, the more likely we are vastly behind the development of any intelligent species. Class A is trillions of years more developed than class M. The letter indicates the age. Age and wisdom are not perfectly correlated. Generally, I would pick a universe closer to the age of your universe. Your universe is about 14 billion years old, and your planet is only two billion years. Your home universe is young."

"Understood. We are young."

"I have been to class K. They were superior in every way; physically, mentally, emotionally, and technically. I appreciated many of the advances, but they saw me like a mentally disabled runt. If I am honest with you. I was able to function, but I could not participate fully."

Lazarus knew the feeling all too well. He could spend decades on class M401 and likely never participate as a fully competent adult. Lazarus was six feet, but SF03's wife was over 10 feet. Looking at her finely tuned arm muscles, she could probably throw him 20 feet in the air like a rag doll.

"On one occasion, I saw a video of a class G universe, and I could not follow the technology or the conversation. If Einstein tried to explain his theory of general relativity to a tadpole, that was the experience I had. The tadpole would not understand the point of the discussion, and Einstein would be frustrated. There would be no value to either side of the exchange."

"Hmm."

"There is one other vital consideration. When you port, there is a different flow of time. As an extreme example, when something enters a black hole, the gravity is intense, which compresses time relative to anyone outside the gravitational event horizon. For someone within the black hole, five seconds may pass. For someone outside the black hole, they would see 30,000 years pass. When we port, time will change for us relative to anyone we leave behind."

Lazarus heard the words, but he was processing. If he understood, what he was being told was five seconds for him could be 30,000 years for someone who did not port to the other side of a black hole. He started to panic. What would that mean for his mother, his work, or Diana? Are they all dead in their world?"

"If I was to travel back to Earth, how much time would have passed? Would I be older or younger?"

"For the few weeks you have spent here, they would be older by about 13 years. I don't have the precise numbers, but I could get them for you. This is one of the reasons I am sharing knowledge with you so freely. By the time we visit two universes, everyone you know on Earth will be gone. This is true for my family too. If they live for 200 years, and they may, I will never see them again. Did you not do the time calculations before you ported here?"

"Sadly, I did not design the machine to port to another universe. I designed the machine to enable high-speed interstellar travel, and for the short term, high-speed travel to see my mom on the other side of my planet."

"The time factor is such an established, self-evident fact to us on M401 that I made assumptions I should not have."

"I feel I must return immediately to arrange my affairs at home. I need to say goodbye to my mother. Most of all, I need to pass on some information to prevent the destruction of my species. They may not listen. I don't expect the powerful people to listen, but as a moral duty, I must try."

"That does change things. Are you saying you will not travel with me through the multiverse?"

"I will travel with you. I gave you that commitment. Could you consider this as a time to spend with your family before we leave together? If I go to my planet, arrange my affairs, and return, that may be a few weeks here but gives me 10 years to make a difference."

"Yes. I see. I agree to that arrangement, but you must make me a promise, my friend."

"Yes, SF03. What is your request?"

"You must agree to take the nanobot self-adapting infusion now. This will extend your lifespan to a few hundred years. You will have the time to travel the multiverse before you die. I also have the DNA drug. You can take that with you and consume it when or if you wish."

Lazarus nodded. "You have been kind and gracious. You, your family, your whole species are impressive. I lack the words to say how much I admire what your species have done. Wait, could something go wrong?"

"Not usually. You will probably be fine," said SF03 with a smile.

"Seriously, what could go wrong?"

"Hardly anything. You might be ported into a nearby place, perhaps the sea or traffic-filled road. The calculations across this distance allow for a small margin of error."

"But not into the middle of a concrete block?"

"No, that never happens anymore. No solid objects. You should be fine."

SF03 got up and came back with the case. Lazarus removed and drank the concoction. He was not sure what would change. As they had explained, no one knew. The nanobots would adapt as needed. SF03 put the DNA into the case. SF03 took the amulet around Lazarus's neck, turned it, and slide his fingers up on the left side and down on the right. The amulet backplate rotated revealing flashing LED lights and a few buttons. SF03 pushed the buttons with alarming speed. Lazarus wondered if he would just show up in someone's bathroom or on top of the Statue of Liberty. Wait. He was wearing translucent plastic clothing just like the rest of the people in this world.

"My friend, I will see you again soon. Do not forget your promise," said SF03.

"Could you send the pelican back soon? The bird does not belong here. I would ask you to keep the soldiers here until I return." SF03 nodded and pushed another button. The plate rotated back into position; the amulet was spinning discs within discs. SF03 stepped back. The kids and wife came into the room, and the family gave Lazarus a wave. There was a popping sound, and Lazarus was gone.

Chapter 27 — Chief or Robin Hood

More than a year later on Earth.

Ares and Diana were sitting on a park bench in Central Park. He was different. When she first met him, Ares was aggressive, confident, charming, and quick to bully. He would never have suggested meeting in a park a year ago.

"Diana, I have a confession. I did not expect or care much about the new youth innovation project. My main goal was to use you as leverage against the Professor so I could steal his invention."

"I was able to figure that out after a few weeks."

"Those plans turned to dust. I never got the damn machine. The machine and my best friend are gone. I hired so many people to find the machine. They all failed. I sometimes wonder if that machine existed. No one can find it, and you never hear about the machine. I lost a trusted friend in the effort. Brodie, my security guy, is gone. I don't think you met him, but we had been friends since grade three. I was weak from a childhood lung disease. I had constant asthma attacks. Brodie lived in the house behind me. I helped him pass the school tests, and he protected me. When I grew out of my health issues, I respected power and only power. Utterly ruthless."

"I am sure you were not utterly..."

Ares held up his hand to stop her. "I was ruthless and not just to our competitors. I did not hesitate to frame, blackmail, threaten, beat, or destroy internal competitors blocking my rise to the top. I spared no one, and the result is I have no friends. Brodie was my strong arm and only friend. We were friends longer than any of my marriages. I am old now, and I regret those decisions. The one decision I do not regret is hiring you."

"Thank you."

"The machine has been gone for a year. The Professor and Brodie are lost, but you are here. You are making a difference. You are feeding the poor and making money at it. Your eternal youth cream is making skin young. You give food to the poor and youth to the rich."

"I am pleased with the skin cream. Unlike other skin creams, our cure for old skin works. The competitors' products can be used for a year, and you cannot be sure they did anything. Use our product once, and your skin looks like you are 16 again. Since our solution works, we can charge as much as we like."

"It is sweet. I want to thank you. Your reward is your department will become a spinoff company, and you will be the new CEO. We will issue an IPO so your company will be listed on the stock market."

"I don't know what to say."

"Just say yes. I am enjoying this moment. It is the one nice thing I did all year. "

"This might be a good time to tell you that the youth solution does more than fix fading skin. We can inject it into livers and kidneys, and they regress to youthful organs. We need more testing in clinical trials, and we need government approvals to market. We are also experimenting with regenerating lungs."

"If you can sell youth, you can own the world. You will be richer than Enworld, the largest energy supplier in the world."

"I have a good team."

"You are one of us now, a CEO. Welcome to the club." Ares shook her hand. "I am going for a short walk before I go back to the office." Diana started to get up. "No, I want to walk on my own. You sit here and enjoy the moment." She watched him walk away. He was spry for an older man, but he did not walk the same as before. In the past, he walked in a manner where you were expected to get out of his way. Now, he walked with more patience. He was in no rush. He looked up at the birds and even turned his head for a pretty girl.

"If only he knew it all. She was a CEO, but she was also a Robin Hood. She would take from the rich and give to the poor. Diana remembered reading a book on American native people. They judged wealth not by how much you took from everyone but what you gave to everyone. A rich man who spends nothing lives without tangible wealth. He does not enjoy his wealth, and the community is not rich. A man who gives to everyone in the community is showing everyone his wealth. What good is a mountain of gold sitting in a vault?

Diana went home. She called the office to cancel her meetings, and she started working on the next leadership articles. If the politicians are doing what the rich want, then she would focus on the rich.

Chapter 28 — Love has no rules or reasons

Years later on Earth

"We have been discussing the corporate part of our Planetary Constitution for over a year. I am tired of talking. Today, before anyone leaves, we will decide. Scrap it, change it, or go with it. We can debate, but no one leaves until we decide. Here is our last draft. Look it over, talk it over, then we decide. We don't need 100% consensus, as that is impossible. I suggest we accept 66% as a majority vote," said Diana.

//

Every CEO who fails to comply with these articles within 30 days will be terminated with prejudice at any point after that.

Articles of Planetary Constitution.

2.Corporate Leadership

a. Executive compensation should not exceed 100 times the average employee.
b. A minimum corporate tax rate of 10% is needed as mandatory worldwide. Deductions, loopholes, and subsidies cannot reduce the tax to less than 10%.
c. Corporations may **not** pay any money to political

campaigns.

d. Stock options are banned because of excessive abuse
e. Industry lobby groups are banned as they reduce democracy.
f. Mergers and acquisitions create monopolies, so they are **not** permitted in any industry where profits grow over a rolling five-year period. All parties must include the beneficial owner's name on signage when acquired to avoid a visual pretense of competition.
g. Corporate profits must be published for study in national public databases for any company with more than 50 employees or revenue over 500K.
h. The names of companies must show the beneficial owner with no more than two layers of ownership. Complex webs of ownership are designed to hide the names of dictators and tax cheats, so they must end.
i. No CEO can be the Chairman of the Board and Chief Executive Officer of the same company. The Board's mandate is to provide oversight of management. You cannot provide oversight of yourself without self-interest corrupting decisions.
j. Patents cannot be bought to enable monopolies. Any patent has a use it or lose it end date based on the life-cycle of industry products.
k. Today corporations must care about more than profit or risk losing their corporate charter. Going forward, each corporation must contribute 1% of its profits to some social good. They may choose any social good except political campaigns (e.g., cure cancer, save orphans, feed the poor ...).

l. Some corporations terminate the bottom 5% of employees periodically based on performance. Nations should do the same to corporations. Each year the government will assess if a corporation is providing net pain or gain to the community. The CEO, Board, and executives of the worst 5% of corporations will be terminated and barred from a corporate executive position for 10 years.
m. Corporations make promises they don't keep, such as cleaning up toxic waste from mining or promising not to move a factory if a subsidy is provided. To ensure compliance, funds will be held in trust, and once the promises are kept, the funds will be returned to the corporation.

//

"I like the way we get rid of the most damaging executives. Currently, suppose you care about people and the environment. In that case, your costs may be higher, so you cannot compete with companies that don't care about destroying the environment. Capitalism does not work in this case. It forces everyone into a race to the bottom. Our changes allow all companies globally to compete while doing little or no net harm," said Yasmin.

"I agree that CEOs are helping themselves too much. Corporations are too greedy. We must kill a few so they get the message," said Pi.

"Look, we have a Board to ensure the CEO and the corporation performs," said Milton.

"We know how that works. The CEO uses a Board interlock. I invite you to join my Board if you agree to approve all my unethical compensation. I will join your Board to approve all your unethical greed. Nudge, nudge, wink, wink," said Faith.

"Don't forget, in America 80% of the Boards appoint the CEO to be the Chairman of the Board. The Board exists to ensure the CEO behaves, but the Board is run by the CEO. The CEO approves himself. It is corrupt, obvious self-interest. In Canada, only 60% of the Board Chairmen are also the CEO, which is bad enough," said Diana.

"It is corrupt. I tried raising this issue in a university paper and was inundated with hostility. I was threatened," said Milton.

"How many people know or care about who is a Board Chairman and who is a CEO? We don't have tens of millions in these positions. You saw hired guns aiming at anyone who dared say the super-rich are corrupt. They are not just taking too much. They are taking so much that they are destroying the fabric of society. They must be stopped," said Pi. Everyone was looking at Pi. She never gave big speeches. They were surprised she knew about corporate governance.

Faith burped loudly. "Oh my, I am sorry. I should have skipped the hot sauce."

"You think drug gangs are dangerous. These corporate CEOs are the real danger, the real killers. They wriggle out of paying health benefits, and some employees die. If it saves money, they buy politicians so companies can pollute our air and water, and communities die. Pollution gives you some strange cancer, but no one knows it came from their pollution. Tobacco companies suppressed decades of their own research showing cigarettes kill. Oil companies are doing the same on global warming. We deserve more. We deserve better. We should take on these killers," said Yasmin.

"I don't like forcing corporations to donate a small part of their profits to help people. The public will be misled to believe corporations are kind. We need the public to see them for what they are, expose their violations, and make them fix their pathological social behavior," said Faith.

"We talked about this a lot. If we make them help some group, the executives will need to pick that group, which will mean they have to sit around a table discussing how to help. Those kinds of discussions will change their culture and make them more empathetic. It will begin a process to make them human again. They will be forced to care about more than greed."

"I am glad we are ending stock options. They were abused horribly. They back date them, reissue them with new dates, artificially bump prices using stock buybacks, then cash in options for millions," said Milton. "What I don't get is why you are blocking corporate political contributions and lobby groups?"

"Simple," said Yasmin. "More and more, we see politicians ignoring the public will and doing what benefits the corporate donors. When the public does not get what the majority wants, it's because the politician was bought. He was bought with legal contributions or a bag of cash; it does not matter. The issue is the majority of people are not getting what they want, which is not a democracy. We know democracy is not working. Look at guns. Most people, including gun owners, want reasonable restrictions to prevent terrorists and the insane from buying weapons, but that law never passes. The lobby group has bought the legislature, pure and simple."

"Something smells bad," said Pi.

"I know. Like I say, corruption," said Yasmin.

"Something here, right now, smells really bad."

"Oh, yeah. I smell it too. Wow. That really stinks," said Yasmin.

Faith was looking down. "Sorry. Too much hot sauce."

"Wait a minute. How can we afford to run an election without corporate donors?" said Milton.

"Easy," said Diana. "Big corporations have tens of thousands of employees. If employees at the corporation believe in the politician, they can provide many small donations. We don't need big corporate donors."

"There is an economic meeting in Davos, Switzerland. We should distribute our flyers," said Diana.

"Agreed," said Yasmin, Faith, and Pi.

"Are you going to Davos next week, Milton?" said Diana.

"I don't want to participate in this effort. I care about you, but I disagree. We have done enough. We have removed over 63 dictators, we killed a few, and most quit because of fear. We have done our part to make the world better. We have taken huge risks. I am a father, and I cannot continue," said Milton. "I love you all, especially Diana, but this is where I must stop."

"You know our plans," said Yasmin.

"I won't tell anyone. I can't tell. You know the dictators I killed. I would also be on trial for murder if I said anything," said Milton, feeling threatened. "I won't come to future meetings." Milton picked up his bag and jacket.

"Are you sure you cannot work with us?" said Diana.

"Not on this project. I believe in capitalism. I believe it will auto-correct. Saving democracy was something I was committed to in full. Killing business leaders is not my cup of coffee."

"Cup of tea," said Pi. "Not my cup of tea."

"Whatever. Tea or coffee," said Milton.

"This is about saving democracy," argued Pi. "Corporations are running the world mostly for the benefit of corporations. Corporations own politicians. Corporations promote fake news in the *free* newspapers they give away on the street or promote toxic fake news on social media."

"I t is time for me to leave the team," said Milton. He sighed. He collected his things into the same old knapsack. Milton's shoulders sagged, and he left. The room was quiet. They looked at the closed door, and they avoided eye contact with each other.

"Diana, you know he loves you?" said Faith. "You should let him go."

"What? No. He is married. He loves his wife and child," said Diana.

"He loves you. He always loved you. He was shy in college. He wanted you so much he could barely speak around you. He wanted you so much that he was afraid to ask you out in case you rejected him. He got drunk at a college party, and his wife trapped him with her pregnancy," said Faith. "He was here to be near you."

Diana was frowning. She was thinking of the many college experiences. Diana did not go out much because she always worked in the library. She believed hard work was enough. She had no understanding of how the wind was turning against working people. Diana looked slowly across the room at her friends. She could see in their expression that everyone knew about Milton's unrequited love. How could she have been so blind?

"I have another confession," said Faith. Everyone looked, from Diana to Faith. "I am in love with Leo. I was smitten from the first time I saw him, and I will do anything for him. I have been seeing him since moving here.

Yasmin shook her head. "He is a sleaze."

"He is a liar," said Diana.

"You don't know him as well as I do," said Faith. "I love him."

"Did you tell him about our constitution?" said Pi.

"No. Definitely, no. I would like to invite Leo to replace Milton. He could be an asset. He is smart and charming, and he can speak multiple languages. He wants to make amends to all of us."

"This is too much to process, and it smells in here. I am not good at this romantic stuff. Give me microbes, and I will be fine. I did not know about Milton. I cannot believe you would fall for Leo after you saw all his games. He is a player. He could have really hurt me," said Diana.

A loud ringtone played, and Diana glanced at her phone and then showed her phone to Faith. It was another text from the sleazeball Leo. Diana declined the call and put the phone back on the table. No sooner was the phone put down than it rang again. Diana snorted in exasperation. She picked up the phone again, ready to blast Leo, when she saw the message. Lazarus was back. He was alive! Well, perhaps someone was pretending to be him? Could someone be using his phone? Could it be true? It had been years. God, the guilt she had felt for so long. She thought she'd killed him. She closed her eyes and said a silent prayer, then answered.

Chapter 29 — Lazarus returns from the dead

Lazarus thought he might find himself back in Canada, but he was sent back to the same alley in New York. He was still wearing alien translucent clothes. He did what he could to create a mist around his crotch. As the mist swirled, you could see glimpses of his groin. He had no money, no cell phone, and no credit cards. He was near naked, broke, and vulnerable. Lazarus went into a restaurant and asked to use the phone. They didn't give him a second glance. A clean, well-spoken man with an odd outfit was typical in New York. They shrugged and pointed to the phone on the receptionist's desk. Lazarus tried to remember Diana's number. He dialed and hoped he got it right.

"Diana, it's me. I'm Lazarus."

"Repeat it."

"It is really me. I have things to tell you. More importantly, I am in New York. I have no clothes, money, credit cards, or place to stay."

"Where?"

"The restaurant where you last saw me."

"Don't move. I will be there in 10 minutes. You were gone for 13 years. I thought you were dead. I thought I killed you. I wish you had called. I am coming right now." Diana grabbed her purse and left. She turned back and hurriedly took the black trench coat from behind her door.

"Got to go. Emergency. Please move my meetings," Diana said to her secretary. She went up to the meeting room. "I have to run... a family emergency. Please arrange something with my secretary. I am terribly sorry." Diana ran to the elevator. She watched the numbers slowly move. Diana huffed, then ran to the stairs, moving as fast as she could, going down a few stairs with each step, and jumping the last few stairs. She grabbed a taxi.

The ride was slow because of the traffic. The rain was drizzling. The flashing lights of the city took on a shine through the moist air. She was tapping her leg and jiggling. After a few blocks, she threw a 20-dollar bill at the driver, leaped out, and ran the next few blocks to the alley. Lazarus stood just inside the door. She jumped into his arms and hung on to his neck. She held him crying as a few tears of joy ran down her cheek.

"I thought you were dead. I thought I'd killed a friend. I am so relieved. Look at you. You are here. You look. You look perfect," she said as she took in his whole body. You could see everything through his transparent clothing. She realized, looking at his crotch, that he was a little excited from the hug. She went red in the face. She smiled and gave him her trench coat.

"Thank you. Thank you so much," said Lazarus.

"Let's have a drink. We can talk, and then I want to buy you some clothes," said Diana.

They got a table and ordered a bottle of wine. Diana looked at him again, and he looked exactly the same. Lazarus was about 39 when they flew to Africa, and she was 25. He still looked 39, and now she was 38. She looked and felt like she was 38.

She took his hand in hers. The skin was young, flexible, and flawless. With her new skin product, she knew a lot about skin. She bent over and examined his hand. She knew skin was a mirror into your overall health. Skin can have blemishes and flaws that reveal your health. Skin in older people can be so thin you can see veins. She turned his hand over. She looked at the palm and then up to his face. The skin on his face looked like a teenager. He had a shine and perfect skin. He looked younger than her, handsome, very handsome indeed. He was blond with a full head of hair and big Superman curls about his forehead.

"What happened?"

"You won't believe me, but I will tell you. I was vaporized, but I was not killed. I was ported. Space folds, space-time bends, and I slid into another universe."

"You are right. I don't believe you. I know you were gone, and now you are here. I guess I must believe you. How can that be?"

"It was not my design. Well, not my intentional design. I was trying to create a vacuum, and I did that inadvertently by opening a new dimension for a second or two."

"Why were you gone so long? Almost 13 years! I thought you were dead. I had to file a missing person's report. I had to manage things according to your Will, but you never died."

"I was gone for a few weeks. Time is relative. You had 13 years while I had less than 13 weeks."

"That explains why we look the same age."

"Where is the machine? Did Ares steal it?" said Lazarus.

"No, it is hidden in my apartment. People see it, and people walk by it. They sit near it, and they have no idea that the machine is hidden in full view. Ares could have touched it. He was that close. He came, and he went - none the wiser."

"Do you have my credit cards or cash?" said Lazarus.

"Your credit cards are all expired. Here is some cash. We can get more when we walk to the tailor. Were you a stripper in the other dimension?" She teased him as she pulled his transparent top a few inches away from his skin.

"Everyone wears this stuff there. It is comfortable, and the clothes are smart. They can dry you if you get wet, warm you if you get cold. They can display the time. Look."

"That looks like a lot of circular squiggles. That is the time?"

"Well, time in an alien language. It's about 3."

"Okay. You meet aliens, and you can read their language. What are they like? Let me guess. They are little green men?"

"You don't know how close you are. They are green but not little. Twice my height and strength, and about 2,000 times smarter than me."

"Sure," she said with a laugh.

He smiled. "I have to spread a paramount message. If we do not focus on science, stop our wars, and seriously focus on microbiology and space travel, we are doomed as a planet. We will destroy all intelligent life on Earth. We have limited time. We must stop being greedy. We must stop spending so much money on sports and religion because we are in a race to find enough scientific knowledge, especially microbiology, to avoid going extinct. We are precariously close to self-inflicted extinction."

"Sure. You tell them. You tell everyone. They might listen."

"Look, I know I am not a politician. I am just a Professor of minor repute. I was shown information about the extinction of intelligent species from all over many universes. We are essentially gone if we don't make changes. We have to move away from spending all our time on romance novels, religions, sports, and games and put our energies into science."

"As a microbiologist, I like the idea. You know the challenge you face. You gave me your plan to remove corruption and dictators. You gave me a plan to put people first and remove greed. You have a monumental task."

"I have to try to save the human race. I keep thinking about all the lives and generations to come. The next 10,000 generations have a right to live and learn more about the truth. I must try. I know what will come if we don't. They showed me the millions of intelligent species who have gone extinct and how they died."

"You mean the big green men."

"Yes. Them."

"Okay, finish your drink. We can get you some clothes, and we can stop all sports, beer, and what's the other thing, religion or romance novels?"

"I know it sounds crazy, but I have a plan."

Diana looked at him. "I am sure you do." Diana thought about how she hesitated to talk to him that sunny day in the garage. When you speak to Lazarus, he will hijack your life. She was talking to him again, and now he was hijacking her life again. This time, he wants to save the world and humans. Yesterday, she was the CEO of one of the most promising global companies. During her breaks from work, she killed dictators and fought corruption. What was going to happen to her now?"

Chapter 30 — The secret is the nanobots

"I know an excellent shop near here. We can walk. The tailor is Indian and works out of a tiny little shop but does excellent work. You can get the finest suits, monogrammed, for a good price."

"I would be happy with jeans, a T-shirt, and running shoes," said Lazarus.

They walked together. The misty rain was still falling. The Professor's hair was curling more in the rain. He looked a bit like one of those statues of Greek gods. As they stood at a traffic light, she could see her shoes and pantsuit bottom were wet. For Lazarus's pants, she could see his clothes were completely dry. She put her hand down and touched the leg material, and it was warm.

"The secret is nanobots. Water beads on the material and runs off. Water, mud, snow, soup, anything runs off, leaving no stain or wet spot."

Diana was beginning to realize she should make no assumptions. He went somewhere, and he may have seen remarkable things and witnessed fantastic technologies. She should listen and learn. They entered the shop and walked down one flight to a tiny basement. There were bolts of cloth everywhere. Diana was showing off a bit. Ares talked about the best places to get men's clothes. The tailor had some premade suits and shirts Lazarus could take now. He measured him for a few silk shirts and suits of the best Italian wools.

"After we finish here, I need to go to the Norwegian and Canadian embassies. I plan to talk about the machine and secure their protection. If we sell the machine through a nation rather than a corporation, we can run the program as a sovereign non-profit venture. All the money will fund scientific innovations, environmental protection, space travel, microbiology, the World Court, the World Health Organization, and Human Rights. I will want full control to ensure the machine can never be used for war. You know how dangerous this technology is if misused. The only people who can sell or service the machine will be our sovereign backers."

"I have the machine here in New York. You can pick it up anytime," said Diana. "You can stay at my place until you are settled. I will get you a phone and a key to my place."

"Diana, I have to know. How is my mom?"

"I have been calling her every week. She is 89 now. She misses you. I explained you were missing and hoped you were not injured but could not be sure. She and I are close. When she fell and hurt her neck, I arranged for someone to care for her. I must warn you. She is still mentally sharp, but she has trouble moving. Her joints are arthritic, and her neck often hurts. I send her books all the time. She is a voracious reader."

"That sounds like Mom. I have to call her as soon as I have clothes."

"You should know that we have been working on your plan. We have made progress. The world is different."

"How so?"

"The big change is there are almost no dictators. Over 60 nations have moved from dictatorships or monarchies to a democracy. Not everyone but close."

"Wow. That was unexpected."

"We still have lots of dictators in corporations. We also have lots of issues. Despite improvements in many areas under democracies, the size of the middle-class keeps shrinking. I would like you to join my team in a meeting tonight. We can give you the details and a better summary of the progress. We also have new targets but have not formed an action plan to achieve those targets."

"Wow again. Listen to you. Action plans, targets, achievements."

"I still can't believe you are here. I feel I am dreaming. One day you were gone, and then you pop back into my life as if you went for a coffee. It is so good to see you. I will sleep well tonight for the first time in 13 years."

"I cannot process the 13 years. I left a couple of months ago on my timeline."

"My phone is going berserk. I am going to have to take this." While Diana listened to someone shouting on the phone, she looked up at a small TV screen behind the tailor. The reporter said Ares was dead. He had been killed by a disgruntled employee. He was rammed by a car and repeatedly pinned against a wall until he died. The perpetrator stayed at the scene and proudly confessed. He admitted threatening Ares for months. "Hello," said Diana. She listened for a few minutes, exclaiming with surprise a few times. "I will be right there," said Diana.

"This is a crazy day. I have to go to the office. Ares has been killed, and he named me as his successor. They say he has a poison pill in his succession plan that ensures no corporate takeover will supersede his wishes. If I am not made the new CEO, all his shares and assets will be sold in a fire sale to our British competitor. I can't believe it."

"He did not discuss this with you?"

"No, nothing. The last time we spoke, Ares admitted he had done many bad things. He said he was proud of was hiring me. He liked that my company feeds the poor and makes a lot of money from the rich. He made me a CEO of a small spinoff company."

"Wow again. From neighborhood student to corporate oligarch in 13 years. Should I be scared of you?"

"Don't be silly. I care more about people than profits. I am exactly the same. Almost."

"Okay. I will see you later."

"Look, Professor, I have to run, but I will send a car for you. They will drive you around to the embassies, and the driver will have your new phone. Here are my keys. The driver will know where to take you. I hate to leave, but they say this is a crisis. The most powerful shareholders want to meet me ASAP."

"Well, Diana. You look different, and you sound different. I will meet you and your team later. I cannot thank you enough. Without you, I would be wandering the streets of Manhattan looking like a stripper if I can quote a friend." Diana was already at the door. She gave him a wink, gestured to the sky with both hands, and she was gone.

Chapter 31 — Going to Norway

Lazarus was now wearing a top-quality white Italian wool suit with a double-breasted jacket. He had a silk monogrammed shirt and black tie. Lazarus felt transformed. He was ready for the embassy. The Indian tailor kept looking at the fabric of the translucent alien pants and shirt. The tailor was shaking his head in confusion. A large fellow in uniform and cap came into the store.

"Are you Lazarus?"

"Yes."

"Good. I have to take you to the Norwegian embassy, next to the Canadian embassy, and then to Diana Mars's apartment. I was also told to give you this phone." The two men left. Lazarus took his alien clothes, two new suits, and three new shirts. The drive was near 2nd and 48th street, and they turned down a small road with a Norwegian name. The rain continued. The day was dull, but people in Manhattan never stop their bustling around. It was nice to have a limousine and be dropped at the front door. Usually, Lazarus would walk everywhere in Manhattan because it was rare he had to walk more than 10 or 20 blocks.

He waited for the elevator. Somehow Lazarus had to find a way to prevent the total decimation of humanity from the Stage Up extinction. Could he inspire some countries to explore space for resources? It was not going to be easy to convince a world leader to aggressively invest in space travel.

As soon as he entered, a young man greeted him. "You must be Professor Lazarus? We have a conference room set up, and the ambassador is waiting with our business attaché."

"I'm surprised. How did you know I was coming?"

"We were called by the new CEO of Enworld and current CEO of Omega Biotech. She said you had a significant proposal. We have cleared commitments and are eager to hear your proposal. As you know, Norway is one of the biggest producers of energy."

Lazarus sat down and was pleased with the unexpected good start. They exchanged the usual greetings with tea and cookies supplied. He enjoyed the beautiful view of the city. Diana, bless her, had helped. Once the pleasantries were concluded, Lazarus began.

"I am a physics Professor. I have been in hiding for the last 13 years – completely off the grid. The reason is I have a machine that can travel at enormous speeds. You may find much of what I say hard to believe, but I can provide proof using a prototype model. I will provide a full demonstration of the actual machine at your convenience."

"What do you mean enormous speeds?"

"Interstellar speeds. A key aspect of my proposal is for the machine to mine the asteroid belt for non-renewable resources that are becoming rare on Earth. The machine was designed for a human pilot, but I recommend changing it for crewless flights to the asteroid belt. As you know, China, Japan, and other nations are experimenting with landing on asteroids to take rock samples. This machine can easily eclipse anything they are doing.

Norway will be a world leader in the supply of metals or minerals with supply shortages. I recommend we mine using robots, and the crewless machine will warehouse the minerals on the moon."

"What is missing from this machine? Can you do this now?"

"There are two required modifications. The machine has no heater. Space is cold. We would need to add heat. The machine has a small and primitive supply of oxygen. We need to add a better circulation of air for any crewed flights. Lastly, we need to scale up. The machine is a two-person vehicle not designed to transport large loads. There is work to be done, but the benefits are significant."

"There are many challenges to what you are describing. We have to fly to the asteroid belt. This takes a long time with many costs. We have to match the velocity of the asteroid before we land. The asteroid will be moving in two directions at the same time, moving forward and spinning. I am not sure why you are talking to Norway. We are a small country with almost no expertise in space travel other than a few communication satellites. For example, the cost of fuel alone is prohibitive."

"I agree, but you will understand as I expand. There are two proposals. The asteroid project is the most difficult but the most important. We have eight billion people on Earth and a growing population. Non-renewable resources are, by definition, not renewable. When we have used them all and hit limits on recycling, we will begin a long and nasty journey into world desolation. We may argue about the timing, but the outcome is undeniable. As a species, our success is tied to us being smart enough to use the resources we have to reach the asteroid belt to find more resources. If we squander our metals and minerals on fun, greed, and endless population growth, we will not have enough resources to find more resources. Until recently, I did not fully understand the importance of space travel, but our survival as a species is contingent on the smart use of the resources on our planet. Most of the metals and minerals are from the first formation of our planet."

"I understand and agree with the theory, but you did not answer the cost of space travel. Are you asking Norway to pay for the cost of innovation? What are you asking us?" said Dag, the ambassador. Lazarus was worried but encouraged. He had a chance, perhaps his only chance, to persuade them. The start was good, and Ambassador Dag clearly understood the need.

"The cost issue is covered in the second project. The energy I am using is a bit complex. Essentially, we travel using gravity to move us. I know that sounds like nonsense, but I am talking about switching gravity partially off. Now, if I were you and some unknown Professor wandered in through the front door talking like I am, I would be asking myself if he was crazy? Should you call security and escort him out. Please observe this little prototype. I call it the beetle, which looks like a small machine. I will switch it on and let it hover. As you can see, it sits in the air, not moving. Feel free to check for wires or any other trick you suspect. I will let it circle the room back and forth using my phone to command the motion. If I speed it up, you can see it moves silently. This little prototype has no propeller and is not burning fuel. This little prototype is drawing on gravity for power."

"You can travel without the use of oil, batteries, or wind."

"Correct. As you can imagine, it will change the world. Vehicles will not need oil. Nor will the ocean liners, trucks, or airplanes need oil. Our planet will not be choking on oil fumes.

Our cost for travel, including interstellar travel, will be within reach of every nation using my engine."

"You would destroy our major source of revenue, which comes from oil production. Again, why would you come to us? You could sell the patents and become a billionaire instantly just on the promise of cheap travel."

"It is because of corporate greed that I have been in hiding for 13 years. What I am asking from Norway is protection from corporations. The first corporation wanted to buy my machine. When the purchase was rejected, they tried to steal it. When defensive measures prevented them from stealing it, they tried to kidnap me. They did not want to save the world. They wanted to destroy the machine to ensure they could continue selling oil. While oil is destroying our air, water, and soil, they only care about short-term profits. Profits are the only mandate of a corporation."

"Why do you trust us not to do the same?" said Dag.

"Ah, and that gets to the core of the proposal. Norway puts people first. You care about the environment. You have sold funds in oil and coal mining stocks from your government pensions. When you negotiate trade deals, you focus on protecting your workers instead of corporate profits. Your nation has already committed to ending national oil production by 2050. Correct?"

"Yes. Burning oil destroys our farm production by causing acid rain. Burning fossil fuel destroys our air and water. It causes global warming, which has many devastating impacts, as you clearly know," said Dag.

"Your nation is a leader of leaders. You are stewards of the Earth. You want a world where your children and grandchildren can thrive. You do not put short-term profit ahead of long-term survival. Your leaders negotiate trade deals with a focus on protecting the middle class and jobs. You do not put a focus on protecting cheap labor and copyrights. Your rank in OECD ratings is a top ten country for education, happiness, long life, living standards, health, and equality. I want to have a long and happy life too."

"It would seem, Professor, that you have done your research on Norway."

"What I propose is this project would be different. We would not use any corporation, especially international conglomerates. I could be rich, but that is not my goal. We will set up a non-profit, fully government-owned, sovereign enterprise. As a sovereign firm, you would protect me from corporate raiders, buy-outs, and mergers. You would prevent any corporate dirty tricks like a hijack of Board control to steal a company from the founder."

"We did some research. You are Canadian. Why not take your invention to your own country?"

"I will. I want at least two capable nations at any given time. Let me first highlight another benefit to Norway. China, Russia, and the USA bully smaller nations. They demand you adhere to American laws about trade with Iran, which prohibits a sovereign nation like Norway from making its own decisions. They threaten your trade. They threaten your CEOs with arrest in a third-party nation if they break American law, even if the CEOs abided by Norwegian laws. China is worse. They demand loyalty no matter what evil things they do to their people. You may not say a negative word, no matter how true, to protect Chinese citizens from the Chinese government. Russia is worse still. They deliberately use disinformation to weaken both friends and foes alike. If Norway had almost exclusive control of this machine, your nation would have the bulk of the supply of some precious resources. If you control the resources, you would have leverage with powerful countries. You could make your own demands. You would have the control because, without you, they could not access some critical non-renewable minerals and metals to power their war machines."

"You are saying we run this company, but we would be one of only two manufacturers."

"Yes. All the building would happen in your country with Norwegian workers. No outsourcing, no selling of licenses, and no corporations. We build in Norway and Canada. Any machine that needs service will be returned to Norway or Canada. This helps us protect our technology."

"What stops them from just buying one unit, stripping it, stealing the ideas, and then building their own like they do with everything else? All they need to do to skirt patents is alter one minor component and claim it is a new product. They could, as you say, just bully us by stealing it and ignoring world business rules. The WTO (World Trade Organization) ruled against the USA on softwood lumber in favor of Canada. The USA response was to ignore the ruling."

"Each machine sold will require an inspection every 30 days. I have defensive measures. If a machine shows tampering signs, we will not sell any new machines or service existing machines for 30 days to that nation. It will hurt them. With a second incident, we will not service or sell any machines to that country for 30 weeks. We will randomly disable as many machines as we wish. There will be no service or sales for a third offense for 30 months, and 50 percent of their fleet will be recalled to Norway. If they want their units returned after 30 months, they have to repay the purchase price. The last escalation will be 30 years, and that will disable any ability to be competitive. We control it. If they mess with us, we increasingly shut them down. The agreement to these rules must be signed if they want to buy a machine." Lazarus felt this was the deciding point. They could control a monopoly using unique technology. Was this was the key to win them over?

"What if they don't return it for service."

"We track the GPS beacon for every machine. If they don't get service in 30 days, we can remotely recall or disable the machine. Any machine that loses the beacon signal will automatically return to the factory in Norway."

"What if they get mad and just invade Norway?"

"Do you have an old book you don't care about, and I can demonstrate?"

The attaché Sven gave Lazarus an old book on trade regulations from 1960. It was more of a file folder with about two inches of documents. Lazarus held the book in his hand, and the beetle flew through it, making a clean hole three inches in diameter. "As you can see, the machine is also a formidable weapon. We could turn their entire fleet against them, vaporizing every building, organic lifeform, and rock into the ether. We could utterly decimate them. For this reason, I must insist that the machine never be sold to any nation or organization that engages in aggressive military activities. They can use their military to help prevent a flood, but they cannot invade any sovereign nation. They would not dare touch Norway. Canada and Norway would become the most powerful nations on Earth. Great power, but with a kind heart that cares about helping people, not using power to take more power."

Dag and Sven took a pause. They exchanged words rapidly in Norwegian. Lazarus kept his fingers crossed behind his back. He was not religious but hoped the ancient Viking gods would bless his sales pitch.

"We would like you to meet with our Prime Minister and his cabinet to hear your proposal. When would you like to visit our beautiful country?"

"I can leave tomorrow using the full-sized machine as a demonstration. It is a two-seater so I can take one person with me. We will make the trip in less than 20 minutes instead of the usual seven-hour flight. Please pick someone who likes an exciting ride. This will be proof that I am not a crazy academic but a practical man."

"Why are you using two countries? You could have just built it in Canada?"

"Even the conservative party in Norway puts people first. Your conservatives would be thought of as liberals in Canada. I will not risk working with a truly conservative government. Conservatives do not believe in big government, which is another way of saying they like to privatize government to create corporate monopolies of government services. Conservatives are more militaristic. This machine can never become a weapon as it is far too dangerous. I will always have two countries as sovereign suppliers. If one county has a catastrophe like an earthquake, hurricane, or tsunami, we will continue to operate in the second country. If a county selects a conservative majority government, the nation will lose manufacturing rights to the machine. I do not wish to interfere in national politics. They can vote in any leader, but the machine must remain outside the control of any corporation. The policies are more important than the name. As I say, even your right-wing leaders are left-wing compared to many countries. The key is the government will not attempt to privatize the control of the machine."

"You are very tough on conservatives."

"It has to do with the future. Science is important to our survival as a world and must remain pre-eminent. Conservatives often privilege religious views over science, and corporate welfare over citizen well-being. The corporations often choose might over morality. This is not the time to go into details, but science is needed to ensure human survival. I cannot have a mostly religious, militaristic leader who cares more about money than people, more about God than survival. Your nation is perfectly positioned for the coming changes in technology because it has a people first policy."

Sven and Dag debated who should go to Norway. Eventually, Dag volunteered. Lazarus and Dag exchanged private phone numbers and agreed to coordinate the next morning. Lazarus was surprised at how interested they were in listening to him.

Lazarus had no firm commitment from Norway. He felt happy because the offer to meet the Prime Minister was a form of progress. Lazarus knew he was no salesperson. He lacked the skills to schmooze and charm. He could not walk up to anyone and be close friends in minutes while sharing a beer and talking about sports. Lazarus knew his face told a story. If he did not like an attitude or idea, even if he thought he was impassive, his whole opinion would be clearly written on his face.

The Canadian embassy was next. The story was almost the same. One call from Enworld and doors were opened. The power of these corporations to gain access at all levels was scary. Since this was the second pitch, Lazarus was better at explaining the plans. The Canadian Ambassador Troy was ecstatic about having more influence and leverage over American politicians. He was tired of having to ingratiate himself when bullied. Lazarus was not given an offer to meet the Prime Minister of Canada. The Ambassador promised to discuss the idea with the Prime Minister and call Lazarus with the results.

This was less successful and slower than Norway but a step forward. Since a Liberal government was currently in power, they laughed with smug joy at the idea that the control was available only to left-wing leaders. Lazarus was surprised. Troy explained the government was always getting threats from corporate leaders demanding conservative policies or loopholes to bypass people-friendly Liberal laws. Corporations would threaten to move their tax base or close factories if their demands were not met. Were all governments becoming government by the corporation and for the corporation? Some corporations already had more power and influence than half the countries in the world. Corporate control would be good if corporations had good social intentions instead of the endless, inexorable pursuit of money with no social conscience. "Institutionalized social psychopaths," thought Lazarus.

Chapter 32 — The board

Diana was escorted into the boardroom on the top floor of the building. She had never been in the boardroom. The table was long enough to seat 50 people. The table was an expensive-looking dark wood with a green blotter at every seat, along with a notepad, pen, and glass of water. There was no word for the room except sumptuous given the beautiful chandelier, thick green carpet, and dark green and gold drapes of velvet. Diana wondered if she should carve her name into the table as she may only last ten minutes and that carving would be the only sign she was ever there.

The Chair of the Board was Phillip Sterling. He looked angry and a bit jaundiced. He had all the signs of cirrhosis of the liver. Diana recognized the symptoms immediately because a liver disease had killed her alcoholic father. She tried not to think about her Dad much. He had abandoned her family when she was seven and did not return until he got sick in his forties. Phillip had dark skin spots, noticeable weight loss, and he was jaundiced around the eyes. She suspected swollen ankles, which would confirm her suspicions. Phillip's pants blocked a close inspection of his ankles.

Phillip was at the head of the oblong table. There were about 15 people, all were elderly white men. She recognized most of them from photographs in the newspapers. Most of them were

CEOs of banks, consulting firms, construction companies, and other major corporations. Diana's little Omega company had a board of only three people; Ares, an accountant, and herself.

"We will skip the introductions. Each person can introduce themselves when they have something helpful to say. We are here to discuss Ares's death, or more importantly, the undisclosed succession plan he left. What do you know about it?" said Phillip.

"Nothing. This is the first I heard about it," said Diana.

"Ares did not discuss making you the CEO when he left?" said Phillip.

"No."

"Nothing at all. You expect me to believe that," said Phillip.

"Perhaps he died unexpectedly and thought he had lots of time to discuss it?"

"Perhaps he did discuss it, and you decided you had waited long enough to take over?" said Phillip.

"He did not discuss it. I have told you that more than once. If I tell you something, you should believe it. If you have allegations to make, show me some evidence. Go ahead, I want to see evidence for any scurrilous allegations," said Diana, who was losing her temper.

"Ares left a poison pill to prevent us from circumventing his plans. You have control of all of his assets, including all his shares in Enworld. You are the majority shareholder. If we fight you, he has provisions that would wreck the company. I don't like surprises. I don't like the idea of some woman in her 30s with no senior management experience stepping into one of the most important positions in the economy," said Phillip.

"Did he do a good job? Were you satisfied with the progress when Ares was the leader?"

"Yes, Ares put the company first. He had no family, and I don't think he had friends. Company man, first and foremost. He did what needed to be done without hesitation. He made good choices," said Phillip. Diana remembered the regret Ares had for some of those choices. Ares had regrets for being ruthless. He died friendless, without family, and killed by a fellow employee.

"And I was one of those choices. You have years of proven choices to trust Ares. For some reason, he thought I was the person needed for this job. You should trust him," said Diana. Phillip was quiet but kept a sneer. Phillip rocked back in his chair and crossed his legs. The right pant leg moved up, and Diana could see Phillip's swollen ankles. Phillip kept his bully sneer even when rocking in his chair.

One of the men at the other end of the table spoke. He had a smooth tone, not threatening. "I am Marcus Hydrome, the CEO of Boopont Chemical Inc. We make plastics, fertilizers, pesticides, and other hydrocarbon-based chemicals. Could you tell us about your management experience?"

"Yes. I joined Enworld as a science project leader. My team developed a cost-effective nutrient to feed the poor."

"Humph," grunted Phillip. "Some green energy millennial on a science project. What has that got to do with selling energy to the world? Ares was going soft."

"We make food that costs 1/600th of the cost of beef. We undercut the competitive foods per equivalent unit of energy by 50 percent and keep the rest as profit. Do I have to ask if anyone here likes money?" said Diana, then paused to look the old men in the eye.

"Again, what does that have to do with selling energy. Ares spun off some silly little side business that he can point to when the protesters get nasty about some oil spill," said Phillip.

"The cheap food gives us a quick profit. The coup d'etat is the youth solution. We can make skin young. Not some fake cream made mostly of a mild acid that burns the skin, so it looks less wrinkled when it heals, but an actual working solution that resets the clock on skin."

"Gah. Your big solution for an oil company is a cosmetic cream. Please, give me a break."

"If you will listen instead of grandstanding, I will get to the good part a bit faster. If you see no value in what I am talking about, I will get out of your way, and you can run this company without me. I will be a figure-head to keep the company whole, and you can make the decisions." Diana saw the old farts were pleased that she put the bully in his place. He stared with some hostility but was silent.

"The skin cream is not the end goal. The same technique of altering the DNA to make skin young also works on organs. For example, Mr. Sterling, we are working on liver organs. A person with a serious liver disease like cirrhosis has only a 50% chance of surviving two years and 35% of surviving three years. The only real fix is a liver transplant. Many people die waiting. Those that are lucky and get a transplant must take antibiotics for life to prevent organ rejection. How much would you pay to have an old diseased liver turned into a young, vibrant teenage liver with no chance of rejection because we are turning the clock back on your own organ? Do I have your interest, or should I let anyone in this room who might have a liver disease die?"

Diana paused, and the room was silent. She waited. Phillip's hand was shaking as Diana turned to Marcus. "In the first year, I made a 400% profit on investment with the food product. Since our skin product actually works, we expect to take the entire youth cream market worth billions. We are in phase three trials with 3,000 happy test subjects and no negative reports. For organ regeneration, we are in phase two trials starting with the liver. We expect to follow in about 12 months apart with organ regeneration for kidneys, lungs, and finally hearts. We sell food to the poor and youth to the rich. I am the CEO of Omega Biotech. Who has improvements on that business model? We sell to the poor, and we sell to the rich. We sell to everyone with a product they need most. Anyone got suggestions for improvements?"

"We are an oil company," said Phillip with a softer voice.

"Yes. You are correct. I was taught diversity is a smart financial move. The oil price has sunk to $5 a barrel in the covid pandemic; sometimes, oil sells for $140 a barrel. The $5.00 price cannot cover the $15 shipping cost for shipping a barrel of oil. We lose money with every barrel at that price. Oil is important but volatile. Who here would like a more stable revenue stream when our competitors are bleeding? "

"Thank you," said Marcus. "This is another secret Ares did not tell us. He told us not to bother ourselves with his little pet project. When we asked about the profits," he said your project was just a rounding error that was not worth our time. He did not tell us you are close to selling eternal life. I wonder what other little surprises he was keeping from us?"

"Oil profits are under constant and increasing threat from green energy. I am not here to have a debate about whether global warming is real. Everyone at this table knows that green energy like wind or solar is now cheaper than coal. You may challenge the science, but you cannot challenge the money. We need a backup plan, and Ares gave you one. Omega Biotech is our ace backup, and Ares knew it. Now would anyone like to resign your board position because you don't like my new appointment?"

"I am the Chairman. You do not get to make those kinds of offers," said Phillip.

"I like a collaborative relationship rather than adversarial. Collaboration is not only more productive; it is a more pleasant way to work. I may not be the Chair, but I am a majority shareholder and CEO. If you see me as some little girl, there is the door. You can use it, or I can. If you think selling youth has a business value, you are welcome to be part of my team."

"I'm in," said Marcus. Moving around the table, the old men each concurred.

"Phillip, if you are interested, there are open positions for more test subjects on our phase 2 trials for liver regeneration. If you have three months, phase three is safer and looking for candidates?"

"How did you know about my liver?" Phillip whispered. "Did you investigate me?"

"I did not know about Ares or the succession plan until you told me today."

"I would like to volunteer. The sooner, the better," said Phillip.

"I will let the team know."

"And Diana, thank you," said Phillip. "I had to see if you had the mettle for the job."

"Gentlemen. I need to come up to speed quickly. Please continue without me while I become familiar with the issues and challenges. I would only slow you down, and you cannot stop making decisions to explain every project. I will leave you in the capable hands of our Chairman."

Diana left. Damn. What a pack of wolves. Those old men thought the childless, lonely, friendless Ares was an asset and not a psychopath. Sheesh. Good thing Diana and the team included Article B in the Planetary Constitution. A percentage of profits must go to a public good from any corporation.

Diana walked down one floor to Ares's office. They had already packed up Ares's few personal belongings in boxes while a painter was putting her name on the door. As soon as the administration team saw her, they hurried from their desks to greet her. The secretary gave Diana a pass to the president's parking spot and a new company credit card with no spending limit. She was given keys to her new desk and the executive safe. Diana spent time getting names and roles from each person in her team.

Ares secretary was trying to hide she had been crying. She was an older woman, very proper and efficient with a robotic coolness. Diana always felt the secretary disliked her. Diana felt like the woman saw her as a corporate climber trying to use youth and sexuality to win Ares' favors. Now, the woman was almost fawning. She walked Diana to the safe, showed her the mechanism to unlock the safe. She offered Diana her loyalty and help at any time, day or night. Diana kept thinking, I was precisely the same person yesterday, and you wouldn't greet me in the elevator. We both know you knew my name, but I was a nameless nobody to you outside of Ares's office.

Diana perused documents from the safe. The safe was the size of a large man, about six feet by four feet. You could walk into the safe. Diana assumed the really nasty secrets were the most hidden, so she started at the back of the safe and worked forward. There were several patents for batteries that could provide more power for a longer time and less heat. Batteries were tricky. It was a tradeoff – more power but shorter life, or more life but less power. You risked a fire if you did not design the battery correctly. All of these problems were solved multiple times in different ways. Innovative materials, imaginative designs, and in a few cases they invented using technology she did not understand. Diana knew from the Lazarus incident how determined Ares was to squash any threat to oil sales. She wondered about these marvelous scientists and what dangers, bribes, and blackmail Ares had used to destroy their dreams.

She found an unholy trinity. Preservatives put in foods that caused cancer, and treatments for those cancers that would keep you alive but never cure the disease. Chemical, medical, and big pharma ruining lives to make more money. They make you sick, and they keep you alive for as long as it takes to strip your family of everything. The more she read, the sicker she felt. Whatever low opinion she had about corporate management was multiplied by x4000. If all you care about is money, you create a heartless, cruel, and brutal world that sees people as piggybanks. No empathy. No feelings. Show me the money. Somehow this corporate monster devoid of all emotion was considered a *person* by the courts. She felt dizzy. Diana walked over to the executive bathroom and threw up. She felt dirty just being in this room.

What blood was hidden in the red carpet? She could only guess and knew whatever amount she picked; it would probably be too low a number.

Chapter 33 — Call home

"Can you see it?" asked Diana.

"No"

Diana laughed. "Unlike others, you know it is here. Look harder."

Lazarus looked carefully. This was no student apartment. The condo was large by any standards and enormous for Manhattan. Modern decorations were all about, and a massive dining table dominated the room. The table had a beautiful linen cloth with intricate Chinese red and gold designs. There was another wooden table, dark walnut, near a window for more functional desk work or snacks. The artwork was modern, mostly realistic paintings of flowers and parks. There was one large seascape painting with an underwater perspective of tropical waters. He looked but could not see the machine.

"The machine is under the table, upside down, just below the tabletop and off the ground."

Lazarus got on one knee, pulled the cover back, and there was his machine, his life work for more than a decade. He trusted Diana but was still comforted knowing the machine was safe. Lazarus smiled with the pleasure of being home on Earth and not surrounded by superior alien beings. The smile disappeared as he suddenly realized an opportunity was slipping away.

"Diana. You should test my microbiome. Collect a full-spectrum test of all the bacteria in my gut and anywhere else."

"Why? Are you feeling ill?"

"Microbiology is one of the most important fields for the survival of our species."

"I thought we were running out of non-renewable resources."

"Yes, resources are the first stage where most intelligent species go extinct during Stage Up. The second most common reason for the extinction of intelligent species is Stage War. This is where a nasty microbe kills everyone. The aliens are advanced in microbiology. They purified my human microbiome before I could mingle with the locals. I had hundreds of types of predatory microbes in and on my body. You should do a complete microbiome. Any bacteria common to most people but missing in me are likely dangerous. I expect every minute I am on Earth I become more contaminated."

"Interesting. Is that why you look so damn good? You seem vibrant, alive, and almost perfect. Follow me to the bathroom. I have a few kits in there, and we can take some samples. I will also give you some specimen jars. I will need urine and poop samples."

"Once you have those samples, I won't look perfect anymore. My poop still smells."

"If you are free of bad bacteria, this would be a fantastic opportunity. You would be the benchmark. We could label any bacteria on you now as most likely safe, and we could study the difference. You are right. This would help us classify hundreds of bacteria types from innocent bystander to possible dangerous predator." As Diana took blood samples, she was forced to stand closer to him than usual. She was touching his arm. She thought of him as old, but he was not old anymore. He was her age. He was smart and a near-perfect male specimen. He could actually be a candidate for mating with someone her age. She wrinkled her face. No, no, no. He may be beautiful, but those thoughts did not feel right.

She had to change the subject. "My team will be here in about 30 minutes. Have you called your mom?"

"No, I wanted to call Mom all day, but I was running around trying to save the world. I kept putting it off. How can I explain a 13-year absence?"

"You should put her on speakerphone so we can both explain it. The story would be easier to believe coming from both of us."

"What story?"

"The truth, of course. That story."

"You are right. I want to tell Mom the truth, but the truth is so fantastic she might think I was lying."

"Have you ever lied to her?"

"Never, perhaps once when I was four. I played in a field and was cut just above my eye by a nail sticking out a rotting plank of wood left in tall grass. There was a lot of blood. You can still see the scar." He pointed to a small scar above his eyebrow.

"What was the lie?"

"I was crying. This other little kid told me I did not have to cry. He said a wise man was paddling down the sunset rays to heal the wound and make the pain go away. I believed him. The sunset was huge that day, providing a massive view of fiery glowing red light. It did feel better looking at the sunset. When

I got home, my mother was in a panic. The blood had covered half my face. She thought I lost an eye. She asked me what I was doing. I told her I was waiting for an American Indian, and he healed me. She was annoyed and demanded I tell her the truth and not some story. At the time, I thought the story was real."

"Well, she will believe you now. I know her much better. We have been talking weekly for many years." Diana dialed his Mom and put the phone on speaker. It rang more than 10 times, but Diana whispered that it takes her longer to answer now as she moves more slowly.

"Hello. Denise speaking."

"Mrs. Solomon, this is Diana."

"Oh, lovely. Nice to hear your voice, Diana. Any news from Lazarus?"

"It's me. Lazarus. I am back from the dead."

"Oh, thank God. I was so dreadfully worried. Are you okay?" said Denise.

"I am better than ever. I know that is a cliché, but it is true. I am really well."

"We thought we lost you. Diana wasn't sure where you went."

"I did not choose to leave. I did not choose to stay away for so long. I could not call."

"That does not matter now, my boy. You are back now, and that is all that matters."

"Thanks, Mom. I will tell you all the details when I see you. It is one of those 'life is stranger than fiction' stories. I have trouble believing what happened, and I lived it."

"When can I see you?" said Denise.

"I have a few things to take care of to get my life back. After 13 years, my credit cards have expired, my job is gone, and my life is upside down. I need to take control. I will call you again in a couple of days. The priority was to let you know I am well and home on planet Earth."

"I am so happy. Welcome back to planet Earth. Where did you go, Mars?"

"Ah, Mom. I told you it was a strange story."

"Get your life in control, and then call me."

"Will do," said Lazarus.

"One more thing. Please don't disappear for another 13 years without calling me first and letting me know where you are going."

"I will. I will call you in a couple of days."

"Goodbye, Lazarus. And Diana, thank you again for all your help. Did you make him call me?"

"I will never tell," said Diana with a gleeful chuckle.

Lazarus pulled his hand through his hair. Diana noticed it was a gesture he made when he was stressed. She grinned that he was more stressed calling his mother than negotiating with prime ministers and CEOs. The door intercom buzzed. Diana looked at the lobby camera and buzzed up the group.

Chapter 34 — Patents for free

The team entered Diana's apartment carrying boxes of pizza. Yasmin had a case of beer under one arm. Milton was also there with two boxes of desserts. Diana raised one eyebrow at Milton but acted as if nothing had happened. People were comfortable in Diana's kitchen. They knew where everything was and helped themselves to dishes and cutlery.

"I hope everyone remembers Professor Lazarus from 13 years ago?"

"How could we not? Lazarus gave us the speech about listening to what is not said because the part left out is usually the most important part," said Yasmin.

"He also proved to us democracy is not what our country does most of the time. We don't vote for religious leaders, corporate leaders, and project leaders though they greatly affect our lives either directly or indirectly by influencing our politicians. We praise and fight for democracy, but we rarely practice democratic processes," said Faith.

"Someone was listening. You remember that 13 years later?" said Lazarus.

"Yes, because I use it whenever someone gives a talk," said Faith.

"I need to give a quick speech," said Milton. He continued when everyone turned to him. "Last time, I got upset and left the group. I want to contribute today. I want to apologize for my actions last time. Also, I have some good news."

"What?" said Diana.

"I was looking up the statistics. When we started, there were 26 wars across the world, depending on which conflicts you count as a skirmish, terrorist attack, or a war. Today, we have no wars for the first time in millenniums. Some wars were power grabs by dictators. Some wars were labeled terrorism but were trying to replace dictators. Some terrorists wanted to be dictators. When we removed so many dictators, we changed many things. We have less crime, less corruption, and fewer wars."

"This team removed dictators?" said Lazarus.

"Yes, over the years, we must have killed 20 or 30 dictators using your little beetles," said Milton. "Most of the remaining dictators quit rather than make the kill list."

"You were following the plan, the articles of planetary constitutional leadership?"

"Yes," said Milton.

"Things are changing. This team is not some little ideological group of university radicals doing nothing but complain about a cruel world that does not understand how enlightened you are. You are all effective change agents," said Lazarus.

"Yes," said Diana. We are here today to issue the corporate planetary constitution. I thought we could distribute it in Davos, the World Economic Forum, where all the most powerful financial people gather. We could, once again, distribute the flyer putting the wealthy leaders on notice."

"The plan is good, but we need to pick our distribution person," said Yasmin.

"I will be in Norway tomorrow. The journey to Davos, Switzerland, is not far. I could do it," said Lazarus.

"Unless someone has a better idea, that will work," said Diana.

"I would like to use the same method to misdirect security. You know, what I call the rabbit hole approach. If we are consistent, we will build on the narrative I created," said Milton.

"That would be fantastic, Milton," said Diana. "Everyone agreed?"

"Are you sure you want to be involved, Milton" said Faith.

"Yes, you are my family too. I just want to draw the line at taking any corporate leader down," said Milton.

"Today, we are in a race to the bottom. I like your plan, Professor. The plan makes the rules planetary, preventing international corporations from moving to the next nation with the weakest labor rules. With this new plan, corporate leaders have to behave because we will leave them nowhere to go," said Pi.

"I have an announcement. Today, as you may have heard, Ares died. I was named as his replacement. I just came from my first challenging Board meeting,"

"Oh wow," said Milton. The group gave her applause with much shouting and hugging.

"Thank you, I think. As a CEO twice over, are any of you going to kill me?"

Everyone laughed weakly.

"Professor. You look exactly the same as you did when I first met you. In fact, you look a lot better. For example, your skin is perfect. I cannot see one blemish. Your hair is rich, thick, and curly. You are a bit of a hunk," said Faith.

"I agree," said Pi. "You look really, really good, and I don't compliment people much."

"If I was honest, you look the same age as me," said Milton.

"Thank you. It must be all the meditation and yoga," said Lazarus.

"While we are together... Hmmm. Damn, this chocolate cake is good. Thank you, Milton," said Yasmin. They looked at her, waiting for her to finish. She kept eating. Yasmin waved her hand. "Hmm, this cake is good. Sorry, I forgot what I was going to say." Everyone laughed again.

"I have something. As CEO, I was able to dip into the treasure chest of Ares's safe. What I found made me sick. He had many documents, for example, new types of batteries. These batteries would reduce costs and improve performance. He was buying technologies to prevent the world from moving away from oil, even if it meant total planetary destruction from the global warming crisis. He chose short-term profits over the survival of our species. It made me literally sick."

"You are looking behind the screen door, and one peak shows it was worse than our fears?" said Yasmin.

"Yes. One of my first acts as CEO is to fix it. I can think of no better person to assign this job to than you, Milton. I want you to go through the safe, look at every document, and tell me the best way to fix it. For each battery patent, I want you to talk to the scientists. Can you find out if they were rewarded, beaten, or cheated? I want their ideas published and to give them credit for their breakthroughs. I want the scientist, or if Ares killed the scientist, the scientist's family to share in any royalties. I think this exercise may give you a different view of the corporation of today versus the corporate mythology found in textbooks."

"It sounds like I will be doing some good," said Milton.

"Yes, you can improve the world for everyone. You can right some wrongs. We can share amazing insights and move technology forward for everyone. I must warn you. Looking at these documents made me angry, then sad, then physically sick. When I think of all the harm done to millions of people to protect one dirty industry's revenue stream, I want to cry. This will be your contribution to our planetary constitution. I will never ask you to kill someone no matter how evil," said Diana.

"I can do it," said Pi.

"Milton, can you call Leo? I want him to work with you. Take him to each meeting with the scientists. He should see what was done by Ares. He can talk to the damaged people involved. If my suspicions are correct, you will find that Ares promised scientists great wealth but paid them nothing for their inventions. He probably offered them 10% or 20% in royalties. They believed they would be millionaires when a big corporation sold their inventions across the world. As soon as they signed the papers, Ares buried the technology and sold it to no one. If you pay 20% or 200% in royalties on zero sales, you pay nothing. He got the invention and patent for zero dollars. He stole it, and the scientists did not become famous. The scientists spent decades of work for naught, and they may have died as paupers. Their families are probably suffering because the scientists spent their time and energies on a promise of wealth instead of actual compensation. Ares cheated them." said Diana.

"Scum," said Pi.

"Worse than scum," said Yasmin.

"And Ares was paid millions in rewards. We live in a society that is upside down. Our most talented author gets a 5% or 10%

royalty, while the mega-corporation that prints the book and distributes it gets 85%. What genius talent does the corporation offer the world that it takes 85% and leaves the author doing all the creative work with 5%?" said Lazarus. "I know there are printing and distribution costs, but the bulk of the money goes to the corporation, and the bulk of the work goes to the author. Work and money should go together."

"Well, friends, let's enjoy the beer. Tomorrow, Lazarus goes to Norway. In a few days, Davos people will get their notification of new governance rules," said Diana.

"Did you know that the membership fee to join the World Economic Forum is $60,000, and to attend the Davos Conference, another $27,000 is needed for one ticket? They spend more money on one conference than most people get to support an entire family for a year. It does make you think, given how poor I was when I graduated," said Milton.

The team drank too much beer. Diana was not as thrilled as the others by her promotion. She was intensely worried she would lose her soul, integrity, and maybe they would kill her if she made poor decisions.

Milton had worried about the team taking him back or not for a week. He was back, but this assignment could threaten his world beliefs. If capitalism was evil, what would replace capitalism? Communism was worse. Diana had suggested with her Russian example that any system was terrible if the leader was terrible. Was it that simple? The system is fair, fix the leaders, and all will be well? Diana was no wimp. What was in those documents that would make her throw up in a toilet?

Lazarus had visions of himself standing with German protestors at Davos handing out flyers until the police took him to a cold dark cell for 20 years. Should he have volunteered for such a dangerous task? He escaped Ares' wrath. Now he was taking on a thousand people just like Ares? The team drank too much beer, and the night clock kept ticking away.

Chapter 35 — Care for a game?

Lazarus spent the night on the couch. Diana was gone before he woke up. He had some fruit for breakfast and tried to get into his email. The account still worked, although he saw thousands of messages and spam. Starting with the new emails, there was a note from Milton, who had sent boxes of flyers to his hotel room in Davos. Most of the emails were no longer relevant. Any message about meetings or discounts from years ago could be deleted.

After removing hundreds of useless emails, Lazarus went over to an online chess website. He wanted to test if his intelligence had improved. He wanted to know if the improvements would last since he no longer had access to the alien bouncing ball game. He registered as a beginner and played the computer. The ratings for chess were respected worldwide and followed a proven and fair system. A beginner could start at 100. Social chess players would rank between 800 and 1200 points, and above that, you moved into a group of serious players. Club players would play competitively and read chess books. The highest rating in chess is 3000, but no one, not even world champions, attained 3000.

Lazarus turned on the rating system, set the game for tournament rules, and the system gave him a starting rating of 800. The tournament rules prevent you from taking back a silly move made against the computer. If you win a game, the rating system gives you points based on the skills of the person you were playing. The stronger the opponent's rating, the more points you get if you win, and the fewer points are removed if you lose. Lazarus won five quick games and moved to 900. The 800-point players made the occasional silly mistakes by putting pieces where you can just take them. Lazarus found the games took a little longer, and his opponents made fewer ridiculous moves as the levels increased to 1000 points. The system was good at finding opponents at your level somewhere in the world. Lazarus won five more games.

Playing opponents above 1000 was more challenging because they knew some tactics. These players would not make simple blunders. You had to be a bit clever to win. Suppose you executed a fork, where you threatened two pieces simultaneously. In that case, they can only move one piece to safety, so you can take the other piece. You could also win a piece with a tactic called a pin. A pin attacks two pieces stacked in a line. If they move the first piece, you can take the second piece. The games took longer and were more fun. Lazarus also found he could ignore the suggested opponent at his level and take someone a hundred points above his or her rating. With stronger opponents, he could move up his rating faster. In just over an hour, Lazarus moved his rating to 1200. If you are above 1200, you can enter an official tournament as a rated player and go against local or national champions. Lazarus had won 15 games in a row with no losses. He smiled, but this was to be expected. He was not a beginner. He had played chess casually for years. If the alien technology made him smarter, he could not tell. The chess games were a fun distraction to stop him from worrying about his tasks in Davos.

Diana came over for lunch, and they worked on removing the machine. The table was purchased with the primary goal of hiding the machine. It took some time, some sweat, a few curses, but they carefully got the machine down without damage.

"Knowing the machine was here, Iwas tempted to use it. I would have loved to fly around the world to see the sights, visit your mom, and just enjoy the thrill of the speed. However, with Ares on the hunt, and likely border agents on the alert, I did not dare risk more exposure. Where there is one Ares, there are probably a hundred. I could not risk it."

Lazarus nodded in agreement. They turned the machine on, and it worked. By angling it, they could get it through her doorway. It was much easier with two people. Once in the passage, they took the freight elevator to the parking area below the building. Diana pulled a tarpaulin over the vehicle. Once covered, the machine did not attract attention any more than the hundreds of other vehicles of all shapes and sizes.

Diana couldn't stay. Diana's cell phone was ringing every few minutes with work issues and even the odd journalist wanting to do a story on the young female head of one of the largest corporations in the world. The Norwegian Ambassador had agreed to meet in the lobby of Diana's building at 3 P.M. Lazarus had time to renew expired documents.

Lazarus looked online to plan his journey. He tried to respond to government requests for missing tax filings, renew his driver's license, and do other paperwork. He took another look at chess. The website chess.com included over nine million players at all levels. They had lessons on the most common openings used by experts and lots of information about upcoming tournaments. There was one world-class tournament, the Tata Steel tournament, that included world-class players, experts, masters, and even international grandmasters. Someone called Tata, the Wimbledon of chess.

You needed at least 30 rated games to enter the Tata tournament so they knew what opponent level would be suitable. The tournament was in Nederland in a small village called Wijk ann Zee, not far from Norway. The timing was right, but Lazarus did not have 30 rated games.

Lazarus began playing more games online to test his intelligence with more challenging opponents. As he played, Lazarus noticed he was not always making the most decisive move possible. You could not be cautious and wait for better players to hand the game to you by making some silly blunder. These players did not make stupid errors. You could block an opponent at this level by squeezing their pieces into smaller areas, so vital pieces had less range of motion.

Lazarus found his mind moving into overdrive. He started to look for ways to take the initiative. With the initiative, the opponent responds to your threat. You make another threat. The opponent has to react to the new threat. You control the game. The opponent can only answer and cannot make plans. The opponent does not have a chance to plot some devious multi-move combination to take you down. Lazarus found new ideas flooding into his mind. He needed to take control of the center of the board to easily switch attacks from one side of the board to another. He needed to keep the opponent guessing where the next battle would focus. With skill, Lazarus could attack the side where his opponent had fewer defenders and keep switching sides until he found the defense weak spot.

The game seemed more comfortable than he remembered. He was now playing people with a 1500 rating, although his rating was 1390. He felt confident until he was bitten by his first loss. He took a piece, thinking he was ahead. The piece turned out to be a sacrifice to put his opponent behind in pieces but ahead in position. This was a brutal lesson. You cannot focus exclusively on the material gain by looking at how many pieces you capture. Lazarus needed more finesse to win at these higher levels.

Lazarus was wondering how many of these chess lessons he could use when negotiating with Norway. How many of these lessons would prove valuable in handling corporate executives? For Lazarus, the goal was not making money or small gains in leadership but avoiding the destruction of human existence. He must ensure his focus stayed on what matters most, saving the world. Losing the king in chess is the end of the game; you have failed regardless of how many material pieces you capture. This is a lesson from this game for dealing with corporate culture. Corporations focusing on short-term material gains may lose everything in a pandemic from some nasty fungus. A trillion-dollar asset base where everyone eventually dies is a pyrrhic victory of absurd proportions.

Lazarus went to the lobby as arranged, and Dag arrived. They shook hands and went to the garage level. Dag, like everyone, had a first look of skepticism. Those childlike bicycle wheels supporting the machine did not earn his respect. Lazarus did not have to help him with the seat belts. Dag had spent some of his youth as a rally car driver. Dag enjoyed high-speed driving, which was his reason for asking to be the test subject. Lazarus pulled the strap to bring over the windshield. Pulling a leather strap was technically backward, and Dag looked distressed. Dag was calmer when the cabin hermetically sealed.

Lazarus drove out of the parking area and onto a street near Central Park. He was moving at street level. Dag was relaxed now. When the traffic got heavier, Lazarus moved a few feet higher and flew over the cars and across to a road in the park.

"That was convenient," said Dag with a wide grin. "I love how the machine makes no noise. This is like driving an expensive car.

"A commercial flight takes 10 hours or so, but I planned to make the trip in about 20 minutes. We will be moving at an intense speed. Are you ready for that kind of excitement?"

Dag laughed. "I may be old, but I love speed. Show me what you've got."

"Good. My speech was just words. This is well beyond a pretty speech. Your initial thought will be we are going to die, but I have done this many times."

"I am ready. When I go to a new speed level, it is always exciting. You always feel like you are going to die at any second. The danger is part of the excitement."

"Here we go." Lazarus pushed the button for the second phase engine. As always, the initial feeling was nothing happened. Dag was holding on hard. After about 10 seconds, he turned and gave Lazarus a curious look. He was about to speak when the machine drifted upwards and backward above the park as they gained altitude with increasing speed.

Dag closed his mouth. He watched in growing horror as the machine flew above the clouds, and the Earth began to look smaller. The planet kept moving away and getting smaller until Dag looked panicked. Then gravity reengaged. Gravity tension built, much like an elastic band, with the familiar burst of speed forward as the Earth caught the machine in a gravity embrace. The speedometer did the typical dance as the numbers spun from hundreds to thousands to tens of thousands.

Dag opened his mouth and closed it. He was speechless as they traveled at 33,000 Km/hour. He gripped the armrests so hard his hands were turning white, but his face was turning a little green. The machine dropped to the upper level of the clouds. Dag could see ships as small dots below, and he could see a jet airliner up ahead. They passed the commercial jet as if it was stationary.

"Whew. My God, that was intense. I did think I was going to die. I never thought the trip really meant a journey into space. Is that the actual speed?" said Dag pointing at the speedometer.

"Yes, just fast enough to do the trip in 15 minutes, and I added five minutes to get you to some specific street in Oslo."

"We will meet with our Prime Minister Erna at the Storting Building, which is what we call our parliament. We will have a few ministers in attendance. There is the finance minister, transportation minister, and other key staff."

"Great. I will bring the machine down to about 500 meters when we get close, and you can direct me?"

"That would work. I would enjoy showing you some of the landmarks. People think Oslo is boring, but we have wonderful architecture and parks. You will enjoy the city."

"I look forward to it. I have never been to a Scandinavian city. I planned to stay for a few days in Europe."

"Excellent. I set the meeting for 4:30 P.M. today. I am embarrassed to admit that I told them not to expect us today. I did not believe a 10-hour trip could be made in 20 minutes or even 200 minutes. The speeds needed would exceed all known speed records. They will be surprised to see us on time."

"I thought I might visit Nederland. They have a chess tournament."

"Yes, the Tata tournament is the most famous. I am also a keen chess player. You should enter if you can. They take all levels from grandmaster to class D players. The world champions often play there but are separated from the rest of us. Most tournaments do not mix grandmasters and ordinary players. The Tata tournament is open."

"Sorry to interrupt. Is that Oslo ahead?"

"Yes. I am surprised you do not have some impressive graphics GPS autopilot stuff?"

"My focus was on the speed and the engine. It took me 16 years to come up with the engine. I also spent time on security once I realized how dangerous the machine could be if used for harm instead of help. With the collaboration of Norway and Canadian engineers, we could add modern gadgets common to commercial airplanes. As you can see, I have no radio. I cannot communicate except my cell phone."

"Okay."

"When they invented the airplane, I read the engineers were excited and told Mahatma Gandhi that they could fly medicine and doctors to anywhere in the world as needed. Gandhi replied that they could also fly soldiers."

"Yes, he was wise. Technology is not good or bad. Technology adds power. It is up to us to use the new power to help or hurt," said Dag. "The big park in the middle is Vigeland Park. There are famous statues and a museum in the area. In the middle is the King's palace. As we approach, you can see on your right the Akershus Fortress. If your eyes follow the long tail of the park, you will see the round building we call the Storting Building, which is where we are going."

Lazarus followed the park past the palace, and they moved slowly around a large fountain in the park. They dropped to street level for the last few yards to the Storting building. When they pulled up to the building, Dag took a diplomat insignia from his briefcase and left it on the windshield. The two men stepped to the ground.

"Now we are back on solid soil, I can revel in the most exciting ride of my life. I had no expectation we'd go into space. I know you told us it was an interstellar craft, but I felt you were exaggerating. The beetle was convincing. Your story checked out. You are a respected Professor who went missing for 13 years. You gave us just enough facts and demonstrations to entertain the possibility you were a sane genius. Welcome to the Storting. I will get the Prime Minister in a few minutes. I set up an hour for you to win her approval."

Lazarus played over the speech in his mind. He needed to use what he had learned in chess. Lazarus needed to take the initiative and watch any positioning.

Chapter 36 — Meet the prime minister

After all the introductions, Lazarus began his speech. He took the initiative. He gave the first part of the presentation about the benefits to Norway. He ended that section with a question about whether Norway could succeed in getting political approval. He explained how only two countries would make and service the machines. After explaining there would be no corporate involvement, he ended with a question asking if Norway had the funds to set up the factories and train the workers. Each part of the speech ended by taking the initiative with a question. The Prime Minister was the one trying to convince Lazarus that Norway had funds and political will. Was Norway the best choice? Could Norway provide the needed security?

Norway agreed to allocate land and buildings for the project. They would provide Lazarus with a safe haven from corporate thugs trying to steal his machine. Every country in the world would need to come to Canada or Norway if they wanted to travel fast without using petroleum. Norway would add standard airplane technology to the machine, such as radio, flight tracking, GPS, heater, and autopilot. Norway would provide a method to file flight plans.

Lazarus now had the backing of a sovereign nation as protection. A government and an army would protect the machine from corporate raiders. More importantly, they agreed the project would be non-profit. Lazarus would be provided with a generous salary and a one percent royalty for his work, but he would never be a billionaire. Profits from the Norwegian operation would go into organizations such as Amnesty International, the World Court, or the World Health Organization. Norwegian leaders would decide. The first meeting was a success. He expected Canada would be a more complicated discussion because of the clause blocking conservative governments.

Dag was bubbling with enthusiasm. He showed Lazarus the sights of Oslo, and they toured the Viking museum. The Vikings sailed the world long before Christopher Columbus or Vasco De Gama. The Vikings had landed in North America around 800 A.D., which was long before Columbus.

Lazarus decided to take a train to Nederland to avoid attracting attention. The machine would remain in Norway until he returned. When Dag had to leave for government commitments, Lazarus remained in the park. The day was sunny, and Lazarus enjoyed the weather. He sat on a park bench and watched the water from the Vigeland fountain. Lazarus always found himself relaxing when he watched the water move. Lazarus smiled. He had traveled from New York to Norway, met with a Prime Minister, and brokered an international deal in a single day. Life was strange. Lazarus Solomon, a global innovator, was determining the flow of wealth and power. He laughed at the absurdity that he would have any control beyond his classroom and his little projects. After a short walk, Lazarus began his trip to Wijk ann Zee in Nederland.

He had one day before the chess tournament. He spent time getting his number of rated games up to 30 for the required number for entry. While always enjoying chess, he was never a star. He memorized a few openings. Chess openings have been cataloged for years to provide the best possible moves given almost any variation. Over millions of games, the openings are part of a system where you can move fast. You do not have to think much because standard openings are played by everyone and recorded for anyone to learn. He had moved up to a 1600 rating. He was not consistently winning, but he won four out of every five matches. Lazarus was not eligible as a class B player. If he could get to 2200, he would be a chess master. SF03 was correct. The brain exercises had added intelligence. Typically, it might take 10 years, and you might never reach a class B player level. Lazarus had taken about 10 days to go from 800 to 1600. How far could he go? Could he go from a social player to a chess master in a few weeks?

Wijk ann Zee was a small town surrounded by rolling green hills and was alongside a beach. You could see horses eating in a field. You could sit on the beach in a deck chair and enjoy the view of the water. From the beach, you could see the large Tata steelworks belching smoke just over the hill. Lazarus rented a room in a Dune Beach House.

He enjoyed wandering the streets of the small village. The park had numerous giant iron sculptures, windmills, and a few dogs basking in the sun. Eventually, Lazarus found the chess tournament venue and signed up for the tournament with some trepidation. This could be a road to misery and defeat. He may suffer constant humiliation and then go to Davos. Could he drop those flyers without being detected or arrested? This could be his last days of freedom, so he should make the best of the beach.

Lazarus enjoyed the sun warming his toes. Casually, he pushed his toes into the sand. Life was good. A young man about 30 years old walking by said something in another language. When Lazarus seemed confused, the young man tried English.

"Good afternoon."

"Same to you." Lazarus had to shade his eyes with a hand as he was blinded by the sun.

"I saw you at the chess venue. I think I also saw you at the fountain in Vigeland park earlier today. You just came from Norway?"

"Yes."

"I am also from Norway. I see you brought a chess set. Would you like a game?"

"Sure." The two men unfolded the board, set up the pieces, and played. The first game did not go well. Lazarus was crushed in a methodical and aggressive attack. They changed colors, and in the return match, Lazarus lasted a bit longer but was again defeated in the middlegame.

"I am not doing well. You are teaching me humility in large dollops," laughed Lazarus.

"You don't know me?" said the young man.

"Should I?"

"How long have you been playing in tournaments?"

"This is my first. They put me in the B class."

They played another match. Lazarus put his head in his hands and focused. He tried to think at least 10 moves ahead. It took imagination as he saw the positions of the pieces mentally moving around. This game was different. It took longer. The young man still won, but it took much longer. Lazarus made it to the endgame with only six pieces left on the board.

"You are improving quickly. You seem to learn with every move I make."

"I am trying my best, but my best is not good enough." They played a bit more, enjoyed the sun, and then the young man got up to leave.

"I am Lazarus. What is your name?"

"Magnus. Nice to meet you, Lazarus. You played well for a B player. I will see you at the tournament."

Chapter 37 — Cheer, cheer, cheer

Diana's office was more prominent than her entire apartment, so the meeting with her friends was moved to her office on the 54th floor. The ceiling was at least 20 feet high. The room was huge with a personal desk, a small meeting desk, a coffee table, couches, and chairs. She was reluctant but added Leo to the group because it was so important to Faith.

"Give us the update on the battery inventors." She looked at Leo and Milton.

"It was an emotional but productive effort. All of the inventors were promised great wealth in royalties because Enworld would promote technology across the globe. All of them were paid less than one penny after they signed the deal. One killed himself. They willingly acquired major debt because they expected a big payoff. They were living in horrible conditions and struggling. They had all signed non-disclosure agreements, so they could not whisper about their technology breakthroughs. Once we informed them that the technology would be promoted, they wept, hugged us, and danced. One sang. We told them that they would be published as inventors and become famous for their work. We have done a good thing," said Milton.

"Tell me about the results," said Diana.

Leo said, "We maximized the impact with a small public relations campaign for each invention. A mid-sized newspaper would interview the inventor. We encouraged everyone to speak freely, have photographs taken, and promote their breakthrough. As soon as the story appeared, the science press picked it up and carried the story. Through the magic of syndication, the story was widely circulated by mainstream media. The inventors are now famous. More importantly for us, our stock gets a bump up with each announcement."

"That is a bit surprising to me. We are an oil company. If batteries work better, that will mean more electric cars and trucks, which will mean fewer sales of oil," said Diana.

"What happened is our stock went up because we own the battery technology. Our oil competitor's stock went down because our energy is cleaner than oil. They will sell less oil. We might sell less oil, but we will sell a lot of batteries. Our stock did not just go up; our competitor's stock went down, and our competitive positioning is improved."

"Sounds good," said Diana. "We will also remove millions of tons of pollutants from the air. This initiative will help the planet breathe, and our children survive."

"Is the global warming threat as big as they say?" said Milton. The whole room groaned.

"We have eight billion people. If each person burns one log of wood a day, we are making too much pollution. You do not need any more information. Common sense says any number multiplied by eight billion is a big number. Yes, global warming is real," said Pi. "Sometimes I wonder why economists are thought of as scientists?"

"Hey, I was only asking because, in economics, you call climate change a *negative externality*. Negative because climate change is bad. External because economics does not include calculations for global warming. There is no market for pollution, so we cannot price polluting the air," said Milton.

"I get angry when I hear things like that," said Yasmin. "Just because you don't know how to price it does not mean it is not real. What is the price of love? Is love real?"

"Okay, okay. Sorry I said anything," said Milton. "I'm just saying capitalism does not put a price on pollution, that's all."

"We know capitalism is flawed. You just proved how incomplete capitalism is in giving us a happy life. We need Capitalism 2.0. We need a system that cares if people live or die," said Yasmin.

"What is happening with the youth serum?" said Diana.

"Phase 3 liver candidates are doing well. We have no side effects so far. That big shot board of director guy is also improving. We have a winner with this serum. We just need to keep going through the government approval cycles. For the youth cream, we cannot keep up with shipments, so we doubled the price. The public got a scare that we might run out, which led to a run on buying. People were stockpiling the youth cream. We tripled the price to reduce the demand closer to our manufacturing capacity. We are still selling massive amounts. All I can say is that there are a lot more rich people than I thought. It costs $3,000 an ounce, but we spend only $3 to produce it."

"Wow. This is going to make us rich. The magic of a monopoly. Of course, we went for more than 10 years earning no profit and spent a lot on research," said Diana. There was a long pause as everyone started to think about how much money they might get. "I have been thinking about the Davos Planetary Constitution. Enworld needs a project that is for the public good. Our Davos flyer demands I find a way to give five percent of our profit to some social good, or you will kill me. I don't want my friends to kill me as the CEO so we need a good idea. I was thinking of developing a new antibiotic or curing blindness in Africa."

"We have antibiotics," said Milton.

"Yes, but bacteria are becoming resistant to the antibiotics we have. People are dying from syphilis or a simple finger cut infection because some superbugs won't respond to any antibiotics," said Yasmin. "The issue is if we spend a lot of money finding a new antibiotic, the more we use it, the faster bacteria will adapt to beat it. If you don't use your product, it will work, but you are not selling much. If you do use the antibiotic, you sell more, but bacteria build a resistance. The formula does not work for a profit-focused corporation. You can make lots of money for a short time or make a little money for a long time. No companies making money want to invest in new antibiotics."

"That is crazy. Tens of millions will start dying," said Leo.

"Capitalism and economics do not solve everything. This is another example of wiping out the human race if we don't improve capitalism," said Pi. "Why do we have a Nobel prize for economics if we already have a Nobel prize for literature?"

"That is not funny. We don't make things up," said Milton. "What is the blindness thing, and why Africa and not here?"

"There is a cure for blindness that occurs in Africa because of a parasite. A pharmaceutical company has a cheap cure with pills that cost less than $20 to produce. The company won't sell the pill and won't release the patent so someone else can provide the medicine. The cure works, and people need it. Africans are too poor to buy the medicine even at cost prices. The company with the patent says they can make more money providing medicine for American dogs than curing blindness for Africans. It comes down to money. Africans do not have as much money to spend curing blindness as American pet owners have to spend on dog breath."

"It is obscene," said Yasmin. "This is just another example out of millions that your system of capitalism is not as good as you think. Every system has some strengths and some weaknesses. Capitalism is not a panacea. Capitalism does some things well, but it has some evils that come along for the ride. It may do some things well, but it does not do everything well."

Milton looked distressed as he fumbled with his pen and dropped it. Leo was quiet.

"Please give the ideas some thought. I don't want to be killed by my friends for not following the planetary articles I helped make. I suppose that wraps things up for today. Let's meet again back here in two days for another update," said Diana. People started leaving. Milton and Faith did not get up.

"You can go first, Faith," said Milton.

"Just a quick thank you for adding Leo to our group. I appreciate it, Diana," said Faith.

"I am reluctant. I almost gave Leo my heart when he was manipulating me. He is a liar," said Diana.

"I understand your concerns. Just give him a chance. He has changed. You won't regret it," said Faith.

"Well, he is here now. We will see. I hope you are right," said Diana.

"That is all I ask," said Faith and she left.

"Diana, I have been trying to find a way to tell you this for a long time. I made a bad mistake. I need to confess," said Milton.

"What?"

"When we first started this journey, I was poor. I was in debt and being evicted. I was desperate until you hired me. My landlord kept harassing me. He came to the house. He threatened me. He said he would put my whole family onto the street. At one point, he suggested I should prostitute my wife to him for a night to buy some time. I totally lost it. I took a beetle and vaporized him from the waist down."

"You committed murder. This is something the whole team has to know because it impacts all of us."

"I buried what was left of him in the backyard."

"But that means the body can be traced back to you. The method of killing will match the method used to kill the dictators. This is the first link between dictator killings and everyone in this group. We are all at risk."

"I know. I made a horrible mistake."

"Why are you telling me now? Did someone discover the body?"

"No one discovered the body. I am telling you because I finally have enough courage."

There was a knock on the door. "Time for your board meeting, Diana," said the secretary.

Diana stood up. "Milton, you have to tell everyone at our next meeting, and we need a good plan to protect each other." Diana grabbed her coffee mug and notepad. She headed out of the room for the one flight of stairs walk to the boardroom.

As Diana entered the room, the directors gave her a full round of applause that lasted a few minutes. The reception was a surprise. "Hip hip hooray," shouted the directors three times.

"To what do I owe this honor," said Diana.

"Our stock price is jumping every week with each new battery announcement. You have made tens of millions in equity gains for the people around this table and our investors. We are thrilled at your leadership," said Marcus.

"Ares bought those battery patents. He did not realize that he was building a monopoly as he bought more and more of them. Each patent allows no competition. Since we did not sell batteries, the authorities were not aware we were creating a battery technology monopoly. Battery manufacturers did not pull us into a bidding war. We have years of no competition. Everyone talks about the wonders of the free market, but no company really wants a free market. All companies want what we have, a big, stinking, money-generating monopoly," said Diana.

The board of directors cheered again. "She is not just improving the stock; she is saving my life with the youth serum," said Phillip. There were more cheers.

"My daughter asked me if I had any input into the battery technology changes. She said it would make a difference to the global warming crisis," said one of the directors.

"What did you tell her?" said Marcus.

"I took credit, naturally. I always take credit for other people's work." The directors laughed, but Diana did not find it funny. She did not care about the accolades. What she saw was a fat, corrupt, old, white man who lied to his daughter. This board had to go. Diana wanted a board representing the actual population, young and old, workers and managers, women and men, black and white, straight and gay, the whole big melting pot. She would start by replacing that antediluvian jerk.

"Have you seen this," said Phillip. He showed her a copy of Time with a picture of Diana on the cover. The caption said, "The face of the most promising CEO in corporate America."

"No," said Diana.

"That is because it does not hit the stands until tomorrow. I am on the Board at Time-Warner. This is tomorrow's copy being printed as we speak."

The directors cheered again. They shook hands and laughed.

"Is this the crisis that summoned me to an emergency board meeting? I was worried, gentlemen," said Diana.

"I admit it was my fault. We just had to congratulate you on the best performance we have seen in our lifetimes."

"Just a quick update before I leave. The youth serum is popular. We have doubled and tripled the price. It is selling for $3000 but costs $3 to produce. Our quarterly results will be good," said Diana.

The directors cheered again and slapped each other on the back. They hugged in a group.

"Diana, I was very cross that Ares forced us to take you on as CEO. I was mistaken. You are a gift, and God bless, Ares. You are amazing. You are a lifesaver. I give you my gratitude," said Phillip, Chairman of the Board.

Diana went back to her desk. The Board was happy and no crisis. This was a high point. Milton's mistake meant the team could be sent to jail for murdering 50 or 60 dictators. It would be jail for a thousand years. Next, the Davos flyers would be sent, and then the oligarchs will go bat-shit crazy. She was concerned about Leo and Milton. She did not trust Leo, and Milton had made a terrible mistake that jeopardized everyone.

Chapter 38 — Security circles

Within 120 seconds, when the first journalist picked up a Davos flyer, the story was published by every media organization in the world. This kind of story sold newspapers. Every radio station, TV channel, and talk show invited pundits to analyze every possible dimension of the planetary articles. When the first Article of the Planetary Constitution about political leadership was distributed to the United Nations, most security organizations considered the document a hoax. Thirty days later, when world dictators started dying across the world, the threat was taken seriously.

Most dictators had fair elections and complied with the new constitution. Many dictators who did not have fair elections died in the days that followed. Every world leader expended extreme efforts to appear to offer full democratic rights to citizens. The newly elected leaders did not want to spend money pursuing who killed the dictator they replaced. For the few remaining dictators, their national security efforts worked intensely to protect them within a fortress of walls, checkpoints, and protocols. Dictators who were afraid to leave the building were essentially putting themselves in jail.

The Davos articles on planetary *corporate* leadership appeared to be from the same organization as the *political* articles. It might have been a copycat document, but no one wanted to take a chance. Every major corporation hired more security. There were shrill outcries from the wealthiest people. Rich people own the most shares and did not like being told their corporations had to pay a fair share in taxes. They did not like planetary rules because they could not keep forcing everyone to lower taxes by moving the head office from one nation to another. They claimed 5% of profits would cause massive layoffs, and many factories would close.

The threat that the business would close was one of those mainstay threats used over hundreds of years whenever the rich were asked to pay one penny more in salaries. If corporations controlled governments, they could use their corporate power to ensure governments worked for corporations instead of for people. The shrill cry grew louder. The world would end if bosses had to pay the same tax rate as the janitors. If companies could not make weapons, how would anyone survive? A world without guns or wars would be too dangerous!

Rich people everywhere started bankrolling security employees, bodyguards, and assassins. The rich bought bulletproof cars, surveillance equipment, and mercenaries. The rich worked alone, in groups, and organizations. They used their 30 days with gusto. The focus and determination would have solved any world problem from global warming to curing cancer if some social good was their goal. Sadly, their goal was to ensure they did not have to share five percent of their wealth. They liked hiding their names in numbered offshore accounts. They liked owning politicians. They paid as many academics as they could find to promote the benefits of the rich staying obscenely rich. The debunked trickle-down theory was repackaged with new slogans. The trickle-down approach never worked, but somehow the best way to help the poor was to give the money to the rich. The only issue was the rich always kept the money, and nothing would trickle down to the poor, which is why the rich are rich. Rich people excel at taking money from everyone near them and keeping it for themselves. Their motto is 'greed is good'. Excessive greed is excessively good. If one cherry tastes good, two million cherries must taste better - except in the real world, it doesn't.

How many people were working all day and all night to find the authors of the planetary constitutions? Millions were most likely on the job to find the authors. This was a direct threat to the ruling class, not the puppet politicians. The curtain was opened. If you thought the rich did not interfere in your democracy, there was no hiding it now.

The Colonel wanted daily updates from Anna Ivanovitch. Guy Lacan at the UN was not seeing more security activity. The focus had moved away from political leaders. Guy found his only challenge was keeping his security experts from leaving for better jobs in corporations. Chris Gota at Homeland Security was overwhelmed by more than 200 emails and 50 calls every hour from influential people asking for help, leads, or insights. Interpol set up a special task force and gave them unprecedented powers. The threat to political leaders was like a hiccup compared to the demands made now. Chris was so busy explaining his progress to one powerful group and hearing after another, he could not do the real work.

"What do you think, Anna?" said the Colonel. "Is this the same group that helped get rid of those dictators serving lifetime appointments?"

"You mean the Mountain Men, funded by Russia, and a group pretending to be ISIS, which is the group pretending to be pretending?"

"Yes, that group? Same people?"

"Not really. The rabbit hole is much deeper. There are now multiple right-wing think tanks that are claiming to be the architects of the planetary constitution. The rabbit hole suggests that each of these right-wing groups is funded by right-wing billionaire families like Koch, Mercer, Sadler, and others. What makes it hard to track is how largely factually correct information is mixed with partial truths and factual omissions. Many of these billionaires actually fund these think tanks; however, we know that rich people do not want the new constitution. What we see is some truth about the funding, but a conclusion that is not true. Think of it as truth without truth. What is sad for everyone is the poor cannot make the rich richer if the poor have no money. The rich never seem to understand their wealth increases if they help the poor just a little."

"Keep the political commentary to a minimum."

"We help fund the NRA (National Rifle Association) lobby group because they make Americans afraid and weak. The NRA thinks every crazed American and visting terrorist should buy a gun. What better way for Russia to make Americans afraid? The NRA has lots of funding from right-wing people, and many right-wing people issue death threats to leaders of all kinds. On the dark web, I find links between billionaires, think tanks, and lobby groups. I see links to hate speech from right-wing groups, ISIS, and the Mountain Men. By selectively quoting hate speech correctly from the think tanks and lobby groups, but omitting the context, you have a perfect storm."

"What is your summary? Can we get to the point?"

"As fast as I find a trail, I find myself going in a circle. If I was to guess, I do not think we are chasing a person. I think I am tracing the flow of money and rhetoric from a sophisticated artificial intelligence bot. This whole exercise is a waste of time. Billionaires do not want to be nice to people. Right-wing think tanks do not want to ban war and guns. This is all nonsense."

"What do we do?"

"We have to go old school. We find a death, find evidence, and follow the trail of the evidence. You could spend a million years tracking false leads and bread crumbs that take you up and down and round and round. Entertaining and useless. I almost pity the analysts trying to track this stuff down. The bot loves to feed people who are hungry for misinformation and disinformation. The deeper you dig, the deeper the chain. Take me out of this basement. Let someone else run this team of 500 analysts. I need to get into the field."

"Hmm," said the Colonel. "You want to leave Cuddly Bear Inc. and explore America? It may not be as fun as the pictures. Okay, Anna. I'll put Sergei in charge. You can explore. Our cover as a social media company works well in Nashville, Tennessee. Now, we will see if you can do more operating like the Russian spies of the 1950s. You can find the person or group, bring them here or kill them. Bring them here is best. If they worked for us, we'd be doing better. We might convince them that they are working for an American social media startup. Half the analysts in this building still believe that lie. Funny how none of these American programmers find it odd that half the building holds Russian programmers."

Chapter 39 — Playing games

Lazarus looked at himself in the mirror. He kept changing. He had the mature face of a middle-aged man, but the skin, hair, brightness of his eyes, and everything else looked like a teenager. He looked young. He felt young and fit. He decided to go for a run, something he had stopped doing years ago because of his knee pain. Now he felt stronger. The run went well. He sprinted at the end and felt good. He had a warm shower followed by a brisk walk to the chess tournament.

The room was full of a few thousand people. Chess was more popular than he expected. He saw Magnus surrounded by a small crowd and gave him a wave, which the young man returned. Lazarus found his table. There were two groups, the masters and the challengers. The masters were famous players. Lazarus was one of about 2,000 challengers. He brought a chess set; however, it was not needed. The opponent was seated, clock and pen at the ready, just waiting for Lazarus. Lazarus was a bit nervous. Why? It was not like this was as important as a job interview. This was just a game. Lazarus smiled at himself. He even brought his *lucky* pen to annotate the moves. He was about to start, but the opponent stopped him. This was not protocol. You can only begin when the event officially begins.

"My first tournament," said Lazarus. The opponent gave him a wry smile that was more like a grimace. "Why should I suffer these fools," was what that attempt at a smile said to Lazarus. Lazarus looked around the room. A decent mix of ages and people. There were not many women.

The start call was made, and Lazarus began the clock for his opponent. The first 10 moves followed a standard opening and took only a few minutes. Lazarus played an opening called the French Defense, perhaps suitable given he was in Europe. Once the game moved into the middlegame, the pace slowed down. Lazarus was a bit bored, so he got up and walked around a few times. He could see Magnus in the section for experts.

Lazarus won without too much effort. The games on the beach helped as he focused on thinking five to ten moves ahead. The next three games followed the same pattern. Lazarus won by being careful, focusing on position, initiative, and thinking far in advance to predict what he would do for any opponent move.

With four wins, Lazarus was becoming more comfortable. The fifth opponent was a boy of about fourteen. The game followed the same pattern, with Lazarus playing black and the French Defense. Lazarus was winning, and the young boy looked increasingly sad. Lazarus felt badly. He was beating a young boy who looked like he would cry. The emotion split Lazarus's determination to win. The small advantage evaporated, and Lazarus lost narrowly in the endgame. The boy was thrilled, but Lazarus felt stupid. The object of the game was to win. He cheated himself by playing less than his best. He cheated the boy by giving him a win because of sympathy instead of his chess skills. The skills the boy should develop were chess skills, not puppy dog eyes.

The remaining tournament went well. Lazarus finished with only one loss. He played against Class B players, but his rating was closer to Class A. Lazarus was convinced his intelligence was much higher. He had moved from a rating of 800 to more than double that in less than two weeks.

Lazarus was surprised to find the event was live. People could see your games online. He did not wait for the prizes since he knew he didn't win a prize. Playing games was a time-wasting activity unless you could transcribe the experience into strategies and tactics for the game of life. He had to get to Davos. Davos was the real objective. All this chess was a subconscious diversion from facing what could be arrest and shameful exposure.

Of course, Lazarus did need to call his mom. He called her from the lobby of the hotel. They spoke for perhaps an hour. He told her how he met the Norwegian ambassador and Prime Minister. He would not have believed himself with such a wild story; however, his mother never doubted him. Whatever he said, she knew it to be true. He did not tell her about his terrorist objectives because one always needs a few small secrets. Lazarus packed his bags and began the journey to Switzerland.

Chapter 40 — Nobel guIllotine

The research was published. For the first paper using jellyfish biology to understand aging, Pi and Diana were the authors. The first paper was not referenced often. Pi and Diana's second paper on organ regeneration was an academic success measured by the number of citations. How many scientists cite your study is the standard measure of academic success. The reports were scientific and did not discuss the practical applications. Pi presented the paper at a few conferences, although at least part of her motivation for the speeches was picking warm, fun places to visit for free. Enworld paid for approved conference trips.

The Nobel people first contacted Pi as she was the lead author. Diana and Pi had won the Nobel prize for physiology/ medicine. Diana was reluctant. "You did the brilliant work, Pi. I don't deserve this honor. You are the genius. It comes as no surprise to me that you won this prize."

"You are humble. You researched jellyfish for years before I got involved. You always pointed me in the right direction. Every discussion we had, you contributed something valuable. Besides, I would enjoy your company," said Pi.

"I don't know. On my own, this would never have happened. It is your triumph."

"Without you, I might still be unemployed. I might be washing bottles for some snotty Ph.D. Professor in some backwoods laboratory. At the same time, he would take credit for my work. You deserve it as much as me. More importantly, we get the prize whether there are two names awarded or one."

"I feel a bit uncomfortable, but you have convinced me."

"Good. Stockholm, Sweden for us. An 18-karat gold medal, fame, and almost a million dollars. Not that you need the money," said Pi.

"I was lucky at money, but I am not lucky at love. I am almost 40. I have no husband, no children, and no prospects for love."

"It is hard to meet men if you are working all day and all night."

"The men I meet are not what I am looking for," said Diana.

"You want someone brilliant, handsome, and single. You want no emotional baggage and someone about your age."

"Yes."

"How about Lazarus? He is all of those things. I forgot how good-looking he is. When we first met him, he was just too old to consider. He is aging really well. He is clearly brilliant. And he is up to your standard, a highly moral person who kills evil people just like us."

"Not funny. Lazarus hasn't killed anyone," said Diana.

"But he is brilliant and handsome."

"He is beautiful for a man, but you make it sound like not killing bad people is a flaw."

"Do I?" said Pi as she fluttered her eyelashes and tilted her head in a cutie pose.

"Sometimes, you worry me, Pi. You are brilliant, but you seem to enjoy killing."

"Did I tell you that big pharma killed my mother? They started charging $7000 a month for her medication that used to cost $19. The company was bought by a bigger corporate predator precisely to charge more for the patented medicine. They essentially killed her and thousands like her for profit. Why? Because they could get away with it. Profit is more precious to them than life. I want revenge. I would love to kill those evil bastards."

"You are scaring me. We want to kill as few as we can. If one death ensures fair elections, less corruption, fewer wars, then that will suffice. That is why we gave them 30 days to hold a fair election. That is why we only killed a few and then waited to see if we could stop. We never wanted to kill anyone."

"They are the killers. They killed my mom. They kill for profits. I kill for revenge. They made enemies when they killed for profit. Now is the time for justice. I want payback. I want them all dead."

"Pi, I did not know about your mom. You are so quiet. You seldom speak, and when you do speak, you speak softly. Passion, revenge. Where is this coming from?"

"From the moment they broke my Dad's spirit with debts for my mom's medications, they made my Dad feel that he was killing my Mom by not having enough money to keep her alive. We should kill them all then nationalize big pharma."

"Pi, I am not sure I know you as well as I should, considering we have been working together for more than 10 years."

"What did you say last time? Big pharma doesn't develop antibiotics because the profit is not good enough, so indirectly let tens of millions of people die. Life is too precious to trust to those greedy pigs. All pharma must be non-profit. As a non-profit, they would make better decisions."

Diana was taking stock. Milton had killed a landlord. The first killing that could be traced back to them because he had access and a motive. Pi wants to kill as many assholes as she can. The world is full of assholes. You would be on an endless killing spree that would indubitably take a few innocents. What did they call the French Revolution? Reign of Terror. What have I done? Once the guillotine falls on the corrupt and greedy monarchy, it is hard to stop the guillotine machine."

Chapter 41 — Davos

Lazarus needed to plan how he would distribute these flyers Milton shipped to Davos. Lazarus had many ideas, and none of the notions were good enough. He looked around the hotel lobby. A few security guards were moving up and down, talking to each other, and checking doors were locked. Lazarus wondered how many people looked like hotel guests but were actually working as security plainclothes officers. Was he paranoid?

He expected there were store and hotel cameras everywhere. You might notice a few, but you only needed to miss one to have your image captured. He looked at the box of flyers. It was the size of a suitcase. He decided to take a walk and have lunch while he thought about the problem.

The day was perfect. Switzerland was picture-perfect and remarkably clean as he could not see any litter on the streets. The homes were immaculate and as pretty as the postcards. The Swiss did not just paint a house. They also painted a boutique of beautiful flowers on the walls. Most homes had flower boxes filled with flowers on windowsills. There were mountains and valleys in every direction.

Lazarus sat down on a patio of a small restaurant near the hotel. It must have been strawberry season because every restaurant offered strawberry and vanilla ice cream sundaes. They would put a whipped cream dab on the top and then add a small wafer. The dessert was delicious. He asked for a lemonade and ice drink.

While enjoying watching the bustle of people ambling in the walkway, Lazarus decided to look at the menu. He had trouble reading, so he took off his glasses and rubbed his eyes. Lazarus could read the menu correctly without glasses. He looked around and tried to read any text in the nearby shop windows. He could read them all easily without glasses. About 20 yards away, inside the enclosed area of the café, was a TV on the wall. He tried to read the text scrolling below the picture. It was clear and easy to see despite the distance and small size of the text. The text said two Americans had won the Nobel prize for medicine and physiology. Both winners were women, and the award was for innovation in organ regeneration. He waited for the next line to scroll. The women were Diana and Pi. He looked up at the pictures, and yes, there she was. It was Diana and her friend Pi. This was amazing.

Lazarus immediately wore his glasses and started to write a text message to Diana on his phone. Again, he found the small text blurred. He removed the $800 glasses that corrected his myopia and stigmatism. The perfect vision must come from those self-adapting, self-learning nanobots SF03 had given him. He had forgotten about the nanobots. SF03 said the nanobots would make improvements but could not say what or when changes would be made. SF03 said the changes are what you need as determined by how you live. Since he did a lot of reading, the bots corrected his vision.

Every day he felt a bit different. He had more energy, more strength, and stamina. He had small and subtle improvements in speed and balance. The bots were probably making little changes all the time to improve oxygen uptake, add muscle mass, and other improvements. This was a good day. Strawberry sundae, improved vision, and now a friend has won the Nobel Prize. He kept smiling about the Nobel. What a lifetime achievement! He remembered when she was one of four students living next door and taking introductory courses. She did resonate when he started talking to her about jellyfish regeneration. A jellyfish could look young but theoretically have regenerated 100,000 times to live a life of perhaps a million years.

The longer he sat at the patio, the more he realized how intense the security was becoming as the time approached for the World Economic Forum. The occasional passing policeman now included patrolling soldiers. He should have expected this change. The waitress came by and replaced the menus. The food was the same, but the prices were higher. A $20 meal changed to $55. When he looked at the sky, he realized what was missing. There were no hang gliders or paragliders today. The air space was being tightly controlled. With worldwide leaders and CEOs in one small ski resort, tight security should be anticipated. The issue of distributing flyers was getting harder and harder with every minute. Lazarus paid the bill and was grateful he got the old price.

Lazarus walked around what was a small town. He could see on the map there was one nearby lake, the Griefensee. The main attraction of the municipality was the magnificent mountains on every side of the town. He stopped to look in the window of a jewelry store. They wanted $80,000 for a watch, and that was not the most expensive watch on display. The prices were astronomical, and he should know given his time in space. The most expensive watch was over $160,000. Lazarus wondered if the watch prices had doubled over the last hour but expected these were the usual jewelry prices. As he walked, he became more concerned. The police were setting up roadblocks. They were checking cars and bags when people moved in the direction of the forum.

The odd aspect was anyone who could afford $50 for a hot dog and $500 for a hotel room could come to Davos. The resort was open to the public. Lazarus looked up to see private jets landing regularly and noticed police snipers setting up on top of some buildings. The security was becoming too much. Lazarus went back to the hotel without any new watches. The $50 Ironman Timex met all his needs. He did pick up about 30 flyers on travel and tours in the area from different storefronts.

Once Lazarus was back at the hotel, he bought a suitcase in the lobby. He opened the flyer box and put the travel flyers across the top to cover the planetary constitution documents. He put the entire box intact into the suitcase. He checked out of the room and rented a car in the lobby. This would save paying $500 for one extra night. The car was a small Fiat. The car was popular in Europe but too small to be sold in North America. A small car was suitable for the many narrow European streets. He put the suitcase with the flyers on the back seat so you could see it contained pamphlets. He put his bag with clothes in the trunk. The trunk was so small it was full with a tiny suitcase.

Lazarus drove out of Davos toward the small lake. The roads were not busy. The security checkpoints were focusing on cars coming into Davos and gave little attention to people leaving. A security person took a quick look in the window and waved Lazarus on. He did not ask to look in the trunk because only cars going into the town were given careful inspections. Lazarus was glad to leave. The lake, unlike Davos itself, was calm. The mountains were green with huge peaks and massive green forests. The road around the lake was not busy. The lake road was not the main thoroughfare.

Lazarus went exploring by driving up the side of the mountains. He kept going until he found a narrow dirt side road that looked unused given the bushes and branches in the street. There were no broken branches on the side of the road, so it looked vacant. Lazarus got out of the car and put his small suitcase on the car. He balanced the box on the suitcase. Next, Lazarus put four beetles under the box, one under each corner. Lazarus then turned on the beetles and raised the box a few inches above the car. He placed the last beetle in the middle to support any weight at that point from the flyers. Lazarus folded the top but did not tape the box closed. Next, he programmed the beetles using his phone and downloaded the instructions. When done, he clicked the Go button.

The box soared up until Lazarus could no longer see the box some 2,000 to 3,000 meters above him. If he programmed correctly, the flying box would move horizontally at a slow pace until roughly over Davos. The box would then drop altitude at speed to about 500 yards above the ground. Two of the beetles would move in a 180-degree arc to flip the box over and empty the contents without slowing down. Once the box was flipped, the beetles would return at high-speed to Lazarus.

There was a risk the box would be spotted, and a sniper would shoot. If a drone were in the air, a bullet hitting the drone directly would destroy the drone. A sniper bullet into a box of papers would probably damage a lot of flyers but not all. Once the box tipped the content, the flyers would spread in every direction so the sniper could only damage a few flyers. A direct hit to the beetle would be a significant problem, but how likely would it be that a bullet aimed at a 15-inch box hit the two-inch device supporting the box? It was a chance, but the beetle would be so destroyed it would not be useful evidence. Any radar would be scanning for metal, something large such as a military drone, not a flying cardboard box of papers. Lazarus was careful to not touch any flyer in the box. All the tourist flyers he touched were in the car.

Lazarus did not have to wait long. The little beetles, all five of them, returned to him in a few minutes. The box was gone, and the job was done. He sent Diana a text. He was confident at least some flyers would be picked up by the abundant media people.

Chapter 42 — Going home

When Lazarus got back to Norway, he found Dag had resigned his post as an ambassador to lead the new machine organization. Dag was eager to show Lazarus the site for the new factory and head office. They would repurpose one of the petroleum buildings until a new location could be built to specifications. The initial project was to mine the asteroid belt and use funds from that work to bankroll the rest of the projects. Startup funding was in place to begin work. Lazarus was impressed.

Canadian officials were calling Lazarus to meet with junior politicians. The officials wanted Lazarus to file funding applications for a small business startup. The officials offered a few thousand dollars of matching funding and partial salaries if you hired up to two students. When Lazarus asked for a meeting with the Prime Minister, the officials laughed and found it amusing. Norway had approved the project, signed documents of understanding, allocated a senior leader, set up a credit line of ten million dollars, and provided a building. If Canada was going to be a player, Lazarus would need a new approach. He needed to go to Canada and talk to his local member of parliament.

Lazarus downloaded some blueprints from his website of flowers and gave them to Dag so Norwegian engineers could study how to add the robotic pilots and mining technology to the existing machine. Lazarus was careful to build his machine in components, essentially replaceable, standard parts, so you could work on one aspect of the device without knowing about the rest of the engine.

Dag was overflowing with enthusiasm. He spent almost 10 hours showing Lazarus all the progress they had made in the few days since the Storting meeting. Lazarus thought the meeting would take an hour, not 10 hours. At 7 P.M., Lazarus was tired, but Dag was on rocket fuel.

"Could someone file a flight plan so I can fly the machine to South Africa to see my aging mother tomorrow?"

"Sure. I can take care of that."

"How was your trip to Nederland?"

"I enjoyed the Tata chess tournament. I did not win, of course. This was my first tournament, so I was just getting the *lay of the land,* as they say. I met a Norwegian, a young man called Magnus. We played a few games on the beach."

"Did you beat him?"

"No, he crushed me in every match. I lasted longer in the last game but still lost."

Dag laughed, "Yes, we are proud of Magnus. He is the reigning world chess champion, you know?"

"Oh. That Magnus. I have seen his name. I knew he was important because he was playing in the special masters and grandmasters section. I was with the thousands of peasants."

Dag laughed. "We should come up with a good name for our company and the machine."

"Yes. You pick the company name. I will find a product name for the machine. I have been calling it the machine for almost 20 years," said Lazarus.

"We have a deal. Did you see what happened when you were gone? The Davos thing?"

"You mean the planetary leadership contractual thingy?" said Lazarus.

"Yes, the planetary articles of the corporate constitution."

"What do you think?" said Lazarus.

"My friends like most of the articles. We hate rich people hiding behind numbered companies. We like the idea of corporate interest in social improvements. We love the end of war and weapons. I had to laugh at the death sentence and carving up of corporate assets for the naughty companies. Is that the correct word, naughty?"

"Naughty works for me," said Lazarus.

"Enjoy your trip to see your mom. When you get back, expect to see progress."

"The machine only flies during the day since it has no headlights or navigational equipment. Just so you know," said Lazarus.

"Here is a company credit card to access the company line of credit. Hotels are expensive in Oslo."

Lazarus spent the night in a nearby hotel. He had strange dreams about prime numbers. He was trying to find a formula to generate prime numbers. The equation that had eluded all mathematicians for thousands of years. The dream started simply. No number can be prime if it is an even number except number two. He removed all even numbers. No number can end with a digit of five and be prime except the number five. This left just numbers ending in 1,3,7, and 9. There are ways to work with numbers divisible by three or nine. These little rules are easy to understand for any grade school student.

Since prime numbers cannot be generated by an equation, there are large prizes over $100,000 in a race to find larger prime numbers. In the dream, Lazarus kept finding methods to look for the prime number formula. He created a map in a rectangle of the numbers with the prime numbers highlighted. He dreamt of turning the rectangle in different directions to find the formula. The rectangle did not work. As numbers become bigger, the gaps became larger among primes. He imagined turning the two-dimensional rectangle into a three-dimensional box but that did not work. Given the broader gaps in larger numbers, he turned the box into a cone to allow larger gaps at the cone's bottom. He changed the cone's circular base radius, so the primes lined up as the cone got larger in height. He dreamt of using multi-dimensional shapes to generate the next prime number.

The dream morphed into finding primes for cryptology. Given there is no formula for prime numbers, security systems use prime numbers as part of the encryption methods for keeping passwords secure. At this point, with various shapes of sine waves and cones, Lazarus awoke. Strange dream. Who dreams about mathematical formulas?

Lazarus got into the machine and flew to South Africa for the second time in 13 years. What was supposed to be a weekly trip became a journey to other worlds beyond his imagination. The trip was uneventful. No rogue rockets tried to kill him, and no pelicans flew into the machine. He enjoyed the trip. He enjoyed watching the magnificent animals of Africa walk across the veldt. Since the engine had no noise, the animals were not spooked and running away. He could just admire them as they gracefully moved.

When Lazarus saw his mom, she looked much older. Her hair was completely gray, and she used a walker to move about inside her small cottage. Mom had a handrail along all the walls for support. She had nurses come twice a day to check her blood pressure and help her with compression stockings. Mom was mentally sharp, but her body was failing.

"My boy, you look wonderful, Lazarus. You look so young and strong. Your skin is so perfect. Blond curls. No glasses. You were always good-looking, but now you look like a movie star."

"Aw, Mom. You always think I am wonderful. The smartest boy in the class. The future leader of the world. I can do no wrong."

"That is because you *are* wonderful."

"Every mother is proud of her children. I am not so special," said Lazarus.

"Allow me to be right, just this once."

"As you wish, but only if you allow me to make you some tea," said Lazarus.

"Then you win. What is that wonderful smell? Is that you?"

"A lot of people have been telling me that recently. I don't know what they are talking about. I can't smell anything different about me." Lazarus dipped his head to his armpit and sniffed loudly. "Nothing. Smells the same."

"No one can smell themselves. Your nose adjusts to smells. You can only smell new smells," said Denise.

"Okay. I am making tea. Remember when your friend Joanna came over. I made her tea and gave her two teaspoons of salt instead of two teaspoons of sugar?" said Lazarus.

"How could I forget? She tried to be polite and drink it before she admitted you made the worst tea in the country."

"You did have the salt in a sugar bowl. I could not see the difference between the two white crystal additives. Shows how smart I am," said Lazarus.

The two laughed as they remembered the look on Joanna's face as she tried the tea. Joanna was too polite to complain, but the tea was unbearable. Lazarus spent the night in the guest room. He made his mom her favorite breakfast, porridge, and fresh fruit. Lazarus hated the porridge, but he ate with her. He told her about his recurring dream. For two nights, he kept dreaming about geometrical shapes and prime numbers. He also told her he was feeling much more active. He needed to take up some sport like judo, swimming, or perhaps tennis. He was no longer comfortable just walking and reading.

Chapter 43 — Blame Higgs-boson

Diana had the next team meeting at her home so they could relax more. She got so many interruptions at work and was always tense that someone may hear their more dangerous plans. The team came up to the apartment in one big group. Leo was with them.

"Welcome, everyone," said Diana.

"We bring wine and good cheer," said Leo.

"I was wondering if we could go around the table and get any concerns from everyone?"

"I'll go first," said Milton. "The activity on the dark web is stratospheric. We have a major viral buzz, as Leo would say. As a form of protection to distance ourselves, I never post anything. I use a little machine learning program, a neural network, which can self-learn. The program creates deeper and deeper circles of fake postings from fake accounts. The fake postings point to real accounts of right-wing think tanks, extreme right billionaires, and militia groups. Militias like to talk about killing people, and right-wing social media often send Democrats death threats. It is easy to make these groups look like the authors of a leadership constitution that kills leaders. I have them chasing their tails. A hungry snake that eats its own tail. This was actually fun. What is scary is the number of page hits has gone up by millions. Removing dictators got some attention, but any program threatening the rich is in another league. There are now millions of followers focusing on finding us."

"That is some update," said Yasmin.

"Since we are confessing sins. I confess a sin. When my Toronto landlord wanted to evict my family, he started harassing my wife and demanding sexual favors. I killed him using the beetle. I know it was wrong. It was done more than 10 years ago, but I constantly worry about it. I also worry that my actions will lead back to this group since he does have holes in his brain."

"Oh, no. What did you do with the body?" said Faith.

"I put him in a metal tub, coated him in acid, then slid the whole thing into a hole beneath a garden shed in the backyard."

"By now, the whole brain would be gone, eaten by bugs and acid. The body could point to you, but it should not point to this group," said Yasmin.

"I would like to go next," said Pi. When the 30 days expire, I volunteer to remove the first four or five CEOs to prove this was no idle threat. They can behave with empathy or die without mercy. I don't need help because I have a good plan. Does everyone agree to let me proceed?" The team nodded. They were relieved they did not have to take on some risky missions.

"Everyone understands that while I am part of this team, I will help in other ways, but I cannot kill corporate leaders?" said Milton. Again, the team nodded.

"My main concern is that Diana is in charge of everything. We naturally turn to Diana to be our leader. I think that is wrong," said Yasmin. "I would like to lead too." The room was quiet. Each person was processing. What would it mean to switch leaders? What would change, and what should they expect? Why now?

Eventually, Diana spoke. "I never wanted to lead. I miss the lab. When I took the job, I knew it was not a real job. Ares hired me to use me to find Lazarus and steal his machine."

"That was all true. Ares sent me to find some way to get the machine. I suggested Ares hire Diana because it would make her part of the team, and he could use her to find Lazarus," said Leo. "Once I met Diana and got to know her, the whole episode has been my shame to carry. Once I met her, I started falling in love with Diana for real."

"I only took the job because I wanted to pay off my student loans. I also wanted to help all my friends get jobs. I did not know if I could manage Ares, but I tried to help everyone do better while desperately trying to keep Ares from controlling me. I had to fight daily for any integrity by turning intellectual cartwheels to balance demands," said Diana.

"This is a good time for me to speak up. I know Leo was not totally honest at first, but he is now. I love him, and I want everyone to commit to being more respectful to Leo," said Faith.

"It is fine. I know I lost everyone's trust. It can take years to build trust and only one minute of stupidity to lose it. All I ask is a chance to prove myself," said Leo.

"It is not fine. Not at all. If any of you love me, then you love and respect my decisions. Leo is my decision. As for you, Leo, you never told me you fell in love with Diana," said Faith.

"That was years ago, and we never got past the first kiss," said Leo.

"Look, I somehow managed to prove to Ares, once he hired me and got to know me, that I was a worthwhile employee independent of Lazarus. We have built something valuable here for all of us. We have done amazing things for the company, each other, our customers, and the world. I don't want to lose any of you," said Diana.

"Nice speech, but you are still in charge. You have a big job. You are a CEO twice over. You run this group even though no one asked you to lead our group. You won the Nobel. You get the big perks and all the big decisions," said Yasmin.

"I never asked to be CEO. If you want to lead that is great. How about you lead Omega Biotech. You can be the CEO of that company."

"No," said Pi.

Yasmin gave Pi an angry look then turned back to Diana. "Why Omega and not Enworld?"

"Because the board of directors at Enworld are ruthless bastards. They lie and are proud of it. They admit they like taking credit they don't deserve. They are a bunch of fat, immoral miscreants. They will do everything they can to block you. Prove yourself at Omega, and you'd have a better shot at taking over Enworld."

"Because I am black?" said Yasmin.

"I don't know, but it would not surprise me. The board would also dislike you because you are a woman, and they won't like that you are young. If they treat you like they treat me, they will threaten you, try to intimidate you, make insane demands, and act like privileged spoilt children. They will offer little support or counsel, which is the reason they are on the board. Combined, they represent all the prejudices behind a thin veneer of educated conversations and expensive clothes," said Diana.

"What about religion?" said Pi.

"You think they'd hate me because my parents are Muslims? I am an atheist. I believe in science, not the supernatural," said Yasmin.

"I would not be surprised if they disliked you for being an atheist and for having Muslim parents. What they love most is themselves. The more you are like them, the less I would like you, and the more they would like you," said Diana.

"Why don't we have articles in the planetary constitution for religious leaders?" said Leo.

"What is wrong with religion?" said Faith.

"Religions are not transparent. They do not post their finances online for the world to see. They say they want money to do God's work but spend money on things like protecting pedophile priests or buying corporate jets for an evangelical minister," said Pi.

"They have little regard for women. They promote dismissive ideas about women in Catholic edicts and Madrassas. The law of the land is that women are equal, but they have no Catholic women as bishops, priests, or cardinals. If a woman wants the job, she has a right to apply according to the law in this country. The job should go to the person with the most merit. Why do religious people get to pick what laws they want to follow, and the rest of us must follow all laws? It is nonsense. If they don't hire a woman for a leadership post, they can prove in court that the guy had more merit. If they fail to prove he was more qualified, they can pay $10,000 a day until they correct the error," said Yasmin.

"That is blasphemy," said Faith.

"What is blasphemy? That is saying you can never improve. If there is a better idea, you can never talk about it because any change to Middle Age ideas would be blasphemy. Any change to any idea, any little bit of progress, would be blasphemy," said Leo.

"You. You are supposed to be on my side," said Faith.

"I lived in the Middle East as a child. They kill people for the blasphemy of daring to have a different opinion," said Leo. Diana noticed people were talking faster and louder.

"My religion shows me the love and respect of God. Religion gives me divine guidance. I get satisfaction being part of a religious community. I have spiritual experiences of transcendence," said Faith.

"You are a biologist. These sacred texts don't understand basics like evolution. How can any scientist believe these pre-medieval myths? There are no real answers in these sacred books. These books do not explain if an experiment on black holes is moral, or what Higgs-Boson particles are?" said Pi.

"Why are we talking about quantum mechanics," said Faith.

"The Higgs-Boson is called the God particle because it can create something from nothing. These religious books are a waste of time. They talk about concubines, camels, and slaves, not genetic modification and nanobots. The questions I want guidance on are not about concubines. I want to know if it is safe to create a Higgs-Boson particle in a cyclotron? The Bible has no answer. These texts are not relevant to the key questions of today. Besides, we have no proof prayer works," said Diana. "I have read many experiments testing prayer. Do any of you know about that famous experiment that proved prayer is real?"

"No," said Faith. "Did someone prove prayer works?"

"If there was any proof, we would hear people quoting the famous experiment daily. The scientists would be celebrities. How is it possible that no scientist produced a single replicable experiment that prayer works in thousands of years? Is there zero proof? We cannot say with any confidence level that there is any evidence to prove prayer works."

"That's it. I am done. We are leaving. Come on, Leo," said Faith.

"I want to stay," said Leo.

"Fine, you asshole. I just defended you but stay if you want," said Faith. She slammed the door when she left.

"This meeting was not successful. We did not solve any issues. We mostly vented frustrations. I am concerned the team is falling apart. We cannot move into this next phase without helping each other. The most powerful people in the world are mobilizing, and they want us on a barbeque spit. I am not sure if that is my fault or not," said Diana. "Yasmin, could you convene the next meeting and lead it?"

"Sure," said Yasmin, "and thank you, Diana."

Chapter 44 — Prime number dreams

Lazarus flew back to Canada. For the first time, he had not attracted too much attention from the border and security people. This time he flew outside of national borders staying more than 200 miles off the coastlines. He followed the sea up to the coastline and landed in Greenland. Using his contact with Dag, he got a flight plan to Canada. When approaching Canada, Lazarus kept the machine ten feet above sea level to attract less attention.

Lazarus tried for a week to make progress in Canada. He called politicians, government departments, and old friends with connections. The sum of the efforts amounted to some good conversations and some offers to work with an industry partner. He could tell from the conversations that many of these people thought he was a crank. He sent many emails and kept a folder of all the contacts even if they were dismissive.

The best plan would be to help Norway mine minerals in space and start selling the engine for use within national borders. Once Canada saw the economic boon to Norway, they would be eager to pursue him. He considered but rejected the absurd idea of asking the Norwegian Prime Minister to promote his machine to the Canadian Prime Minister on behalf of a Canadian citizen. The second national license was not in Norwegian interests, so the request would be too embarrassing.

He had daily video chats with Dag and spent the mornings answering questions from the engineers. They had a timeline to do the first exploratory missions within 12 months. The plan was for a robot machine to fly to the asteroid belt, distribute 100 shoebox-sized beetles to hop about prospecting asteroids for precious resources. There would be no mining. This would be a prospecting and cataloging mission to tag and scope opportunities. Lazarus wondered if Norway could claim asteroids as sovereign land by leaving behind a flag.

What went well in Canada was Lazarus got his banking, passport, and other documents finalized. He would no longer have to use a temporary passport or driver's license. Now, he was a real person in the great book of the bureaucracy rather than a missing or presumed dead persona.

Each afternoon, Lazarus would play a few chess games online, and he took judo lessons. For chess, he was reading the top five books and playing in online tournaments. Lazarus kept improving his chess rating inexorably. He was now 100 points short of the expert rating of 2000.

On paper, he was a man in his fifties. He felt and looked like a fit man in his mid-thirties. Lazarus was faster and stronger than the other people in judo class, but Lazarus downplayed his abilities. He spent his attention learning the techniques of the throws and falls. Since he was not working much, he was able to go almost every day. He was pleased to move from a white belt beginner to yellow in two weeks. Lazarus was not sure if that was faster or slower than most, but the judo helped keep him fit.

He also continued to have dreams about prime numbers. He played with ideas on the computer. He looked at discussion papers about Mersenne numbers, decomposition, and weights.

He did not find any elegant solutions but was baffled by some suggested answers. There were prizes posted. If anyone could find a prime number with more than 100 million digits, a group called the Electronic Frontier would pay over $100,000. The most anyone had found was a prime number with about 23.2 million digits. He kept dabbling with graphic solutions because no one had found a numeric pattern to prime numbers.

For Lazarus, the main goal was to ensure survival for the planet. Lazarus hoped his work with Norway would prevent the Stage Up extinction. He needed to talk to Diana to work on the Stage War extinction from some microbe. The antibiotic project was one she planned to fund using 5% of the Enworld profits. He needed to talk to her more about the importance of that work. Lazarus decided to take a train to New York.

Lazarus still had the DNA enhancement product from the aliens. They had said there was a small chance it would kill him. They also said it would be painful at times. They said the risk was small enough it was logical he should take it. He did not like the idea of pain. The aliens talked about a bit of pain when they burnt his toe fungus and cauterized his colon growth. The aliens had a casual attitude about pain. He was a wimp. They would not have insisted on him taking the DNA enhancements with him if it was not the right thing to do. Before he had time to change his mind, Lazarus opened the case, took the vial, and drank the potion.

Lazarus waited for the pain. Nothing. He waited to see if another arm or eye grew out of his body. Nothing. Did he have any ability to climb walls or fly? No. He felt and looked exactly the same. Was it a test of courage? Who knows what the aliens thought? Well, it is done now. If I wake up tomorrow with six hairy legs, I guess then I will know. Six legs would have some benefits.

Chapter 45 — Take a walk in the park

Diana called Lazarus. She wanted company. She spent all her time working and her friends were not too friendly since the last meeting. Lazarus was her calm water. He could give her guidance, which she might consider, but he could give her support, and she needed lots of support. She felt attacked on all sides. The Board members were like sharks swimming around waiting for a meal. Her friends had different and conflicting needs. They were not cohesive, and she could not fix the issues alone. The problems were too fundamental to who they were and who they wanted to be.

She had cared for Lazarus's mother and maintained his home for 13 years. He could give her some support. She invited him to stay a few days, or a few weeks if he wanted. She was working most of the time, so they would only have a few hours in the evening to talk. It would be nice to have a friendly smile at the large apartment. If he turned her down, she could get a dog. However, dogs need walks, and she was gone so much it would not be fair to the dog. It would be better to get Lazarus for a few days. Lazarus was less maintenance than a dog.

Lazarus was intrigued and accepted her offer. He felt like a tourist on Earth. The journey to his home planet was not intended to be permanent. He promised SF03 he would return, and Lazarus had never broken a promise. Your word is your bond. Your word is your reputation as a professional and as a gentleman. Mom had made sure he was first and always a gentleman.

Diana and Lazarus had a glass of wine. She put on the gas fireplace and sat on the couch with a blanket over her legs. She had lots of wine as she seldom had house guests. She could let go for the first time in years.

"The project is going well in Norway but has no traction in Canada. The Canadians don't take me seriously and don't want to take risks on my crazy ideas. In Norway, they will be prospecting the asteroid belt within 12 months. Given the current pace, perhaps sooner."

"That is a great success. This will prevent human extinction from Stage Up," said Diana.

"Yes. The next stage of extinction is Stage War. The war is not with other humans but with the trillions of microbes around us. As a biologist, I was hoping I could count on you to manage the microbes?"

"Another job. Hmm. I have one plan in the works. Omega Biotech, my little startup, will develop new antibiotics. We will allocate 5% of our profit to this cause."

"I have a suggestion. We know that the bacteria constantly evolve to defeat any antibiotic we design. Why don't we play the same game? We don't focus on one antibiotic that kills one kind of nasty bacteria. Instead, we develop an antibiotic microbe that keeps changing before the nasty bacteria can develop herd immunity."

"That is an excellent idea."

"My thought is to focus as much on our method as the product. We work on speeding up our method of inventing new antibiotics. I am not explaining the idea well. We should assume things will change. We should assume changes will keep coming faster as microbes learn to adapt faster. We are not just designing a new product; we should also design a faster process to exceed the microbes' pace of change. If our pace of change is faster than the pace of change of the nasty bacteria, we win."

"You explained that perfectly. It is amazing how someone states the obvious, and once said, it is obvious to everyone. The thing is that before you stated the obvious, it was not obvious to anyone."

"That sounds a bit convoluted. I am not sure I am as smart as all that."

Diana laughed, "Seeing the obvious is not a skill many have. Would you like to take a walk in the park? It is just a couple of blocks from here."

"Sure."

"Just let me take off these work clothes and put on something comfortable."

As they left, she looked more closely at him in the elevator. He was getting more handsome each time she saw him. He also had this elusive scent that she found irresistible. Did he always smell this good, and she didn't notice because he was so old? She found the smell addictive. It was nice to be near him just for the scent.

The night was clear, so the stars and moon were bright. They walked into the warm night. She felt happy, truly happy, for the first time in years. All those years, she thought she'd killed him, and here he was just talking and walking down the street.

She grabbed his hand. "Come on, let's run," she said. She ran, and he ran with her. She picked up speed, tugging him along.

She let go of his hand and ran down the path into the park. He vaulted the three-foot stone wall passing her and waited at the bottom. She came up to him, a bit breathless, while he looked unperturbed.

"You don't seem winded?"

"I have been exercising. Judo on most days."

It was dusk. The couple wandered the park listening to a musician somewhere near playing the trumpet. The music was excellent, and the birds were singing their evening song. They settled on a park bench. Diana sprawled, sticking her legs out, her arm along the top rail of the bench. She looked up at Lazarus. He smiled. She flicked some hair from his eyes.

"Did I ever show you the golem?"

"No. I don't know what a golem is. You have other inventions?"

Lazarus took out his wallet and removed a square three-centimeter piece of plastic. "This little plastic square can be unfolded into a pyramid with a square base. The material is unique. This was one of my early failures when I tried to find a way to solve a high-speed collision without injury. This material is unique in how it absorbs the energy of a collision." Lazarus unfolded the plastic to form a pyramid. Diana reached for it, but he pulled back. "This little thing is dangerous. It is highly effective at absorbing energy. Any pressure, light, heat, or impact will be absorbed. It will protect whatever is inside. This was the design. I wanted to protect anyone in the machine from a collision or air friction."

"That doesn't sound dangerous. It sounds like a success. This was exactly what you would want for the machine moving at high-speed and hitting a pelican."

"You are not familiar with the story of the golem. The golem is a little boy made from clay. An inanimate boy brought to life by magic. The golem is a friend. The golem can protect you by killing your enemies. The golem grows and keeps growing until it becomes huge. The golem is big but clumsy. A huge golem could kill you by falling on you. A golem could starve you by eating too much of your food. My little plastic golem absorbs any energy. The energy has to go somewhere. The law states energy cannot be destroyed or created. Each hit, shock, or burn makes the golem bigger. The issue is how do we make the golem smaller? We cannot crush it. We cannot burn it in a fire. It can only grow bigger with every exposure to energy. This is the danger. This is why I can never use it."

"What happened to the golem boy in the story?"

"In the Jewish mythology, you bring the clay boy to life by writing a magic word on his forehead. The word is *truth*. You kill the golem by erasing each letter from the last to the first. Unfortunately, my golem material does not have a forehead or the word truth inscribed. I have no way to destroy it. Whatever I do makes it bigger."

"I see the problem."

"This is why I carry it. It is my burden. I am the maker, and I must carry the golem." He put the small plastic item into a small tin container and back in his wallet. A woman in tight yoga stretch-pants came jogging on the path. As she got closer, she winked at Lazarus.

Diana got angry. The brazen woman could see he was with someone. The woman just flirted with him like Diana was invisible. Some people have no class. New Yorkers are aggressive. In New York, with 10 million people on a few little islands, if you don't take what you want quickly, it will be gone in a few seconds.

"Did that woman just wink at you?"

"Woman. What woman?" said Lazarus. Diana smiled. He was oblivious, a dreamer, and a visionary. If he was focused on some concept, he might not know the year.

"Let's find the musician?" she said, taking his arm, squeezing it, and putting her head on his shoulder for a few seconds. It felt good to be alive. She was happy again despite the golem story with the unhappy ending. The trumpet player was professional. This was the joy of New York. You could walk down a street and hear Miles Davis playing the trumpet in the park. The song was *Summertime* from Porgy and Bess. It was an uplifting song. She was so glad she called Lazarus.

They found a small group of people around the musician. Diana put a dollar in the hat at his feet. The songs were smooth and fit with the starry night. "This was a good idea," Diana said. "I am glad you came. I was feeling down." They were enjoying the music. The guy was talented.

Three teenage girls came up to Lazarus and stood directly in front of him. When Lazarus noticed, the bigger girl said, "My friend Susan likes you. She is a virgin."

"Don't tell him that I am a virgin," said the smaller girl with a distressed look.

"My friend Susan still likes you. She is a bit of a slut."

"Oh, my God. How can you stay that!" said the smaller girl, mortified.

The three girls burst out laughing. "Virgin, virgin," sang two of the girls while their fingers pointed at the small girl's head. The little girl ran off, and the others kept laughing as they skipped after her.

"New York!" said Diana aloud, but she thought that women young and old wanted Lazarus. He was not that old Lazarus playing with engines in a dark garage any more.. This Lazarus was hot and fit. When she was with him in public other women eyed him, flirting openly, and men carefully averted Diana's glances fearing they might annoy her robust partner. Looks aren't all that matters, but Lazarus was smart and caring too. More and more Diana felt herself drawn to him. Pi was right as always.

Chapter 46 — Ignore the papers, eat on the floor

Diana made sure to leave the office early. She wanted to see Lazarus. She had been glancing at the clock all day. She was embarrassed to admit she kept thinking about him. When she finally got home, she opened the door to a huge mess. Lazarus was on the floor drawing diagrams. There were hundreds of pages of papers on every chair, table, and floor. Lazarus did not look up when she came in.

"Sorry. I made a bit of a mess. I will clean it all up. I think I have cracked the code," Lazarus said without looking up.

"What code?" said Diana. This was not her plan for the evening.

"The prime number code," said Milton as he came out of the kitchen eating cold spaghetti from a tin.

"The what?"

"Your Professor has found a formula for prime numbers. He is a genius. It has something to do with the shape of multi-dimensional conical topologies," said Milton. "Come over here, Diana. I will explain it to you." Milton grabbed a chair and removed a small pile of papers, some crunched into balls and some with red marks, circles, and formulas. "You are going to love this idea. There is a $100,000 prize to generate a 100-million-digit prime number. The record to date is a

23-million-digit number. Lazarus has generated prime numbers of 100 million digits, 200 million digits, and 500 million digits. The formula works."

"Why are you here?" said Diana.

"The security code protecting computer passwords will be vulnerable if people can easily test for primes. Lazarus does not want to publish the formula until there is a method to secure passwords. Without secure passwords, we would have worldwide chaos. He has designed a system using irrational numbers from Euler and other sources to replace the prime number codes. The method is clever because he combines methods. First, he takes a compression algorithm to make documents smaller. He then encrypts the smaller documents, which run faster because of the smaller file size. Encryption is harder to break because the method has multiple layers. A simple but clever method using two large irrational numbers and not just two large primes."

"And this will allow the world to keep their secrets?"

"Much better than that. If you want security, you give the new Lazarus website the document and a password. The system will protect information from everyone. For individuals, they get free access. For organizations, they pay a fee that is based on how many documents they have. Most people get total security for their messages and financial transactions for nothing. Big companies pay big dollars.

The endless ability of hackers, mostly government agents prying into their own citizens, will be stopped. Non-government hackers trying to steal will be stopped too. The government cannot see the document because the irrational numbers keep changing. Lazarus can see every message and every transaction for anyone in the world if they use his system. When he publishes his formula in a science journal, the Lazarus website will be the only site to secure secrets adequately. Eventually, someone will build a new security system around some huge irrational number."

"Could the government just seize his servers?"

"No, for multiple reasons. No server has all the code used to encrypt. The code is broken into segments across servers dispersed in many locations. Any nation that tries to take down a server will lose encryption services for weeks. All the citizens of those countries will be transmitting money and messages that can be decrypted by almost anyone."

"I see."

"Do you see the whole picture? Lazarus claims the prize. He published the formula for academic triumph. He makes trillions of dollars protecting our worldwide secrets. He has full ability to disclose evil-doers anywhere and everywhere. Your government can no longer spy on you. Pure genius. Lazarus has asked me to build the servers and programs. Can I work on this and pass my official Enworld projects on to my backup person? Please say yes. This is just so amazing."

"When?"

"Now. Right now. Today?"

"As long as your backup person can call you if they get stuck. You have two weeks to provide any help needed. If you trained your replacement well, then you won't have any work. If your training was poor, you are going to be busy."

"Totally agreed." Milton threw his hands around Diana's neck and hugged her. He gathered up all the documents on the kitchen table and left. "This is just so awesome," he said as he walked around picking up a few more specific papers.

"Sorry for the mess," said Lazarus. He looked exhausted.

"Did you eat anything today?"

"I am not sure. I don't remember."

"Good, I brought some Chinese takeout for us. There is a Chinese place nearby that is scrumptiously good. Don't worry about the mess. Have something to eat and recharge. Here. We can clear this little space on the carpet."

"Hmm. This does smell good." Lazarus stuck a fork into a chicken ball and munched away. He closed his eyes. "I am hungry. I got a bit obsessed. I know you have a big deal job. I will clean it all up. I will be the perfect guest when you come home tomorrow."

"You made a mess, did you? She reached out and squeezed his cheek. "I might have to spank you."

"If you had told me about the spanking, I would have misbehaved sooner."

"Clean it up to my satisfaction, and I will give you a kiss." She felt awkward flirting. She had no flirting skills, and she knew it. She had spent years talking to Milton and never once suspected he loved her. All she knew well was the world of microbes.

They enjoyed the meal and kept laughing. They told stupid jokes and anecdotes. She laughed and enjoyed the stories even when they were not that funny. "How do you make an apple pie from scratch?" said Lazarus.

"I don't know?" said Diana.

"According to Carl Sagan, first you need a universe." It was silly, but they both found it funny. She was giggling. Happy, happy, happy. It was so good to be alive. She was exhausted when she came home. The place was a mess. Now it was much later, and she was fully energized. She wanted to talk for another hour.

Why go to bed? If it was her choice, she would fall asleep in his arms on the carpet.

Chapter 47 — It has started

The next morning newspapers were running stories about the deaths of five executive officers in the pharmaceutical industry. The deaths happened at the lobby headquarters of PhRMA (Pharmaceutical Research and Manufacturers of America[1]). In addition to the executives, five security bodyguards and two senior lobby group managers were killed. The deaths were similar to the dead dictators. Each victim had multiple holes throughout the body. The demise was caused by brain trauma due to large holes in the brain of each victim.

The articles did not just discuss the deaths. Most media mentioned the one billion dollars PhRMA spent on elections and the high price of drugs when pharma-friendly legislation followed the bribes/donations. Some of the more liberal media also discussed the possibility of collusion and anti-competitive behavior, given the executives were all attending the same meeting. Given the date, 31 days since the Davos flyers, it was clear there was a bounty on any executives who thought business as usual would not be risky.

Article 2d of the planetary constitution clearly stated no corporation may pay money to political campaigns. Lobby

1. https://en.wikipedia.org/wiki/
Pharmaceutical_Research_and_Manufacturers_of_America

groups always pay and lobby politicians. The vastly improved security of the last 30 days did not provide any protection.

Diana was angry because Pi had removed two managers and five security people. No one agreed to collateral damage. Pi had dispatched everyone in the room even though security people do not control changes to corporate governance. All the changes needed could be done without hurting security people if the mission was planned correctly. Diana called Pi, but there was no answer. She waited less than a minute and called again. She called three more times in 20 minutes, and finally left a message saying 'we must talk as soon as possible'. This kind of slaughter would lose supporters. The team knew from public polls that an increasing majority of citizens supported the removal of dictators and wanted corporate leadership changes. This kind of killing would undermine the constitutional goals.

Diana ate her breakfast of two walnuts and a banana. She could hear Lazarus in the shower. As she looked out the window at the sunny day, she fantasized about stripping and joining Lazarus in the shower. She thought about him holding her, soaping her body, and taking a towel to dry each inch of her body. She gave herself a squeeze, shook her head, and started packing her bag for Stockholm. If Pi did not call her back, she would have to talk to her in Stockholm when they got their Nobel prizes.

Lazarus came into the room. He wore jeans and no shirt. He looked taller. She must be wrong. You don't grow taller when you are 40, but you might grow more rotund. He had slightly wet hair. He was big with defined muscles. Ripped.

"What's up?" he said.

"Pi killed 12 people yesterday. Five CEOs from big pharma, five bodyguards, and two senior lobbyists. She is engaging in war. I told her not one person more than needed. We only need to remove one or two CEOs as an example, and there will be improvements. We should never have collateral damage."

"Talk to her," he said.

"I tried. Pi is ignoring me."

"Or, she is moving through a tunnel. You will see her in Stockholm."

Diana rushed up to Lazarus and put her head on his bare chest. She looked up at him. "Why don't you come with me? We can take the corporate jet or fly in your machine."

"We could see the progress in Norway. Would you have time to join me on that trip after your momentous award?" said Lazarus.

"I'd love to. I cared for that machine for years. We are old friends."

"I have selected a name. We don't have to keep calling it the machine. What do you think of Herald?" said Lazarus.

"Herald. A word meaning a sign something is about to happen. Good choice."

"Let me send the 100-million-digit prime number to the Electronic Frontier for the prize money. The file is big, almost one gigabyte. I also need 10 minutes to pack a bag, and I'll be ready to go."

"I thought you did 200 and 500 million digits as well? Anyway, take your time. The beauty of a corporate jet is it won't leave without us."

"I will just send the 100." Lazarus threw a few things into a bag, put on shoes, and he was ready.

Diana was in a rehearsal for the award. Lazarus went to the Rockaden Chess Club, the most prominent chess club in Sweden. The club was hosting a speed chess tournament, with each player having a maximum of five minutes per 60-move game. The game would be over in less than 10 minutes. Lazarus loved it as the first game was fast, ferocious, and fun. You could make a mistake, but the quicker the game, the more likely both players would make a small error. It was possible to recover from a mistake. The game was a knockout tournament, so each round, half the players were eliminated. They started with more than 80, but the ranks thinned quickly. Lazarus was having fun blasting as fast as he could. There were players of all ages. Most players were much younger than Lazarus. The size of the crowd watching grew as quickly as the size of the players left became smaller.

Move, hit the clock, move, hit the clock. Pitter patter. The moves were like rain pouring across the board. With a rating of near the 2000 expert level, Lazarus was holding his own. He was the great unknown. He managed to make it to the final match; however, he made a midgame error. The opponent took control and never gave it back. Lazarus was beaten but came in second. Apparently, speed chess was not just for fun as prize money and ratings were included. Lazarus was now on the map. Photographs were taken. People cheered the winner, a young man from India who was already famous in chess circles, although he looked like he was still in high school.

When Lazarus left the club, around 11 P.M., he saw a message on his phone. Diana was having coffee with some of the Nobel winners in the hotel lobby bar. There was also a message from the

Electronic Frontier. They were wildly excited by his submission. If proven successful, this would increase the largest prime from 24 million digits to the aspirational 100 million. They were running a Lucas-Lehmer test hoping to verify the prime number. They wanted to meet as soon as possible, anytime and anywhere. Lazarus wrote back, offering them Oslo or Stockholm if they wanted to meet in person within a week. As he was answering, there was another email from Milton. He was making progress. Following the plan was not complicated, as each server set up was taking less than a day. The code was done. He expected to be ready in a few days for a test, not in weeks or months.

Lazarus could see Diana through the street level window as she sat amongst six distinguished older gentlemen. They looked the part as each man had years of experience, gray hair, and some with beards. Diana was young, pretty, and brilliant. Everyone else looked like a wise old academic. Naturally, she was the center of attention. The men, given how they sat around her, were competing for her attention. Lazarus found watching her pleasing to the eye. Lazarus went in and pulled up a chair to squeeze in next to Diana. He got a dirty look from the guy winning the peace prize. There are no rules in love or war, thought Lazarus. Diana put her hand on his and gave it a small squeeze.

Lazarus looked up and saw the writing at the bottom of a TV. CNN claimed there had been another assassination. Breaking news headlines scrolled that two CEOs and the President of the NRA (National Rifle Association) gun lobby had been killed. The method of killing was the same as the large pharma killings.

"Was Pi at the rehearsal?" Lazarus whispered in Diana's ear.

"No. I told the Nobel committee that Pi might not make it, but I could accept on her behalf. She is on a dedicated mission from hell and does not care about prizes and glory."

Lazarus brought up the news on his phone. The top story was about the NRA, which he showed to Diana. She stayed with the jovial meeting, but her mood was different. The laughs and smiles were more subdued. She was tense, and the smiles were tighter.

Chapter 48 — A kiss in the dark

Diana was on stage for her award. Along with the wives of the other winners, Lazarus was in the front row of the audience. Diana looked spectacular. She was the glamourous movie star of the Nobel ceremony. She wore a black velvet evening gown that flowed to her ankles. She had a string of pearls as a choker around her neck and her long hair in a French bun style. She wore simple pearl earrings. She walked gracefully. He noticed, compared to the others, her posture was regal. She sat straight, head up, as the princess of all and sundry below.

She accepted the medal and began her speech. "I accept this award humbly. I started my trajectory because I had a casual conversation with a neighbor who was thinking aloud about how to find the age of jellyfish since they can reverse biological aging. This chat created an obsession with the intricacies of longevity. Once on this trajectory, my destiny was set. My collaborator Pi is sadly not here. I am accepting on behalf of both of us. The genius of the practical gains belongs to her. My contribution was only theoretical. I was the sounding board to Pi's breakthroughs. I feel Pi deserves this award more than me. I wish she could be here. In science, we live in a space-time continuum with all times and locations equally available. In my life, time moves only forward, and a choice once made is a fulsome commitment. My work creating Omega Biotech was again a result of what I thought was a minor commitment to testing a new engine. From that moment, I had made my choice. My work creating Omega began. I would like to thank my team, my friends, and most of all, Professor Lazarus. My team made me who I am today." The audience clapped.

Diana's words reverberated in her mind. She understood how much Lazarus was the architect of her life. He imparted so many glorious ideas that hid away in her mind and were at her disposal when she needed them to guide her toward new discoveries. A small decision was continuously magnified each day.

After the awards and speeches, some speeches too erudite to follow, Lazarus and Diana walked around the building to explore. They passed into a dark corridor, and Diana gave Lazarus a full kiss on the mouth. He returned the kiss with passion. They lingered and kissed again. They were a little breathless when they returned to the reception foyer. She took his arm as they walked. It felt comfortable. Her hand linked to his arm; it was precisely the right thing to do. She was exactly where she should be and with exactly who she should be with. She looked up at him. He was growing. The rented tuxedo was dashing, but he was over six feet now.

The Electronic Frontier had booked a conference room in Stockholm to meet Lazarus the following evening. Milton sent a long email with too many details about the new website. Milton said the servers were ready and could launch in the morning.

Yasmin said she was unable to arrange the team meeting. Pi was not responding. Faith was still angry at everyone. Diana was out of town picking up her Nobel. Milton had disappeared but was at least responding, saying he was too busy this week, but next week would work. With some embarrassment, Yasmin admitted that she was wrong to ask for the leadership role. People are not like working in the lab. People are unpredictable and unreasonable. People get upset if you don't give them things, and if you give them things they asked for, they can still be upset. She admitted she was the proof. She wanted to be the manager. Now she had the job; she hated being a manager. Budget fights galore. Faith won't talk to Leo. Milton is too busy for everyone. Pi won't speak to anyone. Diana commiserated, "Welcome to my world."

At the hotel, Diana and Lazarus walked by a wedding reception in one of the hotel's ballrooms. They could see the dancing and laughing family. A guy emerged from the room and spilled his drink down his jacket. The chandelier and wine were sparkling. Diana grabbed Lazarus and pulled him onto the dance floor. He effortlessly swung her around him. They were not good dancers. They were a scientist and professor who spent their time thinking and reading instead of dancing. They made up for their lack of skill with bountiful enthusiasm. The two of them were jumping and swaying. They did not pretend they knew what they were doing. Two people having fun, enjoying the beat, and enjoying a kiss before retiring to their room. Diana was glad she had booked one room with one double bed.

Chapter 49 — All my clothes are shrinking

The next morning Diana felt wonderful. The world was beautiful, the hotel was wonderful, and the sunny day was wonderful. The birds were singing again. The coffee was wonderful. As the song goes, "what a wonderful world". She did something she never did. She relaxed. She went to the balcony, took her coffee and danish pastry, and sat enjoying the weather.

"They call that a continental breakfast. Coffee and a pastry. I call it a snack," said Lazarus.

Diana smiled as she beamed joy in his general direction. "Were you ever married?"

"I had a few tiny romantic adventures. I am not adept at noticing the subtle signals of mating rituals. I am usually daydreaming about some intellectual challenge. I think I might be love retarded," said Lazarus.

"Funny you should say that. I found out recently that someone I saw almost every day for four years in college was in love with me. It was obvious to everyone, but I was unaware," she said.

"I could see how that might happen. Everyone is in love with you, so the behavior seems perfectly normal from your perspective. People love you. All systems are normal."

"Very funny. I am almost 40, childless, and not married. In a few years, I will be a confirmed lonely spinster," she laughed.

The TV was on. There was another spate of executive deaths. A financial investment conference for primarily hedge fund managers had been targeted. The CEO of Goldman Sachs Bank, two other executive bankers, and the CEO of three hedge investment funds had died. All the deaths occurred in the elevator of the conference center. Diana and Lazarus watched the story unfold.

They showed a clip of a clearly shaken executive asking for time. "We will pay our share of taxes. My bank has agreed to return all tax subsidies. We also like giving five percent of profits to social good. Beginning next week, we will give Amnesty International a weekly stipend. As a bank, we do not buy or sell weapons, but we have some mutual funds, including gun manufacturer stocks. We will be selling our investments to defense manufacturers. I would ask whoever is responsible for these killings to give us time to adjust."

Another executive was demanding action. "We need to find these people and bring them to justice. They are challenging our American way of life. We need to hunt them down and bring them to justice. NOW." The pundits debated endlessly, as usual.

"Turn it off. I can't stand it. I am not killing people, but I still feel responsible," said Diana.

"You told her... you told everyone to remove as few people as possible, then pause to see if changes were forthcoming. You never promoted a systematic execution of all wrongdoers. You wanted as few egregious perpetrators punished as possible to promote better behavior. You cannot blame yourself. You never wanted daily executions," he said.

"Why is any of this necessary? Why would leaders not want to live in a rich community and a rich, successful society? Why do they want to take so much? The leaders create a much better world for the top 0.01% and a much worse world for the other 99.99%. It should never have come to this," she said.

"I'm turning off the TV. We cannot stop Pi. We don't know where she is. She is not listening, and we cannot make her listen. We can at least enjoy our day."

Diana got up and put her arms around his neck. "You are right. We have today. We never know how long we have. We should enjoy our few perfect moments." They spent the day together. The time moved quickly. Without any effort, the time disappeared in an aura of magic.

Lazarus spent some time preparing for the meeting. He started by submitting his prime number formula to a science journal. It would take them a few weeks or months to peer review and publish the article. Next, he compiled documents he would share with the Electronic Frontier group. Diana was dealing with the infinite number of calls and emails any CEO could expect. When Lazarus started getting ready to go, he realized more and more of his clothes were shrinking. He should pay more attention to washing in hot water rules to prevent shrinking fabrics.

"Your clothes are not shrinking. You are getting bigger and stronger," said Diana.

"You may be right."

"Here. Stand against the wall. I will use my cell phone to measure your height." Diana fiddled with the phone. "You are about 6 foot 4 inches. You are getting bigger, which is odd for someone almost 40. Your muscle tone, your skin, everything about you is improving. I expect you are much smarter too."

Lazarus thought about the DNA concoction he took. He decided not to say much because he knew nothing about it. He thought about the nanobots self-adapting to make him better. He had no idea what they were doing. He knew from the bouncing red ball exercises that his intelligence quotient was perhaps the highest in the world and at least equal to a grade five alien. He wondered if the DNA concoction was making him smell better. The DNA changes may be trying to improve his chance of breeding by improving his smell? Flowers used scent as part of the breeding process. The new smell was attracting women around him. Women were definitely treating him differently. Women wanted to be near him. He assumed it was the smell.

When they got to the meeting, Lazarus looked for the room. They were not sure which way to go. Diana pointed to a placard in the hallway. "That's you in the photograph. Look how old you look." They had a placard with Lazarus's photo, an announcement in purple and gold glitter over the prize amount, and an arrow pointing to a ballroom. When they got to the meeting, they found the room had about 200 people in the audience. The stage was a long table for a panel of experts, a microphone, and a few flowers and notepads.

"I expected to see around five people," said Lazarus.

"Looks like it is your turn to be the hero," said Diana.

The whole event must have taken planning. How did they find all these people in such a short time? There were many announcements, some applause, and many strangers came up to shake Lazarus's hand, pat him on the back and praise him.

He was not used to this attention and was unsure how to take it graciously. The event was built with speakers discussing the organization and its goals. With hoopla, they gave him an oversized cheque for $100,000. Many people were posing for photographs, and Lazarus was invited to speak.

"I did not prepare a speech. I did not expect a big crowd. I should say I was lucky more than brilliant. I had a compelling dream that pointed me in the right direction. I am sure almost everyone in this audience is better at mathematics than I am. I do not have a mathematics undergraduate degree or graduate degree. My Ph.D. is in physics. You could all ask me some mathematics questions I could not answer. I will, however, keep the trophy and the money. The money will be given to help improve learning analytics in grade school. I do have a small question. Is there a prize for a 200-million-digit prime number?" The audience clapped with vigor.

"We have not decided. We were basking in your glory for the 100 triumph. We have no second goal," said the organizational spokesperson.

"I have a 200-million-digit prime number on this small USB memory stick." The audience thought he was joking and started to laugh. "I have a 500-million-digit prime number on this second USB stick." The audience stopped laughing. They realized he was serious. "I need two sticks because the 100-million-digit number was a large file, almost 1.2 gigabytes. The 500-million-digit number is a much bigger file because the numbers are longer, so I needed 20 gigabytes. When I say I was lucky, I mean the kind of luck that comes in threes. As math people, you probably like to measure luck in numbers. The

Electronic Frontier can have the first stick if it agrees to pay a prize for the first stick and offer a second stick prize."

"I'll pay $20,000 US for both sticks?" said an audience member. "I am from the US military. We offer $10,000 for any new prime number as part of our encryption effort."

"Would you take 50 Euros for the first stick?" said the host from Electronic Frontier as he counted the loose cash in his pocket.

"Yours," said Lazarus.

The audience went crazy. Someone screamed, "I will offer 200 Euros for the second stick if you give it to the Electronic Frontier."

"Done." Lazarus gave both sticks to the Electronic Frontier. The audience cheered while the military guy sat down chagrined. Lazarus left the stage and went to Diana, but he was repeatedly stopped for hugs and handshakes. He finally reached her.

"I am glad I was not the speaker to follow you. That would be a hard act to follow."

Diana and Lazarus left after about 20 minutes. The people kept milling around Lazarus, but he was eager to go. Some attention was enjoyable; too much attention was uncomfortable.

Chapter 50 — Exposure

Lazarus and Diana drove by rented car to Oslo. The trip was less than five hours. When they stopped for a snack, Lazarus bought a newspaper. Diana took a turn driving while Lazarus read the headlines of the main stories.

"There are stories of more deaths amongst CEOs. Some oil executives from Brazil, Russia, and the Middle East are dead. They were having an OPEC subcommittee meeting on a ship offshore of Portofino, Italy. As an oil CEO, you know OPEC is a lobby group and organization to control oil prices." I guess they must have felt safer being at sea. They were wrong. The headline on the front page says, "Is the CEO a dying breed? Could CEOs become extinct?" This headline says 14 countries are putting some planetary corporate leadership articles into national law. Here is another headline, "WTO (World Trade Organization) will vote on several articles such as no hidden ownership using numbered corporations. They also have agreed on a limit to how much a CEO is paid." This article on page two says hundreds of corporations agree with many of the articles and are creating plans to implement them."

Pi's mass murder is morally unforgivable, but one cannot deny the impact. She is shaking up the world. Influential people are taking less. World organizations are doing more to stop a few powerful people from trapping billions of people in poverty. The method is utterly unacceptable, but the outcomes may improve billions of people's lives. The fat cats needed a prod. I just wish it did not have to be so bloody. Why does it have to be a revolution to get the rich to behave? Could we not slowly evolve to a better life for everyone and avoid blood on the street?"

Diana's phone started ringing. "Can you check that for me?"

Lazarus glanced at her phone. The message was displayed on the phone. "It is a message from Faith. She is resigning from Omega Biotech. She wants to be a grade-school teacher in a small town in Niagara. She wants to stay friends but is no longer committed to the inner circle. There is a postscript. She is moving on her own and starting fresh."

"I wish she had talked to me first, but I cannot blame her. Things are out of control. I feel complicit and guilty for things I have not done. I should have seen the CEO slaughterhouse on the horizon and positively redirected the energy."

Lazarus gave her knee a little pat and then left his hand on her knee for a bit of warmth and support. Diana glanced at him and smiled. She was worried. Each death would bring more attention, more law enforcement, and raise the probability of being caught. This could not continue without ending badly for the team. What upset her the most was it was unnecessary. You stand up to one bully; if you hurt him enough, everyone will treat you respectfully.

They pulled up to the factory just outside Oslo by mid-afternoon. Dag was ecstatic. He quickly greeted Diana and Lazarus but was eager to show their achievements. He showed them the trucks first. They had removed the torus so the trucks could not be used as a weapon. They had also removed the second engine button so the maximum speed would be 1,600

Km/hour and not allow ventures into space. The truck was not a big 18-wheeler but midsized. "We are ready to sell these to any citizen of Norway. They can fly at low altitudes as long as they stay above a highway. The rule is 20 feet above traffic going east, 30 feet going north, 40 feet going west, and 50 feet going south to reduce crashes. We put in a good GPS and a collision detection system used on high-end cars. This vehicle will drop fuel usage, dramatically reduce pollution, and improve the speed of delivery. We can open up air corridors once we have more experience. All very exciting. Can you tell me a bit about the security you included, Lazarus?"

"The vehicle can only be operated by a person with the key FOB. If someone tries to steal the engine without the FOB, the machine will jump 10 meters into the air. The machine will keep jumping another 10 meters higher if the person without the FOB is near. The owner is the only one who can climb in and operate the machine. If someone tries to tamper with the engine by opening or scanning it with electromagnetic beams, the machine will automatically return to the factory.

If the machine cannot return home because of some restraint, an encapsulating blanket around the engine will spray acid on the computer chips turning them into goo in seconds. Finally, the chips have code designed to mislead or camouflage their functions. There are layers of coding that do nothing but act as a redundancy check. Code checks against random segments of the nothing code to ensure the machines are authentic before operating reliably. I expect any hackers will go insane trying to figure out the purpose of the nothing code.

If someone builds their own machine using our components, the code has elements similar to a biological virus that will randomly distribute minor, deliberate errors each day. Every day the compromised machine will function with increasingly unpredictable behavior. This is not all the security protection, but it should give you confidence that the vehicle cannot be stolen or replicated.

We also have a universal recall. With this feature, every machine will notify another within a set boundary to return home to the factory. If you want to disable every machine sold to Russia, you send a single remote command to any machine within half a mile. Each machine would spread the order to other machines until all machines within the set boundary are notified."

Dag's eyes kept getting wider as Lazarus provided more details. "I can see you gave it a lot of thought. Now let me take you both to the Space Wing." The walk went on and on. Dag kept chatting. "I saw the Nobel Prize ceremony. I did not know I would be meeting with a Nobel winner today. Lazarus always sends me on some new wild trajectory that utterly changes my life."

"I can vouch for the same experience," said Diana.

"I did not see the prime number award on TV, but I did hear about it on the radio today. Were you there, Diana?"

"I was."

"It sounds like another wild trajectory. Lazarus wins the competition, then springs a submission for the next two contests that had yet to be announced. I would have loved to see that announcement. You need top presentation skills to get mathematicians cheering and whooping," said Dag.

"It was not that big a deal. Get the next publication of Science magazine, and you will see the prize was the easy part," said Lazarus. The walk through the long underground corridor finally ended at the destination. The sign above the next door was understated as The Space Wing.

"We need golf carts, electric scooters, or something to cross back and forth. It takes too long," said Dag.

"As you can see, here we have a few hundred mining beetles about the size of a shoebox. They can fly from one asteroid to another after tagging potential mining locations. For transport, we have a driverless truck with the torus and the T-bar controls for space travel. We have no need for oxygen, given no humans are on the machine because the controls are done remotely. We plan to shuttle the truck with any valuable findings between the asteroid belt and the moon. Our find and tag methods were developed and have been tested in space. This was the most exciting moment. We have explored space for minerals. As you can see on the big monitor on the wall, we have a catalog of opportunities. There is a snag. The mining itself is difficult."

"Why?" said Diana.

"We cannot push a drill into the rock. With almost no gravity (microgravity) in the asteroid belt, pushing forward would result in the pusher flying backward. Every action has a reaction. We have to somehow tether to the rock before pushing," said Dag.

"I could solve that. Use microbes. Microbes could process away materials and leave the good stuff to be scooped up. Microbes feed on all kinds of things. We could genetically modify the microbe with the CRISPR machine to eat, ferment, or deposit your desired rock. In the same way, microbes produce beer from hops or make a carpet from DNA-altered E.coli. We can process rock," said Diana.

"That was easy. Could Omega Biotech help us? We are not allowed to work with a corporation or make a profit. You would have to loan us an employee. We could pay their salary."

"Of course. I will call one of my top people, Yasmin. She wanted to do something new. This would be a project where she could show off her skills. In college, she took E-coli bacteria, one of the most common microbes, and converted the bacteria to generate electricity by processing sewage. The experiment failed financially, but your project would be easy for her. I will call her today. If she agrees, she can contact you tomorrow. She could leave Omega and join the Norway venture. Lazarus tells me the Norway venture will prevent the extinction of the human species, so your mission is more important than the Omega mission," said Diana.

"As you can see from the big monitor, we have found enough precious metals in enough volume that we are ready to mine. If the mining proceeds, we can start bringing back resources and supply non-renewable resources immediately."

The rest of the day was polite and fun. Dag asked Lazarus about his chess games in Sweden. It was not a headline news item like a Nobel prize, but an unknown person placing second in a speed chess tournament was making news in the chess circles.

"You are keeping secrets from me," said Diana.

"You were doing your Nobel rehearsals, and I thought you'd find my chess game boring in comparison."

"Did you think of a name for the machine?" said Dag.

"I thought we could call it the *Herald*. I see the machine as a foretelling of a better future," said Lazarus.

"Sounds good. I have been calling it the machine for so long, I may not successfully convert to Herald," said Dag.

"I know. I am the same," said Lazarus.

"And me," said Diana.

Diana and Lazarus departed the factory. They tried to decide whether to take the machine back to New York or wait for the morning. The original machine still had no headlights or cabin lighting. The sun was setting.

They found themselves in a small café in Oslo, having sandwiches and a Pepsi. Diana was trying to catch up with her endless emails while they ate. Lazarus was looking out the large storefront window at the people passing.

"Oh, no. I was afraid of this," said Diana.

"What has happened?"

"Milton. He is in custody. The Royal Canadian Mounted Police are in New York and want to extradite him to Canada. They say he is a person of interest in the homicide of a Sebastian Carlos, an alleged slum landlord."

"Did he do it? What do you think?"

"He did. He admitted it to me. The landlord was trying to use unpaid rent as leverage to abuse Milton's wife sexually. He kept coming to the house when Milton was working."

"He is in trouble then."

"I can get him a good lawyer, but that is not the main worry. He used the beetle to kill the landlord. This could give the security people a lead to those who used the same methods in the dictator and corporate executions. The whole group is at risk of exposure."

Chapter 51 — Anna makes progress

Since the Davos threat, there has been unprecedented sharing among the usually taciturn security departments and organizations. Most efforts were not productive. Mercenaries, national defense organizations, CIA, Homeland Security, Interpol, MI5 in England, and all shapes and sizes of private contractors were trying to find a lead.

There was never an assailant in the room when the leader was killed. There was never a weapon left behind. There was never an ax, arrow, or knife lodged in the victim. The entrance and exit wound showed no straight line of entry and exit, as you would expect from a bullet. An exploding shard of shrapnel would not enter a lower extremity and exit from your brain. The pattern of damage left no burn or gunpowder. There were no clues, such as a fallen hair, a button, or a snippet of clothing. There was never mud from a shoe or a trail of blood after the attack. It was always the same – no evidence. You have one or more victims and no perpetrators in the vicinity. All scans of video cameras showed no people coming or going to be involved in a killing. All the people in the building could not be tied to the crimes in the building. The national security organizations had many experts, data, and opinions that did not help.

They had lots of suspects from postings and electronic communications. The leads on the web were in the millions.

The leads and opinions, even books by experts, kept growing in volume, but none helped solve the growing number of deaths. Slowly, experts like Anna Ivanovitch were turning away from all the tantalizing online theories. The online leads were an exercise in futility. Misinformation and disinformation were endless and the opposite of helpful.

Anna got her first big break when she started looking for travel patterns. She linked all travel to any airport within 300 kilometers of the death of a leader. The list was in the millions. As the number of killings grew, the number of people in the same city at the same time who were not residents kept getting smaller. Anna suspected she was not looking for an individual but an organization. Once the CEO killings began, the list of potential executioners started to get smaller with each new death. The list most national security teams used was now under 20 people of interest. Some 20 people had the same travel patterns before the killings began. This process of elimination narrowed the names to three people. Two were men in the security business, and one was a young woman in biotechnology research in New York.

Chris Gota from Homeland Security provided the next insight. A death from 15 years earlier in Canada had a similar wound pattern. He discovered the connection by accident. One of the Canadian detectives was his friend. Chris and his Canadian friend worked on a peacekeeping mission in Bosnia while in the military. The two men shared a few beers one evening when the discussion about the strange head wound surfaced. The suspect was also an employee of the same New York biotechnology company. He had been in Disney World when the North Korean dictator was killed. From the damage to the body from 15 years of decay, there was not much to go on, but the wound's pattern was similar.

Anna knew she did not have long. The sharing of information to solve this international crime was high. Some perhaps many people, would be on the same trail soon. The reward for finding the killers of rich people was now over $100 million. This kind of bounty upset many professional security people. The fear was that many captured and killed individuals would be innocent but gunned down or arrested by overly determined people trying to collect the reward. There was a temptation with that big a prize that someone might be set up to look guilty and then killed for the money. No matter how many judges, lawyers, or politicians complained about the bounty's size, the CEOs were determined to find the killer.

This would be a career triumph for Anna if she could catch the killer. She was looking for a serial killer of over 50 people, all of the victims famous or, more correctly, infamous. The world was now clearly less tolerant of executive abuses, and everyone knew the sins at the top. Anna felt a killer is a killer, and justice must prevail. Anna wanted to capture the guilty person, and if that came with a $100 million payment, the money would be nice. She would be free and able to retire.

Chapter 52 — Swatted like an insect

Lazarus took the machine to New York. The engineers in Norway had fitted the machine with an airline tracker and filed flight plans so no fighter jets tried to shoot them out of the sky. Diana was prepared for the thrill of exiting Earth's atmosphere and reentering into orbit. It did not matter. The experience always struck fear into her bones and took her breath away. Lazarus followed the traffic in Manhattan at street level and pulled into their parking spot. He draped the cover over the machine, and they walked to the parking elevator.

As they waited, a few people came in from the north and south doors. As soon as the elevator doors opened, the men behind them grabbed Diana and Lazarus around the waist trapping their arms at their sides. They were handcuffed, hooded, and carried to a van that pulled up to the parking door. The security people tossed them into the van, jumped in, and with a screech of tires, the vehicle drove up to the street. The whole thing took only a few seconds. Lazarus did not have time to shout or kick. He had some big oaf sitting on him, keeping him immobile. Lazarus's first thoughts were concern for Diana.

The van moved and stopped frequently. Lazarus tried to count the turns. He had no idea where they were, but from the sounds, and the feeling of speed, he was sure they were going through a tunnel and likely being driven into New Jersey. After about 40 minutes, the van stopped and then backed up. Lazarus expected they were in a building. The men dragged him, one on each of his arms, into the building. They went up an elevator. Diana made a muffled sound but stopped when someone kicked or punched her. They removed the hoods. Lazarus and Diana were both taken to a chair. There was a metal table with an iron rail welded above one edge. Lazarus and Diana were handcuffed to the table rail.

"This is not good," said Diana.

"Shut up," said a woman with a gun pointing at Diana. The attackers left, locking the door behind them. A few minutes later, a young man in a blue suit came in. He had an ID Badge that read "FBI, Agent 3019, Jim Connor."

"You are both in a lot of trouble. If you cooperate, if you help us, we will go easy on you." He waited for a response. In his experience, many people chained to a desk would panic and babble endlessly. He couldn't keep them quiet. The challenge was to direct their conversation. Diana and Lazarus did not speak but waited for him to go on. "We suspect you belong to a terrorist group that has killed more than 50 leaders of nations and industry. You are the CEO of Enworld. You have a technical lab technician, Pi, and a computer person, Milton, on your staff. From your email and phone messages, you work closely. Don't bother to deny it. We have Milton in custody for the murder of a landlord 15 years ago. We suspect he may have been involved in the murder of the North Korean Tim Bit in Disney World. We do not have Pi, but we want her. You must help us locate her quickly before she kills again. It is imperative." He paused. Again, no response.

"I know Milton and Pi. You already know that," said Diana.

"Can I get you something? Would you like some water or a coffee?" he asked.

"Sure. Water would be nice," said Lazarus.

"I can do that. I can be nice. I want to help you if you help me. I can make your life hell. I can charge you with so many violations I am unsure where to start. Violation of airspace rules. Accessory to murder. The list is long. Espionage. For now, help me find Pi."

"I would like you to draft a document that gives us a full pardon, irrevocably, for all crimes in the past if we assist in the successful capture of Pi. I would also like you to bring us something to eat, like a grilled cheese sandwich or hamburger. I will sign the document, and I want my lawyer present. I can help you if you help me," said Lazarus. Diana was going to interrupt, but Lazarus gave her a knowing look, so she waited.

"Let me confer with my captain," said the agent. "I will see what we can do." He left the room.

"Diana, I am sure you know they have a microphone here. Whatever we say, they can hear. I don't see any video cameras, probably because they don't need them. I think the tinted window is a one-way window. They can see everything we do. I also think this is probably a secure room. I would guess if I put six bullets from some big gun into that door or window, neither would break. We are trapped. They've got us, and there is no escape. When he opened that door, it looked like a two-inch steel door with a plastic veneer." As Lazarus talked, he gave Diana a double wink so she knew what he was saying was for them. He motioned to his handcuffs and glanced at the beetle resembling a button on his tweed jacket.

Diana knew. Lazarus could use that beetle to vaporize their handcuffs. He could vaporize the door, the window, and the attackers. Lazarus was also huge. He was about 250 pounds, six feet five, and incredibly strong. Lazarus could probably swat that agent away like a little insect. She watched him as he drew a word on the table with his finger. The first word looked like a *lull*. The next word looked like *guard*. It was hard to be sure because he was gesturing and talking nonsense to hide what he was doing. She understood he wanted to lower the guard of the attackers before he worked on their escape.

They sat handcuffed for hours. Their answers were a bit helpful and a bit vague. They provided Pi and Milton's cell phone numbers and addresses because the security people certainly had that information already. Some questions were not because the security team wanted to know the answer. They already knew the answer. The question was a test to see if Diana and Lazarus were answering correctly. They did not know where Pi was and had tried for days to contact her. Diana showed Connor her phone, so he could see she had sent message after message asking Pi to get back to her.

Diana portrayed Milton as a friend from college who was good with numbers. She said he pretended to be a skilled computer person but that was more false bravado than actual skill. Despite Connor's efforts, he revealed information. He said Milton lived alone. He had been separated from his wife for years. The wife called the police about Milton killing the slum landlord after an argument about custody of their children.

As the interview went into the night, they had to go to the bathroom. They would undo the handcuff on one person at a time and escort them to and from the toilet. They would wait outside the stall until you were done. They would take you back and put the handcuffs on again. Lazarus noted when he went that only one security person was outside the interrogation door. Lazarus saw one guard at the elevator. The emergency stairs were blocked with furniture. He suspected they had another guard on the ground floor and likely another near the vehicle.

Lazarus looked out the window of the holding room and saw a few lights. They must be in some remote industrial area. He was sure real FBI agents would have taken them to the nearest FBI building in New York. There would have been other agents from the CIA and Homeland Security asking questions. The room would have been much more secure. This was not the FBI. The woman who said 'shut up' had a European accent, something from Eastern Europe like Belarus or Russia. This was the reason she did not talk much. The badges looked real, but the clothes were European. The suits had that double flap at the back that the British and other Europeans wore. Americans almost always wore a single slit in the back middle of the jacket. One or two agents may prefer a European style, but how likely would all the agents be wearing European clothes. These people were not from the FBI.

Lazarus expected the questioning would be pleasant until they got nothing new. They agreed to any document Lazarus requested because they were not FBI, so the document would be fake and meaningless to authorities. He was sure this was why they did not negotiate for better terms on the amnesty for past crimes. They would not hesitate to bring out electric prods and knives to get more information if they thought it was needed.

It was late. The sky was dark, and the agents were tired. It was time to go. Lazarus waited for Connor to leave the room to talk to his captain. He quickly used his beetle to vaporize his handcuff off one hand. Next, he vaporized Diana's handcuff. Lazarus got up rapidly and angled the metal chair against the door handle. Lazarus went to the window and vaporized a three-foot hole in the glass. The beetle made no noise except a little click when pushed. Lazarus took every beetle from his clothing. He had beetles as buttons on the cuffs and jacket. He had some in the lining of his coat. He grabbed Diana around the waist, and they dived through the window.

They were about five floors up, high enough to easily be killed by the fall. The tiny beetles worked exactly like the machine and removed some of the gravity of the fall. The beetles were too small to allow them to float down, but they slowed the fall sufficiently so they were not killed. They hit the ground hard but not hard enough to break bones. Lazarus rolled as he hit the ground and was not harmed. The practice of falling in judo proved helpful to him.

Once on the ground, Lazarus ran to the black van. An agent was sitting in the van. Lazarus tried the door by pulling quickly. The door was not locked, so it flew open. The agent twisted his head around. You could see from his eyes he was half awake. Lazarus grabbed him by the collar and, with one quick jerk, swung him out and to the ground. Lazarus put the agent in a headlock with one arm and twisted the agent's arm behind his back in a half-Nelson. "Check his pockets for keys and a phone," said Lazarus to Diana. He looked up and saw lights going on in the interrogation room. He saw someone stick their head out of the hole in the window.

Diana was moving fast. She found the keys and a phone. Lazarus was unsure what she was doing until he realized she was using the man's finger to unlock the phone. Lazarus and Diana got in the van and started driving. She could hear bullets hitting the ground as someone shot from the hole in the window. The shots were not close. Pistols were not designed to accurately hit targets that far away.

Diana pulled up phone maps to see where they were. Lazarus took a guess at the first minor road and turned left, hoping they would not have to turn back. They drove fast but not too fast. Diana gave him some directions while she scrambled around, looking for clues in the vehicle. There were some Russian documents. She could not read them, but she recognized the alphabet letters. Lazarus drove into the first small town. He pulled into a parking lot for a local bar. He picked this spot because there were so many cars. He left the van running.

"Are we stopping for a beer?" she said. She looked at Lazarus like he was insane.

"They are looking for this van. They can likely trace the phone you are holding. We want someone to steal the van, so they are chasing the thief instead of us." Lazarus took the phone and made a quick call, then tossed the phone onto the van seat.

They crossed the street from the busy bar and entered a small grocery store attached to a gas station. They got a coffee and sat on the bench and watched. People were continually coming and going from the bar. A few people walked up to the van, peered in, walked around, and walked away. One of the guys did a quick walkaround, jumped in, and backed up. A few friends came up, got in, and drove off. Only a few minutes later, two vans and a black sedan pulled up. They rolled down their windows, talked to each other, and then the two vans sped away after the missing van. The sedan drove around the bar and followed slowly after the missing van.

Diana and Lazarus watched all the action. "Now," said Lazarus. The two of them walked quickly out of the grocery store. There was a big Ford F150 truck pulling a mobile home. Lazarus crouched down so he could not be seen from the gas kiosk. Lazarus tried the door of the mobile home. It opened. The two of them slipped in and shut the door behind them. They had no idea where they were going, but the fake FBI people would not find them in a mobile home being driven down the road. They sat on the floor and waited.

The truck pulled off. The couple was lucky the owner had not noticed. Whenever the truck stopped for a traffic light, Lazarus would peek out the window to see if he knew where they were. They had another lucky break as the truck was heading toward Manhattan. They sat in the dark. Diana was a bit cold and spooked by everything that had happened. Once the truck pulled into Manhattan, Lazarus and Diana tried to sneak out.

"Hey. Did you enjoy the ride?" said the truck driver. "I saw you get in. I had my own issues with the law. Not sure what trouble you are in, but best of luck to both of you," he said, tipping his cowboy hat.

"Mighty fine of you," said Lazarus.

"We need a plan. We cannot go back to your apartment or work building. They will be waiting for us at the obvious places. Any ideas?" said Lazarus.

"We need to get the machine and get the hell out of Dodge," said Diana. "We will never be safe here. We need to get far away."

"Assuming the machine is still there, they will surely be waiting there. If I were them, I would expect we'd risk capturing to regain our machine."

"This time, we will have beetles at the ready. They won't just grab us from behind. We will blast them into the *not-here-anymore* place."

"A brute force attack - could something that simple work? Just run in with beetles blasting?"

Chapter 53 — Live or die in the fast lane

"What day is it?" said Diana.

"Wednesday."

"The cleaners will be there tonight. I was always friendly with them. We could mingle with them to surprise the guards." They ambled to the wrong building. From across and down the street, they scouted the area. When she saw the truck with the cleaners, she waved them down. They talked a bit and gave Lazarus a wave. They got in the back of the truck with the cleaners. An older fellow gave Diana orange overalls to dress like the rest of the cleaning crew. The truck drove into the parking garage of Diana's building. The cleaners unloaded a vacuum cleaner that looked like a small tractor. The team worked quickly while Diana and Lazarus stayed in the truck. The men tipped garbage cans upside down into a device like a wheelbarrow with an added compressor.

Diana could see people in the parking garage who were not walking to cars, not coming or going. There must have been at least five mercenaries. Two were close to the machine, one by the garage door and one on each garage floor. About 20 yards from the guy near the machine, Lazarus got out of the truck. Lazarus kept his back to the guy and swept with a broom. While cleaning, Lazarus glanced sideways and quickly turned and vaporized the man from the waist up. The legs dropped to the floor. Diana had also slipped out and moved bent over and alongside a wall. When the security woman noticed her companion was gone, she started to walk toward the machine. She was looking at Lazarus, who was sweeping again, and she kept walking toward him. Diana was 90 degrees to the woman's left and a few feet behind her. Diana vaporized her quickly. Lazarus moved incredibly fast to the machine and pulled the big tarpaulin off like a small napkin.

He jumped into the machine and started it while Diana ran 20 yards to the machine and vaulted into the passenger seat. Adrenaline hormones were powering her. She was scared but more scared of not getting away. Lazarus turned the machine and bolted forward. They rounded the first level, and Lazarus ran down the first security guy before the guy could pull his gun. The torus vaporized him from the waist up. The second guy was smoking as they zipped past him. He shouted as they drove by him. The guard at the door must have heard the shout. He stood in the middle of the road with a gun ready. The guard fired twice directly at Lazarus. The machine's torus vaporized the bullets and vaporized the guard.

Lazarus pulled onto the street and pushed the button. The machine sat briefly before drifting backward and away from the planet. Diana was finally calming down despite the Earth looking smaller and smaller. "I guess fear is relative. Afraid of being lost in space is not as scary as some guy shooting at you."

Within a minute, the machine was flying at 30,000 kilometers an hour. "Where would you like to go?" said Lazarus.

"Brazil. They have no extradition for rich people."

"As long as we are together," he said.

If she was honest, she knew their whole plan would come to this in the end. The apartment, fancy job, and impressive awards were all melting away. She knew one day, there would be a price to pay for saving the planet from extinction. The rich would not rest until they had complete control. She knew her old life was gone. I have lost the material world, but I have the love of my life. I still have my guy.

"You know, I never liked being a CEO. I like making scientific discoveries. Science moves us closer to the truth. The real truth of nature and the universe. The truth will remain. The money could always disappear in one night or one minute. Who needs all that money? You cannot take it with you. Is it a grand accomplishment to leave the world knowing you didn't share your wealth? Some wealth is good; unlimited wealth shows you have unlimited greed. You are missing a soul if you believe unlimited greed is good. Eat a cherry, and it is nice. Eat unlimited cherries, and you will get sick. Anyone who wants to eat unlimited amounts of anything is psychologically damaged," said Diana to Lazarus but primarily to herself.

Chapter 54 — The end of the beginning

Lazarus and Diana shared their lives in a glass home high in the mountains and deep in the Brazilian jungle. The house was far from any town but quickly accessible with the machine. A huge glass window allowed them to see a small waterfall to the west. They fed well off the bounty of a rich jungle. With money from one of Ares Panama offshore accounts, Diana had rewarded enough local officials that the couple was safe. They enriched their community. The native tribes were given access to lawyers to protect their lands.

A typical day would find Diana experimenting with new foods and exotic blooms in her greenhouse garden. Lazarus spent his time playing Bach and Beethoven on a synthesizer. In the afternoon, he would run in the jungle, talk to the elders of a local tribe, or just explore. He would write poetry or work on some little mathematical problem. Lazarus's current project was using abstract mathematics to generate music.

This life was grand for almost five years or a few weeks in alien time. Of course, eventually, the mercenaries closed in. Perimeter warning signals beeped. They could see infrared signals from people surrounding the glasshouse. The situation was hopeless.

They had planned for this inevitable outcome. Lazarus took the small plastic material from his pocket and unfolded it into a three-inch square pyramid. He took a small vial of thick liquid and dripped it on the material from the top. He placed the material on the floor and then hit the pyramid with a hammer. The little pyramid golem grew. Lazarus hit it a few more times, and the pyramid golem doubled in size. He continued to hit it rapidly until it was about six feet square. Diana held up her arm. A brightly colored parrot flew and perched on her arm. Lazarus called his little dog. Lazarus took another vial of thick liquid and dripped it across one side of the pyramid. He put his hands on the wet portion and pushed his hand into the pyramid. He pulled both hands apart to create an opening. The family stepped into the pyramid. They had to sit on the floor because Lazarus was now over seven feet tall, so he could not stand up.

Lazarus sealed the pyramid with the same liquid. They sat waiting. The security people came crashing in from every side in less than 10 minutes. They rushed the pyramid while shooting. With each bullet, the material grew. One soldier pelted the pyramid with a machine gun. The pyramid kept increasing until the peak touched the ceiling. Diana and Lazarus could now comfortably stand. The soldiers could see the couple standing unperturbed. The calm of their targets infuriated the soldiers. They radioed, and a soldier came in with a massive sniper rifle carried by two people. He set up the 50mm rifle and pumped a bullet directly at the Professor's head. The pyramid cracked the ceiling as it poked through the roof. The soldiers had to move back as the pyramid kept spreading across the floor.

The commander was unwilling to admit defeat and had explosives set at each pyramid corner. The soldiers left one lookout and took cover outside the house. The charge detonated, and the pyramid remained intact. The house had a large hole in one wall. The pyramid was now about 100 feet high and 100 feet wide, but Lazarus and Diana were unharmed, calm, and smiling. The pyramid was buried about 15 feet into the side of the mountain.

The commander came and surveyed the situation. You could tell she was concerned about the stability of the whole structure. The house was broken in every direction and could tumble down the mountain in a landslide at any moment. The mountain had one slope partially displaced by the pyramid. Lazarus and Diana were in the pyramid's center, which was increasingly far from the commander.

The commander, Anna, photographed the couple with her phone. She was sorry she had allowed them to escape from the industrial park so long ago. She was grateful that they had so enriched the people of the world. The momentum on fixing corporate leadership never relented, even after the two disappeared. The execution of corrupt corporate leaders continued unabated. The articles of the planetary constitution were being adopted internationally. The five percent tariff on corporate profits had provided trillions of dollars to improve the human condition. These initiatives changed the culture of greed. Executives had to think about what and where to improve society. They were forced to think about people and help them. The discussions were changing the leaders' identities. They were different when they focused on helping people rather than greed.

Blindness in Africa was improving. Better battery technologies were pervasive. Lazarus had exposed the secrets of the rich and powerful everywhere. Anna had seen many national security teams destroyed when people realized their information and lives were being abused. Infections were being cured using the dynamic antibiotic microbes from Omega. Omega was feeding most of the poor and extending the lives of the rich. Omega was the most powerful corporate entity in the world. Humans were exploring space in ways never imagined. New and fantastic minerals and metals had been found in the asteroid belt.

Anna laughed as she recalled the fallout when the Science journal published the formula for prime numbers. All the lies, deceptions, and crimes by nations against their own people were exposed. The crimes by the famous and the unknown alike quickly arrived on the web. Transparency revealed so many hidden evils and monsters who were pretending to be pious or pretending to care. The same openness revealed many hidden or imprisoned heroes. Anna hoped the world would build a monument to Diana and Lazarus. She knew Diana and Lazarus were already heroes. The villains could no longer lurk in the shadows.

Anna Ivanovitch gave her two targets a military salute and called her men. Lazarus and Diana watched them gather their equipment and move away. Anna would radio her location and the situation to the Admiral. She expected they might send a bunker-busting bomb into the pyramid. She hoped they would offer them amnesty and safe harbor in exchange for new technologies such as this pyramid defensive material.

"Are they willing to just walk away? Defeated by technology once again," said Lazarus.

"It does not matter, my love. It is time. You have a promise to keep," said Diana.

"If they drop a bomb, this golem will be the biggest structure on Earth."

"We did our part. It is up to the people now. We should go to your friend, SF03."

Lazarus gave Diana a deep kiss. He stepped back and ported Diana and her parrot. Lazarus slid the back of his amulet open, punched the buttons as instructed, and was ported with his dog. Lazarus kept his promise to SF03. He did his best to save his planet and win his girl's heart. It was time to return to SF03. They were ready to explore the multiverse.

THE END

Acknowledgements

My thanks to Shelley Lynch, Carol James, Phil Forestall, and so many others for their help and support.

Printed in the USA
CPSIA information can be obtained
at www.ICGtesting.com
BVHW040241090823
668343BV00002B/6

9 780991 868629